survival

For Polly

with best wishes from

survival

DAVID FLETCHER

Matador
9 Priory Business Park,
Wistow Road, Kibworth Beauchamp,
Leicestershire. LE8 0RX
Tel: 0116 279 2299
Email: books@troubador.co.uk
Web: www.troubador.co.uk/matador
Twitter: @matadorbooks

ISBN 978 1800463 660

British Library Cataloguing in Publication Data.
A catalogue record for this book is available from the British Library.

Printed and bound in the UK by TJ Books Limited, Padstow, Cornwall
Typeset in 11pt Adobe Garamond Pro by Troubador Publishing Ltd, Leicester, UK

Matador is an imprint of Troubador Publishing Ltd

For Iris

one

Alex stared at the iceberg. It was huge and it was painfully beautiful; an exquisite blue-white jewel set in the blue-white world all around. It was about two hundred metres from the ship, and it was the nearest of a whole swarm of icebergs, all laid out on the blue, mirror-smooth water of the channel and all sparkling under the bright Antarctic sun. Beyond it were the snow-covered peaks that formed the west side of the channel, their form sculpted by time and their surfaces now coated in every shade of blue and white. They were exquisite themselves – framed by a clear azure sky above and that silver-blue sea at their feet. And their scale was enormous.

Before he had come to Antarctica, Alex had never experienced such scenery. There had been that brief excursion to the north of Norway where he'd been immersed in a similar palette of just white and blue, but that had been different. There it had been just chilling and a little soulless, just a great expanse of featureless white under a glaring blue sky. But here, here in this southern polar setting, what was outside the cabin window was not just truly exquisite but almost alive. Out there were shapes, contrasts, textures and reflections, and out there was that huge, scintillating iceberg, a great blue-and-white fragment afloat in the channel but looking as though it was anchored to the Earth. It was as still and as fixed as the peaks all around it.

The whole wonderful spectacle deserved to be gazed at forever, but Alex had other things to do, and he began to turn his attention away from the view through the window. However, just as he did so he observed a little movement in that outside scene, and his attention was captured again. How could it not be? That movement heralded the arrival of whales…

There were four of them, four humpback whales in a tight group, spoiling the glassy-smooth surface of the channel with their rising, blowing, diving and splashing. Although whether they were feeding, bonding, playing or just relishing their existence, Alex couldn't tell. But it didn't matter. To observe any whale in its natural environment was a joy and a privilege. To observe a quartet of them at close quarters – as these were now – was literally captivating. Alex couldn't take his eyes off them, as first a shiny black back surfaced from the water and then a huge, handsome fluke rose to join it, soon partially obscured as another of the quartet sent forth a tall, misty spout. In fact, it was only when he observed this spout that it occurred to Alex that he should call Debbie to join him. Wherever she'd got to with her preparations, she'd no doubt want to see these wonderful sea-going creatures.

'Debbie, there's some whales out here. Four humpbacks. You should come and see them. They're really close.'

Immediately, Debbie appeared. She'd been in the bathroom and she was now walking towards Alex, her hands to her left ear, clearly still trying to secure a reluctant second earring into its lobe.

'Four of them?' she inquired.

'Yeah. Just to the left. Over there.'

She had now joined her husband, and, having convinced that second earring that it should just acquiesce and take its rightful place in her earlobe, she was peering through the window to locate the promised cetaceans.

'Ah, yes,' she exclaimed. 'Fantastic. And look, did you see that fluke? It was pale underneath...'

'Well, if it wasn't, you'd be a bit concerned. They are humpbacks, and their flukes are supposed to be pale underneath. Just like we're supposed to have a crease in our bum.'

'Don't be vulgar,' responded Debbie. But her words were delivered with a smile, and then she made another observation.

'Just look at them,' she said. 'Aren't they sublime?'

'Sublime and... happy. At least, they look pretty happy. And I must say, it's difficult to imagine that they're not. After all, they've got this wonderful place to live in and they've got each other as well.'

Debbie turned from the view of the whales to face her husband.

'Just as *we've* got each other,' she said. 'As I'm sure you've not forgotten...'

'Sorry,' responded Alex, 'it's just...'

'…time we got ourselves ready,' interrupted Debbie. 'And I'm nearly there.'

'So am I,' declared Alex. 'I just want to put my boots in the wardrobe and sort out the safe…'

And here he stopped. He had at last taken in his wife's appearance. His boots and the safe would have to wait just a while.

'Debbie,' he pronounced slowly, 'you look beautiful.'

And she did. No longer young, she still retained the looks that had attracted him to her almost fifty years ago. Furthermore, she had spent a useful few minutes on her face, doing whatever it is that women do in front of a bathroom mirror, and in her brand-new wine-coloured dress and her favourite wine-coloured shoes, she looked like the proverbial million dollars. And half of that generous total must have been invested in her eyes. They were as sparkly as the iceberg outside.

'Thank you,' she responded. 'I thought I should make an effort.'

Alex hesitated, and then he went into the walk-in wardrobe, and was soon back out again, holding in his right hand his bright-blue linen jacket.

'Might not be up to your dress, but I've brought it this far, and it hasn't got that many creases in it. As long as you don't look at the sleeves…'

Debbie grinned.

'It'll do just fine. I mean, just absolutely fine. In fact, I think that together we will be the best-dressed couple aboard. No matter how many creases…'

'Bloody right,' confirmed her husband. 'Absolutely bloody right.' And then he approached her, threw his jacket on the bed, and embraced her tightly – and held her in this embrace for quite some time. When he finally released her, he then spoke.

'I love you,' he said slowly. 'I always have and I always will. In fact, I may love you more now than I've ever loved you before. And if that sounds stupid…'

'It doesn't,' interrupted Debbie. 'Because I feel just the same. I mean, I really do. So… it can't be stupid, can it?'

Here she gave her husband a generous smile, and then she reverted to the inescapable practical.

'But I now think that while I go and check on my face, you should sort out whatever you're doing with your boots and the safe. Then we might just be ready. And we should get a move on. You said so yourself.'

Alex got the message. He again embraced his wife, less tightly this time. And then, when he'd disengaged, he took his boots into the wardrobe, and after that he knelt before the cabin's dresser that housed the safe. Here he began to fiddle with the safe's contents before locking it closed. When he'd done this, he put on his bright-blue jacket.

Outside, the whales were still cavorting and the iceberg was still sparkling. Inside their cabin, the good-looking Debbie and the now relatively well-dressed Alex were finally about to embark on their plans for the evening.

seven weeks earlier

two

Nobody was fat. Alex just couldn't help noticing. Nor could he help himself thinking that, of the ninety-two people seated in the ship's lounge, few if any would balk at applying the term 'fat' to other people. After all, whilst there were maybe half a dozen of the assembled throng who were arithmetically middle-aged, the vast majority of the ship's passengers listening to the safety briefing were more euphemistically middle-aged, and they must have all grown up in a time when fat people could be called fat without it risking censure from others. The average age of the *MS Sea Sprite's* human cargo, Alex thought, must have hovered somewhere around seventy. And their body shapes fell somewhere in the range of slim to well-fed, with here and there just some overwide hips and the odd minor paunch.

It was not that unusual for Alex to find himself in the company of people like himself: not-fat, old – and white. And this was because he had spent the past quarter of a century travelling around the world on wildlife holidays, and he'd discovered that the majority of those who shared this interest in wild animals and wild places (and could afford to indulge this interest) were... not-fat, old and white. However, here on this ship, there were just so many of this sort gathered in one place, and they weren't just the majority but they were the overwhelming majority. This was going to be a predominantly old-age pensioner expedition, where youth, obesity and any sort of diversity would hardly feature at all. Or at least it wouldn't in respect of the passengers.

The crew and the expedition staff were a different matter. The captain (Captain José) was a youngish Panamanian and his crew were mostly fairly young Filipinos. Then the members of the twelve-strong expedition team, who without exception were from Britain or from one of its former 'Anglo' possessions, came in a variety of ages. But, of course, just like all the passengers and all the crew on this vessel, not one of them was fat.

These team members had all introduced themselves before the safety briefing had got under way, and they had all done this with a mix of humour and irreverence. It would take some time for Alex to remember all their names and what their specialities were, but a few of them had already established themselves in his mind. There was Nick, a professional Australian ornithologist, whose long lean body put one in mind of a stork, but whose facial features had more in common with those of a hawk. One only had to look at him to be reassured that he really knew his stuff, and no doubt all the stuff he would ever need to know about the birds to be seen on this trip. By way of contrast there was then Mike, an ex-Royal Marine, who had fought in the Falklands War and who, more recently, had worked on anti-piracy assignments off Somalia. He didn't owe his body shape or his looks to any bird, but instead he put Alex in mind of a bull. He was big and he was solid. Then there was Tony, a stocky Scottish geologist, who had apparently worked in the Antarctic in his youth and who, despite his attempts at humour in his self-introduction, looked and sounded so dour that Alex wondered whether he was still suffering from some sort of Post-Antarctic Stress Disorder. Or maybe it was just because he was Scottish...

None of these notable three had been selected to demonstrate the use of an immersion suit. That was what was going on at the front of the lounge just now. Two others from the expedition team had drawn the short straw to do this. One of them was a younger, slimmer ex-Marine called Terry, and the other was a bearded Canadian naturalist called John. And they were both now attempting to show how relatively effortless it was to encase one's body in a fully enveloping immersion suit in the event of one having to immerse oneself in cold Antarctic waters. However, they were not having much success. As it appeared that, even after training as a Marine, it was hellishly difficult to deal with these awful insulated onesies without the help of somebody else. And that wasn't the plan. One was supposed to be able to don these life-savers without assistance in the same way that one was supposed to be able to don one's conventional life jackets on one's own, and even that wasn't easy.

Alex could not imagine himself ever rising to the challenge. He was slim, but he was also tall and not very coordinated. He knew he would still be tangling with his onesie as the *Sea Sprite* slipped beneath the waves, and he would just have to put his faith in the successful operation of the lifeboats and hope that not even a life jacket would ever be needed. Indeed, he had already paid a great deal of attention to the location of his and Debbie's muster station and to the location of their designated lifeboat. Both of these had been shown to them before the lounge session, together with an explanation of what toots on the ship's whistle meant 'gather' and what toots meant 'abandon ship'. There didn't, he'd noticed, appear to be any toots to announce that the wrong toots had been used in the first place and should now be ignored.

Well, with the immersion-suit demonstration now concluded, the safety briefing was nearing its end, and was finally drawn to a full stop by an announcement by the cruise director. This was a woman in her fifties, who went by the name of Jane, and who had the shape of a sergeant major and a demeanour to match. And her announcement concerned the promise of a forthcoming mandatory lecture on the subject of biosecurity for the duration of the cruise. As with this safety briefing, she informed her audience, names would be taken of those attending in order to identify those who needed to be tracked down to attend. And just like names, there was no way that prisoners would not be taken. Jane, it appeared, expected everyone's full cooperation. Or else.

Back in their cabin, Alex and Debbie discussed Jane's rather severe attitude, but they ultimately decided that, on a voyage to the Antarctic such as this, there was a need for such severity. Someone had to emphasise the importance of safety on board and of the need to keep the places to be visited safe – from alien species and from any other sort of damage. And in any event, it was no less than they had expected. The tour operators were hardly likely to have put some sort of softie in charge of this trip. Nor would they have countenanced the trip being late getting under way, which was why the *MS Sea Sprite* was now edging away from the dockside in Ushuaia and manoeuvring itself to commence its passage down the Beagle Channel. This would take it into the South Atlantic, where it would then make its way to its first destination: the Falklands.

Alex and Debbie donned their fleeces and stepped out onto their modest balcony. They wanted to observe their departure from Argentina's southernmost port, and they wanted to relish what this meant: nearly three weeks at sea in a fabulous pocket-size vessel, visiting what promised to be some of the most pristine and most breathtaking places on the planet. It would also mean a long, welcome sabbatical from all the nonsense of the oppressive and dispiriting world; a feature of the trip that was reinforced beyond doubt when Alex and Debbie returned from the balcony and Alex turned on the cabin's TV.

They had satiated their interest in their departure from the rather scruffy end-of-the-world settlement of Ushuaia, and Alex had wanted to discover from CNN – which was one of the two external channels on the ship's TV system – just what they would be abandoning for the next three weeks of their lives; what aspects of the world would not be accompanying them on their trip. None of it, it transpired, was much of a surprise. For it appeared that for twenty-one days they would have to survive without a continuous commentary on the latest turmoil in the Middle East, without an account of the latest predictably inane utterances of the resident of the White House, without the latest episode in the coverage of the latest flu outbreak in China, and without any repeated bulletins on the latest egregious behaviour of either Russia or Iran. For a little time at least, Alex and his wife would be insulated from the soul-destroying reality of the modern, human-dominated world, and would instead be able to savour the unadulterated delights of the world as it was meant to be; one that was largely free of unwelcome human interference but one that was still able to elevate the human spirit though its untrammelled natural beauty. Even if it might involve the intervention of a highly capable ship's crew and the skills of a team of talented chefs and solicitous waiters. Whose skills were just about to be put to the test.

Alex and Debbie had undertaken a token amount of unpacking and had then readied themselves for dinner. And, as it was now 7.30 in the evening, it was time to confirm whether they had readied themselves sufficiently – by dressing themselves in fleeces, insulated jackets and hats. Because this first meal of their voyage was to be taken not in the elegant but cosy lower-deck restaurant, but in the ship's exposed outside restaurant at its stern. There they would join all those other passengers who had decided that a view of the dramatic scenery to either side of the Beagle Channel was well worth the exposure to a temperature only a little above freezing.

It was, inevitably, a good decision, not least because neither Alex nor Debbie had ever before sat down to a three-course meal that would be consumed with a ship's wake to their rear and snow-capped mountains to their left and to their right. With the added benefits of a calm sea and an unavoidably light evening, it proved a wonderful overture to their Antarctic adventure. Even if the company of their table companions was not universally enchanting.

The *Sea Sprite* operated a seating arrangement, in both its interior restaurant and in its exterior 'lido' restaurant, of shared tables – accommodating four, six or eight diners. This was supposedly designed to underline the intimacy of the expedition experience it offered. And it succeeded in this aim. Four years earlier, Alex and Debbie had sailed on the *Sea Sprite's* virtually identical sister ship when it had made its way through the islands of Melanesia, and this ship had employed exactly the same system. One had to be careful though. As they had discovered very quickly on that expedition, an intimate relationship with every passenger – even if restricted solely to shared dining – was by no means a good idea. Certain of one's fellow travellers could easily drain one of the will to live, on occasions even before the main course had arrived, and one therefore needed to choose carefully where one sat. This, of course, was not easy, especially at the commencement of the voyage when all of one's dining companions would be complete unknowns and potentially very bad news. On that earlier voyage, Alex and Debbie had dealt with this hazard by carefully avoiding those of their shipmates who had already been found to be wanting, while at the same time cultivating a close relationship with a handful of the ship's guests whose company they had found stimulating and rewarding. By then arranging to eat with this select group virtually every day, and especially in the evening, 'good meals' were maximised and 'poor meals' successfully minimised.

When Alex and Debbie stepped onto the lido deck for their first on-board dinner, they had not forgotten this earlier experience, and fully expected that they would have to embark on a similar strategy – of identifying those whom they wished to avoid, those whom they wished to embrace, and, of course, quite a few more who would fall somewhere between these two extremes. In that it barely recognised how others would evaluate them, this was undoubtedly an arrogant sort of strategy. But it was a strategy that had worked before, and there was no reason to suspect that it wouldn't work again. Indeed, after ten minutes at the table they had chosen, Alex had confirmed his belief in this strategy and he could see that Debbie had as well. Here, seated around them, were four fellow adventurers who were to be avoided and two who deserved to be… ensnared.

The four to be avoided comprised a couple from Dartmouth who had pleasure-sailed all their long lives and who had clearly lost both their curiosity and their manners somewhere in the English Channel, and another couple from Dulwich who were simply more earnest than they were engaging. And neither couple could discuss much more than themselves, their offspring, and then more of themselves. Anything remotely interesting was, for them, of no interest at all, and they were really hard work. The two other diners, Derek and Elaine, were, by contrast, near perfect. They were engaging, stimulating, interested as well as interesting, and they didn't even mention whether they were parents.

Derek was about the same age as Alex, but in appearance terms a complete contrast. Where Alex was tall and slim with a narrow tax inspector's face, Derek was quite short with a barrel chest, and his face was the face of a satisfied libertine, worn and lined but with the unmistakable glow of someone with no regrets. His wife, Elaine, was similarly short but she had the same trim body as Debbie, and a face that was made to smile and one that could never look entirely serious. Maybe it reflected her relationship with her husband, or the impact of some of his past disreputable behaviour. But however they looked, they proved themselves to be ideal table companions and, in Derek's case, the sort of ideal table companion who would not win many plaudits from the world's liberal-minded elite.

It became clear very early on that Derek regarded being forthright (with the emphasis on 'right') as being rather more important than being circumspect or restrained. This was confirmed when, later on in the evening, the table conversation had landed on the topic of the less-than-laudable behaviour of neighbouring countries, probably because on one side of the channel through which the *Sea Sprite* was travelling was Argentina and on the other was Chile. And Argentina and Chile hadn't always seen eye to eye, particularly regarding the ownership of some of the islands near the Beagle Channel. Like most other countries on Earth, they had found very little problem in identifying something about which they disagreed, and they had nearly resorted to war to settle – or sustain – their disagreement. Neighbouring countries that actually love their neighbours, it was decided at the table, are by no means the norm, and the more normal relationship lies somewhere between resentful tolerance and out-and-out hostility, with a simmering sense of superiority on either side to ensure that genuine rapprochement and mutual respect never really take hold. Derek did not argue with this conclusion, but he did have something to add.

'May I just suggest,' he started, 'that whilst I agree wholeheartedly with what has been said about the behaviour of neighbouring states, there is some merit in considering how their behaviour is a product of their functionality. And what I'd like to propose is that the more dysfunctional the state, the more likely it is to act aggressively towards its neighbours. Switzerland, for example, is, in my opinion, very unlikely to pick a fight with any of its neighbours. Primarily because it clearly doesn't need such a fight. Its economy and its culture are both ticking over very nicely, thank you very much, and its neighbours can be left to live in peace.

'But then you look at a car crash of a place like Russia, and it's a different matter altogether. Not content with annexing part of Georgia, it's now annexed part of Ukraine, and as far as I know, it's been messing with places like Estonia for years, and will no doubt continue to do so. And, of course, on top of all that, it isn't satisfied with screwing up just its immediate neighbours, but it's quite happy to reach out and bugger up places like Syria as well.

'And why? Well, because it's a rotten-to-the-core nation that needs to distract its peasants from its rotten nature. And to convince them that they have some sort of standing in the world, when they clearly haven't. When all they can offer the world are various forms of malicious behaviour, quite often involving the use of rockets, artillery, malware, or sometimes even radioactive poisons. Hell, being effing malevolent and spiteful is now what defines Russia. And incidentally, that's why it's not just its immediate neighbours who should be concerned, but the whole bloody world.'

One of the sailing pair tried to interrupt at this point, but Derek carried on.

'There are, of course, lots of other examples of how dysfunctional nations make bad neighbours, and whilst it's not quite in the same league as Russia, there's one over there...'

Here, he was pointing to the Argentinian side of the channel, and he continued his commentary as soon as he had lubricated his throat with another slug of wine.

'You know, at the start of the twentieth century, Argentina was the sixth richest country in the world. All that meat and all the other resources it had. And then one day it decided to embark on a journey to become one of the most economically dysfunctional countries in the world. And it succeeded. It has now had to deal with more financial crashes than its homemade Pope has had to deal with paedophile priests. And you know, it's been able to do this without its people stringing up its leaders by its deciding to pick on one of its neighbours. Not Chile, but a rather smaller, more distant one – way off its coast – and one that it didn't think would fight back.

'Of course, it got that wrong. Or should I say it got Mrs Thatcher wrong? But, nevertheless, it still has the Falklands in its sights, and it still uses this focused aggression – in intent if not in action – to distract its hopeless citizens from their hopeless performance. And if you think I might be egging it a bit there, might I just remind you that when it attacked the Falklands it demonstrated without a shadow of doubt that it couldn't organise even a piss-up, let alone a successful invasion. Because, like most others that pick a fight with their neighbours, Argentina is a country that is highly flawed and intrinsically inept. In other words, dysfunctional.'

Alex nodded in agreement, but then immediately made an observation.

'Some dysfunctional countries focus on their citizens rather than on their neighbours,' he suggested. 'Just think of Venezuela, for example. Sometimes it's easier to attack your own people than somebody else's.'

This observation had the desired effect. It sparked a two-way discussion between Derek and Alex on the various behaviours of dysfunctional states, and this ultimately drew in Debbie and Elaine. But not the other four diners at the table. (They seemed far more interested in their food.) Of course, this was exactly what Alex had wanted: the beginning of Derek and Elaine's ensnarement. And this was pretty well complete by the end of the meal. It was even them who suggested – quietly – to Alex and Debbie, that they should dine together again tomorrow. Possibly, they also suggested, with a new choice of other companions.

It made for a great end to this first day at sea, and it filled Alex with a great sense of anticipation. What would Derek and Elaine's views be on the age of so many of their travelling companions – and on the shape and the colour of them all?

three

The next morning was the start of a day 'at sea'. The *Sea Sprite* would be crossing the Argentine Sea on its way to the Falklands, and the only scenery visible from the ship would be the ocean and the sky. This experience wouldn't be a first for Alex and Debbie, as they had encountered this total absence of land for a whole day two or three times on their cruise through Melanesia. However, it was still a novel experience, and it made Alex consider what it must have been like for early maritime explorers, many of whom would often have had no idea of how many 'at sea' days they would have to endure, or indeed whether they would ever see land again. He could only conclude that they must have been very brave, very desperate or very stupid. Or a touch of all three. And they wouldn't even have had the delights of a modern cruise ship to enjoy, or the promise of a series of presentations to distract them. Alex and Debbie had both. And before the first of those presentations (the mandatory one) got under way, they wanted to explore their new ship to ensure that they knew the locations of all its delights. And they did this immediately after breakfast.

This meal had been consumed in the ship's indoor restaurant situated at the rear of its lowest public deck, the 'Magellan Deck'. This was a handsome room whose wood-and-brass decor echoed that of a private yacht, and indeed this same decor was to be found throughout the entire vessel. It was there in the corridor outside the restaurant that led to the doctor's surgery and to a dozen or so passenger cabins, and it was all the way up the stairwell that took them to the deck above. This was named after another explorer and was known as the Columbus Deck. Here was the reception area of the *Sea Sprite,* and another corridor running towards the bow of the ship between twenty other cabins. This deck also housed the stern-situated principal lounge, the home of safety briefings, biosecurity briefings, the planned programme of presentations, and indeed any sort of 'public' gathering. It boasted a similar decor to that in the rest of the ship, but the presence of rather too many upright easy chairs set out in well-ordered ranks made one think that one was no longer on an elegant yacht but instead in a care home. Even its carpet and curtains looked as though they had been chosen to provide no unwanted excitement to its enfeebled patrons.

It was all rather better on the deck above, this one named after a third explorer, in that it was known as the Marco Polo Deck. This housed twenty more cabins towards the bow, but at its stern there was a very inviting club-lounge-cum-bar that had not even a hint of care home about it. No, this had more the ambience of a country house, and this ambience was reinforced by the provision, at the back of the lounge, of a small library. This was accessed through two pairs of glass doors from the lounge and it was stocked with a healthy collection of both novels and reference books. Alex made a mental note to revisit it soon.

However, there was a little more of the ship to check out first, and before that mandatory presentation commenced. So, he and Debbie climbed up to the next deck, which was the Erikson Deck and the deck that was home to their own (starboard) cabin. Theirs was one of eight cabins on this deck, and it was situated at the far end of the corridor that led to the bridge – and that was closed off just beyond their cabin by a door in the corridor itself. Beyond this were the chief engineer's and the captain's cabins, a radio room, and then the bridge. Happily, this was not an out-of-bounds area, and if the corridor door was displaying a green indicator, one was allowed to pass through it and join the crew on the bridge. Only when there was a red indicator showing – to signify that the captain and his men were engaged in something tricky, like docking the vessel or negotiating a path through icebergs – was one not allowed to observe their operations. Instead, one might then want to take oneself to the rear of this deck, and there relish the view from the ship's outdoor lido restaurant – or alternatively one could climb to the top deck of the ship, the Explorer Deck. Here one could make one's way to a small observation terrace above the bridge, but what one could not do was examine the ship's ten zodiacs. These were stored in a restricted area at the rear of this deck, ready to be craned down to the sea whenever required, and they were entirely out of bounds in this situation. One would only be allowed in them when one was about to commence an excursion, and when, of course, one had been enlightened on all matters pertaining to biosecurity requirements in this part of the world. Yes, it was mandatory lesson time, and after a quick pit-stop at their cabin, Alex and Debbie made their way to the care-home lounge in readiness to receive their essential instructions.

Jane, the cruise director, was in charge of proceedings, and she started by emphasising the need for constant vigilance; for the need to be aware that, as a visitor to these southern realms, one was a 'real and present' hazard; and that the fauna and flora to be found here had not evolved to withstand an onslaught by unwanted alien invaders. What this meant in practice was that one had to take particular care with whatever one was wearing, and ensure that it carried no undesirable soil, seeds or other potential threats to the legitimate plant or animal residents of the places to be visited. Alex could well understand the importance of this approach, but he was yet to become fully aware of what it would entail in practice. Especially when the *Sea Sprite* delivered him to South Georgia.

Having got her basic message across, Jane then spent some time explaining that the assembled company was on its way not to a benign set of islands in the South Pacific, but to a very inhospitable part of the world with notoriously unpredictable weather. What this meant was that, on every shore visit, the passenger-carrying zodiacs would be preceded by one or two zodiacs carrying just emergency survival kit, kit that would enable the pupils in the room to survive for twenty-four hours should the weather prevent their return to the ship for this length of time. Oh, and this kit had been employed on numerous occasions in the past.

This was a salutary message, and Alex took it to heart. Just as he did the warning that fur seals could often be really dangerous, and that a bite from an elephant seal was to be avoided at all costs. Apparently, they don't have just teeth in their mouths, but also a thriving colony of bacteria known to be harmful to humans. Not quite a case of rabies, Jane said, but something you'd probably not wish on your worst enemy. And, in all likelihood, the medication you'd require would mean that you couldn't imbibe any of the ship's all-inclusive wine. And Alex found that prospect more than a little disagreeable.

What he also found disagreeable was the fact that included in the 'how to behave towards wildlife' guidance, there was now, as well as 'Don't get within X feet of an animal or bird', 'Don't block their path' and 'Don't alarm them', a call to 'Don't ever feed them'. This, it appeared, had been added to the list of 'don'ts' ever since ships visiting this region had brought with them hordes of Chinese. Alex found this depressing but not surprising, and wondered whether the authorities had been obliged to consider extending this new exhortation to include the request 'Don't ever eat them' as well. God help the wildlife here, thought Alex, if there's a whole tidal wave of China's terrible-tourists about to overwhelm it.

Anyway, it was now time to conclude his exercise in offensive but justifiable racial profiling, as Jane's lecture had been completed and it was time instead to collect one's ship-issued boots and one's ship-issued windbreakers. Because, although Alex and Debbie had kitted themselves out with a whole wardrobe of thermal underwear, insulated trousers, waterproof trousers, inner gloves, outer gloves, inner socks, outer socks, neck warmers, beanie hats, heavy-duty fleeces and down jackets, they still needed a windbreaker to protect them from… the wind, and some sturdy waterproof boots that would enable them to make landings in the surf and even traverse the odd shallow river. Encouragingly, for both of them, the boots and the windbreakers seemed to fit well, although Alex did wonder whether, as well as a life jacket and a dangling pair of binoculars, he could really cope with five layers of clothing on his upper body. He normally wore only one…

He was still pondering this conundrum when he and Debbie returned to the lounge to listen to a presentation by Nick, the bird man, on *Birds of the Falklands and South Georgia*. They both had more than a passing interest in birds, but they both also knew that their knowledge of the birds of this region was sadly lacking. And especially in respect of those that are inconsiderate enough to spend most of their lives at sea and are therefore really difficult to observe. They needed a crash course in identifying the relevant species, and that was just what Nick was about to provide.

He was a natural. He was a good speaker, and he was so knowledgeable about his subject that he could well have been on autopilot. The lecture just seemed to stream out of his mouth without any effort at all, and in a way that made it particularly memorable. How he did this, Alex was at first unsure. But then he spotted the trick. Put up an image of Bird A on the two screens at the front of the lounge, talk about it for some time, explaining how to identify it and where it is likely to be found, and then and only then reveal its name. It was an excellent way to capture your audience's attention and to keep it captive. And Alex thought it should be promulgated within the entire teaching establishment back in Britain as a way of (possibly) capturing the attention of the rather younger audiences they had to deal with there.

Anyway, stuffed with an abundance of knowledge about storm petrels, southern giant petrels, cape petrels and three dozen other birds, Alex and Debbie retired to their cabin to don what they thought might be the required amount of cold-weather gear to allow them to conduct some bird-spotting from the rear of the ship. They would install themselves on the sheltered area beyond the library on the Marco Polo Deck, and attempt to find and identify some of the pelagic birds that Nick had assured his students were to be seen in this area. Fortunately, when they arrived at their chosen location, it was not only as sheltered as they'd hoped it would be, but it was also equipped with that knowledgeable ornithologist. Nick was there with four other passengers, pointing out – and naming – a whole range of avian escorts. There were four sorts of petrels, the occasional shearwater and albatross, and even the very occasional penguin, carving its way deftly through the water. And these last chaps were probably from a colony somewhere in West Falkland – hundreds of miles away. The natural world, concluded Alex (again), was just remarkable beyond belief. So too was the spotting ability of one of Alex's fellow passengers at the back of the ship. His was up there with Nick's.

His name, it transpired, was Roy, and Roy was a single traveller who, as Alex would soon discover, had the singular good fortune to possess a gigantic brain that contained a whole library of facts not only about birds, but also about butterflies and many other sorts of insects – and about plants, literature, world music, world politics – and flags. Here was a man, in his late sixties and with the build and the face of a retired prize fighter, who could follow an instructive discourse on snowy sheathbills with an explanation of the colour choice for the Argentinian presidential flag, and how its design had subtly changed since its first manifestation in the summer of 1812. Fortunately, his encyclopaedic abilities didn't preclude him from having a sense of humour and an interest in just about everything. And Alex and Debbie discovered this when they had lunch with him – in the lido restaurant. They would have to try to get him to join them for their evening meal, and introduce him to Derek and Elaine.

Before then, however, there was some more unpacking to do and another presentation to attend, this one given by a real-life professor called Colin – on the Antarctic Treaty System. Alex had particularly wanted to see this, but the travels involved in getting to Ushuaia and their busy first day aboard the ship had left him feeling a little tired, and he wondered whether it might be better to just rest in their cabin. When he made this known to Debbie, she reminded him that all the ship's presentations were carried on one of the TV channels, and if one chose to, one could listen to the presentations and even see the visuals being used without leaving one's cabin or even one's bed.

Perfect! Alex would learn all he needed to know about the Antarctic Treaty System while propped up on a pillow. Just as soon, that is, as he'd identified which channel on the TV he should use. And it was as he was doing this that he discovered that, as well as the in-house presentations channel, there was another that showed the view from a camera on the prow of the ship, three more that showed films and various nature programmes and two more that were still carrying twenty-four-hour news coverage! How on Earth he had forgotten his experience in Melanesia – where similar news portals were always available – he could not understand. But, of course, technology had now progressed to the point where it was actually more difficult to be out of the range of world events than it was to be within their range. And no doubt CNN – and BBC World News – would accompany the *Sea Sprite* even if it decided to drag itself over the icy expanse of Antarctica to the South Pole itself. There was, therefore, only one thing to do: accept that 'the news' was still very much there, and resort to his normal habit of watching far too much of it. Even down here in the southern world. And he would start with a healthy dose of BBC World.

Not surprisingly, he soon discovered that he could have written the news himself. President Assad was still busy dropping barrels full of high explosives and assorted nuts and bolts onto small children, and was well on his way to reducing a country that Alex and Debbie had once visited to a blood-soaked wasteland. President Trump had just tweeted – with little in the way of grammar but with lots of capitals – another pile of garbage. President Xi Jinping had released an announcement that China's latest homegrown flu epidemic was now succumbing to the power of his all-powerful Communist Party. And President Putin had reiterated his claim that the Malaysian Airlines airliner downed over the Ukraine quite some time ago was the work of a bunch of inebriated, trigger-happy Ukrainian soldiers, and that Russia had always made a point of never pointing any of its armaments at anybody, let alone at a plane full of innocent people. Oh, and neither had Russia ever engaged in any sort of cyber warfare.

Alex touched on these remarkable Russian revelations when he was seated for his evening meal; a meal that would be shared with his and Debbie's carefully selected companions: the forthright Derek, the charming Elaine and the human database, Roy. This fifth conspirator had been welcomed into the fold by Derek and Elaine with open arms. They must have spotted almost immediately that he would make for very good company, and that he might also prove to be a fount of information on any number of things. In fact, soon after Alex's brief dissertation on the innocence of Russia and a brief round-table exchange on the afternoon's presentation, Roy won the attention of all those around the table by pronouncing on the comparative risks of dying on a cruise ship versus on an airliner. This wasn't one of his normal areas of interest, he explained, and he hadn't been able to perform a rigorous check on all the relative data. Nevertheless, he was still able to reassure them that reputable cruise ships were safer, in unscheduled mortality terms, than even the super-safe aircraft in service today. Although he did go on to provide a caveat concerning the heightened dangers arising from any floating vessel's proximity to an iceberg.

It should be emphasised that, whilst he clearly knew what he was talking about, his revelations were presented as a light-hearted contribution to the table talk and in no way came over as nerdy. Roy might know his facts, but he also knew how to relate to other people and how to amuse them. Furthermore, he knew when to listen; as, for example, when the conversation had wound its way around to human rights – via the threatened rights of Falklanders to live in peace – and Derek was being his now predictably forthright self.

'They're a bloody menace. A bunch of ridiculously ambitious, apparently inherent entitlements that exist in a vacuum and are about as anchored in reality as Alice in effing Wonderland. I mean, let's be clear. Just like every tiger, civet, worm and cockroach, no human arrives in this world with any *inherent* rights. To suggest so is just as stupid as saying that they arrive in this world with some sort of Original Sin. And we all know how bloody stupid that is. No, what happens is that the society into which they're born confers on them some *civil* rights, and it is these sorts of rights that actually mean something.

'I do accept, of course, that certain societies confer a lot more rights than others. I wouldn't, for example, wish to make my way through life with a set of Libyan civil rights, and certainly not with a set of North Korean civil rights. But that doesn't detract from my main point, which is that, to mean anything at all, rights of any sort whatsoever have to be conferred – and policed – by a nation state. To expect a whole set of nebulous human rights, detached from reality and from any sort of real legitimacy, to actually work is just wishful thinking. Remember, these rights are not rooted in any real society, *and* they often conflict with a particular society's legitimate *civil* rights. I mean, just think of some of the dafter human rights and then think about how they prevent us from deporting some bleedin' terrorist. It's just bloody stupid.

'And one last thing. By constantly emphasising the importance of human rights, we successfully ignore the importance of human *responsibilities*. And this is because the existing UN canon of improbable human rights requires in reality no responsibilities on the part of those who demand them. After all, they're inherent, remember. Whereas with civil rights… well, they involve all sorts of responsibilities, not least the responsibility to maintain the societies in which they exist. So, in short, human rights encourage people to think selfishly about their entitlements, often at the expense of others. Civil rights promote an understanding of the responsibilities that all rights entail.'

Alex was impressed. He could have scripted that little speech himself. Albeit he might have waited to deliver it when everybody at the table had taken a glass or two more. Serious issues of the sort just addressed were always more easily digestible, Alex thought, if they were preceded by more than a soupçon of lubrication. That said, he had enjoyed that further dose of Derek's candid thinking, and it seemed to have gone down well with all the other diners at the table. Debbie, in particular, had drunk deeply from the well of Derek's discourse, and as Alex was thinking, she was talking – to Derek – about the epidemic of human rights lawyers. She seemed to be questioning why they tended to spend so much of their time in benign jurisdictions such as Britain and not in places where their services might actually be welcomed, places, for example, where things like female genital mutilation were commonplace. Maybe, she herself suggested, the fees and the wine bars in those sorts of places were not nearly so attractive…

Anyway, ultimately the dinner came to an end, and all five diners returned to their rooms, having promised that they would dine together again – given, of course, that, despite Roy's careful calculations, the *MS Sea Sprite* hadn't come to grief overnight. Even if it wasn't yet near any icebergs…

four

When Stuart had applied for an overseas posting, he'd had in mind somewhere like the Caribbean or maybe somewhere in the Far East; somewhere that was the antithesis of boring old Gloucestershire. After all, his team leader had made it pretty clear that these were the two likely destinations. And he'd definitely said nothing about a desolate, windswept island in the South Atlantic; a place where the principal differences from Gloucestershire would simply be more sheep and more rain. And as for the opportunities for romantic encounters in this god-forsaken place... Well, they were just about as rare as encountering any excitement here. It really was the dull capital of the world, and he was stuck here for a whole eighteen months!

His mistake had been to neglect that he was fluent in Spanish, and that this fact would hardly go unnoticed by those who organised overseas postings. It just made their job easy; as easy as Stuart's present job was difficult to endure.

As soon as he'd arrived here, he'd begun counting down the days. And not even the odd day in Joe's eight-metre yacht would stop him doing that. He did love sailing, but taking account of the long hours he worked – and the vicissitudes of the local weather – he could indulge this love on only very rare occasions. Most of the time he had to entertain himself with just reading, listening to music, and drinking. And avoiding the blasted wind. If only he'd not applied in the first place, or had not learnt Spanish, or had used his degree in botany to become a botanist, or had taken up a career as a sign-writer. Or if he'd developed an allergy to sheep...

However, he *had* learnt Spanish, he *had* taken up a career in intelligence and he *had* applied for an overseas posting. Without first developing an allergy to sheep. So, he just had to accept his present predicament and look for ways to make the best of it. Especially during his long hours at work. That would not be easy. There was, after all, little possibility that any of the intercepts he had to pore over every day would help him in any way. Most were just mundane, and some barely reached even that threshold. They were even duller than the dull capital of the world. But what could one expect? South America was still something of a backwater in terms of world affairs, and communications between even the Presidents in this continent tended to be just parochial in nature, and would be of very little interest to anybody in the rest of the world. They were certainly barely of any interest to anybody back in Gloucestershire.

In fact, Stuart had decided that the only people who might find a genuine interest in everything he saw each and every day would be scholars; academics who had chosen as their field of research the comparative characteristics of different South American nations. Very soon, for example, they would have discovered that Uruguay's character was that of a well-organised city gent, reflecting its status as the well-ordered Switzerland of the southern continent. Whereas that of Paraguay was that of a paranoid recluse. This country had yet to shed the isolationism – and paranoia – instilled into its very being by its first dictator back in the first half of the nineteenth century, one José Gaspar Rodríguez de Francia, whose political ideas were novel to say the least, but also very long-lasting.

Then there was Brazil. Too big a country to be run effectively and coherently by any Brazilian, as was only too obvious from every intercept Stuart had ever seen. And then, of course, Venezuela; a country with 'learning difficulties' that Stuart could never imagine being able to live a normal adult life. Especially now that it was drowning in corruption; a feature of its character that was blatantly obvious in so many of its internal communications. Argentina wasn't anywhere near as bad, but it was bad enough, and certainly bad enough to convince Stuart that it no longer represented the threat it had in the past. And what's more, most of its population probably knew this as well. So, its claims on the Falklands would now probably ossify into the same lifeless corpse as Bolivia's claims on Chile for a means of access to the sea. Where Bolivia now pays homage to its own cadaver by holding an annual *Día del Mar* (Or Day of the Sea), Argentina holds a *Día de las Malvinas* to honour just its fallen in the Falklands War, but not yet the demise of its hopes to annex this faraway prize. In due course, Stuart believed, it would. And then Argentina might even begin to sort itself out.

Mind, that certainly wouldn't happen before Stuart had done his time in dullsville and returned home to Britain. And meanwhile it was just 8.30 in the morning, and now he was ensconced in his boxlike office he had some intercepts to deal with. In fact, he had a whole library of the buggers to get to grips with, and with not even the prospect of finding something interesting to look at. Just more of the mundane, more of the duller-than-dull and maybe the occasional 'entirely incomprehensible'. As in his own entirely incomprehensible behaviour that had brought him to this windblown, sheep-infested rock. It was no good. He would just have to forget his self-inflicted misfortune and get on with his work.

Maybe Bolsonaro had dropped another bollock, and Stuart would be the one to find it. Or maybe the flight coming in from Brize Norton today would contain a contingent of Pre-Raphaelite beauties, but not necessarily with all their clothes. Or maybe the wind would just continue to blow and Stuart would simply become one day older and one day closer to getting back to Britain. Without much else happening at all. He was pretty damn sure he knew which of these three options it would be…

five

The walk-in wardrobe in Alex and Debbie's cabin contained two of those impossible immersion suits and four life jackets. Two of the jackets were of the bulky 'ship at risk of sinking' variety, and had been test-worn prior to the ship's original safety briefing. The other two were examples of lifesaving gear that was much less bulky, and that was designed to be worn by the ship's passengers whenever they were aboard a zodiac. These had not been tackled before. But, as it was now time to prepare for their first zodiac ride, Alex and Debbie were currently trying to secure these two encumbrances over their shoulders, and over five layers of clothing. This was not easy, and it only added to the overheating that had commenced as soon as they'd each encased themselves in the full twenty-one items of clothing that made up their cold-weather kit – while still situated in a warm and cosy cabin. Alex could well understand how self-insulated haystacks could quite easily get so hot at their centres that they burst into flames. He didn't, of course, think that he ran much of a risk of spontaneous human combustion, but there was definitely the risk of minor heatstroke. And grappling with these damn life jackets certainly wasn't helping matters at all.

Needless to say, as soon as they had both overcome the life jacket challenge, they decided to leave their cabin and station themselves at the rear of the outdoor lido restaurant. Here, in much cooler conditions, they would await the call to board one of the zodiacs when these had been readied for use. From their chosen vantage point they could observe these craft being prepared. All ten had now been craned down from the top of the ship and, including the two that had already been used to take the survival kit to shore, they were all now loitering around the stern of the ship. Soon, one of them had been stationed next to the landing stage three decks below, and the boarding call was made – for just starboard cabin passengers, in order to avoid an unseemly jam. So, Alex and Debbie began to make their way down, interested to see what the loading procedures would entail. They soon discovered that they entailed a check of their life jackets, the stepping into a bath of some sort of disinfectant, and then the presentation of their electronic ship-passports to enable Jane to ensure that, in due course, all those she had let loose ashore had eventually returned to the ship before the ship steamed away. It was apparently regarded as poor cruise practice to leave a string of abandoned cruise passengers in the wake of one's passage across the seas.

With all these procedures completed, one was then allowed to step – with just a little steadying help – into one's zodiac, and one then found oneself seated on one of the inflated sides of the zodiac, with ultimately three others on one's own side, and four on the side facing. At which point, the zodiac's engine was put into gear and its team-member driver began the process of taking his craft to its destination. Which on this occasion was a beach maybe five hundred yards away on a small island that formed part of West Falkland (the barely inhabited half of the Falklands that lies to the west of… East Falkland). Alex and Debbie, it appeared, were just about to embark on the exploration part of their voyage. And they were suitably filled with excitement.

The island was Saunders Island, and at that moment, whilst there was a strong wind blowing, any potential rain was just sitting above it in some threatening grey clouds. It was dry, and the only moisture settling itself onto Alex's waterproofs was spray from the sea. This he was happy to accommodate, just as he was more than happy to see that his zodiac was being escorted to shore by a pod of playful dolphins. And they were dolphins he had never seen before, because they were Commerson's dolphins; a species found around the tip of South America and out here in the Falklands. And because they have a black head, dorsal fin and fluke and a white throat and body, they are also known as piebald dolphins or panda dolphins. And with their propensity to swim close to the surface – and very close to any available zodiacs – they made this first landfall in West Falkland one that Alex and Debbie would not easily forget. Nor would they easily forget the time they were about to spend on Saunders Island itself…

It was like a sliver of the Hebrides – with penguins. Grass-covered, treeless, windswept and unavoidably beguiling, it provided an ideal home for some of these enchanting birds. To start with, Alex and Debbie came across a colony of gentoo penguins, many of them in horizontal mode as they 'sat' on the pile of pebbles they called their nest, incubating their eggs. They were captivating – and unbothered; a pair of features of the wildlife in this part of the world that would become ever more obvious as Alex and Debbie made ever more landings. The Magellanic penguins were just the same. With their bullseye-inspired coats and their rabbit-like burrowing habits, they could not fail to enthral any observer. And then there were the rockhopper penguins, who – with their red eyes and their punk haircuts, complete with yellow side spikes – had the appearance of the sort of bird one might encounter after taking magic mushrooms.

No such psychedelic association would be inspired by the next birds Alex and Debbie observed, because these were not more penguins but albatrosses; black-browed albatrosses, a whole colony of them spread out across the steep slopes of a narrow bay. And they were simply elegant beyond words; genuinely tear-inducing – and mesmerising. As, in their own way, were a family of upland geese encountered on the walk back to the zodiac, and a pair of striated caracaras, two angels of death perched on a rock above the rockhopper colony, and waiting to exploit any of its unguarded moments. And all these birds really were as unconcerned by a party of visiting primates as it was possible to be. It was something Alex loved to observe; a reminder that, from other animals' perspective, the species known as *Homo sapiens* wasn't necessarily the most interesting species on the planet. And neither, on this occasion, did it look at all graceful or in any way composed.

This was not only because the island's terrain was in places quite demanding, but also because the earlier wind had dropped and the temperature had risen. Quite noticeably. If one was therefore still dressed for true Antarctic conditions as one was scrabbling around that demanding terrain, it was all too easy to appear rather distressed if not a little ridiculous. Alex and Debbie would have to learn from this excursion and in the future dress accordingly.

This they did immediately after lunch and before they had embarked on another zodiac ride to another destination in West Falkland, known as West Point. And it was as well that they had discarded some of their insulating apparel, because on the island of West Point they were faced with a two-mile hike across a moor-like stretch of land, with some of that hike inevitably being uphill. It was, however, worth it. Because at the end of that hike they were able to get within feet of a mixed colony of rockhopper penguins and black-browed albatrosses, and once again experience the complete indifference of the island's residents to the presence of humans. It was a wonderful and very humbling experience.

In a very different way, so too was the visit to the home of the only human residents of West Point: a farmer and his wife who lived in a tin-roofed wooden farmhouse just up from the island's only jetty. Here Alex and Debbie found a flagpole with a pristine Falkland Islands flag flying from its top, and a less-than-pristine dwelling, in the sense that it looked very weather-worn and more than a little in need of some thoughtful TLC. That said, it was sheltered behind a wall of venerable (planted) cypresses, and it had a charming garden full of plants like lupins and hebes, with even a clump of honesty by the kitchen door. Furthermore, inside the kitchen was a large table groaning under the weight of a huge spread of home-made cakes and biscuits; an overload of sustenance for the *Sea Sprite's* passengers to sustain them all till dinner.

It was no doubt a commercial arrangement between the tour operators and the farmer's wife, but it was delightful all the same, and very welcome after the afternoon's walk. It also reinforced in Alex's mind that the Falklands are no more than a little slice of Britain sitting in the South Atlantic, occupied by a bunch of people who could easily be living in some of the remoter parts of the British Isles. It was indisputable. These folk, with their scones, lemon sponges and tiered cake stands, might not be true endemics of the Falkland Islands, but they were true natives of this place, and true British natives to the core. Indeed, Alex decided that he wouldn't be in any way surprised if he saw more clear evidence of Britishness when the *Sea Sprite* docked in Stanley the following morning.

However, that was tomorrow, and there was still an evening to get through; a task that would prove not at all difficult as the weather had transformed itself from dull and overcast to bright blue sky, and the *Sea Sprite's* course towards East Falkland would now take it through sheltered waters; an ideal combination for another spell of al fresco dining...

Gathered around a table for six this evening were Alex and Debbie; Derek and Elaine; Roy, the database; and Nick, the ship's ornithologist. This promising combination saw Roy and Nick engage immediately on the etymology of various bird names, in which, unsurprisingly, Roy had a particular interest. The others around the table became mere interested bystanders to this exchange, up until the point where they had to take sides on the origin of the name 'gentoo'. Nick was fairly convinced that it was simply derived from another name for this bird, which was 'Johnny penguin'. And 'Johnny' in Spanish is 'Juanito', which sounds vaguely like 'gentoo'. Roy, on the other hand, thought that it was a straight steal of the Anglo-Indian word '*gentoo*', a word that was used to distinguish Hindus from Muslims, and was applied to this particular species of penguin because of the supposed likeness of the patch of white on its head to a… turban. When a vote was taken, Nick won by a margin of four to nil. None of the voting panel, it seemed, could ever imagine the rather modest patch of white on this penguin's head ever putting anybody in mind of a turban. Roy conceded defeat gracefully, and he didn't even protest when his reference to two world faiths caused the conversation to abandon birds entirely and instead dive headlong into the highly risky waters of religion.

This topic engaged all six around the table for quite a while, but did little other than confirm that they all had very little time for redundant superstitions, and that none of them could really explain why, in certain 'religious' cultures, piety and depravity seemed always to be joined at the hip. Their failure to resolve this question did, however, lead to a further discussion about which countries in the world they would no longer be prepared to visit.

There were many, and a lot more, they all agreed, than there had been twenty or thirty years ago. So, added to all those that had never had much to offer in terms of natural wonders, there were now a whole raft of countries that were too touristy, too 'developed', too authoritarian or too bloody dangerous (generally thanks to their being infected by some form of diseased fundamentalism). In fact, Debbie made the point that there was definitely scope for an imaginative map-maker to produce a map of the world that would replace all these totally unappealing countries with just sea. By doing this he would find that he'd have a ready market amongst all those planning where next to visit in the world that wasn't on their mental no-go list. The map would also, suggested Elaine, have a lot of blue on it. And nobody disagreed with that. Although Derek did point out that he wouldn't buy it unless China was one of the countries replaced by a patch of blue...

Nick made the mistake of asking why this was so, and he was soon to find out. Derek's antipathy towards China, it appeared, was multi-faceted and the product of a whole stack of issues that he had with the behaviour of this giant country. This was all too apparent in the answer he provided, one that was as uncompromising as it was savage.

'If Earth were a galaxy,' he started, 'China would be a black hole: one of those mysterious and frightening astronomical phenomena that suck in all that's around them. And, of course, provide no illumination whatsoever. I mean, just think about it. Over the past thirty years it's been sucking in much of the world's intellectual property – illegally – to help it suck in much of the world's manufacturing, along with all those millions of manufacturing jobs. Put another way, it has managed to make almost an artform out of copying, imitating, cheating and simply stealing a whole range of technologies, and then throwing in the odd bit of counterfeiting for good measure. And, all at our expense. And it's also, of course, been sucking in shedloads of resources from all around the world; all the coal, iron ore, assorted minerals, timber and any other stuff it can get its hands on to feed its new-found insatiable appetite. It is a ghastly black hole.'

Here, Alex interrupted.

'You can't leave it there!'

Derek smiled.

'I was just drawing breath. Just before I tell you what really makes me loathe this giant soddin' vacuum cleaner, and that's the way it hasn't just been sucking up the world's resources, jobs, secrets and wealth, but also its precious wildlife. There's not one part of this world that hasn't felt the impact of China's shameless interest in harvesting whatever's rare and irreplaceable. And the rarer the quarry and the closer to extinction it is, the better. More chance then that it will command an exorbitant price in some exclusive Beijing restaurant, or maybe a ridiculous price if it can be claimed that its skin or its spleen will cure you of cancer and at the same time stiffen your willy. So, if you're a sea cucumber off one of the Galápagos Islands – essential to the whole ecosystem there – forget it. You're just too bloody tasty. And it's not a great deal better if you're a turtle or a tiger or a pangolin or a poor soddin' bear. And if you're an elephant, you'd just better hope that your local African government hasn't signed a deal to let the Chinese build a new road in your country. Cos if that road comes anywhere near you, so too will the poachers and then the middle men; those grubby little bastards who'll be shipping your tusks back to China before you can say, "effin' ivory trinkets".

'And as for rhinos… well, they're on their way out. And again, it'll be that black gaping hole called China that'll cause their demise. Just as it'll soon be responsible for eliminating every last shark on the planet. I mean, you cannot carry on killing one hundred million of those wonderful creatures every year, and then expect them to survive for very long. And for some soup, for God's sake! For a bowl of effin' soup! It's just barbaric; pure, unadulterated barbarism. Or, if you're in China, just the highlight of a nice night out, probably rounded off with a live snake skinned at your table followed by a restorative dose of bear-bile puree. It makes me sick. It makes me feel physically sick...'

'You wouldn't believe what they try to bring into Australia,' offered Nick. 'They'll try and sneak in anything. And without any thought for the risks it might pose. Or, I might say, for our own Aussie culture...'

Well, this was becoming something of an exercise in overt racism, but it wasn't over yet. This time it was Roy who added to the assault.

'That flu thing they've got at the moment – I bet I know where it started. Just like all those other flus from the East; stuff like SARS and all those other coronavirus epidemics...'

'Wild animal markets,' interrupted Alex. 'Those sickening places where you can find your next interesting meal cowering in a tiny, filthy cage – next to hundreds of other tiny, filthy cages – and not feel one ounce of sympathy for the poor animal's dreadful plight. After all, it's just a civet or a snake or a bat or some other miserable specimen of worthless wildlife. And it's only got any worth at all because you're going to steam it and eat it. Just before you take that potion of donkey-skin gelatine that you so much adore. And meanwhile, back at that market, a new animal virus decides that, for a change, it'll choose a human as a host, and the next lethal pandemic will be unleashed on the world. In fact, infectious diseases are about the only things that China gives the rest of the world in exchange for everything it sucks out of it. If you ignore the lessons it provides on how not to run a country…'

'You mean…?' prompted Elaine.

'I mean the way it's constructing an Orwellian surveillance state. The way it's incarcerating all those millions of its own people whom it doesn't regard as properly Chinese. The way it's seeking to intimidate its neighbours, either by seizing faraway islands or by making direct threats. And the way it's ensnaring countries all around the world with its promises, its "assistance", its finance – and ultimately its debt. Yes, if one had to design a nation that was a truly malign influence on the rest of the world, one would probably come up with something like Russia as the prototype and then refine it until one had something that was indistinguishable from China. I too would definitely want that map with that… huge black hole replaced by just sea.'

Derek raised his glass to Alex, and Alex raised his, and then he asked Derek a question.

'You don't think we're being just a little bit harsh? You know, you can't write off a whole country. There must be millions of decent Chinese.'

'Yeah. And they're making themselves known, aren't they? Out on the streets every day, calling for all those markets to be closed and for all their restaurants to take shark-fin soup off the menu. Or maybe they're not. Maybe they have other priorities. Like making a god out of President Xi. I'm sorry, Alex, but as you may have noticed, I don't like to get too tangled up in nuances and any sort of mitigating arguments.

As far as I'm concerned, China is the pits, and I suspect that, if they knew what's in store for them, the last remnants of the world's wildlife would hold that very same view.'

Well, that pronouncement more or less wrapped up the dismemberment of the most populous nation on the planet, and the conversation then drifted on through the dangers of sobriety and the merits of chicanery before concluding for the night. Alex had enjoyed it all: the not-entirely-charitable discussion, the company at the table, and the meal itself. All he had to do now was return to his cabin where, with Debbie, he would make one last inspection of their boots before preparing himself for some much-needed sleep. After all, tomorrow promised to be a busy day. The *Sea Sprite* would be arriving in Stanley, one of the few capitals of the world yet to fall under the hegemony of China. And it would be necessary to confirm that it was unlikely to do so in the near future. Even if it hosted a Chinese takeaway. Which it probably didn't…

six

What Stanley did host was a bust of Margaret Thatcher. Mike, the former Royal Marine, enlightened Alex with this information while they were waiting to disembark the *Sea Sprite* in Stanley's modest port. And he also confirmed that it *didn't* have a Chinese takeaway, but instead just four very English pubs, of which The Globe Tavern was the most iconic. Or at least the most popular choice amongst all the military types who served on the island. He, of course, knew these important facts because, as well as having fought in the Falklands War, he had been back to this remote place several times since. He had lost too many friends here to dismiss it from his life entirely.

Alex made the mistake of asking him whether it had all been worth it, and had received in response an emphatic 'Yes'. Mike was unmistakably a natural warrior. Even though he was now past fighting age, with his solid build, his massive arms and a discernible air of both strength and resolve, he could have been nothing else. But he was a thinker as well. That 'yes' was followed by the rather desolate admission, 'But I survived it, didn't I?', and then a distinctly wry smile. Alex wasn't sure how to respond, and settled on a feeble 'I'm sure you're right. And I'm sure you've given it a lot more thought than I have.' Mike gave an indeterminate nod to acknowledge this platitude, and then Alex was saved from any further embarrassment by a call to disembark. He, Debbie and about twenty other shipmates were about to set off to visit a farm…

There wasn't much wildlife within excursion distance of Stanley's port, so Jane had organised three options for the passengers of the *Sea Sprite* that entailed no tracking down of wildlife at all. One was a visit to the site of a Falklands War battleground, the second was a guided walk around Stanley, and the third was a visit to a Falklands sheep farm to get an insight into how the locals made a living out of the local unforgiving terrain. Alex and Debbie had chosen this third option because there would still be an opportunity to stroll around Stanley after the farm visit was concluded, and the advertised attractions of this farm included some peat-cutting and a spot of sheep shearing, both of which sounded marginally more interesting than trying to find any tangible evidence of a now-ancient battle.

They boarded a coach to take them to the farm, situated some thirty miles outside the Falklands capital, and it initially took them towards Stanley itself, which was no more than a mile or so away. The road was tarmacked, and it was still tarmacked as it skirted the suburbs of this mini capital, and apparently for quite a few miles after that. This, their local guide informed them, was because the British government had decided that a proper surfaced road was necessary to connect Stanley with the enormous airbase it had built after the Falklands conflict. And this stretch of road on the way to the farm was the beginning of that new highway. Their guide also informed them that his principal job was as a disc jockey on Falklands Radio, but of far more interest to Alex was his mention of that substantial military establishment, the positively named RAF Mount Pleasant.

Before he'd embarked on this trip to Antarctica, he'd used Mr Google to do a little research on this place, and had been intrigued to discover its size – in population terms – compared to that of Stanley and to that of the whole of the Falklands. Because it was reckoned to be home to about 1,200 people, most of whom were service personnel engaged in manning and maintaining the aeroplanes on the base, along with the missile systems, and whatever other protective and monitoring assets were housed in its eight thousand acres of land. That meant that Mount Pleasant had a population only seven hundred fewer than that of Stanley, and that it constituted over a quarter of the entire population of West and East Falkland combined. It was an enormous investment by the UK, but one that was thought vital to guarantee the self-determination of the locals, and to protect the Falklands' fish stocks and its potential offshore oil riches, both of which some dastardly South American nation might claim as its own. It was now an established outpost of the British military, and one that provided it with all sorts of training opportunities that were simply not available at home (such as the availability of empty, demanding countryside, and, of course, equally empty skies). And there was also, according to the oracle, Roy – who knew most things about all things – a listening post somewhere on the base that was run by GCHQ or some other agency, and that monitored communications throughout the whole of the South American continent. Roy did emphasise that he could not be entirely sure that this was correct, but over breakfast he had assured Alex that the base definitely did have its own library, cinema, swimming pool, gym, climbing wall, golf course, kart-racing track, cricket ground and even a Costa Coffee shop, such was the need to keep the troops happy in their enforced isolation. Alex would have dearly liked to visit the place, but that wouldn't happen today. Instead, the coach driver finally found a turn-off from that tarmacked road to Mount Pleasant, and one that would eventually deliver his passengers to Long Island Farm, a rather smaller establishment than that military base – with a population of... just one.

She was waiting to greet the coach as it arrived, a rather weathered-looking lady who called this secluded outpost masquerading as a farm, her home. It was West Point all over again, except her farmhouse, in its exposed coastal setting, was even lacking the shelter of some much-needed trees. The wind was blowing strongly, and Alex soon formed the view that it probably blew continuously as well. It would have sent him mad within days.

Anyway, the lady of the farm had not just the company of the *Sea Sprite* visitors today, but also that of her (arithmetically) middle-aged son who had travelled from his home in Stanley to assist her in the hosting of her guests. And it was this sensible son who invited the coach-load of visitors to join him in order to observe some peat-cutting. He, it transpired, was the peat cutter, and whilst his skills were impressive, Alex soon decided that peat-cutting did not really constitute a spectator sport. Neither did the unsuccessful sheep-herding with a semi-retired sheepdog, conducted by the mother. And it wasn't until the son took the band of visitors into the sheep-shearing shed that things began to get more interesting. He, of course, was the sheep shearer as well, and he was very good at it, and much better than he was at defending the general sheep husbandry in these parts, which seemed to involve letting the sheep roam wild until they died of either starvation or cold. Perhaps, thought Alex, there *were* some differences between Falklanders and Britons after all. Nevertheless, the lady of the farm proved to be another champion in the preparation of home-made cakes and biscuits, and when the visiting party had eaten enough of these – in the lady's peat-heated house – it was time to be returned to Stanley to consider the comparative merits of urban and rural Falklands.

There was no competition. Whereas rural Falklands was clearly a very close neighbour of purgatory, Stanley gave the impression of being within sight of the uplands of heaven. It was clean, ordered, relatively attractive, and it clearly provided its residents with a peaceful and comparatively effortless life; at least compared to those who struggled to exist on any of the surrounding sheep farms. It also looked prosperous; not outrageously affluent but just really very comfortable, due in part, no doubt, to all the wealth that seeped out from that huge military base thirty miles up the road. Maybe the Argentinians had done the Falklanders a favour. They had unintentionally provided them with a permanent source of additional income, courtesy of the UK taxpayers, which could only add to the gratitude of the locals to that faraway place off the coast of Europe.

They were certainly grateful to Margaret Thatcher. Alex and Debbie had treated themselves to a drink in The Globe Tavern – but no lunch, as this rather basic drinking dive did not sully itself with anything so bourgeois as food – and had now walked along Stanley's esplanade towards its Government House to arrive at the handsome and expansive war memorial. And there, no more than twenty yards away (and just as promised by Mike), was that bust of the Falklands' saviour, situated in the most prominent position possible: at the entrance to 'Thatcher Drive'! It was a likeness in bronze, thought Alex, an image of which had probably never been shown anywhere in Argentina. He also thought that it was probably time to get back to the ship. A shuttle service had been laid on to take the Stanley wanderers back to the *Sea Sprite*, and the last shuttle left at 3pm, just one hour before the ship was due to leave Stanley for its two-day voyage to South Georgia. And neither Alex nor Debbie wanted to miss that.

So very soon they were back in their cabin, and very soon after that they were taking in the view from their ship, first of Stanley Harbour and then of Port William, the large inlet on the east coast of East Falkland that would allow them to proceed to the open sea. They were now embarking on a journey to an even more remote part of this planet, and they just couldn't wait to get there. Even more than they just couldn't wait for dinner...

Tonight, it would be taken in the indoor restaurant on the lower deck with the usual suspects, joined on this occasion by John, the naturalist and immersion suit demonstrator. It was he who kicked off proceedings by asking the other five at the table what, if anything, had impressed them about their time in the Falklands. Elaine was the first to respond, and she did this by stating how English the whole place felt. And not British, but specifically English, an impression assisted to no small degree by her sighting a Waitrose van during her guided tour around Stanley. On hearing this revelation, Alex nearly choked. Not only, it appeared, were there English pubs in Stanley, but also England's premier grocer. Even if, as John explained, there was no Waitrose supermarket as such in Stanley; just a conduit for some Waitrose goodies in the form of that mobile Waitrose-branded van. What the logistics of this might involve, Alex could not imagine. But that there was a Waitrose presence here legitimately underlined Elaine's contention that the Falklands were indisputably English before they were British.

Debbie's contribution was to point out how even 'downtown' Stanley was very peaceful and quiet, and how this was in part probably due to the absence of teenagers. She had not seen one. And this was not because they were hiding away in their bedrooms with their smartphones, but because they were at school – in England. That's what happened to many of the local children, who then might stay on in England to attend university. It was a feature of life not uncommon even in the remoter parts of Britain, but in the Falklands it was the norm. And very noticeable.

There were further contributions from around the table that addressed the hardships of life outside Stanley, the practical difficulties of living somewhere that was quite so remote, and the insecurity inherent in living somewhere that was claimed by another (hostile) country. Since the establishment of that Mount Pleasant facility, the Argentinian threat had been barely a threat at all, but it would never go away entirely. And this, it was proposed, must make life in the Falklands a little like living on the slopes of an inactive volcano. Which will still always be a volcano.

Then Alex made his contribution to this discussion, and it concerned the Falklands' modest population and how this compared to the overcrowded conditions in much of the rest of the world. However, he didn't applaud the sparseness of *Homo sapiens* on this land mass, but instead suggested how much better it would be if there were no humans there at all.

'I mean,' he concluded, 'I've nothing against the Falklanders. In fact, quite the reverse. I think they're a model of decency and stoicism. But I do have to say that I think this stoicism element is in part due to how they've had to live. They've had to scrape a living out of the sort of environment our own species was never designed for. And they've only been able to do this by screwing up this environment – with swarms of sheep. And they can only really survive, even now, with all sorts of outside help. I mean, think how much they depend on Britain for stuff like education and defence. And even delicacies from Waitrose. No, in my mind, there's no doubt about it. The Falklands would have been better off left to its own devices rather than it being… well, spoilt for the sake of three thousand souls. Or should that be over four thousand, if we include all those airmen and soldiers…?'

At this point, John made his own contribution.

'I tend to agree. The endemic plant life on the Falklands has been all but buggered. Though I have to say, that hardly makes the Falklands a unique case. Everywhere we go we bugger things up.'

'Don't be so technical,' joshed Debbie. 'We aren't all naturalists and we might not all understand.'

John chuckled, and then he apologised.

'Sorry. In plain English, *Homo sapiens* does tend to have an impact on natural flora. And fauna. A quite considerable impact.'

'Nobody would disagree with that,' ventured Derek, 'but it's all about numbers really, isn't it? If there were only a million of us on this planet, we would find it very hard to make much of an impact at all, no matter how careless and profligate we were. The natural world would overwhelm and absorb our puny efforts without raising a sweat. And it's only because there are now nearly 8,000 million of us that the natural world is on the back foot. Or in some places it's flat on its back and struggling to breathe. And you know, this is so often not at the centre of the debate. But it should be. Our out-of-control population is the root cause of all the world's major problems, from resource depletion through rampant pollution to our old friend, climate change. We are an infestation, and we are destroying our planet.'

Derek would find no one to disagree with him. On every group wildlife expedition Alex and Debbie had ever joined, sooner or later this subject of overpopulation and its impact on the world would arise, and every time it did, there was barely a debate. After all, it was difficult to debate a fact, even if the fact was as far reaching and fundamental as the deadly impact of a plague of humans. More often it was just the chewing over of some subsidiary facts, such as the tripling of the world's population in the lifetime of most of those doing the chewing. Or maybe the fact that every three days, the number of new humans popping into the world was equivalent to its entire population just twelve thousand years ago. Or there again, it might be the likening of the explosive increase in our numbers to the sort of behaviour observed in other animals – such as rats or mice – which was then always followed by a catastrophic collapse in numbers. Populations increase exponentially – as ours was doing – and then they spike, and then they crash. Which, if we do as well, might be good news for the world if not for us.

Maybe it was this last common theme of these discussions that led Roy to make a pointed contribution to the proceedings, and this concerned the control of our out-of-control population.

'Interesting, isn't it?' he observed. 'When we're faced with a burgeoning population of any animal that might threaten our interests in any way, we resort to culling or maybe even eradication. But we never see that as a solution for ourselves. Even though it might be better not just for the world, but for us as a species. I mean, by culling ourselves we might just avoid a cataclysmic crash.'

He grinned. He was, after all, being plainly provocative, and this became even more evident as he carried on.

'Culling, of course, might be a little difficult in practice. I mean, how would you do it without causing untold psychological damage to those who survived the culling? And what would be the criterion one used to select those to be culled? Age? BMI? IQ? Political persuasion? Or maybe even sense of humour. I mean, there are just so many miserable bastards out there...'

Derek guffawed, but Roy carried on.

'No. I think eradication would be better. I mean, it worked in South Georgia. It took them a few years, but by dropping baited poison from helicopters in a very controlled and ordered way, they got rid of every rat on a huge island that hadn't been rat free for over two hundred years. Ever since the whalers introduced them back in the late eighteenth century. For once, humans actually succeeded in undoing some of the harm they'd done in the past…'

'You're going to eradicate us all?' inquired a smiling Elaine.

'No, just a lot of us – in selected areas. So, we'd have not just the Falklands as a human-free spot in the world, but maybe most of Asia, some big slices of Africa and most of the New World. And that'd give the million or so of us who survived plenty of places to visit to enjoy the wildlife.'

'And how are you going to achieve this laudable eradication?' asked Debbie.

'Easy. Poisoned Big Macs dropped from helicopters. With, of course, a few Quorn burgers for the vegans and the vegetarians…'

That answer initiated a wave of laughter around the table, and an observation from Alex that Roy ran the risk of ending up with a slimmed-down humanity consisting largely of helicopter pilots, and that might not be the best result for our species in terms of diversity or even gender. Roy countered that challenge by first brushing it aside as a mere detail, and then suggesting that, even if *Homo sapiens* ended up as a collection of helicopter pilots, at least that would be better than it ending up extinct. Or possibly not…

Alex had witnessed this before: people who thought just as he did, burying under a mound of humour their real feelings about what their species was visiting on every other species on the planet. Whether it had legs, wings, fins or roots in the ground. It was all so dreadful, so dismal – and so beyond hope – that this was the only way they could possibly deal with it. And the darker the humour, the more likely it was to entomb their darkest of fears, at least for a while. Until that next time when they looked at the world and were confronted with the reality of its rising inundation by mankind.

Fortunately, for all those aboard the *Sea Sprite,* that next time was some way off. This was Alex's thought as he slipped into sleep, back in his cabin. Because if there was one place in the world that hadn't yet been swamped by mankind it was the Antarctic, along with its satellite rugged outposts. And that's where they would be spending their imminent future, starting with the rugged outpost of South Georgia. Alex could hardly wait. Even though he'd been informed that South Georgia could boast no Waitrose presence of any sort...

seven

Last night, Stuart had gone to see *Gravity*. The cinema in Mount Pleasant normally got its hands on new releases very quickly, but this was one that had eluded its grasp for years, and it was now showing it for three nights in a row. Stuart had expected it to be very popular, which was why he and his soldier mate, Gill, had decided to turn up early for its first night's showing. But they needn't have bothered. The modest cinema auditorium had been less than half full, and by the end of the film Stuart could well understand why. Clearly, word had got around – although not to him or to Gill – that *Gravity* was the new *Citizen Kane;* another Emperor's Clothes film, lauded by the critics but about as stimulating as a dose of Rohypnol. Why anyone would think it was other than tedious in the extreme – and so damn ponderous – he could not understand. Unless, of course, as he'd long suspected, there was some sort of film-makers' cabal, a secret coterie of these guys who simply manufactured an overblown reception for their wares, designed to distract the paying public from realising that what they were being fed was nothing more than a load of old crap.

Stuart was only thirty years old, but he had already decided that if he wanted to watch a genuine cinematographic masterpiece, he would have to seek out a film made somewhere between the '40s and the '70s. He would have to look for a genuine silver-screen rush by watching a film that was nearly half a century old, or maybe considerably older. In fact, to guarantee that he ended up viewing a production that had outstanding dialogue, polished acting and a well-written screenplay, he knew that, as often as not, he would have to resort to a black-and-white movie (other, of course, than *Citizen Kane)* in which all the characters filled their non-speaking intervals by lighting a fag. *Gravity*, most certainly, even with all its colour and all its technical wizardry, was not in this bygone premier league. Nor even in the league four rungs below. Instead it was a fifth-rate misuse of everybody's time, and that included all those involved in its production and all those unfortunate enough to have chosen to watch it rather than taking a nap in the bath. It was awful, and he wished he and Gill had gone for a pint instead. Maybe accompanied by a game of cribbage. And he also wished that it wasn't just 8.30 in the morning and he now had to deal with a whole day of boring intercepts. But he did, and he knew he had to get started. There was already an unusually large backlog...

He had noticed a little rise in the traffic over the past few days, partly as a result of an undue number of exchanges on a new bit of bother in Venezuela, and partly due to an increasing number of less-than-illuminating briefings on the new Asian flu. More and more officials around South America were, it appeared, taking an interest in the likelihood that the next unwanted present from China would land on their mat. However, today that little rise had become a big rise, and as Stuart worked his way through the morning it became crystal clear that this surge in communications had nothing to do with Venezuela but everything to do with the potential of an epidemic to become a full-blown pandemic. Everybody wanted more information on this threat, but nobody, it seemed, was able to provide this information. And the reason for this, he began to gather, was that no information was now coming out of China. Where initially that country's masters had been 'fully transparent' and 'uncharacteristically open' in their communications, they now seemed to have reverted to type, and little if any information was emerging from the infected empire.

This was more than a little odd, and Stuart began to think that he might have the seed of a worthwhile report to HQ. But then he thought not. If he'd observed this behaviour by scrolling through these intercepts, it was inconceivable that the Death Star back in Blighty hadn't picked it up as well, and that it wasn't already attempting to divine what it all meant. And anyway, maybe it was no more than the sort of mass panic that overtakes everyone when they're not quite sure of what's going on. It was probably just human nature on show and nothing more. There was certainly no evidence to indicate that the epidemic was getting particularly worse, and indeed there was not even any evidence that it was spreading around the world. Quite the reverse. The emergence of new cases in other countries was being closely monitored, and there seemed to be none at all. Which surely must be very good news and hardly a reason to indulge in a bout of indecent panic.

Nevertheless, Stuart would keep a close watch on developments. It was what he was trained to do and why he'd been posted to this windswept corner of the world. And who could tell? What might emerge could prove to be a great deal more interesting than watching Sandra Bullock and George Clooney pootling around in space. In fact, it could hardly prove less…

eight

Alex and Debbie shared their breakfast with two retired teachers. One had taught maths; the other, his wife, had taught physical education. Neither of them, it appeared, had fully recovered from their experience. It was in their manner. It was as though, thought Alex, they expected him or Debbie to become disruptive at any time or even to report them for inappropriate behaviour.

So, Alex tried to assuage their potential concerns by steering clear of discussing anything that could be construed as controversial or that might lead to any sort of conflict. The condition of the sea was, he thought, a safe topic to introduce, and he asked them how they had dealt with the swell, a gentle but obvious swell that had developed overnight as a result of the *Sea Sprite* moving into open ocean. They both confirmed that this hadn't been a problem during the night, and that it still wasn't now. Indeed, they apparently felt entirely OK, and they thought they could probably cope with these sorts of seas indefinitely. Alex responded that he and Debbie felt the same, but didn't confide that what was uppermost in his mind at the moment was whether he could identify – very quickly – a new safe topic of conversation, because this current swell one was on the point of drying up. He need not have worried. The maths teacher took up the task. By asking Alex and Debbie whether they had any idea what a 'life coach' did.

After a little hesitation, Alex said he thought that they helped people in some way, but he really wasn't sure. The maths man then revealed what he believed a life coach did, which was 'to help people attain their goals in life'.

This caused Alex to ignore his toast for a moment and to ask the single-word question 'How?'

This is when it soon became apparent that nobody around the table knew the answer to this question, and that the real purpose of life coaches being introduced into the conversation was to illustrate the proliferation of jobs that were something of a mystery to all those who didn't do them. Life coaching was an extreme example, but what do 'community development officers' *actually* do, asked the maths man, and didn't the world used to spin on its axis without an army of 'social media managers' to help it, or indeed without a single 'existential therapy counsellor'; who, according to maths man, was somebody who helped his clients to gain new insights by changing the way they saw the world.

Well, this had been an entirely unexpected start to the day, and a frivolous one as well. However, frivolity of any sort was soon to be dispensed with, because Jane had organised another mandatory presentation on biosecurity in anticipation of her charges being let loose on South Georgia in two days' time. And that meant more lounge time after breakfast for another briefing on how not to screw up a fragile environment. And this briefing was, in many ways, a re-run of the first biosecurity briefing, but it was designed to underline just how special and how super-fragile the environment of South Georgia was, and how easily it could be damaged. Those who were responsible for this environment might have cleared it of introduced rats – and before then, introduced reindeers – but this hundred-mile-long refuge in the southern Atlantic still ran the risk of an assault by new alien invaders, and particularly an assault by a multitude of unwelcome seeds. It had already been colonised by a number of alien plant species, and there was now a real effort being made to prevent any further foreign wildlife setting up home there. Accordingly, Jane went to great lengths to explain that everyone's kit would have to be near antiseptically clean before its owner was allowed to set foot on South Georgia, and that immediately after her briefing, there would be another kit inspection, where every outside piece of wear intended to be taken ashore would be rigorously examined.

She hadn't been joking. Alex and Debbie, along with all the other passengers from the Erikson Deck, had to report to an inspection point on this deck, where their boots, waterproof trousers, outer jackets, gloves, hats and neck warmers were all given the third degree. Not just a cursory perusal, but a full-blown 'invasive' examination, with particular attention paid to the rubber soles of their boots. These were the favourite hiding place of seeds, and needed to be screened for the smallest particle imaginable

– that might just be a seed. It was not quite what Alex and Debbie had expected: an almost draconian scrutiny of one's clothing, where there was a real possibility that one would be ordered back to one's cabin to scrub one's trousers or to take a paperclip to the soles of one's boots, and thereafter report back for a further inspection.

They were OK. No aliens were located on their boots and no suspicious residues needed to be scrubbed from their trousers. They were therefore free to spend the rest of the morning at leisure – or, if they so wished, attend a non-mandatory presentation on how to take the best photos in South Georgia and the Antarctic, given by the ship's official photographer, a willowy young lady called Rosie. This was mildly tempting, but not tempting enough. Debbie wanted to catch up on a number of minor chores, and Alex doubted that anyone could improve the way he just pointed his clever little camera at the object of his interest and then pressed the button on its top. So, while Debbie stayed in their cabin, Alex took himself off to explore the ship's library, where, sitting in one of its handsome easy chairs, was Roy. With nobody else in this elegant sanctum, they soon decided that it was in order to have a conversation, and so Roy abandoned his tome on *Flags of South American States and Provinces* and engaged the new visitor to the library in an exchange on alien species…

'It just breaks the habit of a lifetime,' he started. 'I mean, all this checking for seeds.'

'I'm not sure I follow,' offered Alex.

'Well, it's one of the things that define us: our propensity to introduce alien species into an environment where they'll wreak havoc. And now we're going to all this trouble in an attempt to stop something like a marginally harmless cress setting up home on a rock in the South Atlantic that's already been invaded by stuff like buttercups and daisies. It just seems a bit... well, futile.'

Alex must have betrayed the shock at what he'd just heard, because Roy immediately went on.

'No, I know it's not futile, and I'm just as fanatical as anyone when it comes to preventing the further screwing up of an environment. But I was simply trying to make the point that it's quite funny that the most practised agent of alien invasions – our *Homo sapiens* mob – is now going to such great pains to reverse the habit of hundreds of lifetimes...'

'Well, they did get rid of the rats – and the reindeer...'

'Yes, they did,' conceded Roy. 'But from an island in the middle of the Atlantic. And that's not to underestimate their efforts. But set against what we've done all around the world, it's hardly going to register. And there's no way *they* – or anybody – are going to be able to repeat that success on any major land mass.

'I mean, how would you go about undoing the work of that guy in the States? You know, the one who thought that New York would be "more cultural" if its Central Park were home to every bird mentioned in Shakespeare's plays, including the starling? And that's why starlings are now a ubiquitous pest from Alaska to Mexico, and one that won't ever be shifted no matter how many helicopters we might deploy.

'Mind, that's hardly the worst example, is it? Think about all the other species we've introduced stupidly or unwittingly. All those that haven't become just pests, but an actual existential threat to the indigenous wildlife. I'm sure you know already, but there are just so many examples of introduced species first establishing themselves and then going on to compete with the native species. And knocking the shit out of them. You know, by introducing pathogens or parasites that either kill them directly or by screwing up their habitat. Or, of course, they might just miss out the middleman and simply eat them themselves…'

Alex did already know, and, as Roy continued his indictment of mankind, in his mind he reeled through possums, cane toads, fire ants and pythons.

'And don't forget all those chaps that have gone feral all over the place. And all those plants: Himalayan balsam, Japanese knotweed, kudzu, rhododendron, purple loosestrife… I mean, you can go on and on. And, of course, it's still happening. All those tree diseases that are cropping up everywhere, courtesy of our neglect and indifference, with no doubt more in the pipeline.'

This was all valid stuff, thought Alex, but it was going nowhere. They both knew only too well just how destructive invasive species can be, and how humans had been so instrumental in facilitating the whole process of the wrong things being in the wrong place. So, Alex thought it was time to widen the discussion, first by registering the fact that *Homo sapiens* has so often played the role of invasive species itself.

'Let's not forget ourselves,' he started. 'Ever since we decided to take a stroll outside Africa, we've been busy invading everywhere else, and doing everything that's expected of a noxious invasive species. We've killed the native species directly, for food or even sport. We've fucked up their environment or simply removed it. And, of course, we've introduced whole armies of domestic animals to displace the native wildlife. To the point that, in most of the world, the only animal of any size that you're ever likely to encounter is one we intend to eat. In fact, we've been not so much an invasive species as an ecological steamroller, squashing flat the natural world as fast as our stupid careless attitude will let us.'

This was no good. This was turning not into a debate, but into some sort of mutual reinforcement of Alex and Roy's deep-seated beliefs, and matters were not improved by Roy's further observations that by using all our skills to eliminate fauna and flora so adeptly, we were already an established extermination event. That, at the rate we were going, we were on course to wipe out half of all animal and plant species by the end of the century. And that would be as a direct result not just of our invasive species habits, but also of our love of overfishing, forest clearance, mining, hunting, contaminating or building on the natural world, and, of course, our buggering up of the climate as well.

It was time to draw this exercise in reciprocal breast-beating to a close, and Alex did this by asking Roy how long he thought it would take for the human dreadnought of destruction to arrive in that one part of the world that it had yet to violate: Antarctica. It didn't take long for Roy to respond.

'Well, I assume you don't mean Antarctic waters, because the Chinese krill fishers are already there…'

Alex nodded his head.

'Yes, I was meaning the continent itself. What's currently protected by the Antarctic Treaty…'

Roy again responded immediately.

'The groundwork's already started. Just look at how many so-called "research stations" there are where there is probably bugger-all real research going on. No, loads of them are just stakes in the ground, evidence of a pre-existing national presence to allow a national claim to be made when the starting whistle's blown. I mean, you're never going to convince me that Ukraine's "research station" has been established to forward Antarctic research. Or how about Romania's, or Pakistan's! And then there are a whole clutch of Argentinian stations and a crop of newcomers, countries like South Korea, India, the Czech Republic and Belgium, all of whom have suddenly developed an intense interest in Antarctic research. Most of which, I suspect, has yet to be published...'

'When will the starting whistle be blown?' interrupted Alex.

'As soon as our insatiable world decides that it's a mere extravagance to ignore the Antarctic's untapped riches. And that date isn't too far off. Just think of all the minerals that could be mined there. And, of course, without any disturbance to human settlements, and largely out of sight. There won't be many witnesses to an open-cast iron-ore mine at the bottom of the world.

'Although, there again, I suspect the first wounds will be as a result of mining to extract some of the rather more exotic stuff. After all, if the world's already bingeing on smartphones and it plans to power everything on four or more wheels with a battery, it'll need a hell of a lot more lithium to start with, to say nothing of cobalt, nickel and some other really rare metals. And none of this stuff, as far as I know, grows on trees. And soon not enough of it will be found underground – unless we raid our precious larder of last resort. I'm sorry, but I think Antarctica is already on borrowed time, and however the starting whistle gets blown, as soon as the shrill blast is heard, the prospectors and the miners will be in there before you can say, "Devastate, despoil and devour." Antarctica, as we know it, will no longer exist.'

Alex didn't quite know how to respond. Especially as he could again challenge nothing that Roy had said. It was more or less what he himself thought would be Antarctica's fate. And he certainly agreed with him on the rather suspect proliferation of so-called research stations on the continent, and the remarkable interest in Antarctic research shown by so many countries so far from Antarctica that had shown no such interest in the past. Or maybe Romania really *did* want to push forward the understanding of this frozen continent. He couldn't, of course, be entirely sure that it didn't...

Anyway, it was now coming up to lunchtime, so Alex avoided an immediate response by suggesting to Roy that they rendezvous in a few minutes time in the lido restaurant, where, with Debbie, they would be able to gauge whether outside dining was feasible despite being in such an exposed part of the planet. It was. And over lunch, Debbie was treated to a synopsis of their earlier discussion before she rescued them both from their self-inflicted melancholy by steering the conversation in the direction of workplace romances. Where, she wanted to know, would men and women meet each other in the future, now that workplace dalliances seemed to be on the verge of being bracketed with stalking and sexual assault? Especially those men and women who were allergic to discos and nightclubs. Neither Alex nor Roy knew the answer to this puzzle, although Roy did suggest that if they weren't able to meet, it might provide a partial solution to the world's population problem.

Fortunately, this discussion and all other conversation was put on hold when the three diners reconvened after lunch to partake of a slice of birdwatching from the stern of the ship. Instead, they tried between them to distinguish the albatrosses from the petrels and the petrels from the shearwaters, and really only felt confident in their identification skills when they were treated to the sight of diminutive storm petrels feeding off the surface of the sea as they pattered across it. They were, the party of three agreed, too small to live in this endless watery environment, and barely credible in their choice of feeding habits. How, by dining on the minuscule creatures they found on the surface of the sea, could they possibly derive enough sustenance even to fuel their never-ending dance across the waves?

Equally puzzling was the fact that the Falklands had once been located off the east coast of the tip of South Africa. But that, according to Tony, the expedition team's miserable geologist, was where it was back in Gondwana days, before South America had bidden farewell to Africa. And, as he was keen to point out in his afternoon lecture, just because a chunk of Africa cleaves off, spins around and ends up closer to South America than it does to the Africa it has left, it doesn't make it part of South America and it never will. The Falklands, he announced, were not only culturally detached from South America but geologically detached from it as well. It wasn't only Alex, it appeared, who was mildly jingoistic when it came to the claims on this disputed Atlantic territory. And this was a point he readily admitted to when, with the other members of the famous five, he turned up for dinner later on.

Alex and his little clan had gathered in the inside restaurant – and had very soon been joined by Tony. This made for a less-than-stimulating meal, simply because it was impossible to ignore the pall of gloom that Tony cast over the table. And if he wasn't being gloomy, he was being unbearably tiresome, and he achieved his outstanding level of tedium by continually talking about various impenetrable aspects of geology, to the exclusion of virtually everything else. It was just as well that Derek was occasionally able to illuminate the murk of Tony's presence with a few contributions of his own. Delivered, of course, with his trademark lack of inhibition.

One of the 'less provocative' of these that Alex would not easily forget concerned a safari holiday in Namibia where years ago he and Elaine had been taken to a hide after dark to observe leopards. This was on a private reserve, and leopard sightings could be almost guaranteed because the owners of the reserve would put out food to attract these scary felines. It was, as Derek conceded, by no means a natural spectacle, and had more to do with a zoo experience than a true safari event, and indeed this zoo flavour of the arrangement was emphasised in the design of the hide. This was a long, half-submerged construction, giving a dozen or so clients an opportunity to view the action.

However, as Derek went on to explain, even with this 'zoo' arrangement, leopard sightings were not absolutely guaranteed. And this was because these creatures have very sensitive hearing, and if they detected the presence of humans in the hide, they would not make an appearance.

Accordingly, Derek and Elaine and the other occupants of the hide – all of whom were British – complied with the instructions they had been given before entering the hide not to make a sound or even to whisper to each other. And consequently, they were rewarded with the sight of two leopards. It was just after this successful viewing that the manager of the reserve told them that very often a contingent of Italians would visit the hide, but on not one occasion had they seen a leopard. Italians, it seemed, when in a group, no matter how small the group, could not refrain from chatting to each other for more than about thirty seconds. And to expect up to a dozen of them to remain silent for thirty or forty minutes was to ask the impossible. It could be, he concluded, that no Italians had ever set eyes on a leopard, and they never would until they abandoned their stereotype and learned to shut up.

That, Roy suggested, would be a very long way off. And before this politically incorrect stereotyping was drawn to a close, he went on to remark that at least the Italians had *wanted* to see leopards. And not just reduce their bones to powder for use in ineffective medicines and potions. Nor would they have regarded the abuse of such a wonderful wild animal as anything other than barbaric.

So, another day at sea ended on a familiar theme, and Alex and Debbie retired to their cabin, buoyed by the company of three of their dinner companions and wondering whether the fourth would benefit from the attentions of a life coach…

nine

For the first time since he'd arrived at Mount Pleasant, Stuart was actually keen to start his day. It was why he was sitting in his tiny office at such an early hour. At seven o'clock in the morning he was normally trying to decide whether to have another half-hour in bed or to get up in the hope that lurking somewhere on the breakfast buffet would be at least a couple of pieces of edible bacon and maybe one sausage that didn't put him in mind of an overfilled condom. Where, he had often wondered, did they get these monstrous obscenities, and were they really what servicemen actually wanted, or were they just designed to look engorged and therefore suitably macho? He might never learn. Just as he might never learn what his new crop of intercepts meant. But it wouldn't stop him trying.

There were more than ever. The volume of traffic had risen through the whole of yesterday and it was now even higher. And Venezuela's local difficulties had dropped out of sight.

Almost every message, every signal and every exchange of information now concerned what was going on in China. Or, more precisely, what might be going on in China, now that it had apparently stopped communicating with the rest of the world. It was unprecedented. The most populous nation on the planet had taken a vow of silence – and more. As well as imposing a radio silence and a social media blackout, and unplugging itself entirely from the internet, it had stopped all flights out of the country, and – through its complete silence – was not giving clearance for any flights into the country either. And all shipping movements had come to a halt as well. It seemed to Stuart that China had either decided to engage in some form of extreme self-quarantine, or its all-powerful communist clique had a really serious problem on its hands; something it just couldn't control.

The more Stuart pondered these conjectures, the more he concluded that they were both highly improbable. Why, if you had a serious epidemic on your hands that warranted a massive self-quarantine exercise, would you not tell the rest of the world what you were doing? They would probably be extremely grateful and very relieved, and might even offer you some help. However, on the other hand, something so serious that it could break the grip of the communist regime was just about inconceivable. When you're able to monitor all your citizens, ignore the law as you wish, and lock up or otherwise dispose of anybody causing you a problem, nothing could be that serious. Even the outbreak of a really dangerous flu would no doubt be brought to heel. No matter how draconian the measures adopted to achieve this might be. And no matter how many people might need to be dealt with…

Stuart began to feel he was getting nowhere. There was now a mountain of intercepts to deal with, but he felt that even if he successfully scaled its heights, the view from the top would be no clearer than it was for him now. How could it be when the mountain was made up of just questions, suppositions and concerns but no real information whatsoever?

However, just as he'd become hopelessly despondent about not being able to discover anything of any use at all, he read an intercept that had originated in Madrid and that referred to a number of fires. It appeared that somewhere in that huge, inscrutable country, there were blazes that were visible from space.

He reread it, and he reread it again. And what struck him was that it didn't appear to be just supposition or rumour. There were references in it that seemed to confirm that it was a factual report based on genuine intelligence. It even gave the locations of some of the blazes. They were in Shanghai, Hangzhou and Nanjing. That, of course, was significant – and alarming as well. These weren't forest fires or scrublands ablaze, but presumably huge conflagrations within urban centres. And if so, why weren't they being put out? What were those cities' fire brigades doing?

This had to warrant a report to HQ. Even though Stuart was absolutely certain that if anybody in Madrid knew about these fires, then there was no way that they wouldn't also be known to 'the family'. Indeed, it was inconceivable that it wasn't a family satellite that had first picked up these inexplicable conflagrations. Nevertheless, he had to do it. Protocol would not allow him not to report it. Just as his curiosity would not allow him to do other than buy a couple of wraps and a bumper bottle of water in order that he could eschew the canteen and stay at his post. And that wasn't just his professional curiosity. It was a deep sense that he should find out everything he could as soon as he could to satisfy his own personal curiosity. After all, in his mind, life so far – as in the life of the entire human-dominated planet – had been a series of non-events and damp squibs. And despite the odd conflict and the odd insurrection, nothing of any great import had ever happened. There had been absolutely nothing to set his own pulse racing, or indeed to upset the monotonous self-satisfied rhythm of a deeply self-satisfied world.

Well, maybe something was going on that might finally cause the onset of some serious arrhythmia. Maybe he'd at last know what it was like to witness something so far out of the ordinary that it might give the human world the sort of shock that it had never experienced before.

Or… there again, it was not beyond the bounds of possibility that spending all this time marooned on a bleak and desolate outpost, with only soldiers, airmen and sheep to keep him company, was finally getting to him. One intercept about some flames in a far-off land, and he'd let his imagination run wild. In fact, he began to have second thoughts about putting in that report, protocol or not. And maybe he should just see whether anything else developed. Eat his second wrap and just monitor the chatter. And maybe later this evening, try and come to terms with mundane reality again with the aid of a late pint of beer…

ten

Alex and Debbie were learning about flags. They were having breakfast with Roy, and Roy had just enlightened them on the use of colours in national flags, and how only one nation on Earth has a flag that features neither red, white nor blue. This nonconformist, he told them, was Jamaica; and clearly he was not going to end his lesson there. To start with, he reminded his audience that the Jamaican flag consisted of a gold saltire dividing it into four sections, two of which were black and two of which were green. (As any cannabis enthusiast would probably know.) He then went on to explain that the black was supposed to depict the strength and creativity of the Jamaican people; the gold, sunlight and the wealth of the country; and the green, its agricultural resources, and hope.

However, his lesson in vexillology was not over yet. Because Roy then informed his audience that before August 2017, Jamaica had had to share its title with Mauritania. It seemed that, before that month, the Mauritanian flag had consisted of a gold star and crescent on a green background, and was therefore similarly deficient in red, white or blue. However, following a referendum, a change was made to the flag to sandwich the green and gold between two red stripes, to symbolise the blood shed by the country's patriots in its struggle against its French colonisers. That struggle had resulted in independence back in 1960, which, suggested Roy, did indicate a degree of tardiness in recognising the patriots' heroic efforts. But, he went on to say, given that Mauritania is a country which still embraces slavery and still imposes the death penalty for atheism, maybe this failure to move very quickly – on anything – was only to be expected.

Well, there were no Mauritanians in the restaurant to take Roy to task on his defamatory comments, and there was no way that Alex or Debbie would take on this role themselves. Instead, Alex suggested that Jamaica was highly unlikely to add even one red stripe to its flag, unless it wanted to symbolise its favourite beer. Debbie didn't understand what he meant by this until Alex informed her that Red Stripe was the name of Jamaica's very own home-brewed lager, and even when he had done so, she was less than impressed. Indeed, wasn't it about time, she suggested, that, rather than exploring any more vexillological matters, it might be better if they brought their meal to an end and prepared themselves for the first presentation of the day? This was not on flags, but on the conduct of the Falklands War. Mike, the ex-Marine, was going to give an account of his experiences in this conflict. When he was just seventeen…

It was a packed house. The lounge was completely full. Everybody, it seemed, was more than eager to hear what had happened in that campaign – from the mouth of someone who had actually been there, from someone who had been one of those heroes who had 'yomped' his way to Stanley. And to start with, what they heard was how a mere child had undergone the rigours of Royal Marine training to be turned into one of the youngest soldiers to be dispatched to that faraway war. Although, as Mike recounted, when the news was delivered to him and his equally youthful peers, at least one of them wasn't quite so sure of just how far away the Falklands actually were. This became immediately apparent when he asked their sergeant why it was that the Argentinians had mounted an attack on some of those islands off the coast of Scotland.

After that there wasn't much fun in Mike's presentation – as he moved on to talk about his arrival in the Falklands, and the reality of what fighting in a war must inevitably involve. Needless to say, that included injury and death, and huge disappointments, such as when the Argentinians attacked and sank the *Atlantic Conveyor* with the loss of twelve of its crew. This was the large cargo ship that had been requisitioned by the military to bring to the Falklands much of the heavy hardware that the fighters would need to confront their adversaries. So, to the bottom of the sea went not just hundreds of tons of heavy equipment and fourteen Harrier jump jets, but also a mix of eleven Wessex and Chinook helicopters. This was really bad news. It meant that the Marines and their Parachute Regiment counterparts had now lost their means of overland transport, and, with only one operational helicopter at their disposal, they soon realised that they would not be flying to Stanley but instead they would be walking there. That, of course, was where the bulk of the Argentinian forces were disposed – in positions around the town – and to engage them, the Marines and 'Paras' would now have to march (or yomp) fifty-six miles in three days, carrying on their backs loads weighing an incredible eighty pounds.

Alex had often thought about this feat, and could barely imagine it was possible. And now that he had seen for himself the Falklands terrain, he was convinced it really was impossible. How could anyone carry that weight for that long, and in such demanding circumstances? Well, it seemed that after all these years, Mike was still having similar thoughts himself. Even though he was one of those who had performed this remarkable deed. And when he embarked on the detail of the march, one could understand why.

The weather was foul; a constant blast of wind and plenty of rain. The conditions underfoot were dreadful and everywhere was wet. So much so that Mike's army-issue boots were incapable of keeping his feet dry, and his entire Falklands campaign was fought with wet and very cold feet. And swollen feet. He said he knew that he could never take his boots off, because he would never have got them back on again. Indeed, even now, he reported, he had problems with his feet, as well as a degree of permanent numbness in his fingers from their long exposure to cold. These were the sort of injuries, thought Alex, that don't attract the same attention as the loss of limbs or other forms of trauma, but for those who have to live with them for a lifetime, they must be a real burden to bear.

The burden to bear in the form of that eighty-pound bergen was something else that Mike talked about. Because this – on top of as much as forty pounds of other equipment

– was what made that fifty-six-mile hike barely credible and what reduced many of his comrades to tears of despair. They collapsed. They had to be helped by their mates before their mates then collapsed in turn. And this had happened to Mike. He had reached the end of his power and endurance and he had blacked out with exhaustion. When he recounted this aspect of his story, the proverbial pin could have been heard dropping onto the lounge carpet, as everybody was clearly trying to imagine how bad it must have been to have felled this hulk of a man before them. There was a palpable sense of relief in the room when he then went on to explain that eventually he was able to carry on and in due course participate in the successful action against the Argentinian forces. Although his description of this engagement – and the mix of skill and bravery it entailed – again reduced the audience to absolute silence. It wasn't often, thought Alex, that one is in the presence of someone who has demonstrated such courage and who has lived to tell the tale. Even if he might not have perfect feet or fingers any more.

Inevitably, Mike's presentation ran over its allotted time. But nobody complained and nobody left the lounge before Mike had answered a whole raft of questions, the answers to which served to underline just how daring the whole Falklands operation had been. And how daring had been those young men in uniform who were charged with performing the operation. And how lucky were those who had survived it…

Lunch provided an opportunity to digest all that Mike had talked about, and on Alex and Debbie's table this opportunity was made the most of by two Scots. They were the male members of two Scottish couples with whom Alex and Debbie were sharing the table, and they both talked at length about what it must be like to go to war; something that neither of them had ever done. Occasional contributions to this exchange were made by the others at the table, but it wasn't until Alex asked what, if any, dangerous situations his dining companions had encountered that the conversation became one that was properly shared by them all. Everybody, it seemed, had something to say.

It appeared that the perils confronted and overcome included two serious road accidents, one very dicey landing on a flooded runway, one pugnacious drunk in an underpass, one avalanche, one black mamba, one collapsing chimney stack, and two incidents involving unstable extendable ladders. Given how many years the assembled six had spent on Earth, this litany of mishaps impressed nobody, and Alex definitely thought it did no more than demonstrate what cushioned, sheltered lives they had all led. Nothing had come their way that had even approached what Mike had had to tackle in the Falklands and the risk to life he had faced on that campaign. And how likely was it, thought Alex, that any real danger would arrive to meet any of them this late in their lives? It was almost inconceivable. Just as long, of course, as one of Roy's icebergs didn't get some other ideas...

Back in their cabin, Alex and Debbie reflected on their supremely safe life, and how so many people in other parts of the world lived lives that were little more than an unbroken series of dangers. If they weren't facing the threat of disease or starvation, they were fleeing conflicts or getting caught up in conflicts. And, of course, many of them were succumbing to these various dangers. Because, as Debbie pointed out as an example, not every barrel-bomb could land somewhere else. Alex agreed, and then he was reminded by that barrel bomb reference that he hadn't plugged himself into the news today. Not that much of the 'news' currently being carried by either CNN or BBC World News would meet the definition of this word. It was more in the nature of reiteration, as, over the past three days, both channels were reporting not much more than Putin's belligerence, Assad's evil, Trump's imbecility and Xi Jinping's assurances to the rest of the world that the flu epidemic was totalitarianly under control in modern-day Cathay. Nevertheless, Alex was a bit of an addict, and even if his fix was going to be no more than a warmed-up dose of yesterday's reiterations, he thought he would give it a try. If nothing else, it would fill in a bit of time before he and Debbie took themselves off to listen to a talk by Nick on the subject of penguins. This was a must, and even a report on the outbreak of hostilities between Russia and the US would not stop them going to that. Although the report they were about to hear on China might just possibly make them late...

They tuned in just as a talking head in London was declaring that China's current behaviour was unprecedented and impossible to interpret. It then became clear that Mr Xi Jinping had abandoned his efforts to reassure the rest of the world about the threat of flu, and instead had taken a vow of silence. This being China, so too, it appeared, had the other 1.4 billion Chinese who shared the country with him. This enormous global power was not saying a word to anyone beyond its borders, and neither was it allowing anyone into China or out of China. It was in complete shutdown. No internet connections, no phone connections, no cross-border travel, no cross-border trade, and certainly no responses to the world's rising chorus of questions as to what the hell was going on there. What could possibly be making a country of this size want to seal itself off from all the other nations in the world? (As one of the talking heads said, even China's old mucker, North Korea, was not being told what was going on. And apparently Kim Jong-un was now wetting his spider-silk pants.)

Alex and Debbie had both become transfixed. They couldn't take their eyes off the screen. Not because they were being fed any information, but because there didn't appear to be any information to be fed. It was just repeated appearances by a succession of 'experts' who were doing little more than expressing their puzzlement while at the same time trying to retain their valuable oracle credentials. A couple of them did manage to make one valid observation, which was that, whilst the nation-wide shutdown of China might well be as a result of a deadly flu epidemic, the absence of flu cases outside the country almost certainly meant that the infection was transmitted through close contact and not through the air. However, most of the time these wise men and women were doing no more than making stabs in the dark that were no better than Alex could have done himself with a blunt butter knife. After all, an exercise in self-quarantine, a power struggle at the top of the Communist Party, a gigantic natural disaster and a tsunami of civil strife were all ideas that anyone could have come up with. Although few people would then have been able to support these ideas with any rational arguments. If it was a quarantine exercise, why would China's rulers do this without telling the rest of the world what they were doing? After all, why miss out on the acclaim that such a selfless act of altruism would inevitably attract? As regards a power struggle or an outbreak of civil strife... well, could either of those events really close down an entire country; one that was so huge and one that was bound to have porous walls? Furthermore, civil strife – or even the evidence of a vigorous power struggle – would probably be picked up by a few hundred spy satellites, as would any very large natural disaster. No, something else was going on in China; something mysterious that Alex believed was beyond the imagination of any of those talking heads – and, very irritatingly, beyond his own imagination as well. Unless it was aliens...

He made the mistake of proffering this visitation from another world as a possible explanation for China's comatose state, albeit with the caveat that, given China's population, there would probably have to be an awful lot of aliens. Debbie's response to this suggestion was withering, but she did promise not to repeat it to anyone else. Just as long as Alex didn't betray her own facetious remarks about the shutdown being the result of the world's biggest game of hide-and-seek. Although, in a way, this idea had about as much credibility as all the other ideas they had heard. And, of course, a game of hide-and-seek might not be spotted from space.

It was a frivolous way of dealing with what had been revealed about China's condition. Probably because both Alex and Debbie were not just mystified by this huge dollop of real news, but a little bit scared by it as well. Would they soon be facing a genuine danger, and not as a result of meeting an iceberg, but instead as a result of having to deal with whatever the fallout was from nearly a quarter of the world succumbing to an extreme form of introversion?

Something was going to happen as a consequence of this extraordinary and bewildering event, and neither Alex nor Debbie could see how it might be good – for them. And they weren't even sea cucumbers or civets.

Anyway, Alex reckoned that most of their fellow passengers were a bit unnerved as well. That was probably why so many of them had turned up, along with Alex and Debbie, to listen to Nick's penguin lecture, and to lose themselves in a bit of normality for a while. After that, they could return to their televisions and start to come to terms with the magnitude of what they had heard and try to work out what it might mean for them, here on the *Sea Sprite*, even if at the moment they were about as far out of harm's way as they could possibly be. After all, whatever might be going on in China was on the other side of the world and they were way beyond its reach. God, not even a Chinese Chernobyl could get to them here.

Alex had the very same thoughts himself, and the reassurance provided by the *Sea Sprite's* remote situation did allow him to put his concerns to one side, at least for long enough to allow him to concentrate on Nick's presentation. This shift in focus was helped by the fact that, despite the new China-size enigma in his life, he really did want to brush up on his penguin knowledge, which was currently at the level of embarrassing ignorance. He knew what general shape penguins were, and he now knew a lot more about those he had encountered on the Falklands, but that still left a lot to be learnt, and a lot that could successfully distract him. And it was all interesting stuff. How, for example, the macaroni penguin, with its elaborate crest, earned its name from Maccaronism, a style of men's fashion adopted in England in the eighteenth century, notable for its flamboyant or excessive ornamentation, and earning its devotees the nickname of 'maccaroni' (or 'macaroni'). Then there were the chinstrap penguins, reckoned to be the most aggressive species of penguin; probably, suggested Nick, because they knew that in disrespectful circles they were referred to as 'jockstrap penguins'. And finally, how about the reported fact that massed ranks of king penguins have been known to follow the movement of an approaching helicopter so very intently that when it passes overhead they continue to observe it, and thereby fall over backwards in an act of splendid synchronised unanimity.

There was, however, no such unanimity when Nick's presentation came to an end, and people began to gather in little groups to discuss the Chinese puzzle. Alex and Debbie's little group – which included Derek, Elaine and Roy – certainly came to no consensus on the cause of China's behaviour. Roy was convinced that the Communist Party was in its death throes and had wrapped the nation in some sort of despotic cling film in a last-ditch attempt to survive, whereas Elaine thought that just possibly it was a classic case of mass panic. The flu had wreaked havoc, she suggested, and people were now just looking to their own situation and ignoring everything else. The only thing that was still operating was the state, and this wanted to keep the news of the panic from the rest of the world. Other (very flawed) explanations were offered, but Alex offered no hypothesis himself, primarily because he didn't have one but instead only a firm belief that it wasn't the demise of the party or a case of mass panic or any of the other ideas put forward by members of the group. Nothing fitted, nothing worked, and nothing would be gained by continuing to stumble around in the dark. Which is why Alex decided he should take his wife back to their cabin and watch some people on the telly stumble around in the dark instead. There was another presentation in the lounge on offer – on Antarctic climate research – but Alex knew that this wouldn't do what Nick's lecture on penguins had done: successfully distract him for forty minutes from thinking about China. So, he might as well concede defeat and sit himself in front of a screen to witness a new clutch of talking heads attempting either to comprehend the incomprehensible or resolve the irresolvable. If nothing else, it might provide him with some more possible theories for China's actions, which he could then discount along with all those he had already discounted. And that might assist him in contributing to the inevitable China discussion over dinner.

Well, in the event, dinner was just generally unenlightening and not specifically unenlightening on the subject of China. This was because Alex and Debbie had made a tactical error on entering the restaurant, and had ended up on a table for six with the four people they had been carefully avoiding since their first meal on the ship. They hadn't got any better, and they were certainly incapable of grasping the undeniable significance of whatever might be going on in China. Or its potential ramifications. In fact, Alex had to admit to himself that they were more realistic in their ignorance than were many of those pundits on the telly. In a way, he found their performance perversely refreshing.

It did, however, leave him wanting more. He hadn't quite had his fill of China, and so, at the end of the meal, he convinced Debbie to accompany him to the bar, where he knew he'd find a new crop of both concerned fellow travellers and improbable opinions. And he did. But he also discovered a new snippet of information. It appeared that one of his new acquaintances had heard of somebody who had heard somebody talking about some unspecified sort of trouble on China's border with Myanmar. Well, this second- or third-hand piece of gossip got Alex thinking, and what he thought was that he was thinking far too much about something that was happening on the other side of the world, and that he was on this side of the world with the prospect of arriving in South Georgia in no more than a few hours' time. And whatever delights South Georgia held in store, they would not be affected by events in China. Nor would those events affect his ability to savour these delights. In fact, the only potential impediment to his relishing South Georgia's promised natural wonders would be his not getting enough rest tonight. And, as it was now nearly midnight, hadn't he better take his wife back to their cabin so that they could both go to bed?

Even if, as was quite likely, they might not immediately go to sleep…

eleven

He *had* sent in a report to HQ. Stuart had known it would be futile, but in his organisation one ignored the protocols at one's peril, and he was certainly not keen on the prospect of having to defend his inaction at a later date. Nothing had happened, of course. He hadn't even received an acknowledgement. Although, there again, that wasn't unusual. He'd thought on many occasions that if he stopped putting in any reports, nobody back in Blighty would notice, and ultimately he would be forgotten about completely. Indeed, he had fantasised about this eventuality, wondering whether he could clear off for the rest of his scheduled stay on this island – to somewhere like Thailand – and then just pop back in time to catch his homeward flight to Brize Norton. And nobody would be any the wiser.

However, he was still here, still in one of the dullest places in the world, which had suddenly and unexpectedly exploded with a burst of genuinely riveting interest. That was why he was again in his box, and although it was just ten in the morning of this new day, he had already been at work for nearly three hours. And there was so much to do. And only him here to do it. There had once been three monitors in this station, but the powers back home had cut that down to two, and when those two had reached the end of their posting, only Stuart had been sent to replace them. There was supposedly an active search for another mug to fill the vacancy, but nobody stupid enough had yet been found. And anyway, Stuart suspected that they weren't looking very hard. This monitoring set-up duplicated a lot of what could now be done back in Britain, and if one factored in the quality and the relevance of what was being monitored, it had to rank as one of the least significant sets of eyes in the whole organisation, and one that might one day be relegated to a stand-by function, only ever activated if Argentina showed any signs of getting stroppy again. And that was unlikely, and even less so now, now that its regime, like all the other governments in South America, was fixated on what was going on in East Asia. Yes, it wasn't exclusively China in all those signals any more, but also Myanmar, India and Nepal.

The first indication that China's syndrome was on the verge of leaking into neighbouring countries was another report from Madrid that spoke not just of more fires in more Chinese cities, but also of confirmed fighting on China's border with Myanmar. This, the report said, involved Chinese border guards and what were presumably Chinese citizens, and was interpreted as the Chinese authorities trying to maintain the integrity of this border. Or, in other words, they had decided to shoot their own people rather than let them escape from the country.

This was very significant, and one would not have needed extensive training in intelligence work to realise that it was very significant or, indeed, to realise that it pointed to the presence in China of something that people wanted to avoid at all costs. Even if it might mean getting shot.

And then it got a great deal worse. Similar reports were being made about shooting being heard – and observed – on the country's borders with Nepal and India. It was only a matter of time, thought Stuart, before more reports emerged from maybe places like Vietnam or Mongolia, or anywhere with a common border with China that offered a gateway out of that troubled country.

He also thought that he should again make a report to HQ. It would be just as meaningless and futile as the one he'd submitted yesterday, but simply composing it might help him to assemble his thoughts and come up with his own tenable theory of what might be going on in China. It might even help him to compile a theory on what might be about to happen next. In the event, it did neither, but it did make him think about one aspect of the flu that was now beyond doubt. In fact, he'd even seen it confirmed in a discussion he'd caught on the canteen telly, and this was that the flu could only be transmitted from person to person. After all, there had been no reported cases of this flu in any other country. And taking account of the fact that nobody was being let out of China, that had to mean that it was this person-to-person route and that it wasn't being transmitted through the air. The epidemic was trapped within China's borders and it wasn't being given the chance to become a world-wide pandemic.

Yes, the guys on the telly were right. It had to be person to person. That's the only form of transmission that made any sense. Until, that was, the late afternoon. This was when Stuart came across an encrypted message to the Peruvian government – from that country's ambassador in London – mentioning an unconfirmed report of multiple deaths in India and Pakistan. There was very little detail to accompany this bombshell, but it did make clear that those who had died had not died as a result of bullets or some other munitions, but as a result of some invisible affliction, something probably airborne and something that brought about death very quickly.

As he finished digesting this latest piece of information, Stuart put his hand to his chest. It was as he thought. His heart was racing. And then he realised he was feeling just a little bit nauseous. He therefore sat back in his chair, took five deep breaths and then supped from the bottle of water on his desk. He was a professional, he reminded himself. And professionals do not have an attack of the vapours. Particularly when they have another futile report to compose. And when they have to prepare themselves for a late night of monitoring followed by an early start to a full day of monitoring in the morning.

Maybe, thought Stuart, it was a really good job that he hadn't taken himself off to Thailand…

twelve

The mat of giant kelp writhing in the swell put Alex in mind of liquorice; in particular, the shiny black liquorice straps he used to buy as a kid. Of course, this kelp, with each of its 'tentacles' up to twelve feet in length, was on a rather different scale to the sweets he remembered. But as it slithered around below the algae-covered rocks, it could have been a giant version of that tempting black confectionery, gone wild on the coast of South Georgia and now adding to the distinctly 'other-worldly' feel of this magical place.

That feel had become apparent as soon as the *Sea Sprite* had arrived at the western end of this huge, elongated island and had begun to make its way along the island's rugged north coast. It was all forbidding-looking cliffs, capped with thick, low clouds and punctuated by just one massive, sprawling glacier that had made it to the sea. And it was this glacier that underlined not just the other-worldly nature of this place, but also its scale. As Alex studied this enormous feature through his binoculars, he realised that the multiple tiny specks below it were seals and penguins. What he'd thought was a really large slab of frozen water was in fact a gigantic slab of frozen water, and the cliffs were on a similarly massive scale.

This was even more apparent from the zodiac as it began to make its way around Hercules Bay, a heroic-sized inlet halfway along the north coast, where the *Sea Sprite* had anchored to allow its passengers their first close encounter with South Georgia's scenery, South Georgia's wildlife and South Georgia's kelp. Alex had boarded his zodiac – with Debbie and with a sizeable helping of anticipation – and was now relishing the experience of finding himself in this remarkable lost world. It wasn't just the giant kelp and the giant cliffs towering above his tiny craft, but it was also the whole ambience of this place; a secret inlet on a secret island, sheltered by a low grey cloud that obscured the tops of its enfolding cliffs, and filled with so much wildlife that it was difficult to know where to look.

On the rocks above the kelp were numerous fur seals, some looking grumpy, some looking indifferent, and some – the testosterone-fuelled males – looking both imperious and potentially aggressive. Nearer the end of the bay, below a magnificent waterfall, were more fur seals, a few dozen elephant seals, a clutch of king penguins and, above them, a colony of those delightful macaroni penguins. These guys, thought Alex, must have raised a smile on the faces of the very first humans to visit this island; 'pioneers' who weren't so much interested in observing the wildlife here as harvesting it for their commercial gain. But even they must have been captivated by the appearance – and the habits – of these unavoidably comical inhabitants. With their quiff of yellow feathers and their propensity to embark on climbs up near-vertical rocks, many of which proved unsuccessful, they could not have failed to have captured the attention of the most hardened of hunters and then caused them some serious amusement. There again, there must have been those amongst these early visitors who had observed the unsurpassable skill of these same chaps in the water and, like Alex, had simply marvelled at how something so clumsy and laughable on land could transform itself into such a peerless performer beneath the waves. They might also have stopped to think that, as clumsy on land as these penguins were, through determination and some persistent trial and error, they were – eventually – still able to scale those challenging rocks; rocks that any human would clearly have found impossible. They were quite a thing, and they constituted a fitting end to this first close-up experience of South Georgia before Alex and his fellow shipmates returned to the *Sea Sprite* – and to a world that had looming above it not low grey clouds but instead an ominous red China.

There was no new news. On CNN and BBC World News it was just the same loop of no information and no enlightenment whatsoever from a series of professional gurus, and that meant that a similar loop was replayed numerous times over lunch. Was it a deadly pandemic? Was it an earthquake in the Communist Party? Was it some inconceivable natural disaster? Or was it the world's biggest imminent anticlimax? Would China come back online within hours and announce that normal service would be resumed as soon as possible, and just as soon as the final dregs of that pesky flu thing had been completely flushed away?

Alex was relieved when lunch was over, and when the *Sea Sprite* had taken up its new anchorage off King Edward Point. This was just a few miles east of Hercules Bay, and it was the gateway to South Georgia's most visited site: the abandoned whaling station at Grytviken.

King Edward Point sits at the entrance to King Edward Cove, and is home to the island's tiny resident population of humans. For here is a fisheries research facility run by the British Antarctic Survey, shared with a handful of resident government officers responsible for South Georgia and the South Sandwich Islands – and accommodation for both these officers and the BAS researchers. However, it is Grytviken, at the head of King Edward Cove, that is of real interest to any visitor, because as well as hosting the remains of a huge whaling station – and South Georgia's only functioning church, its only active Post Office and its only museum – it also hosts, just a stone's throw away, Shackleton's grave. This has pride of place in a small whalers' cemetery, surrounded by a low white-painted fence, and blessed with what might be amongst the best views from any cemetery in the world.

That was Alex's thought as he stood in the cemetery, glass in hand, ready, with all the other passengers from the ship, to toast Shackleton's memory with a slug of very welcome whisky. This had been thoughtfully provided by the ship's operators and was designed to pay suitable homage to one of the most remarkable explorers of all time. For here, buried below this cold South Georgia soil, was a man who might not be remembered for a series of outstanding successes, but instead for his courage, his determination, and his unwillingness to give up. What schoolboy, mused Alex, hadn't been inspired by Shackleton's exploits, and in particular, by his eight-hundred-mile voyage in a converted lifeboat that led to his saving the lives of all his colleagues who had been forced to abandon the *Endurance* when it had become trapped in pack ice? While they remained in a makeshift refuge on Elephant Island, Shackleton and five of his companions had set off in their open boat for the faraway South Georgia and, after fifteen days making their way through the waters of the Southern Ocean, they had arrived on this island's south coast. Then, taking just two of his crew with him – and with no proper equipment and no maps – Shackleton had managed to scale the mountain chain that makes up the spine of South Georgia, and finally reach a whaling station – and help. His colleagues on Elephant Island were eventually rescued, and his reputation as a fearless explorer soared. No wonder, Alex concluded, he was so revered. And so deserving of this recognition in Scotch.

Of course, how Shackleton had got on with the local fur seals was not recorded. But Alex thought that if it had been, he would have been less than complimentary about their behaviour. Alex had now made his way, with Debbie and a straggling line of his shipmates, into Grytviken proper, and while the numerous king penguins and elephant seals who had colonised the whaling station were largely indifferent to a troop of wandering humans, the fur seals were a different matter altogether. Essentially, just as promised in that first biosecurity presentation, they were not only inquisitive, but truculent as well. And the young males in particular were just plain dangerous, and had to be discouraged from attacking the *Sea Sprite's* passengers by the use of sticks or loud handclaps. This was apparently better than letting them inflict a bite, but it did mean that for as long as Alex and Debbie were in Grytviken, they had to guard themselves against a fur-seal ambush, and this didn't make for a very relaxing visit.

Nevertheless, they were still able to soak up the remarkable atmosphere of this place, and marvel at the size of the rusting whale-oil tanks and the equally prodigious size of all the kit required to turn whales into whale oil – and grieve for all the thousands of beautiful creatures who would have been butchered in such a despicable way. Not, as Alex thought, that it would have been seen to be in the least despicable then. And the hard-working inhabitants of Grytviken were no doubt upstanding honest folk just going about their honest work, and on Sundays turning up at Grytviken's tiny wooden church to give thanks to God for the bounty he had so generously created. Even if that might be a very human perspective on the purpose – and birthright – of all non-human animals.

Alex and Debbie risked a threatening phalanx of fur seals to visit the church, and found it charming and in surprisingly good condition. The Post Office, the next destination on their city tour, was similarly charming and very well appointed. And the museum was also very smart, as well as being packed with all sorts of interesting exhibits. There was even a replica of the *James Caird,* the twenty-foot lifeboat that the ship's carpenter from the *Endurance* had prepared for Shackleton's eight-hundred-mile mission to bring help to his stranded crew. This nautical chippy had apparently raised its sides, strengthened its keel, given it a makeshift half-deck of wood and canvas and had sealed the whole lot with oil paint and seal blood. But it was still basically a small lifeboat, and Alex could not imagine how anyone would set to sea in such a small vessel in such demanding waters, and without any modern navigational aids to help him find so small a land mass so far to the north – and so easy to miss entirely. Maybe he should go back to that cemetery and toast Shackleton again. Or maybe he should report to a waiting zodiac and return to the *Sea Sprite,* while carefully avoiding a further gang of fur seals who had gathered to ensure that he and his wife were menaced to the very end of their visit. Even if they would escape without a single bite…

Back on board, it was the usual welcome with a warm flannel and a glass of something too hot to drink, and then a brisk walk to their cabin to dispose of most of their layers of clothes. And then it was on with the telly. Had CNN or BBC World any new light to shed on that oriental mystery that up to now had been kept at bay by South Georgia's charms? Well, no, neither of them had, other than an 'unconfirmed report' that something out of the ordinary might be going on where China bumped into Myanmar. And it might even involve shots being fired. Maybe last night's third-hand rumour had been more than just a rumour.

Alex was just about to make this point to Debbie when the ship's tannoy found its voice. It was the expedition leader's number two, Sarah, a youngish women with an admirable body but a less-than-admirable demeanour, announcing that at five o'clock there would be a meeting in the main lounge to address the situation in China. It wasn't, of course, mandatory. But it didn't need to be. Alex could not believe that it wouldn't attract a bumper audience, or that anyone would turn up late.

He was right. When he and Debbie entered the old people's lounge, there was hardly a seat that wasn't already occupied, and they had to position themselves at the back of the room on a couple of chairs that were situated directly under a picture of the *Endurance.* Alex just hoped that what they were about to hear might be rather more uplifting than the message Shackleton must have had to deliver to the crew of his ill-fated vessel. And that it certainly wouldn't involve the use of any lifeboats, even if they'd been upgraded by the use of copious amounts of seal blood. He would soon find out. Jane had just adopted her standard legs-planted-firmly-apart stance at the front of the lounge and was about to speak. When she did it was in a tone somewhere between earnest and ill at ease.

'Thank you all for coming at such short notice,' she began. 'And I won't waste any more of your time than I have to by my coming straight to the point. And the point is China, and whether your captain knows anything more about what is going on in that country than you might have seen for yourselves on the news. Well, I can tell you straightaway that he does not. None of us do. All we know – like you – is that China has unplugged itself from the rest of the world and the reason it has done this is a complete mystery. It might be something to do with the flu there. And personally, I think it has to be. But nobody can be sure, and there seems to be little point in indulging in speculation.

'Instead, I think we should focus on our situation and consider whether the events in China – whatever they are – should have any impact on our cruise. That is to say, any impact on the continuation of our cruise. Should we now curtail it and head back to Ushuaia or should we just sit off South Georgia for a while until things become clearer? Or should we simply carry on – ignore faraway events and just keep to our original itinerary? Now, I know that there are already some very different opinions on this. After all, it's difficult to overestimate the seriousness of a country the size of China isolating itself from the rest of the world. And some amongst you are very worried about what this might mean, and think that the idea of our just carrying on as if nothing has happened is reckless to say the least. You think we'd be simply burying our heads in the sand. Conversely, there are quite a number amongst you who think that abandoning the cruise now would be entirely pointless. What, you ask, would it achieve, and how could it place us in a better position than we're in at the moment: remote from the seat of whatever the problem might be, and still with an ability to monitor developments on the other side of the world?'

At this stage of the address, Alex could see that a handful of people in the lounge were getting a little restless. They had questions to ask and they wanted to ask them now. However, Jane had other ideas, and she quickly pressed on.

'Well, I did say that our captain knows as little about what is going on within China's borders as we all do. He's been unable to discover anything about the reason for China's shutdown. However, he's been far from idle, and he's been in close contact with Stanley – and I mean the authorities there. And he's even paid a visit to the government guys at King Edward Point – while we were toasting Shackleton – to see whether they've got any more information. And the purpose of his efforts – obviously – was to establish whether we should turn back, stay put or carry on.

'Well, ladies and gentlemen, I am happy to report that the firm – official – advice from the authorities in the Falklands, based on the advice they have received from

London – and fully supported by the guys at King Edward Point – is that we should carry on. They believe that there is no danger in our adopting this option, and on the contrary, they think it would be counterproductive for us to return to Ushuaia. That would only invite any number of problems and it would also be completely futile. As in "what would it achieve?".'

'Well, we'd be back in civilisation, to start with,' interjected someone at the front of the room.

Jane glared at him, but she responded in a calm and placatory tone.

'I know what you mean, sir. But I really don't see how that would be an improvement on our current situation; one where, if we need to, we can be back in "civilisation" in no more than three days' time. And as I've said, we certainly do not need to do that yet. All the advice is to… well, to keep calm and carry on. And that's exactly what the captain has decided to do. And I truly hope that when you've given it some more thought, you'll all give that decision your full support. After all, our captain's primary concern is our well-being, and all he is doing is what he thinks is best for us in all sorts of ways. We will remain entirely safe and we will even have the bonus of seeing more of South Georgia and then, all being well, the Antarctic Peninsula.'

The original interrupter had been gently but successfully faced down, but another now found his voice.

'How can he know it's OK to go all the way to the Antarctic Peninsula? Anything might happen.'

Jane smiled, and again answered calmly.

'Sir, I did say, "all being well". Obviously, we will be monitoring what's going on all the time, and if we get different advice tomorrow – or even in the next few hours – we will act on that advice and do whatever is necessary. We certainly won't be sailing off to Antarctica before we know that it's safe to do so. I can only repeat; the captain has our well-being as his absolute priority.'

Alex was aware that there were a couple of mumbles in Jane's audience at this point, but nobody spoke up, and nobody even asked a question when Jane invited these from the floor. She'd done her job well, and was now able to wrap up her unscheduled talk with a promise that everybody would be kept well informed of any developments and that meanwhile she would be very grateful if the assembled passengers remembered that the maintenance of biosecurity measures was still crucially important. And this meant that they should ensure that they'd inspected their boots and all their outerwear before they embarked on tomorrow's planned activities. It was her way, thought Alex, of injecting a little normality into a potentially febrile situation. Or maybe she always used any opportunity that presented itself to ram home her favourite biosecurity message. Indeed, having given it just a little more thought, he soon decided it was the latter...

Over dinner, the intensity of the biosecurity arrangements featured as an early topic for discussion. This was partly due to the fact that the normal gang of five had made a pact at the beginning of the meal that they would talk about anything other than China. This worked very well, and in due course it led to a fascinating debate on the intellectual capacity of certain politicians and how, despite having had a virtual intellectual by-pass, some of them were able to achieve high office if not the respect of their peers or of mere mortal plebs. And without exception, all of them were blind to their blatant inadequacies. This then somehow led on to an exchange about gender politics – and the dangers of allowing any such exchange into the public arena – before Derek decided to vent his thoughts on the subject of 'cultural appropriation'.

Unsurprisingly, he had no time for it and thought it worse than ridiculous. In his mind, the very idea of suggesting that by wearing a Mexican hat one could in some way be disrespecting Mexican culture was no less than preposterous. And what's more, he argued, it ignored the rather old-fashioned epithet of 'Imitation is the sincerest form of flattery.' Why would anyone put a Mexican hat on his or her head if he or she didn't like Mexican hats? He did go on a bit, and he did dwell a little too long on the subject of cultural imposition, which he considered to be a rather more serious issue in England than anything to do with hats. But he concluded swiftly and amusingly by suggesting that the English might successfully undermine the whole concept of cultural appropriation by pointing out that the English language, which is central to all aspects of their culture, has been appropriated by hundreds of millions of people around the world. And would they now kindly desist from this discourteous behaviour. Would they just clear off and find their own bloody language and leave ours alone...

It had been a really good evening. And after dinner Alex and Debbie would have gone to bed happy, if only they hadn't put on BBC World News and heard that there were now several well-validated reports of shooting on China's borders with no fewer than six of its neighbours, and that this or some other issue might be the reason for India's mobilisation of its armed forces.

What, thought Alex, would the captain and Jane make of that?

thirteen

Before he'd crawled back into bed last night, Stuart had picked up multiple reports that all indicated that China's ailment, whatever it was, was no longer just China's problem. To start with, there were more fairly detailed reports of sustained shooting near its borders with countries as far away from each other as Vietnam and Kazakhstan, and then some rather sketchier reports that some of that shooting had crossed the borders. In Vietnam, in particular, there seemed to be a response from that country which involved elements of its military. And whilst nobody seemed to be shooting on India's side of its border with China, there was a report in a number of intercepts, first confirmed and then denied, that India had mobilised its armed forces – or was just about to. Like much of what Stuart was picking up, the credibility and clarity of these messages concerning India's actions rather depended on their source. Those originating in Spain or Portugal were probably the most reliable, but not always.

Those originating from anywhere in South America were the least reliable. And if anything came out of Venezuela, one could almost guarantee that it would be either risible or plain wrong. Like the intercept he'd seen late in the evening, hot off the military press in Caracas, which had claimed that it had now been established that the CIA had infected China with a new strain of Ebola. It had apparently been developed on the orders of President Trump, and it was destined to be released on the streets of Caracas within weeks if not days.

That snippet of light relief didn't do much for Stuart's mood, and he went to bed feeling very concerned, not just about what he had seen throughout the day, but about what might greet him in the morning. He knew that whatever greeted him, it was unlikely to be good news, and it was just a matter of whether it would be simply more bad news or possibly some dramatically worse news. He hardly dared admit it to himself, but he rather thought it would be the latter. And sure enough, when morning came, the possibility of it being just more of the same bad stuff disappeared very quickly indeed. Even before he had reached his den for an early-morning start to his day.

He'd left his sleeping quarters and had made a beeline for the nearby NAAFI shop to pick up a bacon sandwich to eat at his desk, and something was different. He wasn't quite sure what it was to start with, but then it clicked. There were far fewer service guys about, and those who were still about were not strolling or chatting, as they would normally be at this breakfast time of the day, but they were distinctly 'on their way somewhere', and with expressions on their faces that didn't invite even a brief morning greeting. Something must have happened overnight, and whether these people knew what it was or not, they had obviously been told that they had some work to do and no time to dawdle or chat. Stuart felt more concerned than ever. And alone. He might be working for the government, but he wasn't a soldier or an airman, and that meant he wasn't being let in on whatever was going on. He would have to see whether he could deduce anything himself. Just as soon as he'd got his breakfast back to his work-station and plugged himself into the latest crop of intercepts.

He'd taken only one bite of his bacon butty, when he began to understand why Mount Pleasant this morning was very different from the Mount Pleasant he'd become used to. Why its air of relaxed boredom had, in the space of only a few hours, turned into one of determined absorption. It was in the first intercept he read, one to the Spanish ambassador in Buenos Aires, and it simply said that there were now tens of millions of dead in India, and millions more in South-East Asia, all the way down to Malaysia and Indonesia. It was an odd communiqué in that it didn't accompany this information with any interpretation of the cause of all these deaths, or indeed with any other commentary at all. Maybe, thought Stuart, the sender just hadn't been able to come to terms with the implications of the message, and as a result had refrained from adding anything at all to the grisly bare facts. Unlike the sender of the second message Stuart read, who stated categorically that the millions now believed to be dead across a whole swathe of Russia presaged the arrival of the killer flu in western Russia and then probably Europe.

Bloody hell! Europe! Stuart felt his heart thumping again, and he entirely lost interest in his bacon delight. Instead, he brought to mind that thought he'd had two days before; the thought that he might be witness not to another damp squib, but to something that would provide a shock to the human world of the sort it had never known before. Well, this was it. And it was for real. And already, for millions of humans, it hadn't been just a shock, but instead the end; their genuine apocalyptic experience. And for how many more, wondered Stuart, would the apocalypse arrive? And would he be amongst their number?! He might be on a rock in the Atlantic, but at the rate that flu was spreading, who could tell? It might be here any time.

But then Stuart had another thought. How could any flu spread at that rate? He wasn't a medic, but he had done a degree in botany, and that had given him at least a little understanding of infection mechanisms, and certainly enough to know that there was no way that a flu that had previously been confined to just one country could so quickly overcome so many other people in so many other countries. And with apparently barely any incubation period at all. It was ridiculous. But there again, it was real. Somehow, some sort of disease was spreading like wildfire across the whole of Asia and it was proving so deadly – so quickly – that it was difficult to see how it would stop before it had killed millions more on that giant land mass. And after Asia, there was then the rest of the world, which indisputably included the Falklands.

He didn't know what to do. His training had not included guidance on the appropriate response to a supercharged pandemic that was acting in such an unconventional and terrifying manner. So, he retreated to his comfort zone: he dug into the mountain of intercepts and he tried to find some nuggets of good news. Unfortunately, there were none. None whatsoever. Instead there were more references to urban fires and fire storms, and there were a few reports that suggested that the wave of deaths had now reached the UAE. Against this background of carnage and devastation, there were a few further reports touching on the economic meltdown caused by China's withdrawal from the family of nations, which was now afflicting the whole of the world. And there was one message from Ecuador's ambassador to Moscow stating that Quito was one of the cities being considered by Putin's advisers as a suitable 'temporary relocation destination' for the great one himself. No doubt so that he could get a better perspective on events back in Mother Russia and thereby better devote himself to the welfare of any of its surviving citizens.

Stuart actually chuckled at that one. But then he decided it was time to relocate himself. He would abandon his pointless monitoring work – although he might get around to making a pointless report later on – and he would go and seek out his mate, Gill. Gill, after all, was in the Royal Corps of Signals; she was a signaller. And with a role in military communications, no matter how small, she might just know what had been communicated to Mount Pleasant from the authorities back in Britain. And even if she didn't, she might at least know what had been communicated to all those purposeful service personnel on the base; what they had been told to cause them to change their demeanour and their behaviour so very much. And if nothing else, Gill might make him feel not quite so alone. Or quite so afraid...

fourteen

Even before he had got out of bed, Alex had used the remote to turn on the television and tune in to BBC World News. He was more than a little eager to discover whether China was now at war with India and whether hostilities had been launched against any of its other neighbours. Debbie was keen to discover this too. However, it seemed that they might have to wait. Because the members of the panel in the BBC studio were not discussing any sort of military action, but instead they were trying to reconcile the normal, accepted forms of disease transmission with what was now being observed; namely, the rapid spread of China's mystery disease beyond its borders. The monster, it appeared, was now out of its cage. And that made any exchange of small fire – or indeed any exchange of the bigger stuff – pale into insignificance

Inevitably, both Alex and Debbie were soon captured by the discussion of how the monster might advance, and they began to listen intently to what was being said. In this way they learnt that diseases are spread in one of five ways: through direct contact with an infected person, through being showered with droplets from an infected person when that person coughs or sneezes, through indirect contact such as touching a contaminated surface or ingesting contaminated food or water, through airborne transmission, or through a vector – such as a mosquito or a fly. They also learnt that none of these transmission routes could explain how a disease that had been contained within one country – and even a country the size of China – could find its way into so many other countries quite so quickly. Although, as one of the panellists was quick to point out, that was possibly a minor puzzle compared to establishing how the disease managed to be so lethal, and so swiftly. There appeared to be no incubation period at all. Which was not just a mystery but also an affront to every tenet of modern medicine. The world simply did not host a disease that could fell people without even a short period of notice. Although, maybe it now did…

It was just as the panel's deliberations were being interrupted for an update on the number of deaths in various countries – given in millions – that Jane's voice came through the tannoy. It was now eight in the morning, and despite the arrival of Armageddon in Asia, time for her morning briefing. She started with her normal greeting.

'Good morning, everybody. And as you will see if you look out of your cabin window, we have the prospect of a very good morning ahead of us. The captain has brought us to St Andrews Bay, and I can tell you now that the sea is very calm with only a slight swell on the shoreline, and if it remains that way, we'll definitely be able to land you ashore as planned. And believe me, St Andrews Bay is not to be missed. I regard it as one of the absolute highlights of our trip.

'We will start boarding the zodiacs at 9.15, with passengers from the port side first. And I'd just like to take this opportunity to remind you to check your boots again if you haven't already done so. And please don't forget your cameras. I assure you; you will be devastated if you do.'

Here Jane paused, and Alex thought for a second that her message had ended, with no reference whatsoever to the calamity on the other side of the world. But then she continued.

'I suppose I should just mention that some of you may have seen that there have been some… errh developments in Asia, and the captain will be organising another meeting in the lounge later today when he will have a full update on what's going on there and what it might mean for us here on the *Sea Sprite*. I will let you know the timing of that when you're back on the ship. Meanwhile, though, have a really good morning.'

That was the end of her message, and its conclusion triggered an immediate exchange between Alex and his wife.

'One is put in mind of the cricket scores followed by an announcement of an imminent nuclear attack,' pronounced Alex.

'Well, sort of,' responded Debbie. 'But what else could she say?'

Alex mumbled something entirely indeterminate as a prelude to delivering some actual words. And then the words arrived.

'Well, it's just the whole idea of carrying on as though nothing has happened, when we all know something bloody massive has happened. And is still bloody happening...'

'...which we can't do anything about, and certainly not this morning. And if you ask me, it would be plain stupid not to go ashore. I mean, what's the alternative: a morning of more of that telly, or maybe an endless, futile debate with a load of people who have as much idea of what's going on and what to do about it as we do? No, I vote for the zodiacs. And anyway, I've spent so much bloomin' time on my boots...'

That was it. A decision had been made by one of the party – and accepted by the other – and it was now time to sort themselves out before a cup-of-coffee breakfast, followed by the demanding task of encasing themselves in their multiple layers of clothes. Soon after this, they were boarding a zodiac, and a few minutes later they were making a wet landing on the grey-gravel beach of St Andrews Bay. They would now find out whether, over the next three hours, they would be presented with enough of interest in this place to properly distract them from the massacre of millions in faraway lands.

It started well. They had landed in the middle of a menagerie. No need to drive around in a safari vehicle here to catch sight of animals, and no tiresome waiting in a hide. No, here in St Andrews Bay, there were animals and birds all over the place, and so many of them that the task of keeping the recommended few metres away from them was a full-time job. Here, just a few feet away to the left, were a couple of young male elephant seals, practising their fighting skills. With their flabby chests raised from the ground and their mouths open in a fearsome red gape, they were actually more posturing than engaging in real battle, and they were certainly failing to impress their more sedentary colleagues arranged all around them. These particular overfilled tubes of blubber, as grey as the grey beach beneath them, were either asleep or just about awake, but clearly quite indifferent to the activities of their more energetic companions.

Similarly indifferent were the pair of skuas curled up on the ground, and not in the least concerned by the presence of two looming humans, who were themselves more interested in what lay in their path: twenty or so king penguins, who gave the impression of strangers gathered at a convention waiting to be introduced to each other. Some looked into the distance, some looked to the sky, some looked as though they were in a trance, and some were now taking an interest in the new arrivals to the convention: a pair of outlandish visitors who were entirely the wrong colour and entirely the wrong height.

As Alex and Debbie made their way along the beach, they encountered more and more of these penguins, many of whom appeared to take an interest in their presence. Not an intense interest, but just a nosy, inquisitive sort of interest, which might see them waddle towards them, but only far enough to become apparently confused, at which point they would either waddle away slowly or just stand and look. They were charming beyond description, and their company was infinitely preferable to that of the scores of fur seals that also occupied the beach. They were just as threatening and actually aggressive as those encountered back at Grytviken, and it wasn't long before Alex and Debbie were charting their course along the huge grey beach of St Andrews Bay by reference to the disposition of these furry grey thugs. Fortunately, there were far fewer of these bruisers than there were of elephant seals. And whilst the elephant seals were potentially dangerous, in practice they were either just into that mock-fighting between themselves or, more commonly, they were just inert. Clearly, if one spent ninety per cent of one's life dashing around under the sea, one sought to spend the other ten per cent doing as little as possible on land. Particularly if one hadn't been charged with too much of that troublesome testosterone.

St Andrews Bay is a two-mile-long 'bite' out of the north coast of South Georgia, backed by mountains and glaciers. Further along its gravel beach was the site of a king penguin colony, and it was towards this that Alex, Debbie and the rest of the ship's company were making their way. It was quite a walk, and it involved crossing a somewhat lively melt stream about forty feet wide and with a bottom made up of seemingly mobile mini boulders. This was negotiated only partially successfully, in that Alex collected a bootful of water as he made his crossing. However, it was well worth the discomfort because, after a few hundred yards, he and Debbie reached the top of a ridge and there before them was the biggest sentient biomass they had ever seen.

It was the king penguin colony; 150,000 of these remarkable birds spread out to form an entire landscape, and constituting not only a wonderful natural spectacle but also a complete distraction from any lingering thoughts of that blasted life-threatening plague. It was truly spellbinding; rank after rank of white and steel-blue sentinels, all finished off with yellow-orange finery around and below their heads. And within these ranks, animated busbies, the remarkable portly king penguin chicks that were thought by early visitors to this land to be a completely different species. It was easy to see why, thought Alex. Their appearance bore no relation whatsoever to that of their parents, and in his opinion they had more in common with Jeremy Hillary Boob, PhD, one of the more bizarre characters in the ancient *Yellow Submarine* animated film, now long forgotten by most but still lodged in Alex's overstuffed brain. With their brown furry coats and their pronounced penguin beaks, they even had the same slightly surreal and distinctly whacky look. Alex thought they were amazing.

Ultimately, he also thought that he should abandon this most remarkable display of wildlife and guide his wife back to the waiting zodiacs through that gauntlet of fur seals. This he did without recharging his wet boot with more water and without attracting too much attention from any of the delinquent seals. All that then remained at the end of this odyssey was to equip himself and his wife with a life jacket in readiness for their zodiac taxi-ride back to the ship; there, no doubt, to be reintroduced to the first act of the end of the world. And indeed, this was exactly how it seemed to Alex as he stepped off the zodiac and onto the stern of the *Sea Sprite*, his mind now stripped of the insulation against reality provided by St Andrews Bay. In fact, he soon felt the need to tell himself that he was possibly being just a little bit negative in harbouring such thoughts, and he sincerely hoped that when he and Debbie attended the next gathering in the lounge this would prove to be the case. And before then, there might even be some better news on the telly. However, there was none…

The first report they heard was on the economic impact of the 'flu', which was apparently already way beyond disastrous. With China's role in world commerce having been eliminated entirely, there was a catastrophic knock-on effect in the rest of the world, now exacerbated by the Grim Reaper's arrival in so many other countries. Essentially, much of world's industrial activity was grinding to a halt, if it hadn't already come to a standstill. Service industries were also suffering hugely, and inevitably the world's stock markets were in meltdown. The report didn't carry news of how many investors were jumping out of New York skyscrapers, but given the magnitude of the collapse in share prices being experienced now compared to that seen in the Great Depression, they should have been leaping off window ledges in their thousands. Alex wasn't inclined to join them, but he did feel sick to the stomach when he thought of what this news could mean for his own personal wealth. It was just as well that the next report on the telly took his mind off these woes – by it having to digest the news that China now seemed to be empty of living humans…

This was the news that formed the first topic of conversation with Roy over lunch. He was as stunned as Alex and Debbie were that the world now didn't include this giant country. Or that it did, but it lacked any people.

'Just think,' he said. 'Who would have put money on the Chinese becoming extinct before all the world's sharks? I still can't believe it.'

'Maybe they're just "critically endangered",' suggested Alex. 'You know, there must be some of them left, some soldiers or the like hidden away in nuclear bunkers…'

'And politicians,' interrupted Debbie. 'I can't believe old Xi Jinpong has succumbed to the flu. Or many of his top party chums. They'll be hidden away safely somewhere.

Either underground or in one of their secret boltholes in the West. Maybe in somewhere like Burgundy…'

The conversation drifted on like this for some time until, just as the three diners were finishing their coffee, Jane's voice came over the tannoy to announce that the promised ship's powwow would commence in the main lounge at three o'clock, and that it would be followed by a presentation on *Shackleton's Imperial Trans-Antarctic Expedition, 1914-1917*. The first of these lounge gatherings, thought Alex, might prove even more popular than the second.

It got under way with a welcome from Jane, and then an announcement by the captain himself that he still had no further insights into what was happening in Asia, over and above what was being shown on the news. And the official advice channelled through Stanley was still to 'just carry on, but keep in touch for any updates to this advice'.

This message didn't go down too well with a number of the passengers, and one near the front immediately got to his feet to make the point that, considering what was going on, he and his wife wanted to get back to England as soon as possible. They wanted to be with their children and their grandchildren, and it was, this red-faced gentleman said, incumbent on the captain to turn his ship around and get it back to Ushuaia without further ado.

In response to this 'forceful request', the captain said nothing, and it was Jane who stepped in to explain why this simply wasn't going to happen, despite others in the audience indicating that they had similar thoughts to the guy who'd just spoken. For the first time the *Sea Sprite's* passengers were going to witness the real Jane, a Jane stripped of all her tact and with an important point to make.

'I completely understand why you think we should do that,' she pronounced in an uncompromising tone, 'but you *must* understand that if we turn back to Ushuaia now, the only thing that's certain is that we will end up being stuck there. I mean, you must have seen on the news that international flights are in complete chaos, and the probability that we could get you a seat on a plane back to Britain – even if we could get you back to Buenos Aires – is essentially zero.'

At this point the red-faced man clearly had something to say, but Jane carried on.

'So, what you're asking for is entirely impractical and it also undoubtedly ignores the wishes of many of your fellow passengers. I am not going to ask for a show of hands, but I can sense that a large majority of people in this room do not want to go back to Ushuaia – prematurely – and instead they want to continue on an expedition cruise for which they have paid a great deal of money.'

(This statement prompted the nodding of quite a few heads in the room.)

'And sir, whilst I and my team always strive to do everything we can for our guests, we cannot, unfortunately, split this ship in two, and send one half of it back to Ushuaia while the other continues on its way...'

'I think that's unduly rude...' interrupted Mr Red Face, only to be interrupted himself – by the captain. Because Captain José had swiftly equipped himself with the microphone in order to make a short but uncompromising announcement.

'Sir, Jane has made very clear why we will not be going back to Ushuaia – just yet. What I now need to make clear is that the *Sea Sprite* is not under the command of a committee. It is under *my* command; a situation you implicitly accepted when you boarded this vessel. You must therefore refrain from trying to wrest that command from me. In any way whatsoever.'

Here, the captain smiled disarmingly. Then he went on.

'I hardly need remind you, sir, but a rebellion against my authority has a name. It is called "mutiny".'

At that statement, the room fell silent. It also brought to an end any further discussion concerning the possibility of an immediate return to Argentina; and, indeed, an end to the gathering. People clearly realised that there was nothing more to be learnt in this room, but possibly a great deal more to be learnt by returning to their cabins and keeping a watch on the news. Despite its tempting subject matter, *Shackleton's Imperial Trans-Antarctic Expedition, 1914-1917* might, thought Alex, not even attract a quorum.

He and Debbie were certainly intent on flicking between BBC World News and CNN, and by doing this for the rest of the afternoon, they discovered that there had now been countless deaths in the very south of India, and that most North Koreans were now either dead or making their way to South Korea. Neither Kim Jong-un's whereabouts nor his vital signs were known. Nor whether he still had any vital signs…

That Kim might now be dead was one of the first topics to be discussed at dinner with Derek, Elaine and Roy. After that, the conversation explored just about every aspect of China's demise. These ranged from the large sigh of relief from the world's population of wild animals to the potential benefits of having an appreciably smaller world population of humans – soon, by all accounts, to be much smaller still. Roy also introduced the thought he'd expressed over lunch: that he would never have imagined that the Chinese would become extinct before sharks. And this caused Derek to put forward the opinion that it would be the ultimate irony if it was found that the devastating disease that had eradicated a whole nation was one that had been passed from sharks to humans as a result of some of those humans feasting on shark's fin soup. The other diners agreed, but Roy did suggest that the disease – whatever it was – was much more likely to have been picked up from a bat or a pangolin or any of the live animals (formerly) traded in Chinese markets. Elaine agreed, but went on to point out that there might soon be no one to perform the necessary detective work, and maybe soon, no one to care.

It had been a strange meal, and it needed to come to an end. Today's events had been exhausting for all those at the table, and none of them knew how much more exhaustion tomorrow might bring. So, stumps were drawn and the gang of five returned to their respective cabins. And, if they did what Alex did as soon as he was within reaching distance of his TV's remote, they would all have learnt that the fourth Horseman of the Apocalypse had now ridden into Iran…

fifteen

Yesterday had been not just scary, but also really frustrating. Stuart had not been able to find Gill, nor anyone else in uniform who was prepared even to speak to him, let alone explain what might be going on. There had clearly been an instruction given to all the service personnel on the base to keep whatever they'd been told within the military family. And even if you'd been granted Class A security clearance in order to do your job, that didn't make you a soldier or an airman, and you were going to be kept in the dark. The only people Stuart spoke to all day were a couple of civilian contractors in the NAAFI canteen, who, just like him, were at a loss to know what was going on, and more than just a little bit scared.

In the end, Stuart had decided to abandon his search for Gill and for any indication of what was happening on the base, and return to his lonely listening post in the hope of getting an update on what was happening beyond the base. This was when he discovered that China was now a vacant country, which more or less confirmed in his mind that the world was now experiencing an unprecedented, off-the-scale event. It was truly staggering news, and of course it wasn't the only news. By the time he finally went to bed, he'd also discovered that there were many more deaths in more countries; more countries facing the same – still unbelievable – fate as the now-deceased China, and there was seemingly no end to the spread of the killer disease. One communiqué had even made a reference to a small cluster of deaths in Colombia. But that one Stuart didn't believe. It had originated in Colombia. And whilst information generated in that country was about a thousand times better than that dreamt up in its immediate neighbour, Venezuela, it was still almost exclusively unreliable. Even when it related to drugs…

It was now six in the morning of the next day, and Stuart was already dressing himself after a super-early – for him – set of ablutions. And as he buttoned up his shirt, he told himself that today, even if he was still unable to track down Gill, he would find out exactly what was going on in Mount Pleasant. It must, he knew, be in response to the carnage taking place around the world, but he still wanted to know precisely what it was that had caused the base's entire military complement to become automatons overnight, and apparently automatons without a voice. He even repeated this promise to himself aloud, and it was just as he was giving a confirmatory nod of his head to this determined statement that he noticed that there was an envelope on the floor of his room. It was just next to the door, and it must, he thought, have been pushed under it sometime in the night. He also thought that its contents deserved his immediate attention. They did. It was a copy of a short note on air-force-headed notepaper informing him of a meeting to be held in the base gym at nine o'clock, at which all non-military personnel would be given an update on what was happening on the base. It was signed by the base commander, and whilst attendance at the meeting was not described as mandatory, it was referred to as 'strongly advised'. It didn't, of course, need to be. This was one visit to the gym that Stuart wasn't going to miss.

First, though, it was another unhealthy breakfast from the NAAFI to be eaten at his desk, and then another dip into the flood of intercepts that had come in overnight. Not one of them lifted his mood. It seemed that the Chinese pestilence, whatever it was, had now crept into Africa. Although, the more messages and signals he read, the more he realised that this lethal disease wasn't so much creeping into that continent as overwhelming it in a fast-moving wave. Deaths were already being reported in sub-Saharan Africa, and even Madagascar appeared to be succumbing to the scourge. However, there were a number of intercepts that were even more disconcerting – for Stuart. These included half a dozen originating in Europe, and they seemed to confirm that the flu had arrived in Colombia. That intercept from last night had been correct. And there was even a suggestion in these messages that this terrible disease was already moving into Peru. How long, Stuart thought, would it take for it to make its way down the coast of the continent to the south of Chile, and then into Argentina? On the basis of what he'd seen so far, not very long at all...

Inevitably, when he arrived in the gym, he did so with a multitude of other people, all non-military personnel and all wearing looks of apprehension on their faces. There were builders in their work gear, NAAFI workers in their kitchen whites, some guys Stuart recognised as IT workers – in bad T-shirts and jeans – and any number of assorted other contractors and workers, all dressed in all manner of casual or work clothes. There must have been well over a hundred of these civilians, all now seated on canvas chairs that had been set out in rows in the gym, and all eager to learn just what was going on. They did not have to wait long. At nine o'clock sharp, an RAF officer strode into the gym to take his place behind a lectern at the front of this makeshift auditorium, ready to make his address.

Stuart was not sure of his rank, but taking account of the number of bands on his sleeves and his youthful looks, he reckoned he was probably a lieutenant. Or was that a flight lieutenant? Stuart had not been entirely diligent in learning either his army or his air-force ranks, but he did know that officers were chosen very carefully for a particular job. And when someone was required to impart a certain amount of information but no more, a senior officer would not be selected, but rather a competent junior who could easily claim that he didn't have access to further and better information. The civilians gathered here, thought Stuart, were going to be told just enough to satisfy their curiosity for now – and so pacify them – but not a great deal more. It was almost a cert…

'Good morning everybody,' the ginger-haired officer began, 'and thank you very much for attending this meeting and for turning up so promptly. I assure you that I will take up as little of your time as I can.'

Here he tried an ersatz smile, which was presumably designed to conceal his trepidation. It was one thing, thought

Stuart, to confront an enemy of the state, in the air or on the ground; it was quite another to confront an audience of unarmed but anxious civilians. Nevertheless, he had now parked the smile and he was beginning the substance of his address.

'First of all, I want to convey the commander's genuine apologies for having kept you in the dark for so long. He knows – as do all of us serving on this base – that you must have observed our behaviour over the past twenty-four hours, and this can only have added to your concerns as to what might be going on. However – and I'm afraid there is no other way to say this – he and all of us were simply following orders. Only overnight have we received permission to give you this briefing. So, again, please accept his apologies, and I hope that from now on we will be allowed to share with you everything we are doing.'

Stuart thought that final remark might not be quite as genuine as the apology proffered, but no doubt the poor guy was just doing his job.

'OK,' the officer continued, 'you all know that something terrible is happening in Asia. An unknown disease there has already obliterated China and killed hundreds of millions of other people, and there doesn't seem to be any slowing of its progress across the planet. I won't try to hide from you just how serious this is...'

'Well, how serious is it?' bellowed a man in brown overalls. 'Are we all going to die?'

This interjection knocked the officer off his carefully calculated trajectory, and he let his eyes widen far too far. But then he collected himself.

'No, no. I think that's highly unlikely, sir, and particularly when you hear what we've been doing in the past twenty-four hours. You see, we were in receipt of orders to transform this base into what is termed a "super-safe area". And to start with what that means is that we've had to work very hard during those twenty-four hours to set up a secure defensive perimeter around the whole of the base. And this is now finished. And, I can assure you, it is simply impregnable. From either land or from air. Nobody, and I mean nobody, will be able to get in…'

'What about the people in Stanley?' interrupted another man in overalls from near the front of the hall.

'We can't, of course, accommodate the whole of the population of Stanley – or, indeed, the rest of the Falklands. But I can tell you that we have already taken steps to ensure that a handful of our local contractors have been able to bring their families onto the base. The rest have opted to leave the base and join their families in Stanley. Like all those in Stanley who have no connection with the base, they have chosen to stay there. And why wouldn't they? After all, there is no immediate danger, and they are already in a safe – and comfortable – place. Which is, no doubt, in their minds, a much more attractive proposition than being billeted in a not-so-comfortable "super-safe" place. If, of course, the situation changes for any reason, these arrangements might be reviewed. But for now, it is just you – and all us service personnel – who are in a very secure refuge. And a well provided-for refuge. I mean, as well as setting up that secure perimeter, we have been kitting out all our bunkers with enough provisions for over a month, and we've also set up quarantine units throughout the base, should these ever be needed. We've done everything we can to deal with whatever the immediate future has in store. And I hope this means that you're now far less concerned than you were when you entered this room.'

Nobody said anything, but the atmosphere in the gym had changed. Where before there had been anxiety, there was now a mix of relief and confusion. Clearly, being told that one was in a secure refuge might calm one's fears to a degree, but it still left other questions unresolved. Like how long would the refuge be necessary, and what would happen once it no longer was – if that time ever came? But nobody asked these questions, and before anybody chose to, the officer made a further announcement. Having explained to his audience that the base had been turned into some sort of hermetically sealed sanctuary, he then informed them that not all flights into the base would be suspended, as it was possible that certain 'important people' might be flown in from Brize Norton. He avoided using the term 'Very Important Persons', but Stuart immediately thought that what he was talking about was either the Royal Family turning up or maybe even a Government in forced exile. And he found either of those eventualities really very scary indeed. What the hell did that say about what they were expecting to happen in Britain?

Others in the audience clearly had similar thoughts, and they now began to bombard the officer with questions about the expected fate of their home country, and a few more concerning such things as the transmission methods of the flu. But this was where his lack of seniority proved its worth. He essentially had one response, which was that he had not been briefed to answer such questions, principally because, as far as he knew, nobody had answers to these questions, and certainly nobody on this base.

Well, that was it. The bad news was that the world was just overflowing with bad news. The good news – of sorts – was that Stuart and all those 'fortunate' enough to find themselves on this base were now going to be protected from all that bad news – as much as this was possible. And who wouldn't want to stay somewhere that might soon host Her Majesty the Queen or the ruddy Prime Minister?

Stuart left the meeting feeling a little reassured but still very concerned and very suspicious. Had they been told everything? Was there any more to be learnt – either from Gill or from the continuing torrent of intercepts?

An hour later, he had given up on the Gill route. He had established that Gill was on some sort of special duties for the rest of the day, and wouldn't be available until tomorrow. That just left the intercepts route. And armed with a takeaway lunch and a takeaway dinner, Stuart retired to his snooping post to spend what would be a solid fourteen hours looking at more of the world's 'official' chatter.

It just got worse and worse. People were dying in Ukraine, in Nigeria, in Sri Lanka and even in the Maldives. And as the day wore on, they were now reported to be dying in Alaska and in California. And in northern Brazil!

When he finally went to bed, exhausted and more frightened than ever, he wondered whether he should put on a tie in the morning in case he ran into the Queen or the PM. And should he get a haircut...?

sixteen

As Alex was waking up, he began to think about China, and the fact that it wasn't there any more. In place of what had been the world's most populous nation there was now just the largest stretch of human-free land on the planet, and that was almost impossible to take in. He hadn't been a fan of China, and had regarded it in much the same way that Derek had; as a giant vacuum cleaner sucking up the treasures of the world, and especially its natural treasures. China, in his mind, had been the principal culprit in diminishing the planet's store of diversity and enchantment – as often as not, simply to satisfy its ravenous appetite for 'exotic' food and worthless cures. It had been a monster, a voracious beast gobbling up the world's irreplaceable fauna. And now it was gone.

How could that be? How could a giant nation with a long and sometimes impressive history have been extinguished in such a short time? And did it deserve such a fate? Even from

Alex's jaundiced perspective, he had to accept that there must have been countless numbers of decent, honourable people in that country, and probably many who were as much revolted by some of its egregious habits as he was. And surely they deserved better than a premature and sudden end to their lives. And what of what was left behind? As far as was known, this flu thing infected only humans, and not other animals. That meant there would be countless millions of domestic and captive creatures in China that would now be facing an extended period of suffering before they starved to death or in some other way met their end. It didn't bear thinking about, and Alex tried desperately not to think about their plight by instead wondering whether there might just be some humans still alive in that vast and maybe-not-completely-empty country.

After all, as well as possibly thousands of soldiers and officials waiting out the pandemic in hundreds of bunkers, there might be legions of people who were simply immune to the disease, and who were now coming to terms with an *almost* empty country as well as the likely deaths of their nearest and dearest. In fact, the more Alex thought about it, the more he could not believe that China was now a cadaver. Even though there had been repeated reports of there being no signs whatsoever of human life in any part of that vast country. And certainly no communication from within it.

He sighed. Maybe it *was* a cadaver. And if so, what did that mean for the rest of the world? And for him and for Debbie? How would they avoid a similar fate? And would it involve them staying on this ship for rather longer than they'd planned? And would the answer to any of these questions become clearer today? Maybe Jane would have some better news. In any event, she sounded pretty chipper when her voice came through the tannoy and shook Alex out of his early-morning reveries and Debbie out of her sleep.

'Good morning, everybody,' she sang, this time more enthusiastically than ever. 'As you may already have observed, we have another fine day in terms of both the weather and the sea, and our captain has now delivered us to Gold Harbour. And I can assure you that, if you enjoyed St Andrews Bay, you will not want to miss out on a visit here. Gold Harbour is a wonderful site, and we've already checked that we will be able to make safe landings and get you all ashore. Just as soon as you've all had your breakfast and are ready to go. Oh, and this morning we'll start with starboard cabins first, and we aim to get the first zodiacs away at nine o'clock.

'Anyway, I hope I haven't roused too many of you with this call, but I just wanted you to know that as far as I and my team are concerned, this is still very much a live expedition, and if there are any updates to give you on any necessary changes to our planned itinerary, these will be delivered a little later in the day. As and when our captain has further information. So, for now, I would just ask you to make sure you're ready for the zodiacs starting at nine, and also, of course, that your kit is ready as well. I mean, please make sure that you've checked your outerwear for any seeds or any other debris, and that you've paid particular attention to the soles of your boots. I'm sure you don't need reminding, but this morning will see us landing once again on South Georgia, and South Georgia is a very special place. Please treat it accordingly.'

Alex stared into space. He needed a second to satisfy himself that Jane's monologue had actually finished, and just a couple more to decide that at this early hour, the task of reconciling the morning's planned activity with the demise of China and the likely annihilation of much of mankind was simply beyond him. Instead, he decided, he would acknowledge the presence of his wife with a softly spoken 'Good morning' and a softly delivered kiss. That done, he then asked her a question.

'Are you up for more penguins? Or do you want to stay by the telly and probably worry yourself sick?'

Debbie laughed.

'Well, I've no idea what there is to worry about, but I'm certainly up for more penguins. How about you?'

'Oh, I reckon you can see an approaching apocalypse any time you like. But how often do you get a chance to see a whole bunch of penguins? There's no contest. Gold Harbour it is, and the telly can look after itself.'

Alex then gave his wife another kiss, and when he'd done this he went to the cabin window and took in his first view of their intended destination: a small bay with a large glacier to its rear and, on its curved beach, another huge host of penguins and seals. Debbie joined him to have a look herself, and then she immediately retired to the bathroom to begin her morning ablutions. As soon as she was gone, Alex switched on the television, which was already tuned to CNN and which was already pumping out more bad news on China's legacy to the world. The flu, it appeared, was now spreading quickly through the States, and deeper and deeper into Europe. Indeed, Germany had declared a state of emergency. But when the newsreader then began to announce that a pandemic of conspiracy theories had now joined the real pandemic and was spreading like wildfire throughout social media, Alex switched off the TV. He knew he could well do without the suggestion that this deadly flu was either the work of the CIA or of a secretive bunch of reptilians who were running the USA – and who, of course, were themselves entirely immune to the killer bug.

He could also have well done without the company of a singleton traveller who installed herself on his and Debbie's table at breakfast and who started to assault them with her very own conspiracy theory. This involved the intricate choreography of a whole sequence of fake news stories, including the crucial role of the attendees at the last Davos gathering, and what could only be described as an extended programme of mental gymnastics that neither Debbie nor Alex could possibly follow. They both just nodded at what they thought were appropriate junctures in her presentation, and left the table convinced that the *Sea Sprite's* doctor might soon have to deal with the ship's first case of pandemic-induced derangement. They hoped it might also be its last.

Fortunately, this unwanted breakfast-time experience was soon overtaken by a further encounter with South Georgia's remarkable wildlife. It had taken only a few minutes to be transported from the *Sea Sprite* to Gold Harbour's beach, and Debbie and Alex were now walking along its grey-gravel surface in the direction of another colony of king penguins. It was a similar experience to that they had enjoyed yesterday. But different. This was because there were barely any fur seals here, but instead just a host of lethargic-looking elephant seals and a sprinkling of gentoo penguins amidst the thousands of their king counterparts. This made for a much more relaxed perambulation, as there was no need whatsoever to guard against the unwanted attentions of the furry fiends, and one could stand and stare at whatever caught one's eye without fear of ambush from behind. The elephant seals were not just lethargic-looking but also pretty-well motionless.

Alex and Debbie relished their time in this place, and found particular delight in one woolly king penguin chick who was constantly harassing its attendant parent in an attempt to get fed. It did succeed on a number of occasions – in securing some foul regurgitated stuff – but not without driving the adult bird to despair, as evidenced by this bird's constant attempts to move itself further along the beach. And what it must have thought – of being bothered by a child who looked to be twice its weight – was something Alex would never know and could barely imagine. What a life these creatures led, he thought, and did it involve joy, contentment, worry or fear? Probably all, he decided, but not, of course, the fear of a distant, invisible killer that might one day arrive to wipe them all out. That sort of fear was the sole preserve of 'perceptive' humans. Although it could, of course, be set aside for a while if these 'perceptive' beings were suitably distracted by yet more charming king penguins, or by the biggest elephant seals Alex had ever seen…

There were three of them. Three beached, blubbery submarines, each with an elephant nose and apparently no intention of shifting their massive forms much further than an inch. And why would they want to? They were immense, and any measurable movement would surely have cost them an unimaginable expenditure of energy. So, they just lay there, each looking like a huge, recumbent Jabba the Hutt, the *Star Wars* creature for whom they must definitely have been the original inspiration. Even if male elephant seals don't normally turn into greedy and corrupt crime lords.

Alex shared these thoughts on the inspiration for Jabba the Hutt with his table companions for lunch. These were Debbie and Roy and a couple from Kent who appeared not to have eaten for a week. Their appetites were amazing, and they ate more food during lunch than Alex would over the course of the day's three meals. Not for the first time, he was bemused by people's... gluttony, and their ability to stay slim. These two were no Hutts. They were both as lean as all the other oldies on this ship. And just as concerned about their potential impending fate...

'I'm beginning to think we're in real trouble,' said the man from Kent – between chews.

'I think so too,' added the woman from Kent, her mouth now empty for the first time in minutes. 'And I mean real trouble.'

Alex wasn't sure that these statements warranted a response, but Roy decided otherwise. Having now abandoned his earlier theory that what had been happening in China was due to the death struggles of the Communist Party, he now sought to reassure his two Kentish table companions by setting out his new theory. This admitted the existence of a deadly plague – which had probably been passed on to humans by pangolins, which themselves had caught the virus from bats – but stressed the fact that it was not in the interest of this virus to wipe us all out. If it did that, this new human form of the disease would wipe itself out as well. It would suit it much better, Roy explained, if it let a large number of us survive, so that we could then rebuild our numbers and provide the virus-in-waiting with a new pool of victims in, say, ten or twenty years' time. How it would go about sparing a large slice of the human population, Roy was not entirely sure, but he knew that viruses mutated all the time, and he thought the likely route would be simply to make itself less virulent. It would turn itself into something that provided only mild symptoms or no symptoms at all, and in that way it could conceal itself until it mutated back into its deadly form at some point in the future and again wreaked havoc on a replenished mankind. What this all meant, he explained to his captive Kent audience, was that by being so out of the way on this ship off South Georgia, they and everybody else aboard the *Sea Sprite* were destined to be survivors. They might ultimately end up with 'the plague', but they would either experience it as merely a mild cold or not be aware that they had it at all.

Alex thought this all sounded like a quite convincing theory, but only quite convincing and not nearly convincing enough to convince him. The couple from Kent seemed similarly dubious as to their promised good fortune, and it was left to Debbie to show some enthusiasm for Roy's amateur hypothesis with a few well-chosen encouraging words. However, Alex suspected that her words were more to do with bringing the lunch to a timely conclusion and so enabling her to leave the scene of gluttonous behaviour as soon as acceptably possible. After all, the Kent couple had finished their desserts but were now eyeing up the buffet for, no doubt, further helpings…

Back in their cabin, Alex wondered aloud whether the Kent gobblers might now have finally finished their meal and thereby discovered, as he had, that neither of the TV news channels was currently working, and whether the absence of these news outlets would further undermine their belief in Roy's promised route to salvation. It certainly wasn't helping Alex to look at the future with too much optimism, and he doubted that many would turn up to the next scheduled meeting in the lounge looking other than deeply pessimistic, if not downright distraught. Jane had announced this mid-afternoon gathering over the tannoy and even she had sounded rather more downbeat than sunny. And why not? Both those news channels disappearing could not be good… news.

Jane now had a packed chamber in front of her and, by her side, a sombre-looking captain. Alex was already sure that whatever was about to be imparted would not bring cheer to anybody in the room – or, indeed, a great deal in the way of much-needed comforting reassurance. He was about to be proved right.

'Thank you all for coming,' Jane started, 'and may I begin by saying that I really hope you enjoyed your morning. I thought it was fantastic, and I suspect you did as well.'

This reference to the passengers' earlier activity did generate a subdued murmur of assent within the throng, but it seemed that most of her audience had other matters on their mind; and in particular whether they might still be alive in a few days' time. Jane clearly sensed this immediately, and quickly moved on.

'Right,' she continued, 'I'm sure you're all keen to know what the captain's learnt and what this might mean for the rest of our trip…'

'And why the news channels have disappeared from the telly,' interrupted a voice from the crowd.

Jane cleared her throat, and attempted to carry on in a calm and deliberate manner.

'Well, to start with – and to address the loss of the news channels – I am told that this is very likely to be a problem with the satellites. That is to say, we have no reason to believe that either the BBC or CNN have gone off the air, and...'

'...and no reason to believe that they haven't,' re-interrupted the original heckler.

Jane composed herself.

'As I say, I think we can be pretty confident that there has probably been some disruption to the satellite system, and if it was anything other than that, Stanley would have let us know...'

And without drawing breath, she then went on, using this reference to Stanley as her springboard.

'...just as they have let us know that the official advice is still to carry on with our cruise. The only new piece of advice of any sort is that, if we do need to bring our cruise to an early conclusion – for whatever reason – we should sail back to Ushuaia and not to the Falklands. As the authorities there have made very clear, the resources available to deal with the unscheduled return of any number of ships are very limited, and it will be much better if we were to head back to Argentina, where there will be all the resources we will ever need...'

'...if they're not all dead there,' suggested a new voice in the crowd. 'And what about what we want to do? How about asking us where we might want to go...'

'That's enough,' interjected a now severe-looking captain.

Here, he took the microphone from Jane, and immediately put it to use.

'Before this meeting,' he started, 'I agreed with Jane that, as your expedition leader, she should brief you on what we've been told. But I think that might have been a mistake. It seems that some of you may have forgotten what I said yesterday, which is that, as captain of this ship, I have absolute control of its movements and no one – and I mean no one – is going to dictate what I do. So, may I just say myself – as your *respectful* but recognised captain – that I will be taking this ship to Antarctica as planned, until such time as I am advised to do otherwise, when in all likelihood I will take it back to Ushuaia. And my apologies if that all sounds a little autocratic, but ships do not do very well with multiple captains. That's why they go to sea with only one.'

Here, the captain glared at the assembled company, before handing the microphone back to Jane to allow her to resume her role as the softer face of authority. And nobody in the audience said another word. Instead, they listened to Jane explaining that, in thirty minutes' time, there would be a lecture on the early days of the British Antarctic Survey, and that, as most people would have realised, the *Sea Sprite* was already on its way further east and south along South Georgia's coast. This was to allow it to arrive at Drygalski Fjord in the late afternoon, in order that the ship's passengers could take in the splendour of this dramatic seven-mile-deep inlet before they readied themselves for dinner. Furthermore, as this fjord was at the southern tip of South Georgia, it would provide the *Sea Sprite* with an ideal overnight anchorage before it set sail for Antarctica in the morning. Or, just possibly, for Ushuaia…

That was it. After the delivery of no actual bad news but no good, reassuring news either, the lounge was soon empty. And back in their cabin, Alex and Debbie were attempting to process what they'd been told. They would certainly have welcomed some rather more positive news, but they had been heartened to a degree simply by the captain's attitude and determination. He had sounded both competent and confident. Indeed, they both agreed that 'he knew best' and that now, with no access to any outside news via the telly, they had to trust him more than ever to do the right thing. And if this involved ploughing on to Antarctica, then that was quite all right by them. Hell, going to Antarctica was the primary purpose of their coming on this cruise. And, in their minds, Antarctica had a great deal more to offer than Argentina. Like Adélie and chinstrap penguins, and crabeater and Weddell seals – and all those promised icebergs, and so much more.

Derek, Elaine and Roy all agreed. Having taken in the delights of Drygalski Fjord, they were now together at a table, taking in some of the delights prepared in the *Sea Sprite's* galley, and they were all being surprisingly upbeat about their rather novel situation. After all, one could not dispute that if the world was being devoured at great speed by some terrible contagious disease, they were sitting on the very edge of its platter. And, as Roy continued to maintain, the disease might become completely satiated before it employed its cutlery anywhere near them. They might easily survive as the most fortunate leftovers ever.

Alex, back in his cabin and lying next to Debbie, tried to persuade himself that Roy could well be right; that he and everyone else on this ship might be amongst the luckiest people on the planet. But it was difficult. And anyway, he asked himself, weren't most leftovers either consumed later on or just consigned to a bin…?

seventeen

Stuart was awoken by a knock on his door. This had never happened before, and it took him more than a few seconds to remember where he was, let alone to wonder who might be indulging in such an extraordinary action so early in the morning. Nobody knocked on his door at… ten to six. By glancing at his clock, he had now confirmed just how early it was, and this caused him to catch his breath. What the hell was going on? Shit! Was this a call to get him into one of those damn bunkers? Had there already been deaths on the base?

Well, there was only one way to find out. Get out of bed, step into some jeans, and then open the door. This he had done within only a very few seconds, and when he opened the door, he was a little surprised but very relieved to see that it was Gill. His absent friend from yesterday was now his very-much-present friend, and a friend who was clearly expecting to be let in.

Stuart didn't hesitate, and in no time at all, Gill was sitting on the solitary chair in Stuart's room, and Stuart was sitting on his bed. Then Gill spoke.

'Jesus, I'm knackered,' she started. 'I could sleep for a week.'

'I heard. You've all been sealing up the base and God knows what…'

'Bloody right. Thirty hours solid. I've never worked so hard in my friggin' life.'

'I thought you signals guys had it easy – one screwdriver turn every twenty minutes and that was it.'

'If only,' retorted Gill. 'You wouldn't believe what's been going on. And the stuff we've been doing with the comms kit. And all the comms that have been coming in. Well, I've never seen anything like it.'

'Yeah, I can imagine. We civilian types got a briefing from an RAF guy, and he did indicate you'd been a bit busy.'

'Mmm… more than a bit busy, I can tell you…'

And here she stopped herself, before asking Stuart a question.

'What did he tell you about what's going on outside?'

'You mean in Stanley?'

'No. I mean in the rest of the friggin' world.'

'Nothing that I didn't know already. You know, shedloads of people dying. And all over the place…'

'And in Britain?'

Stuart felt a lump in his throat. It made him hesitate for a second, and then he spoke.

'Nothing, but I did infer that it might be really bad news.'

This time it was Gill who hesitated. She was evidently deciding how to proceed. And then she spoke. In almost a whisper.

'I could get court-martialled for what I'm about to tell you. But… well, you're my mate, and frankly, even if they find out, I don't think convening court martials is going to be a top priority any time soon…'

'You mean "courts martial",' corrected Stuart without even thinking.

'Yeah. Whatever. But I've just got to tell you. You see, I've seen some of the transcripts of some of yesterday's comms. And, well… pardon my French, but we're fucked. And when I say we're fucked, I mean Britain's fucked. I don't know quite how bad, but I suspect really bad…'

Here she stopped herself, and looked at Stuart intently.

'Hey, mate, I didn't think. I mean, about your family…'

'Come on. Don't you remember? I lost my parents even before you did. We're both two lonely orphans in a big, bad world.'

Gill looked relieved, if a little bit embarrassed. Then she laughed.

'God. How could I have forgotten that? Too many hours on the job…'

Stuart hardly heard what she said. He was too intent on formulating a question for his friend.

'So, you've seen something which… well, which says that this flu thing has got to England…?'

'And Scotland and Wales, and Ireland as well. I think they shipped some people out to Canada, but I'm not really sure. All I'm pretty sure of is that we've essentially had it. And I doubt any of your lot are still alive. Unless they're all down in some big Cheltenham cellar. Although I'm not so sure that even that would be enough.'

'Christ!'

'Yeah. Christ indeed. A bit more than effing scary, ain't it?'

Stuart nodded in agreement. He couldn't think of anything more to say. Then, somehow, he did have a thought.

'Gill, did any of the stuff you saw say anything about what's actually killing everybody? I mean, somebody must at least have a theory. There must be some sort of info on it. Something that gives an indication of how it spreads, for example…'

'Ah!' exclaimed Gill. 'I've just remembered why I'm here.'

'Why?'

'There was this attachment, see – this super-encrypted attachment to one of the signals to the colonel – that I reckon might have been to do with that very subject…'

'How can you know?'

'I can't. It's just that it was referred to as ultra-secret, and later on I heard that the colonel nearly went white when he read it. You know, after it had been decrypted…'

'So?'

Gill looked untypically bashful. Then she spoke.

'Stuart, we're in a hell of a pickle. We might be in a very out-of-the-way place here, one that's been made as safe as possible. But out there, in the wider world, there has been absolute carnage. And I just don't think anywhere is now quite out-of-the-way enough. Or safe enough…'

'And you want to know what was in that encrypted attachment?' offered Stuart. 'So that you – and I – might… have a better chance of surviving. If it all goes tits up…'

'Yeah. Something like that. Although it might be nothing. Or even if we do find out what's going on, it might be a waste of time...'

'Can you get hold of the message? The one with the attachment?'

Stuart sounded both excited and impatient.

'Yes, I can. But I'm not sure...'

'Could you forward it to... errh, let me think. Yes, I know. Could you forward it to the President of Colombia? If I get you his details.'

'To the President of Colombia?!'

'I should be able to decrypt it. But only if I pick it up as an intercept and use the firm's magic box to do the decryption. And, of course, I can't intercept it unless it's sent.'

'Yes. But to the President of Colombia?'

'Gill, he's probably dead. And even if he isn't, who's going to spend time attempting to decrypt an attachment to a message in English, when outside on the streets of Bogotá there are piles of bodies or some sort of uncontrolled mayhem? We could probably just as safely send it to the FSB. Only Moscow isn't on my patch...'

'Ah, I see,' pronounced Gill. 'I'm with you. I'll get on to it right away. And then I'll start work on my defence...'

'Eh?'

'For the court martial.'

'I wouldn't bother. They'll just shoot you.'

Gill laughed out loud, and Stuart smiled. Then the laugh and the smile evaporated. Nothing about what they planned to do was in any way funny, and they both knew it. No, this was desperate stuff, and only yesterday the idea of broadcasting serious military communications – to Colombia or anywhere – would have been totally beyond their combined imagination. However, that was yesterday, and today the world was not the world they had known, and it never would be again. Sending a message to the leader of a nation noted for its drug exports, no matter how sensitive and how important the message, was now just something that had to be done. The consequences of doing so could hardly be any more daunting than what was happening around the world. And, most important of all, they both knew that it might result in their gaining a real insight into why all this was happening. Which might just be crucial in their attempts to avoid two further unscheduled deaths.

Five hours later, when they met again in Stuart's room, they had indeed gained this insight. Gill had managed to forward the 'ultra-secret' message to Colombia's head honcho, and Stuart had been able to intercept it and then decrypt the all-important attachment. Now they both knew the nature of the beast that was threatening their lives. And maybe even a way to evade it...

eighteen

Alex had been dreaming about Shackleton. He had been with him aboard the *James Caird,* the ridiculously small lifeboat that had been used to navigate the eight hundred miles of Southern Ocean between Elephant Island and South Georgia. There were two others on board this boat. One was Jane and the other was an unknown gentleman with Chinese features and a tendency not to face his fellow crew mates. For most of the time he just looked out to sea. And this was a very rough sea, somewhere, according to the irrational dream script, between Elephant Island and mainland China. Shackleton, it appeared, had decided that the fate of all four in the boat lay somewhere in that ancient country and not on the much nearer, albeit bleak, island of South Georgia.

Jane had agreed with this choice of a faraway destination, and was now dividing her time between cleaning the soles of her boots and toasting Shackleton with a small tot of

Scotch. Alex, in contrast, had not reconciled himself to a trip to China, and was trying to convince Shackleton to sail to the Falklands instead, and there replace the withdrawn Chinaman with Debbie. She, he claimed, knew the way to South Georgia, and she would not look out to sea all the time. Alex's efforts were, however, unsuccessful, and it was only when the coast of China came into view – lined with hundreds of dead bodies – that Shackleton even acknowledged his presence. And he did this by telling him that he didn't like living in that cemetery in Grytviken. It was far too cold, he said – just before Alex woke with a start, and the realisation that he was on a rather bigger vessel than the *James Caird,* but one whose navigation might be similarly problematic. Or possibly even more problematic...

The *Sea Sprite* was still at anchor in Drygalski Fjord, and the ship's position was the first item in Jane's tannoy address, just after her normal breezy greeting.

'Good morning everybody, and, as you are all probably aware, we are still in the shelter of Drygalski Fjord. And I hope its calm waters gave you all a very comfortable night. I certainly slept very well myself.'

At this point there was an unusual hiatus, as though Jane had mislaid her script. But it was only fleeting, and she resumed her address with a piece of vital information.

'At ten o'clock, there will be a further meeting in the lounge, where Captain José will announce his plans and where there will be an opportunity to ask him any questions you might have. Obviously, this is a very important meeting, and I would encourage you all to attend and to arrive in the lounge in good time for that ten o'clock start. Following the meeting, we will be weighing anchor, and our captain will want to do this as soon as is practically possible, and certainly well before lunch. So please, if we can all be seated in the lounge ready for that ten o'clock kick-off, it will be much appreciated. And meanwhile, please enjoy your breakfast.'

Alex had been sitting on the bed listening to this address, and now, at its conclusion, he turned to Debbie, who was sitting at the dressing table, and gave her the benefit of his interpretation of what Jane had just said.

'We're going back to Ushuaia,' he announced. 'I'd put money on it.'

'How do you know?' responded his wife.

'Whatever old José's heard from Stanley, I reckon he wants to get back to a port – any port – and make us all somebody else's responsibility. I also suspect that even Jane has had to admit to herself that the idea of pottering around the Antarctic Peninsula while the rest of humanity is in its death throes might become increasingly difficult to swallow. At some point, we're going to have to engage with whatever is left of our world, and that means accepting that this ride around the bay has got to come to an end. Probably sooner rather than later.'

Debbie sighed.

'Mmm... you're probably right. But I so much wanted to see Antarctica.'

'Me too. But we do need a ship to do that, and I don't think this ship will be going anywhere near it. No, it'll be making a beeline for Ushuaia. There's no doubt about it...'

Irritatingly for Debbie, he was right. It was only seconds into the lounge meeting – this time hosted by the captain, with Jane at his side – when the poker-faced captain announced that the *Sea Sprite* would be retracing its passage along the north coast of South Georgia and, after picking up a number of BAS and government personnel from Grytviken, it would be making its way directly to Ushuaia, where it would arrive in just three days' time.

This announcement created an immediate buzz throughout the room as the entire complement of the *Sea Sprite* absorbed his message and began to consider why he had come to this decision. What had his guiding hand in Stanley told him that had made him abandon his 'just carry on' approach?

They didn't have to wait long to find out. He was just about to enlighten them on exactly what he'd been told.

'As you know, the government in Stanley has been our main source of information – and guidance. And up till now that guidance has been to carry on with our cruise, with the proviso that, if this advice was to change, we would be encouraged to head back to Ushuaia rather than to Stanley. Well, the advice has indeed now changed. It is now to head back to Ushuaia. Which is exactly what we'll be doing...'

'Why? What's happened?'

This was one of a group of four Welsh people on the ship, a comparatively young-looking chap, who was clearly rather more impatient than most of the other passengers. He simply hadn't given the captain any opportunity to finish his explanation. This he now did, somewhat clinically albeit suitably politely.

'Stanley has lost its direct link with the UK. Probably because of problems with satellites. But for whatever reason, it is now effectively blind. And as our friends in Stanley were only too keen to point out, a blind man doesn't make a very good guide. And that's why they think we should return to

Ushuaia. To carry on to Antarctica – without any idea of what was happening in the rest of the world – would hardly be the most prudent course of action. And I tend to agree. Whereas, if we get ourselves back to Ushuaia, we will almost certainly learn what's going on around the planet, and we'll be able to formulate a course of action…'

'What about the military base on the Falklands? They'd still have communications.'

It was the same Welshman, and this time he received a very comprehensive answer to his brief but pointed question.

'Sir, let me first remind you that the human world is rapidly succumbing to whatever it is that originated in China. Indeed, so rapidly that it appears very likely that its devastating impact will now have reached Europe – and Britain…'

Here, there was a collective gasp from the audience.

'Now, the people in Stanley tell me that they don't actually know how bad things might be back in Europe – and in Britain in particular – and they admit that it might be not as bad as they fear. However, what they do know is that the military base outside Stanley has gone into lockdown. And not only that, but the intelligence they were getting from the base has now been terminated. For whatever reason, there is now no more information coming from the military. And I think that means that our chances of getting anything out of the base there are effectively zero. Whereas, when we get back to Ushuaia, we should be able to plug ourselves into any news of what's going on elsewhere.

'So, I hope you can now understand that, as your captain, I have no other choice than to take you back to Argentina, so we can…'

'What if Ushuaia doesn't let us in?' interrupted the persistent Welshman.

'Stanley has assured me that Ushuaia is still letting ships in. And it's definitely already accepted a number that have chosen to return there prematurely...'

'And how long are they going to carry on doing that?' demanded the same questioner.

'As far as we can gather, indefinitely. And Ushuaia, you might recall, is on an island within the Tierra del Fuego archipelago, and it is currently 'disease free', as is, apparently, almost the whole of South America east of the Andes. Sir, I cannot emphasise enough that, given that we cannot realistically continue with this cruise, Ushuaia is our obvious and possibly our only realistic destination. It is somewhere where we can take refuge, and monitor what is going on in the rest of the world. Insofar as that is still possible. And one other thing. I am quite certain that returning there represents your best possible chance of at some point getting back to England...'

'You mean Wales.'

The captain was now finding it difficult to hide what was clearly a growing sense of irritation, and he could only respond with an icy '...and Wales'.

The end of this exchange marked the end of the captain's current interaction with his charges. He clearly had no postscripts to add to his opening address, and his briefest of question-and-answer sessions had drawn to a close. So, with a nod of thanks to his now-silent audience, he made his departure from the lounge – in the direction of the bridge – and it was left to Jane to manage any fall-out from the gathering. There was surprisingly little of it, other than the repetition of the same question in various forms, which, for obvious reasons, could not be answered. This was 'How will we go about getting back to England – or Wales or Scotland – when we get back to Ushuaia?' Jane did her best to be reassuring, but all she could really do was ask the passengers to be patient and to put their trust in the ship's captain and his crew, and in her and her team. Together, they would all ensure the best outcome they could.

Alex thought that all sounded worryingly vague, but nobody in the room pushed Jane any further. No one demanded better information, or even a revised plan. But there again, he thought, how could they? The *Sea Sprite* could not stay at sea indefinitely. At some point it would run out of fuel and provisions and it would have to return to port. That port could not be Stanley. It would not be allowed to dock there. And even if it somehow forced its way in, its crew and passengers would simply have swapped being stranded on a ship for being stranded on an island. And that made very little sense at all. Nor did the idea of seeking a port in faraway South Africa, or somewhere in Australia or New Zealand. It was probably feasible for the *Sea Sprite* to reach one of these distant destinations, but it was highly unlikely that the flu wouldn't have made it there first. It was already odds on that South Africa was now infected, and whilst the Antipodes might still be free of the disease, it made no sense to go that far when this wasn't certain. And if the flu *was* there, the *Sea Sprite* would then be out of options, and all those aboard it would be very nearly out of time. No, it had to be Ushuaia, in the recognition that it was the closest open port, and it gave access to a large land mass, most of which, as far as was known, was still free of 'the scourge'. Indeed, as Alex heard one of the passengers remark as the meeting finally broke up, it was the ultimate Hobson's choice. As well as being a matter of life and death...

Alex took Debbie back to their cabin, and there they both tried to come to terms with what was going on. This was not easy. Up to now, no matter how catastrophic the news had been, it had been news of something going on somewhere else, somewhere far beyond countless horizons, and they had both been able to cope with this well. They had even been able to regard it rather philosophically, and as an 'interesting' phenomenon, or even as food for their shared wry sense of humour. But now – as in three days' time – they were going to be obliged to engage with some sort of deadly pandemic, which, whilst not necessarily within touching distance, would almost inevitably impose itself on everything they did for the rest of their lives. However long these lives might prove to be.

Within twenty minutes, they had made each other deeply glum, and so glum that they decided that they could not face any company or indeed any food. They would therefore give lunch a miss and instead get themselves a drink from the bar – a double gin and tonic each – bring these back to their room, and take them out onto the balcony. Here they would sit in their cold-weather gear and take in the north coast of South Georgia for a second time as the *Sea Sprite* retraced its route back to raw reality. After all, there was no way that there would be a third time...

It was still a fascinating sight, and with the help of their binoculars they were able to make virtual repeat visits to both Gold Harbour and St Andrews Bay before, in the early afternoon, the *Sea Sprite* arrived off King Edward Point.

Here the captain arrested its progress in order to pick up a handful of the base's resident scientists and administrators; an exercise that was conducted remarkably quickly with the help of one of the ship's zodiacs. In no time at all, the *Sea Sprite* had six new passengers who had decided that they preferred the idea of being in South America rather than on South Georgia. Unlike their eight colleagues who had decided to stay put and sit out the world's convulsions in the middle of the Atlantic Ocean. These stay-put eight had gathered on the quayside at King Edward Point to wave goodbye to their colleagues – and to the *Sea Sprite* – and they were still there when the *Sea Sprite* began to move away and out of their lives, probably forever. It was a poignant moment, and for Alex it really rammed home what was going on. People were making desperate decisions, decisions that might prove fateful – or fatal. In fact, in three days' time, he and Debbie might be faced with similarly dramatic decisions, although whether they would involve something quite as clear-cut as what he had just witnessed, he was not so sure. Deciding what to do, having been landed in a port in Tierra del Fuego, was bound to be more complicated; a view that would be reinforced over dinner...

The *Sea Sprite* was now in open ocean again. South Georgia and its complement of amazing wildlife had been left behind. And in the ship's lower-deck restaurant, Alex and Debbie, sitting at a table with Derek, Elaine and Roy, were seeking the views of their companions as to what might happen when their voyage reached its end.

'Do you think we might be "on our own"?' asked Debbie. 'I mean, I can't recall the small print, but I suspect when we're back in Ushuaia...'

'We'll be in charge,' interrupted Roy. 'There are ninety-two of us and only one captain and one Jane. And I suspect they'll want us on board... metaphorically speaking. And that means they'll have to be a little more responsive to democracy than they are at the moment. And they'll certainly have to recognise that you can't have a mutiny when a ship is within stepping distance of a quay...'

'I'm not so sure,' offered Elaine. 'We'll be a boat full of Brits, parked no more than five hundred yards from a memorial to all those Argentinians who died in the Falklands and on the *Belgrano.* And I imagine, if he really wanted to, the captain could... you know, ask for the help of the locals, and they'd be only too pleased to oblige...'

'To do what?' questioned Debbie.

'To help the captain do exactly what you suggested: to help him abandon us...'

'No, I wasn't really suggesting that,' observed Debbie. 'I mean, old José's been a model captain so far, and I can't believe...'

'We just have to wait,' interrupted Derek. 'To borrow from a maritime expression, we're all in uncharted waters. And that goes for our captain as well. And for Jane, and for everybody else on this ship. For all we know, when we arrive in Ushuaia, there won't be anyone alive, and our potential abandonment won't even be an issue. We'll all be far more concerned about how to avoid a similar fate ourselves. If we've got any time to be concerned about anything at all...'

To say that this contribution from Derek had a chilling effect on the conversation would be an understatement. The conversation was now essentially frozen solid. It was therefore fortuitous that Roy was seated at the table with a ready-made means of inducing an immediate thaw. Inevitably, it involved flags.

'Did you know that the official flag of the Tierra del Fuego province consists of a white stylised albatross in flight, with its outstretched wings dividing the flag from the top left corner to the bottom right corner, with a white-starred blue sky above and an expanse of sandy-coloured... sand below? I have to confess that I don't know when it was introduced, and I don't know quite what those white stars are meant to denote. But I do know that it is very rare to find albatrosses appearing on any flags anywhere. In fact, the only other flag I can bring to mind that features albatrosses is the flag of Tristan da Cunha, which together with the blue ensign, has a representation of the coat of arms of Tristan da Cunha. Which, as you may or may not know, consists of a Tristan da Cunha longboat above a Naval Crown, with a central shield decorated with four yellow-nosed albatrosses – and flanked by two Tristan rock lobsters...'

Derek immediately burst into laughter, and he was soon joined by all those around the table, other than a slightly satisfied-looking Roy. It wasn't the first time that his eclectic mind had come to the rescue of an awkward situation, and it probably wouldn't be the last. And on this occasion, it didn't just provide a rescue, but it also provided a reboot. The conversation around the table simply sprang into life. And none of it involved the daunting prospect of what might happen in three days' time, or even any reference to the worldwide pestilence that was assailing mankind. Instead, it kicked off with a debate about lobsters – as food – and how they compared with langoustines and crayfish. It then took a course through inedible foods such as *tête de veau*, after which it made a number of stops at topics such as French underwear habits, the merits of cotton over satin, and the place of fetishism in 'traditional sex', before finally arriving at the unlikely terminus of transgender tendencies in non-human animals.

When, soon after this highly enjoyable – and highly restorative – discussion, Alex and Debbie were back in their room, they gave thanks that they had linked up with three individuals who had not only become good table companions, but who might also prove to be very valuable allies in their fight to maintain their sanity. And their lives. Whatever awaited them in Ushuaia would be that much easier to deal with – and overcome – with, at their sides, a grumpy old bugger and his formidable wife, and a large-framed walking reference book who could confound any enemy on Earth with his super-extensive knowledge of the world's flags. Together, they would no doubt make an invincible team.

nineteen

When Stuart was at university, he had spent one summer vacation working for a builder, and one of the jobs he'd worked on had been the construction of a house extension with a basement. The builder had gone to great lengths to make the basement waterproof, and as well as providing it with a waterproof membrane, he had sought to ease the pressure on this membrane by surrounding the whole construction with land drains connected to a very deep sump. At the bottom of the sump was installed an automatic pump, and this was designed to remove water from the sump as it arrived from the land drains. That way, the ground around the basement was prevented from becoming saturated and the water pressure on the membrane was kept to a minimum.

Stuart had almost forgotten this brief episode in his life, but it had now come back to him. And this was because he was presently crawling through the very same sort of pipe that the builder had used to create the vertical shaft of that sump. It was made from black plastic, it was corrugated, and it was just eighteen inches in diameter. It was, however, not just ten feet long (the depth of the pump shaft). It was, according to Gill, seven or eight times this length and, as promised by Gill, it was far from dry. There were at least six inches of very cold water lying at its base all along its length, and this made progress over its endless corrugations not just painful but also really unpleasant. Pulling a fifty-pound bergen behind him didn't help matters either. It kept getting stuck, and it was just an enormous weight to have to pull along a corrugated channel.

Of course, there had been no option other than to use this route out of the base, just as there had been no real option other than to take the dramatic step of actually leaving the base. For Stuart, it would mean the end of his career, insomuch as a career in an organisation that might or might not still exist had any meaning. And for Gill, who was ten feet ahead of him in the pipe, it would mean actual desertion, in that she'd be abandoning her post without any intention of ever returning. Understandably, it was not a step that either of them had taken lightly. In fact, they had spent much of the day agonising over what they should do, and already Stuart, for one, was aware of the burden not just of that heavy bergen but also of genuine guilt. Should they have agonised some more, and come to a different decision?

It was so difficult. They were in a military environment, and whatever was happening in the wider world, that environment would ensure that rules were followed and that those who broke these rules would be punished. So, making it known to any of the senior officers that a super-encrypted, ultra-secret military dispatch had been interfered with and then decrypted – by two lowly grunts – would not have been seen as just a minor misdemeanour. Both Stuart and Gill would have been marched off to some sort of close confinement before they'd even had a chance to explain their motives. In the unlikely event that they were then allowed to communicate with those in authority, these guys almost certainly would not or could not have changed the standing order for the base. Which was essentially to sit tight behind that supposedly impregnable perimeter and wait. They would very definitely not have contemplated its evacuation. And even if they had, with so many personnel, they would not have been able to do this in the way that it needed to be done. That is to say, by leaving the Falklands and heading south.

So, reluctantly, both Stuart and Gill had come to the conclusion that they couldn't safely share their findings – and the probable consequences of those findings – with anybody, and that they would therefore have to take the ignoble route of abandoning their roles along with all their mates. It hadn't been at all easy. Neither had it been easy to pack two bergens with a whole pile of rations so quickly and so discreetly, and then make it out of their accommodation block at one in the morning without being observed. But these practical challenges they had managed, and Gill had then been able to find her way to that less-than-impregnable section of the base perimeter, where she'd remembered that there was an overlooked, overgrown drainage pipe that would allow them to escape. She'd discovered it by mistake a few months ago when she'd been examining an aerial near the perimeter fence and had gone off for a pee. She'd then later explored it to gauge its potential for a brief spell of unauthorised absence, or even as a possible channel for some unauthorised contraband. She'd obviously never imagined that it might allow her to bring her military service to an end – in an attempt to avoid her life coming to an end. But that was before the world had changed forever...

Well, Stuart had finally reached the end of the pipe, and standing above him in the dim light of a half-moon was his 'comrade-in-arms', Gill. She looked more exhausted – and more 'moist' – than Stuart did himself. And she also looked rather frightened. Maybe, thought Stuart, the enormity of what she'd done was now hitting home. Stuart was merely a civilian who had left his job without the required period of notice; Gill was a soldier in the British Army who had committed the ultimate military crime: desertion. And in the face of impending danger. No wonder she didn't look too elated to be outside the base.

Anyway, both absconders knew that there was no time for regrets and no time even to recover from their passage through the pipe. They had a long walk ahead of them – with fifty-pound burdens on their backs – and they really needed to get their walk under way before the short Falklands night came to an end. Their absence from the base was unlikely to be noticed very soon, but even Gill didn't know what surveillance kit was employed beyond the confines of the base, and they certainly didn't want to be spotted embarking on their six-mile trudge to Choiseul Sound. This was where Joe's boat was moored, just where the sound ran north of Lively Island. And, of course, that was another source of guilt. Joe was away in Britain at the moment, and whether he was dead or alive, taking his boat without his knowledge or permission was hardly the best way to repay the generosity he'd displayed in the past. This was the man who had helped Stuart maintain his sanity by allowing him to join him in sailing the *Bluebird.* And now the *Bluebird* was going to be snatched away, probably for all time, by two miserable deserters. If, that is, they could manage those six miles with heavy backpacks and without being detected by a pair of keen eyes back on the base.

It soon became apparent that the six miles might well defeat them, irrespective of whether they were spotted or not. Stuart was fit, but he spent most of his time at a desk. Gill was probably fitter, but she was a signaller, not a Royal Marine, and the idea of any yomping was about as foreign to her as going about her work without a screwdriver. It just wasn't what she did. And this was now rather more than evident from her gasping for air, just before she sank to her knees and then toppled sideways.

Stuart was at her side immediately, and after he'd quickly sloughed off his bergen, he knelt down beside her and started to speak.

'You OK?' he asked. 'Or you got a real problem?'

Gill turned to face her solicitous interrogator and, before she made any reply, she treated Stuart to a broad, muddy grin. Then she did speak.

'Shit! A bloody office civvy, and you're still bloody standing. Don't, for God's sake, tell the lieutenant. He'll have me doing press-ups for a week.'

Stuart wasn't sure how to interpret this response, but within a split second, Gill was pulling herself up into a sitting position – still with her bergen on – and complaining about the Falklands.

'I mean, who the bloody hell thought it a good idea to cover this soddin' island in this soddin' grass and then soak it in soddin' water? Christ! It's bad enough with this bloody bergen, but there ain't even a soddin' path. Just these soddin' tufts of grass and all this soddin' water.'

The expletives seemed to be doing their job. After taking a few more seconds to gather herself, Gill drew herself into the vertical and then reached down for Stuart's bergen in order to help him hoist it onto his back. She had recovered as quickly as she had collapsed, and Stuart could only think that this was all to do with British military training. Gill might have just deserted from her 'family', but her family had somehow instilled into her something that simply prevented her from giving up. If the body failed, then the mind would take control and ensure that it didn't fail again.

And so it was. When Gill had collapsed, she and her civvy mate were no more than a mile into their yomp. But once she was back on her feet, she only ever stopped in her forward progress to allow Stuart to catch up. For now it was Stuart's sedentary lifestyle that was making itself known, in that he was having more and more difficulty in making his way across the unforgiving terrain of the Falklands, and quite a lot of difficulty in even keeping upright. However, he did manage – just. And in the light of a dreary Falklands' morning, the welcome sight of open water came into view, and in only a few minutes more, Stuart was able to make out the mast of a boat he knew well. The *Bluebird* was sitting at anchor in its normal spot – for which he was supremely relieved – and soon both he and Gill would be able to throw their bergens into the bottom of Joe's skiff and row themselves out into the sound and take control of Joe's lovely eight-metre boat.

It was done. They were aboard the *Bluebird,* they had stowed their bergens below deck, and Stuart was giving Gill a crash course on how to sail a boat of this size without it coming to grief. He had no real idea of how Gill would adapt from being a soldier to becoming a sailor, but he would soon find out. Because before they had even treated themselves to an energy bar, Stuart had cast off and, without much hindrance from Gill, had got the *Bluebird* under sail.

Now all he had to do was take it to the Antarctic...

twenty

The sea was getting rough. So far on this voyage, the passengers and crew of the *Sea Sprite* had been spoilt with seas that, for this part of the world, had been remarkably calm. But not any more. Alex had to steady himself in the bathroom as he shaved, and when he was in the shower, he came very close to being out of the shower, but not at his own choosing. It was only through some instinctive judicious footwork that he avoided exchanging his vertical situation for one that involved being horizontal on the bathroom floor. Debbie had similar problems when it came to her turn to ablute. Although, of course, she didn't have to scrape her face…

Breakfast – with a 'new' couple from Slough – proved a subdued affair, and Alex decided against enlivening it by making any reference to John Betjeman and his invitation to bombs to fall on that unfortunate town. Instead, he attempted to stimulate some conversion around the table by giving his (expurgated) opinions on various members of the expedition team and then offering his views on the challenges provided by very rough seas. He'd chosen this latter theme because the sea was becoming rougher than ever, and how the Filipino waiters were weaving their way between the tables with trays of food and beverages was beyond Alex's understanding. If they had developed sea legs, he thought, then each of them must have developed at least six of them. Because they never needed to steady themselves, and they seemed almost unaware that the surface on which they were moving was itself moving – a lot. It was a quite incredible sight.

No less incredible was the number of people packed into the main lounge to listen to the most miserable man on the ship deliver a presentation on his time in the Antarctic, a time more than forty years ago when, as a young man, he had been dispatched to that cold continent to study its rocks. This, of course, was Tony, the dour Scot, and his talk had been given the title of *Working as a Geologist in Antarctica in the 1970s;* not a title, thought Alex, designed to draw in the crowds. But it didn't matter. Clearly, virtually every one of the *Sea Sprite's* passengers – including Alex and Debbie – was thirsting for some sort of distraction, and a grumpy old Scots bloke recounting how he'd gone about chipping off bits of rock in a cold climate would be distraction enough. In fact, it proved to be more than just an adequate distraction, and instead a genuinely interesting diversion. And this was because grumpy Tony barely made a single reference to the geology stuff, but instead focused almost exclusively on just how demanding it was to be a 'pioneer' member of the British Antarctic Survey. In a time when one's survival was dependent on small simple tents, dreadful rations and one's all-important huskies.

It appeared that Tony had been based at some sort of camp equipped with primitive wooden buildings, but that for most of the time he had been far away from this camp, living in a tent and doing his geological stuff with just a partner and a team of huskies for company. And life had been as basic as it was possible to be. The food was repetitive; it was from cans or packets, and it was very 'uninspired English' in character. Entertainment was just about non-existent, as it consisted of whatever books and puzzles could be squeezed onto one's sledge along with the more vital provisions. And whilst personal hygiene was never ignored, it and all other necessary personal chores would often have to be performed when there was a blizzard blowing outside. How this was done was left largely to the audience's imagination. So too were the intricacies of providing the husky team with its vital supply of raw, recently killed meat.

Alex could just about come to terms with the hardships of early Antarctic life insofar as they concerned Tony and his fellow researchers looking after themselves, but he found it far more difficult when it came to how they had to deal with the grisly implications of having to feed and care for a much-loved team of dogs. There was clearly no room for the squeamish in those early days of Antarctic research, and one had to be prepared not only to tackle butchery duties but also to deal with canine wounds and even the demands of canine births whenever these arose. This was definitely the most captivating aspect of Tony's story: his bringing into the world new huskies in order to furnish the British Antarctic Survey with all the huskies it required for its expanding work.

It was impossible, he said, not to build an extraordinary bond with these new recruits to cold-weather science, or indeed with all the huskies one looked after in Antarctica, on whose efforts and resilience one's life depended.

It was very evident that Tony's audience could easily understand this close relationship forged between humans and their huskies. Heck, hadn't most of them, at some stage in their life, owned dogs themselves, or maybe they still owned them now? So when, towards the conclusion of his presentation, he talked about the complete replacement of huskies with snow-cats – and how the huskies were rewarded for all their years of hard work with a bullet in the head – the mood in the auditorium immediately sank like a stone. But it had happened. Whoever had been running the British Antarctic Survey back then would not countenance the cost and the difficulties associated with repatriating so many dogs, and these dogs were therefore simply shot. Tony had shot a number of huskies himself, but had not been able to bring himself to shoot his own. He'd had to ask somebody else to do that for him.

So that was it, thought Alex. That was why Tony was such a morose and miserable individual. He hadn't got over it. Not after all these years. He had indeed spent most of his adult life with some sort of chronic post-traumatic condition, or at least something that had sucked the joy from his character and left him looking and sounding like a man consumed with gloom. So, for the first time on this trip, Alex felt really sorry for one of his fellow travellers; the man whom, up to now, he'd regarded with disdain, and whom he'd gone out of his way to avoid. He also, of course, felt desperately sorry for all those dogs. We use them, he thought, and when we have no further use for them, we kill them. Just like we killed all those thousands of faithful horses at the end of World War I. Not for the first time in his life, he felt guilty for just being a human. And to be feeling sorry and guilty at the same time was not what he had expected when he had sat down to listen to this Antarctic veteran. But he could do no more about it than he could about the state of the sea. Which was now very rough indeed.

In fact, it had become so rough that, when Tony had answered the last of a series of questions put to him after his presentation, Alex and Debbie decided to eschew lunch and instead settle for some liquid refreshment and a couple of cookies in the bar. This, they had reasoned, would entail less movement around the ship, and therefore a reduced amount of grappling with its lively motion, and it would also reduce the burden on their stomachs should these come under any challenge. Which was by no means impossible. That sea was not about to calm down any time soon.

Indeed, it continued to behave boisterously throughout the whole of their stay in the bar, and so much so that the two light-lunchers decided to eschew any further activity on the *Sea Sprite* that would involve their straying more than a few feet from their bed. It was going to be a cabin afternoon, and no attempt would be made to visit any other part of the ship until it was time to eat in the evening. And even then, leaving their cabin would be by no means a certainty. Their small maritime vessel was now – according to a tannoy announcement by Jane – having to deal with a genuine Southern Ocean storm, and it was quite possible that conditions would deteriorate further. And that might mean that it would then prove an insuperable challenge to deal with a regular dinner, even if the kitchen staff were able to prepare one.

However, that was a decision for later, and once Debbie and Alex had, with some difficulty, made it back to their cabin refuge, the only immediate decision to make was how they might spend their afternoon. There was still a presentation on offer in the lounge, which could, of course, be accessed through the cabin's TV, and its subject was *Wind Speeds and the Beaufort Scale*. It could not have been a more appropriate subject, given the present conditions. Nevertheless, neither Alex nor Debbie thought it would be an ideal accompaniment to their experiencing the real thing, and they decided against tuning in. Instead, having also decided that any joint activities might prove tricky on a bed that was now pitching and rolling in sync with the ship, they wedged themselves against its headboard, buttressed themselves with pillows, and set about some reading.

Debbie chose a historical novel. Alex selected a work on identity, race, religion and gender; a recently published book that claimed it wanted to question what were and what were not 'acceptable' views in each of these four interconnected facets of modern life. It wouldn't be the first time that while Debbie had sought to entertain herself, Alex had chosen instead to scourge himself. And what better way to indulge in a bit of self-flagellation than to expose oneself to some of the most divisive and poisonous issues on the planet? Or what had until recently been some of the most divisive and poisonous issues on the planet before the plague had arrived – back when humans had been able to indulge themselves in the luxury of contemplating their navels to the virtual exclusion of everything else. Including the fragility of their species. And this was what struck Alex as he read through a chapter on transgender rights and the rights of others to challenge those rights.

It was all so narcissistic, he thought. Humanity had been focusing more and more on itself, and no more so than when it had embarked on a debate on transgenderism that had quickly descended into a catechism of transgender rights that could not be questioned. After all, the rights of a transgender male – who now identified as a woman – had, clearly, to trump the rights of any mere natural woman, even if it meant glossing over the fact that there might still be a willy in play. That was what the canons said, and one was a transphobic monster if one held any other (heretical) views. Obviously.

Well, it was all nonsense, thought Alex. Because now, whether you had a penis or not, or whether you wanted to be called 'she' or the inexplicable plural 'they', it wouldn't stop you being consumed by the plague. Neither, for that matter, would it be of consequence whether you were a mild-mannered Church of England sort or a fundamentalist Muslim who looked upon his non-Muslim brethren as a load of two-legged abominations. And as for whether you were a blond-haired Caucasian from the Black Forest or a bushman from the Kalahari, it wouldn't make a blind bit of difference. This terrible pestilence that had already consumed so much of mankind was clearly as indifferent to one's racial antecedents as was the most liberal-minded liberal imaginable. And even identifying as a neutral, pathogen-sympathetic observer wouldn't prevent you from being gobbled up by the disease with no name. If you were human, that's all you needed to be. Your race, religion, gender and identity meant nothing at all. Just as they should have meant nothing at all, thought Alex, before this pandemic arrived. And the fact that they did – and did to such an extent – was merely a reflection of humanity's selfish, self-centred, self-obsessed, self-absorbed and self-indulgent way of thinking. President Trump, Alex concluded, might be – or have been – an extreme example, but at heart every human on the planet was in some way a terrible narcissist. This is when he recalled what had happened to the original Narcissus of Greek mythology. He hadn't been cut down by a disease, but he'd killed himself when he saw his reflection in a pond and realised that he could not have the object of his desire. And maybe, thought Alex, that was what was happening to the entire human race. Unable to live happily with all our differences and all our different outlooks, we had submitted ourselves to the agent of our doom. And after all, it did appear that the plague was something we had inflicted on ourselves...

It was a tenable theory of sorts, but, like the constant pitching and rolling of the bed, it couldn't keep Alex from falling fast asleep. Maybe he shouldn't have had that last drink at lunchtime. And maybe now he shouldn't sleep on, because, as it was coming up to six o'clock, there was somebody else on the bed who had clearly decided that she was beginning to get hungry. Alex knew this when she shook his shoulder and announced that it was time to wake up.

He attempted to rouse himself while at the same time coming to terms with the movement of the bed.

'Jesus,' he pronounced, 'what the...'

'Ah,' interrupted Debbie. 'Shaken *and* stirred. James Bond would be proud...'

Alex wasn't quite awake enough to appreciate Debbie's jest, and instead he just focused on pulling himself up into a sitting position on the bed while trying not to roll off it.

'God,' he observed, 'it hasn't got any better, has it? In fact, it feels as though it's got worse.'

'Well, nobody's announced that dinner's off. So, I suggest we just ignore the weather, and get ourselves ready for some food.'

'Ignore? How can you ignore this? And that isn't just weather, that's a full-blown storm. Either that, or there's something wrong with this bed.'

'Look, we can't just exist on biscuits. And anyway, I'm really peckish. So, come on. Get a move on. After all, I don't want to be late. And as they used to say in ancient Rome, *tempest fugit.* Get it? *Tempest fugit,* not *tempus fugit...*'

Alex gave his wife a mystified look, and then he did get it. 'Mystified' was swapped for 'amused', just before 'alarmed' arrived as he eased himself off the bed. And then it was the morning ablutions all over again, only worse, until finally he and his wife were as ready as they ever would be to tackle the journey from the Erikson Deck down to the Magellan Deck and there secure themselves a seat at a table in the downstairs restaurant. Seated at the table already were Derek and Elaine, and within only a few minutes Roy was there as well.

It was an odd situation. Here were five people, all of whom knew that their destiny was very much in doubt and that their very lives were at serious risk, but who, at the same time, were having to cope with the immediate demands of life on a storm-tossed ship. In the event, it didn't take too long for these immediate – and insistent – demands to take centre stage, and it started with an Elaine observation about the forthcoming meal.

'Well, I bet soup's off,' she said. 'Judging from the way the water in our loo's moving about, I can't believe that much more than a millimetre of it would make it to the table. And I bet the gravy boat's given a miss as well.'

'I don't know,' responded Roy. 'You may not have noticed, but nobody seems to have told the waiters we're in the middle of a storm. They just seem entirely oblivious of it.'

And he was right. Each waiter was still operating on a team of six sea legs, and as the restaurant patrons swayed about in their chairs, their Filipino attendants went about their business as if the *Sea Sprite* were still docked in port. It was a truly remarkable sight, and one that prompted Roy to add an addendum to his original observation.

'Mind, if we're hit by one of those rogue super-waves, I suppose they might notice that. I mean, it'd be pretty difficult to serve the sea bream when the ship was upside down…'

'Roy!' exclaimed Elaine. 'You shouldn't say that. This is a well-built ship, quite capable of dealing with any sort of sea conditions, and the likelihood of it being tipped over is zero. It's got stabilisers, remember. And while they can't iron out the roughest of seas, I'm sure they can go a long way towards keeping us upright…'

'*If* they're deployed,' responded Roy. 'I mean, if the sea's very rough, most captains will keep them retracted. To avoid them getting damaged…'

'What?!' exclaimed Elaine. 'You can't be…'

Roy interrupted her, a generous, wicked grin now spreading across his face.

‘Yes, I am. I’m having you on. Sorry, Elaine, but the way this whole restaurant is moving, it is just about credible, isn’t it? Even stabilisers have their limits. And, to tell you the truth, I’m not so sure they’d be much use at all against a super-wave. But there again, super-waves are really very rare indeed. In fact, I once read that your chance of dying as a result of your vessel being hit by one of these freak waves is less than your chance of dying as a result of being hit by a falling piano. And that’s a pretty small chance…’

The conversation carried on in this vein for some minutes, with rather more prosaic stories being told about rough ferry journeys and trips across the English Channel in bad weather aboard a hovercraft – in a time when hovercraft once plied this route. In fact, the round-table discussion, meandering through various topics, was maintained at a very light-hearted level for over an hour, and it wasn’t until coffee and brandy were being consumed that it took a turn for the serious.

Shortly after these two beverages had somehow been successfully delivered to the table, Debbie made the mistake of wondering aloud what might be going on now in all those countries that had been denuded of their populations. Derek was first to provide his own thoughts on this matter, by proposing that in many urban centres there would now probably be fires. With no fire brigades around – or anybody around – there would be no way that small spontaneous fires wouldn’t have grown into widespread raging infernos. Even as they were sitting at this table, he suggested, New York or Paris might be burning out of control.

This downbeat observation caused Alex to make one of his own, and this was similarly downbeat if a little less dramatic, and it concerned the fact that as electricity supplies failed for various reasons, so too would all the pumping of water that was essential to so much of modern infrastructure. If New York wasn't ablaze then almost certainly its subway system would be flooded, as would the London Underground. This contribution hardly lifted anybody's mood. But then Roy picked up on that mention of the failure of power supplies – because of the failure of power plants – by broaching the subject of one particular type of power plant, and how its failing – across the globe – could end up being rather more serious than any underground flooding. Yes, he was about to deliver a chilling monologue on the fate of deserted nuclear reactors, and he started by providing his audience with a headline…

'Nuclear reactors,' he pronounced slowly, 'do not look after themselves.'

And now that he had everybody's attention, he provided them with his unedited copy.

'I think there are about four hundred nuclear plants on this planet; some of them with multiple reactors. And by now many of these will no doubt have been abandoned. Well, they might run on autopilot for a while, but that autopilot will almost certainly cut off the plant's connection to the grid. What happens then is that any number of diesel pumps kick in to keep water circulating around the core. But diesel pumps need diesel, and without their fuel being replenished they will probably stop working after just a few days. That's a real problem. Because even if the fission in the core has been stopped, the uranium in the core will continue to decay and continue to generate heat. And certainly enough heat to pressurise the coolant water.

Which will then be released by the opening of a relief valve until the pressure is eased, for the cycle to then start again – and again…'

'Until…' interrupted Derek.

'Yes – until the valve decides to stick, or, more likely, the water is entirely depleted…'

'…and then you have your classic Chernobyl,' finished Derek. 'The top of the reactor core becomes exposed and you have yourself a meltdown.'

'And what does that do?' asked Debbie.

'Well,' responded Roy, 'that means that you'll be spilling radioactivity into the air and into any nearby bodies of water. And whilst there wouldn't be a nuclear explosion, you'd have masses of radioactive lava melding with the surrounding steel and concrete, and this would finally "cool" in temperature terms but it would remain radioactively hot almost indefinitely…'

'Yes, I suppose it would,' agreed Derek. 'A congealed mass of danger, lethal to anything that approached it for bloody aeons, and of course something of a testament to human hubris…'

'This radioactivity released into the atmosphere,' interrupted Elaine. 'Is that going to be a danger for us?'

Roy shook his head.

'Difficult to say,' he started. 'But the bulk of those reactors are in the northern hemisphere. You know, in places like the States, Russia, China and Europe. I don't think there are any in Australia, and there's only a handful in the whole of South America. So, we'd be pretty well placed in the south of Argentina. But, there again, I don't claim to be an expert on the dispersal of radioactivity. And with four hundred reactors going into meltdown, I'm not sure anywhere on this planet will be entirely safe...'

Here the conversation suffered a short hiatus. Maybe the other four at the table were absorbing the possibly dire implications of Roy's brief presentation, or maybe, like Alex, they were instead trying to assimilate the fact that even a good outcome to their plight might mean a life spent in Tierra del Fuego. Indefinitely. It was no wonder, then, that the hiatus was drawn to a close by Debbie proposing that, instead of dwelling on the demise of all those faraway reactors, it might be better if the assembled five turned their attention to... gin. In particular, she wanted to know what they all knew about England's 'gin epidemic' in the late sixteenth and early seventeenth centuries, and William of Orange's role in initiating the widespread consumption of this tipple. As she briefly explained, she was interested in seeing what parallels could be drawn between that popularisation of this drink and the slightly different one that had overtaken England in recent years – without the involvement of William of Orange.

Well, it was all a bit obvious. She clearly wanted the meal to end on a trivial high rather than on a literally life-or-death low, but it was actually a very good move, and one that was immediately aided and abetted by Roy. Maybe he was keen to redress the fact that he had cast a nuclear pall over the proceedings, and, not surprisingly, he knew all and everything about England's love affair with gin back in the days of Hogarth.

So, it was another good end to the day, despite whatever might be in store and despite the fact that Neptune was still having a party. Even if not genuinely mountainous, the sea was still significantly hilly, and it took Alex and Debbie all their strength and all their balance to get themselves back to their cabin. When, safely inside, they decided that they might be in for a very rough night indeed. Even if the *Sea Sprite* didn't actually tip over…

twenty-one

It was as Alex was rising from the breakfast table that he felt the movement. During the night there had been lots of movement, up and down and side to side. Then, as the morning had approached and the storm had started to abate, there had been just a noticeable but diminishing swell, and that had now disappeared. Almost entirely. It was, as Alex had thought, quite literally a case of the calm after the (very violent, Southern Ocean) storm. But this new movement was entirely different. It was the movement of the ship turning. Somebody up on the *Sea Sprite's* bridge was taking the vessel through a fairly sharp turn – to the left. Alex quickly worked out that this meant that he was no longer on a ship sailing west, but on one embarking on a more southerly course. And he could not imagine why. Ushuaia, no doubt, was still where it had been since it was established, and travel in any other than a westward direction would not deliver the *Sea Sprite* to its harbour.

All these thoughts were put into words as he addressed his wife.

'Something's up,' he said. 'We're going south. And that wasn't on the agenda. And it won't get us to Ushuaia.'

Debbie nodded in agreement, but she looked a little distracted. She seemed to be processing this unexpected event herself, and at the same time trying to take in the general reaction of all those still seated at the tables, which was a mix of apparent astonishment and concern. These were worrying enough times as it was. To have a surprise piled on top of the worry was clearly not very welcome.

'Come on,' continued Alex. 'Let's get back to our cabin. Maybe we can see what's going on…'

And so, filled with more trepidation than he'd budgeted for today, Alex eventually followed his wife into their cabin, and immediately went to its balcony window. There was nothing to see – other than a sea now at peace – and there was still nothing to see when he stepped out onto the balcony and slowly scanned the sea as carefully as he could. However, he could at least confirm in his mind that the *Sea Sprite* was heading south. A hazy sun, somewhere to the east, was now casting a shadow of the *Sea Sprite* onto the surface of the ocean directly below his feet. And that was a confirmation beyond doubt.

Debbie had now joined him on the balcony, and she offered an opinion.

'There has to be a reason,' she observed. 'Maybe there's a ship in distress. Maybe we're on our way to help.'

'Well, it'd be nice to know,' responded Alex. 'Hell, it's not as though…'

'Ladies and gentlemen.'

It was Jane on the tannoy. She was interrupting Alex remotely.

'As I'm sure you'll all have noticed, the captain has changed our course. And he has asked me to explain why. It's very simple and it's nothing to be concerned about. It's just that he's received a mayday call from a small vessel – a yacht – which has been knocked about by the storm. And we're now on our way to provide whatever assistance we can. No doubt you'll all be aware that maritime law requires us to do this. Although, of course, I'm quite sure that even if this wasn't the case, we'd all want to go to the aid of this vessel. After all, it's what we would want if we were the ones in trouble.

'Anyway, the captain reckons we will be in sight of the vessel in about two hours' time, and meanwhile I'd just like to remind you that at ten o'clock, Rosie, our team photographer, will be giving a presentation on her time in the RAF, during which, as you might remember, she was stationed in the Falklands for nearly two years. It's a really good presentation. I can guarantee it. So, please come along. I'm sure Rosie will be delighted to see you.

'Oh, and of course, I will let you know when we have any more information on our rescue mission. Although that won't be for some time yet.'

And that was it. The on-board oracle had spoken – first of the dramatic and then of the mundane – and Alex could now imagine that, in every corner of the ship, passengers and crew alike were trying to come to terms with this latest twist in what was already a very twisted trip. Nevertheless, this didn't stop him indulging in a bit of light-hearted nonsense.

'Blimey,' he announced. 'A lecture on Rosie's time in the RAF! We can't possibly miss that…'

Debbie punched him in the ribs – gently – and then acknowledged her husband's observation.

'Sometimes I wonder...'

'...how you ended up with such a cool, unflappable dude such as myself.'

'Yeah, something like that,' she responded. 'But you know, sometimes you'd be better off if you were a bit more flappable. I mean, here we are, in the most perilous situation we've ever been in, and we now appear to be going off piste and maybe into even more bloody peril...'

'That, my dear,' responded Alex, 'is to ignore both the laws of the sea and the laws of decency. Just as Jane said. And anyway, I can't think how it can make our present perilous situation any more perilous. The yacht might even be carrying a team of microbiologists. They could be our salvation...'

Debbie let out a small groan.

'Oh, you're impossible, Alex. But, irritatingly, also completely right. We have to go to their aid, don't we?'

'Yep,' agreed Alex. 'And though we don't have to go to Rosie's lecture, I think we probably should. I mean, better to stick with normality while we can...'

This, Alex and Debbie and virtually all the *Sea Sprite's* passengers did. And accordingly, Rosie had a full house – for what turned out to be an extremely entertaining presentation on her role as an RAF communications officer. It even contained photographic proof that she'd been able to climb to the top of a very tall radio mast.

However, just minutes after her presentation ended, so too did the normality. By this time, Alex and Debbie were back in their cabin, and on hearing a brief tannoy announcement from Jane telling them that the *Sea Sprite* was now approaching the stricken yacht, they were soon out on their balcony. And there it was. Not a shiny, sleek, polished-to-the-gunnels yacht such as one sees in select South Coast marinas, but more a comprehensively roughed-up yacht, as in one with no mast, and a deck covered in yacht detritus and a good deal of splintered wood. And sitting in its stern were not a number of white-coated microbiologists, but instead just one young man and one young woman, both of whom radiated exhaustion and relief in equal measure. In due course, Alex and Debbie would learn that their names were Stuart and Gill.

It didn't take too long to get a zodiac into the water, and within only seconds it was off towards the ruined yacht, with Mike at the helm and Terry and John as his crew. It then took them very little time to reach the crippled vessel, and even less time to collect the two aboard it and bring them back to the ship. Alex and Debbie couldn't see it from their vantage point, but the rescued pair were then obviously deposited at the back of the *Sea Sprite*. And when this had been done, Mike, Terry and John returned to the yacht to secure it with a line. Alex wasn't entirely sure what they intended to do, but he'd later discover that the captain had decided to take the wrecked but still floating vessel in tow, and this was how one went about it – by first securing it with a line. He would also discover that the yacht had been completely disabled by the storm; losing not only its mast and much of its superstructure, but its steering gear as well. It wasn't so much a yacht now, but more an elegantly sculptured, untidy raft. It was indeed pretty well useless as a maritime vessel.

Its sorry condition was discussed over lunch, together with every aspect of the middle-of-the-ocean rescue of its crew. So too were the implications of the *Sea Sprite's* resumed westward – but slow – progress. Alex and Debbie were sharing a table with a sailing pair from Dorchester, who, as well as sounding authoritative on the subject of battered yachts, also had their own interpretation of the captain's sluggish progress west.

'He's deciding what to do,' the male of this pair pronounced.

And then his female partner completed their reading of the situation.

'Those two from the yacht must have brought some more news. And he's weighing up what to do.'

Well, as it turned out, they were spot on. But this would not become apparent until 3.30, when the entire passenger complement had been gathered in the lounge for an unscheduled but 'urgent' meeting, for which Jane had issued a three-line whip. At the end of her post-lunch tannoy announcement, she had said very emphatically that everyone – and I mean everyone – should attend. And she hadn't even followed this up with a pleasant platitude or a reflex reference to biosecurity measures. She clearly hadn't wanted to dilute the imperative nature of her message. Nor, as became apparent when the proceedings commenced, did the captain want to dilute the significance of *his* message. And he achieved this end by first introducing the rescued pair, and then by making it very clear that what one of them was about to say was not only of vital importance, but also that it had his full support. It would be, he said, as if he were speaking himself.

That got everybody's attention. And that was all the passengers and a good number of the crew, who had now stationed themselves at the back of the lounge. There was an even fuller house than there had been for Rosie…

The captain's brief introduction had included the information that the young woman standing beside him was a British Army signaller from the Mount Pleasant base on the Falklands and that her name was Gill. And he'd also let it be known that the young man accompanying her was some sort of spy, and that his name was Stuart. He then quickly went on to say that he wasn't a James Bond sort of spy, but instead one of those guys whose job it was to monitor transmissions in order to provide what used to be Britain's security services with intelligence. He then added that Stuart had also been based at Mount Pleasant and that his 'area of interest' had been the whole of South America. And Stuart, it appeared, was the person who would be addressing the assembled throng. This he did as soon as the captain passed him the microphone. And he started with an alarming announcement.

'Ladies and gentlemen,' he began, 'I am going to tell you something that you will find hard to believe. But first of all, could I just say how grateful Gill and I are for your saving our lives. I just hope that now we might be able to save yours…'

'Wow!' Alex mumbled to himself. 'What the hell is he going to say?'

In the event, Stuart had a lot to say – about his job at Mount Pleasant and about how he'd been able to track the spread of 'the plague'. And how he'd become increasingly concerned by the speed of its spread – right up until his colleague, Gill, had been able to give him access to some vital information in a top-secret military document, when he'd then become more concerned than ever.

In telling this tale, he'd had to admit to his and Gill's less-than-laudable behaviour, which in normal times would have earned one of them a court martial and the other an ignominious dismissal. There was then the matter of their running away from their mates. And this, in particular, clearly upset the ex-military members of Jane's team. Mike looked no less than murderous. However, Stuart, although looking very shamefaced at this point, managed to plough on with his story and share with his audience the stunning contents of that hijacked document, and what these contents would mean for them all.

'Nobody could work out,' he explained, 'how a disease could be transmitted so quickly and be lethal so quickly. It was behaving like no other disease ever visited on this planet. And what was finally discovered – thanks to the Chinese ambassador in London eventually coming clean – was that this terrible disease was behaving in this way because it wasn't a disease at all. And it isn't. Of that I am now absolutely certain. Because...'

And here he paused, not for dramatic effect but because he simply couldn't do otherwise. Even though he clearly knew what he was about to say, he equally clearly was finding it difficult to say it. And then he managed.

'...because, ladies and gentlemen, all those millions of people who have died out there have not died as a result of an infection, but as a result of being overwhelmed by fungal spores...'

At this point there was a communal gasp in the lounge, and then Stuart carried on.

'I don't claim to be an expert on the behaviour of fungi and their spores, but I do have a degree in botany, and my reading of the technical stuff in that document left me in no doubt that it had to be believed. Now, I know this will sound literally incredible, but apparently there was a genetically modified fungus produced in China – although we're not absolutely sure why – and it turned out to be extraordinarily generous in its spore production. And I mean *phenomenally* generous. What had apparently been a relatively modest tweak to arrive at this new form of fungus had somehow led to its producing and then releasing into the atmosphere trillions and trillions of spores. And very unusual spores. Unusual in that they were microscopically small, and I mean much, much smaller than *normal* spores. And… they were deadly. Nobody knows the precise mechanism – and nobody probably will – but once inhaled… Well, they kill. And, according to what's in that document, through an attack on the body's nervous system. But not a very "decisive" attack…'

Here he hesitated, but then he went on.

'And what I mean is that it's reckoned that they cause a neurological "storm" in the body. And this storm triggers the onset of some severe – and very painful – muscle spasms, while at the same time more and more of the body's pain receptors are activated. Until ultimately – and we're talking after maybe twenty-four hours or so – the body can't take any more. It is, I'm afraid, not a good way to die. In fact, it is a drawn-out and probably agonising way to die.'

At this point, Alex noticed that one of the female passengers had turned as white as the snow on South Georgia's peaks, and then he noticed that one of the male passengers had done the same. He wasn't in the least bit surprised.

'So,' continued Stuart, 'with these spores...'

'How do they spread around the world?' interrupted that same Welshman who had been bolshie before.

Stuart responded immediately and not resentfully.

'In a word, easily. And that's the problem. They'd soon colonised the whole of the atmosphere over China. And because they're so incredibly small and so incredibly light, they soon migrated to the upper atmosphere and then they started their journey around the planet, descending into the air we move around in and the air we breathe. Everywhere...'

'Yeah. But we have masks. I mean, the military certainly have masks. And all sorts of kit. And bunkers...'

'They do,' responded Stuart softly, 'but I can't stress enough the microscopic size of these spores. Or their vast number. Or their toxicity. They will get everywhere; if not immediately, then soon enough through any air-filtration system that exists, to ensure nobody survives. They are unstoppable. I'm sure you haven't forgotten, but Gill and I did a runner. And I can assure you that we wouldn't have even contemplated doing that if we hadn't both been certain that the spores couldn't – and wouldn't – be stopped at Mount Pleasant. No matter what protection had been put in place.'

Here was where the captain decided to intervene in this doom-filled presentation. And he did this by retrieving the microphone and very forcefully explaining that he had been convinced by Stuart's story as soon as he'd heard it, and then even more convinced when he had read the detail in Stuart and Gill's looted document. So much so, that he now wanted everyone else in the room to be equally convinced.

And if they hadn't been by what they'd just heard Stuart say, then he hoped they would be when they'd all read that document themselves, copies of which were already been prepared for distribution to every individual on board. He then emphasised that everybody being convinced was really very important indeed, because Stuart had something more to say. And what he had to say might mean that they could all stay alive. But it would also mean that they wouldn't be sailing to Ushuaia. At least not for some time.

Alex became aware of his throat. It was arid rather than dry, and he suddenly had a desperate craving for a gin and tonic. However, he would have to suppress the urge. After all, like all the other near dumbstruck people in the room, he had to listen to how he and Debbie might not end up dead…

Stuart had now been equipped with the microphone again, and he began to explain where salvation might lie.

'OK. The bad news first,' he opened. 'It won't be too long before the spores are everywhere in South America. And just about everywhere else in the world that hasn't already succumbed. Places like Australia and New Zealand, if they're not open-air morgues yet… well, they very soon will be.'

Alex thought that Stuart had slipped into the gratuitously dramatic with that choice of words, but maybe he wanted everybody's completely undivided attention. And sure enough, if he hadn't had it before, he did have it now.

'However,' he continued, 'as is shown in the document we "intercepted", there was one place in Asia that hadn't been touched by the spores. And that place was Franz Josef Land…'

'Where?' shouted the Welshman.

'Franz Josef Land. It's a big archipelago off the north coast of Russia, and north of the Arctic Circle. Nobody actually lives there, but there are a couple of Russian bases on a couple of its islands. And it appears that these bases were still transmitting messages – to anyone who would listen to them – well after all their comrades on the Russian mainland had perished. And I mean even those in really deep bunkers, whether under the Kremlin or anywhere else...'

'So why...?'

It was the Welshman again. It was as though he'd been planted to help Stuart along.

'Cold or polar atmospheric circulation, or a combination of the two.'

For Alex, the penny dropped immediately. Cold. Polar. And there were two poles. And when Stuart and Gill had got themselves into some nautical difficulty, they were on their way to the south one – where there would be a similar helping of cold and the same sort of polar atmospheric circulation as found at the other end of the world. They were seeking refuge in the Antarctic. For as long as it took. And the captain had decided that they had made the right decision. Which meant he was now going to announce a permanent change to his present westward course and instead head south. Debbie might see her chinstrap penguins after all.

For many others in the room, the penny didn't drop quite so quickly. Even when the captain spelled out exactly what Alex had been thinking, and then confirmed that he would indeed be taking the *Sea Sprite* to the Antarctic. And when the penny did drop, for certain members of the throng, it didn't have the result that the captain so desperately wanted.

In fact, the gathering descended into something of a bun fight, with on one side people like Alex and Debbie, who felt that there was no choice other than to go south, and on the opposing side, people for whom the idea of hiding in a deep freeze for an unspecified period was no less than unbridled lunacy.

Gradually, however, the Antarctic enthusiasts began to prevail. This was in part due to the captain's assurances that he had enough provisions and fuel to be able to stay at sea for as much as a month if necessary, and to two important contributions from Stuart. The first was that, because of his work as a monitor at Mount Pleasant, he knew a great deal about all the Spanish-speaking research stations on the Antarctic Peninsula and, very significantly, the location of all those that were currently unmanned but full of further provisions. The second was that he had little doubt that if the *Sea Sprite* returned to Ushuaia now, all those aboard it would be dead within days.

This still left open a lot of concerns and a lot of unknowns, and neither Stuart nor the captain could say with any degree of certainty when it would be safe to return to South America – or indeed whether it would ever be safe to do so. Even though, as Stuart emphasised, genetically modified plants of any sort are generally sterile, and therefore as soon as the atmosphere was clear of spores, the danger should have passed. All they could say was that, without a shadow of doubt, it would be lethal if they returned, as scheduled, in just thirty-six hours' time. And the only possible chance they all had was to defer that return for as long as they possibly could.

Eventually, the meeting was drawn to a close, with

the captain reconfirming that the *Sea Sprite* would now be adopting a course almost due south, and for those amongst the congregation who still vehemently disagreed with this decision, he would be hosting a further meeting in the Magellan Deck restaurant directly after dinner. It would, Alex thought, be no more than a sop. And a second further meeting – of the whole ship's company, to be held in the lounge the following morning – would be of far more importance. At this, the captain promised, there could be a detailed discussion of all aspects of their current situation and, more importantly, there could be a run-through of the practical implications of turning an expedition trip into a survival trip. Not least regarding ways in which the passengers and the crew would now have to interact.

But that was for tomorrow. There was still a chunk of today to deal with, and after their first drink at the bar, Alex and Debbie had another before returning to their cabin, where they were able to absorb the contents of Stuart's purloined document. None of what they read changed their minds, but it did persuade them to return to the bar again, where they stayed for such a long time that when they finally descended to the restaurant, they were able to dine alone. Which, for once, was exactly what they wanted to do. After all, they still had a lot to discuss. Just the two of them.

And a lot to digest...

twenty-two

When he woke up, the first word that drifted into Alex's mind was 'implausible'. The second was 'preposterous'. Could it really be, he asked himself, that some previously unknown super-fungus had suddenly spewed an Earth-sized cloud of spores into the atmosphere, and that these spores were absolutely deadly? That once ingested they would kill you – and that they would do so very slowly and very painfully?

Oh, and what about other animals? Why were the reports only of humans being cut down in their millions? It was all just so completely implausible; indeed, so implausible that it was simply preposterous to be running scared to the south. After all, the Antarctic had never been seen as any sort of refuge, and it might more accurately be described as one of the most inhospitable places on the planet. So how the hell had he swallowed all this stuff, and how had he been so easily seduced by the captain's plan to take the *Sea Sprite* to the lands of snow and ice?

He lay in bed for some time, trying to answer these questions. And finally he did. Because he brought to mind what he'd read in that document; that exposé on the fungus that had been so detailed and so authoritative as to be undeniable. And he remembered also what that guy, Stuart, had said. And how he had said it. And how he'd admitted that his understanding of botany had been challenged by the existence of such an extraordinary form of fungus, but not overwhelmed by it. Nature was full of remarkable stuff, he had stressed, and it had the capacity to provide endless surprises. Even when it hadn't been fiddled around with by man. No, it hadn't been a flight of fancy, and there was every reason to believe that everything Stuart had said was true. Just because something was implausible didn't mean it was impossible. And neither was it preposterous to seek safety in an improbable destination, which was no more than Stuart and his friend had been doing when their boat came to grief. Alex just had to accept that there was a menace out there, just as it had been described, and that the only sensible course of action was that being taken by Captain José. There was no other option.

It was this very point that Roy made at breakfast. Alex and Debbie had sat with him for this first meal of the day, and all three of them had confessed to having had a great deal of difficulty in believing with absolute certainty what they'd been told, but at the same time they had all accepted that they had to. However improbable, the existence of a planet-sized cloud of lethal spores was the best theory in town, and they all needed to take this as read.

This, it transpired, was not an exceptional conclusion. When they gathered with all the other passengers and many of the crew for the captain's promised briefing at ten o'clock, the atmosphere in the lounge was one of welcome calm. And it was calm because there was clearly an overwhelming acceptance of what was going on and what needed to be done. If there were any remaining dissenters, they were probably very few in number and they were definitely keeping a low profile. Alex was pretty sure that they wouldn't be providing any sort of challenge at this meeting, and even if they wanted to, they would have to wait until it was the turn of 'Any other business'. Yes, all attendees at this lounge powwow had been equipped with an agenda, and after the captain (flanked by Jane and Stuart) had offered a greeting to his audience, proceedings kicked off with agenda point 1. Which was 'Our new itinerary'.

This was interesting in itself, thought Alex. It could instead have been something like 'The threat from spores' or 'Questions arising from the distributed intelligence document'. But it wasn't, and there was no other reference to the existence of a lethal miasma of spores anywhere else on the agenda. The captain clearly now considered the existence of this threat, and indeed any other aspect of the threat, a closed subject, and he was going to focus entirely on what needed to be done in the face of the threat. Nobody in the room appeared to find this a problem, just as they probably had very little problem in now seeing the captain as their leader and not just as the bloke who drove the ship. Possibly because their situation demanded a leader, and he was the streets-ahead obvious candidate. He certainly had a very clear vision of where he would lead them in geographic terms. As he was now about to set out…

'OK, our itinerary,' he began. 'As was indicated yesterday, there are certain research stations – especially on and around the Antarctic Peninsula – that will almost certainly be empty but will still be stocked with provisions. Some of you will no doubt already know this, but it is not uncommon for many research stations to be left unmanned for most of the year, or for years in some cases. But they are generally not left without supplies. Even if only to be used as a back-up by other research stations. And with Stuart's invaluable input it is these installations that we have now identified, at least four of which we plan to visit. And I'm now going to show you where these four are, and how they will dictate our route over the next few days.'

At this point, Rosie brought up a map on the two large screens at the front of the lounge, which were normally used to display visual aids during more conventional presentations. The map was of the Antarctic Peninsula with, dotted above it, the islands of the South Shetlands and, above them, a cluster of tiny dots at the centre of which was Elephant Island, home to the *Endeavour's* crew for so many months.

'OK,' continued the captain. 'At the moment we're heading towards Elephant Island. That's the island right at the top of the screen. And because we're already trying to conserve fuel – which means we're now going a little more slowly than normal – we won't be passing Elephant Island until sometime on Thursday. That's the day after tomorrow. Anyway, we won't be stopping at Elephant Island. Because there's nothing there to stop for. And instead we'll continue on to Deception Island. And that's the island you should be able to make out at the bottom of the South Shetlands. That's the string of islands above the peninsula…'

Here, Jane moved quickly to one of the screens and pointed out the exact location of Deception Island. Then

Nick, the bird man, followed her lead and did the same on the other screen.

'Now,' Captain José continued, 'we *will* be stopping at Deception Island, because on this island there are two empty research stations. One is Argentinian and one is Spanish. And I'll come to what we will do there under agenda point 4.

'OK. From there we will sail to the peninsula – now being pointed out by Jane and Nick – and we will make for a place called Cierva Cove. And here we will find Argentinian research station number two. Then we will sail down the channel, now being pointed out, and pay a visit to Argentinian research station number three in a place called Paradise Bay. And here we'll review our situation. I mean, by then we'll be almost sixty-five degrees south, and we'll have to decide – or *I'll* have to decide – whether to go further south or maybe stay right there. Paradise Bay is not only as beautiful as its name suggests, but it is also very sheltered and it will provide a very good anchorage for as long as we need.

'So, that's a brief run-through of our immediate itinerary. Does anyone have any questions?'

Nobody did. Or if they did, they were not going to ask them now.

'Fine,' announced José, quite clearly very relieved. 'So why don't we move on to agenda point 2, which is On-board arrangements?'

Here, he gathered his thoughts, and then continued.

'Now, I think you'll all accept that we're now embarking on a new chapter of our cruise; one which is going to be very different from what we've been experiencing so far. Bluntly, we are no longer on an expedition, and instead we are seeking to keep ourselves alive. All of us. You, the paying passengers; my crew; the hotel staff; Jane's team; our friends from South Georgia; and, of course, our new shipmates, Stuart and Gill. So, I'd just like to say that I've discussed this with my fellow officers, and with the hotel manager, and with Jane, and whilst there might very likely be a need for a little more forbearance all round, there will definitely be no need for an upheaval in people's roles. And what I mean by that is that every member of my crew, and all the waiters, chefs, chambermaids and stewards, and all the members of Jane's team, will be more than happy to continue in their roles if you, the passengers, continue in yours. Offering to help out in the galley or offering to take on waiting duties would, I assure you, be entirely counterproductive and would only serve to disrupt order on the ship. So, we – the crew, the hospitality staff and the expedition team – will continue to be... the crew, the hospitality staff and the expedition team. And you... well, I'd like to ask you to please continue to be the passengers. Albeit, as I say, with as much forbearance as you can manage.

'Now, I'm not going to ask for questions just now, because I suspect they will be answered under points 3 and 4. And especially under point 3, which, as you see, is "Food".

'OK. Let's talk about food. We do carry a lot of provisions on the *Sea Sprite*, and we hope to collect a good deal more from our visits to those research stations I've mentioned. But we have to make sure that those provisions last for as long as is reasonably possible. So, from lunchtime today, I'm afraid you will find that the buffet service is suspended, and all meals will instead be plated. And I'm sorry, but it will also be necessary to restrict lunch to one course, and dinner to just two. There will still be some choice, but much less than's been offered before. I know this isn't what you paid for, but I suspect that somewhere in the small print, survival might just take preference over gastronomy, and it certainly takes preference over unrestricted tippling. I hate to say this, but wine and all other alcoholic beverages will now have to be rationed. After all, I'm sure none of you would want to see us running out of *booze.* I hope you understand.'

For the first time during this briefing, there was an audible hum in the room as many of the passengers absorbed the implications of this latest piece of unwelcome news. Quite clearly, for some, the absence of a gin and tonic or a whisky and soda as part of their daily routine would be a terrible cross to bear. And Alex, for one, felt suddenly very despondent.

Fortunately, his despondency was short-lived, because José had now moved on to agenda point 4, which was 'Volunteering', and this immediately distracted him from the threatened absence of gin. For what the captain was discussing was the need to go about the pilfering of stores from the deserted research stations as quickly and as safely as possible, for which he would need some 'auxiliaries' to assist his front-line troops. He explained that certain members of his crew and the ex-military members of the expedition team would lead the assaults on all four of the identified stations, but that their job would be made that much easier if they had a number of able-bodied passengers as their helpers and assistants. And therefore, would all those in the room who believed that they could assist in this way identify themselves by registering at reception before lunch. Not all might be accepted, he warned, but, that said, he would still be grateful for as many passengers as possible stepping forward.

Alex actually grinned. It would be like joining the Home Guard, he thought, only without the uniform and the drills. He would definitely be reporting to reception as soon as this briefing was at an end.

That wouldn't be long. The remaining agenda points dealt with communications (of which, for the time being, there would be none), interactions with other ships (which, in due course, would be 'cautious and limited'), and medical facilities (which would be much as they were at the moment: a fully equipped surgery under the control of the ship's rather lugubrious-looking Ukrainian doctor). Such facilities, explained the captain, would almost certainly prove sufficient for their needs. Nevertheless, he went on to say, in view of the circumstances, he had suggested to the doctor that he should invite all those who had previously worked in the medical profession in any capacity to identify themselves so that he might call upon their services if and when required. The good doctor, it appeared, had agreed, and he now looked forward to hearing from any willing parties who had these appropriate credentials 'as soon as possible after the conclusion of this meeting – in his Magellan Deck surgery'.

Of course, the meeting couldn't come to that conclusion until the captain had invited any contributions from the assembled company that might fall under 'Any other business', and this he did rather hesitantly, and obviously in the hope that there would be none at all. He wasn't to be so lucky. That Welshman was as persistent as he was bolshie, and he immediately stood to his feet and posed the question: 'Should we swap cabins after a week or so?'

He then went on to explain why this should doubtless be done.

'I mean, those on the Erikson Deck have only paid for their cabins up until the 12th December. So, if we're at sea any longer, those of us on the lower decks should have a chance of an upgrade. You know, swap our cabins for ones with a balcony. It seems only fair…'

Alex couldn't work out what had occurred first: the obvious amused incredulity within the assembled company, or the look of bemusement on the captain's face. But whichever it was, the answer to this question was not provided in words, but in the reaction of everyone else in the room – regardless of the location of their cabins. The captain remained silent, and the Welshman fell silent too. He might, thought Alex, now think twice before daring to ask another question at one of these meetings.

Nevertheless, he had successfully discouraged anybody else from asking a question at this meeting, and within only minutes of it breaking up, Alex was registering his willingness to become an 'auxiliary'. As was Debbie. She clearly wasn't about to let him have all the fun…

Roy volunteered as well. But Derek and Elaine did not. Past heart problems for Derek and slightly arthritic knees for Elaine saw both of them having to give up the opportunity to play as pirates, and, in any event, there were already too many volunteers. Dad's Army was oversubscribed well before lunch.

It was now that time; time for the first pared-down, single-course meal (of pasta and chicken) – and this was being 'relished' by the Famous Five. It didn't look terribly appealing, but at least the wine rationing hadn't yet been sorted, and everybody's glass was replenished without question. It was as the topped-up glasses were being assailed that Roy brought up the subject of 'mutual protection'.

The conversation so far had dwelt largely on all those issues discussed in the morning's meeting, and especially the planned itinerary and the planned acquisition of other people's property without their consent. Would the three volunteers at the table really be able to participate in a bit of breaking and entering? And what if the target research stations were not entirely deserted? What if there were some Argentinians or Spaniards still at their posts? What if some violent conduct was called for?

Well, it was possibly that last question that caused Roy to bring up this new subject, and the first thing he did was explain why the subject might be worth considering at all.

'Look,' he said, 'it's all very well to put a plan in place – just like the captain's done – but I can't be the only one to have thought that it will only work if… well, if order is maintained…'

'You mean,' interjected Derek, 'if we're not all at each other's throats. If the jolly Welshman hasn't stirred up a war between the decks, and the crew aren't trying to throw us overboard.'

'Yes, exactly,' responded Roy without the slightest hint of humour in his voice. 'And you see, I thought… well, there's the five of us. And, well, we all get on pretty well…'

'…and we should watch each other's backs,' finished Alex. 'You want us to become the five musketeers.'

Roy looked a little abashed. Maybe he didn't know whether his suggestion was about to become the object of ridicule or scorn. But before he had an opportunity to decide, Debbie spoke up, and what she said was unequivocal.

'I think it's a bloody good idea. No point in not assuming the worst. And if I've got to trust my back to anybody, I think I'd be happy to trust it to you guys. And even to my husband…'

'Me too,' announced Elaine. 'I think it's a great idea. Although I hope we never need to put it into practice.'

Derek and Alex then concurred, Derek with a wry smile on his face, and a warning that his doctor had long ago advised him not to engage in any form of pugilism. But he was still clearly serious, and everybody knew this. So, when all five of them had drained their second glass of Sauvignon blanc, they were all firmly signed up to Roy's idea of mutual protection. Although, as Elaine had said, they all no doubt hoped that it would prove to be a novel sort of insurance policy against which they would never have to make a claim.

After lunch, for those not preparing themselves for an outbreak of mayhem on the *Sea Sprite*, there was bingo on offer. As Jane explained in her tannoy announcement, this might be a first for the *Sea Sprite*. She could not recall this rather mindless pastime ever having been offered before (although she did not use the term 'mindless pastime'). But, as she went on to say, neither could she recall there ever having been such a need for an 'engaging pastime' before. Nevertheless, it was a pastime Alex and Debbie could do without. Their afternoon would be spent reading and dozing. In fact, more dozing than reading. Traumatic developments could clearly prove very tiring.

They were both feeling better when the time came to join the members of their gang for dinner, a dinner that would not be remembered for its culinary delights or its abundance of food. There was no starter, and when the main course arrived it looked no more appealing than their earlier lunch. It was an unspecified fish with boulangère potatoes. The potatoes were quite good, but the fish was completely tasteless. Alex suggested that it had not just the appearance of a congealed cloud, but also the flavour of a congealed cloud. The second course was only a little better, in that the apple and blackberry crumble did have a little colour. Even if only the minimum of both apples and blackberries.

The conversation around the table was hardly memorable either. It consisted largely of a series of unanswered questions concerning their imminent journey south. Would the passenger/crew relationship be sustainable? Would the captain allow any zodiac excursions to relieve their being 'trapped' aboard the *Sea Sprite* for so long? And what about their raiding parties? Would the women really be allowed to join the boys?

Nobody had definitive answers to any of these questions, but they did all have their views on the likely success of their seeking shelter in the Frigidaire south. And the exchange of these views provided a highlight to the table discussion. It would be what Alex would remember long after the rest of the discussion had drained from his mind. Debbie started it, and she did so with a confident statement.

'You know,' she said, 'I have a really good feeling about the next few weeks. They might not be the easiest weeks we'll ever spend, and we might have to deal with far worse than tasteless white fish, but I think it will work. We'll get through this. And whatever we find when we get to the end of it – back in Ushuaia and beyond – we'll be damned pleased that we did what we did. Yes, we're going to come through this. All of us.'

Roy then added his thoughts. Immediately and enthusiastically.

'Debbie, you're right. And I'd go even further. I mean, how often do you get a chance to do something like this: make off for a cold continent on a fabulous ship, with the promise of some real adventure? And not just stuff like breaking and entering, but… well, anything. I mean, like absolutely anything. It's going to be an unscripted excursion like we've never experienced before. God, I can hardly wait to get started. I really can't. And, Hell, when we break into those research stations, I might even be able to "liberate" a few flags…'

This comment set off a ripple of chuckles around the table and drew an immediate response from Elaine.

'Well, Roy, I'd prefer you liberated some toiletries and maybe some toilet paper first. You can never have enough of life's little essentials. Especially if we're not going to be anywhere near a shop for several weeks…'

This caused a few more chuckles around the table, and then Elaine carried on.

'Anyway, I have to say that I'm with Debbie and Roy. This is going to work. I'm not sure quite how, but we will all survive.'

'And how about you, Derek?' asked Debbie. 'What do you think of our chances?'

'Twenty per cent,' responded Derek without a second's hesitation.

'Twenty per cent?!' shrieked Debbie. 'Why on Earth would you say that?'

'Because,' replied Derek calmly, 'I've learnt over the years that twenty per cent is often a pretty sound prediction. Or at least it sounds pretty... sound. And after the event, nobody remembers what you said anyway. And that's why, if you ask me what the probability is of the captain walking into this restaurant in the next fifteen minutes, I'll tell you it's twenty per cent...'

'You're insufferable,' observed Elaine. 'I'm sure we can expect something a little more sensible from Alex.'

Alex sighed. It was clearly his turn, and he wasn't sure what to say. Should he be realistic or optimistic or frighteningly honest? In the end, he plumped for the optimistic.

'Why wouldn't we get through all this?' he opened. 'After all, we're on a roll. First, we managed to end up on a ship literally hundreds of miles from you-know-what. Then we ran into Stuart and Gill. And now, with their help, we've devised a plan to keep us all alive. And I'm pretty sure we'll still be on a roll when we get back to Ushuaia. Why on Earth would we not be?

'So, Derek, I reckon that if you could just find another eighty per cent to top up your twenty per cent, you would be dead on the mark. All of us on board this ship, not just the five of us around this table, are going to come out of this on top. And you'd better believe me...'

And as he signed off with this confident conclusion, he wished desperately that not only would they believe it, but that, at some point, he would as well.

twenty-three

It had been Stuart and Gill's second night aboard the *Sea Sprite* and their second night of sharing a bed. Gill was Stuart's mate, his drinking friend, the guy he watched films with. She wasn't his girlfriend, and even on the *Bluebird* they had slept apart. But here on the *Sea Sprite*, there was only one spare cabin. And an assumption that, if the two of them had been on a yacht together, with the intention of spending an isolated future together, then they could certainly lie on a bed together.

This was a difficult assumption to deny. And, in any event, it would have been churlish beyond belief to have even tried. After all, they had been plucked from the sea and saved from almost certain death. So, they had said nothing, and had merely accepted the arrangements offered without question. And those arrangements were, of course, far more luxurious than those they'd become used to back at Mount Pleasant. It was like being… well, on a luxury cruise.

Furthermore, it had soon become apparent that they were the sort of arrangements that could lead to a development of their feelings for each other. It was early days yet, and their relationship was still strictly platonic, but it seemed to Stuart that they were already seeing each other in a different light. He knew for certain that Gill, although physically the same Gill he had known for months, was now a much more attractive Gill. Especially once out of most of her clothes. And he was now beginning to suspect that this growing attraction was mutual – and quite optimistic enough to believe that his suspicion was more than just a suspicion…

He was also optimistic about their situation in general. After all, he and Gill were now on a substantial ship that was unlikely to suffer the same fate as their considerably smaller 'borrowed' yacht. They were also in the company of nearly 150 other souls who appeared to have signed up to their hiding-in-the-Antarctic strategy. In fact, Stuart had been amazed at just how quickly his explanation of the improbable events had been accepted. And then delighted with the similarly rapid acceptance of his plans for survival. Indeed, in retrospect, he had never felt quite so gratified, quite so important – or quite so terrified – as he had done at the end of that first session in the lounge. And if only there hadn't been that understandable antagonism from the ex-military in the room, his appearance in front of all those people might have ranked as being the highlight of his life so far. But it still certainly beat anything he had done in all those long weeks on the Falklands. By more than a furlong.

Indeed, just like the sausages on offer aboard the *Sea Sprite* beat any of those condom monstrosities in the Mount Pleasant canteen. By miles. And it was now time for breakfast!

twenty-four

Alex awoke feeling tired. He'd had a very disturbed night. Not because of the state of the sea – which was now remarkably calm – but because of the state of his mind. Despite the shared confidence expressed at dinner the previous evening, and despite the confidence he'd himself expressed about the likely outcome of the *Sea Sprite's* passage south, he was full of foreboding. What had started off as a willing acceptance of the 'survival plan' – which had retained its poise, despite an early stumble – was now finding its path increasingly full of doubts and concerns; question marks that even the promise of adventure and a place in Dad's Army could not overcome. He was now on a journey into the unknown, and whilst this journey held out the prospect of all sorts of perils, it held out no firm prospect of a worthwhile conclusion. Even if the *Sea Sprite* stayed in the Antarctic for months, there was no guarantee that safety would be secured when it returned to Ushuaia. In fact, it was more than probable that what would be found there would be an unavoidable and painful death. After all, if the damn fungus had done such a comprehensive job of wiping out the vast majority of mankind, why would it not stay around and kill off any late-to-the-party stragglers?

Nevertheless, Alex knew it wouldn't help him – or his wife – if he let all these leaden thoughts overwhelm him. And in any event, after yesterday's downsized dining, these thoughts were already being pushed to the side by the unavoidable forces of hunger. He was more than eager for breakfast; a breakfast that he knew would consist mostly of victuals that had been either fried or grilled. Today, muesli and yoghurt would be eschewed, and eggs and pig products would take their place. And, though he didn't yet know it, his breakfast would also be accompanied by a generous helping of interest and even some intrigue. Because, as he and Debbie were approaching the Magellan Deck restaurant, they were joined by two others who were also seeking their breakfast, one of whom asked Alex and Debbie whether they might join them. The joint response to this request was an immediate and enthusiastic yes. After all, the two shipmates who were seeking their company were Stuart and Gill...

Alex's first thought, when they were all seated, was that their (possible) saviours were rather ill-matched – physically. Gill looked really quite solid, and she had a countenance that, from certain angles, might best be described as severe. Stuart, in contrast, was more 'comfortable' than solid-looking, and his countenance was anything but severe. With a roundish face and soft, sleepy eyes, he looked more like an overgrown choirboy than a member of a now-defunct intelligence service. And he certainly looked young. They both did. Probably because they were less than half the age of most of the other diners in the room. Their lives had yet to be led, not just looked back on.

Anyway, with orders placed with one of the solicitous waiters, Alex posed his first question – to Stuart. He suspected he already knew the answer to it, but he still had to ask it.

'Stuart,' he began, 'have you any real doubts about this fungus thing? You know, are you really sure that it's going to get to virtually everywhere in the world, and that it's really as deadly as suggested in that report?'

'No, I've no doubts,' Stuart replied firmly. 'Once I'd got over my initial surprise, I was absolutely certain.'

'Surprise?' questioned Alex. 'You mean at its erhh… improbability? And at its… virulence… and its… reach?'

'No. My surprise that it was a fungus and not a pandemic disease. I mean, that's what we'd all expected…'

'We?'

'My… erhh, colleagues. My… community. I mean, everybody who worked in intelligence. And a lot of other people in the loop as well.'

'I'm not sure…'

Stuart looked directly at Alex and then at Debbie. And, after a slightly awkward hiatus, he embarked on a little pre-fry-up enlightenment of his older table companions.

'OK. Accepted fact. China has seen itself for years – or should I say *had* seen itself for years – as not only the greatest civilisation on the planet, but the one most wronged. Primarily by all those inferior specimens in the West. It had therefore been seething with resentment for years, and had been directing all its energies into returning to its rightful place in the world. That is to say, as the world's number-one power and the world's number-one undisputed master…'

'Undisputed master…?'

'Alex, there are academics in China who promote the belief that the Chinese people are a separate, superior species to the rest of mankind. Resentment can breed irrationality, and if it's not held in check by what we regard as morality and humanity, it can easily get out of hand…'

'But…'

Stuart was clearly not about to brook any interruptions, and he carried on.

'Well, it's hardly a secret how China had been forcing its way to the top in economic terms. Or how it had been able to do this so quickly by cheating in every way possible; you know, by pinching anything it wanted and by just generally not playing by the rules. Which, of course, is quite OK if you're resentful enough and not burdened with too much in the way of principles. It's what also allows you to ravage the world's resources, and not just its wildlife…'

'And this was sort of the official view?' managed Alex.

'Yep. And so was the fact that China knew very well that it would still take years to impose itself on the rest of the world through its economic power alone, and that its military wouldn't be much use either. America would do anything it took to make sure of that…'

'So…'

'So,' echoed Stuart, 'if you want to impose yourself on the rest of the world sooner rather than later, you have to do more than shower the world with exports, lend money that can't be paid back to every poor country in the world, and grab islands in the South China Sea. You also have to weaken the rest of the world to the point where it's completely exhausted and therefore unable to do more than accept a future of indefinite serfdom. It won't then just be a case of China being number one. It will also be a case of there being no number two, but just a load of has-been and now subjugated countries.'

Alex could barely believe what he was being told. But his credence was to be challenged even more. Stuart was just about to explain how the enfeeblement of the rest of the world might be achieved.

'So, what if you first kit out your country with a surveillance system that is so powerful and so invasive that it can track not only what all your citizens are doing but also the progress of any epidemic? Whether this epidemic arises unintentionally in one of your filthy wildlife markets or, heaven forbid, if it's *created* and then unleashed *intentionally*?

'Easy then to track its spread through a few thousand or a few tens of thousands of your own expendable citizens, and bring it to a halt, while the world's airlines transport it around the globe – to all those inferior countries where an embrace of liberty and a rejection of state surveillance mean that it will be spread without check. And even if what has now become a pandemic doesn't kill millions, it will still incapacitate their economies to such an extent that they will never recover. Only your own superior country will remain untouched and only it will have the resources and the wealth to keep the world from falling into ruin. And hey presto! As well as your becoming the number-one country in the world, you're now the master of all you survey. Your ancient empire has prevailed, and it's now been restored to its rightful position. And it's an unassailable position. Never again will you have to feel demeaned. Or resentful…'

Alex felt as though he was gulping for air. He wasn't physically, but in his mind, he was struggling to breathe. This guy at the table wasn't some mad advocate of conspiracy theories; he was a representative of a renowned intelligence service that had only recently ceased to exist. And it was all so… alarmingly credible.

'So,' continued Stuart, after a slight pause, 'you can see why I was so surprised. No pandemic, but instead the fungal equivalent of a Triffid, only a million times worse. And so bloody worse, it killed off its "keepers". Which I suspect wasn't part of their plan. After all, it's quite tricky to be the masters of the world if you've all kicked the bucket…'

Alex gathered himself. He had one final mental gulp, and then he asked Stuart another question.

'Are you saying that China engineered this thing, but somehow got it wrong?'

Stuart smiled.

'Well, let's just say that the Chinese ambassador, for whatever reasons, was not definitive on that point. You'll have seen that in the report. But my reading of that document leads me to believe that he was expecting some inferences to be drawn. And that's all I've done. A "GM accident" leading to the annihilation of mankind is extremely implausible. A miscalculation with a genetically modified, maybe human-specific weapon is only highly implausible. You may or may not agree.'

Alex felt stunned. What he'd just heard hadn't just reinforced his prejudices and more; it had also lifted the lid on quite how dangerous his species could be when it devoted itself not merely to the extinction of other species but also to the enslavement of most of its own. Then, it could not only miss its target, but it could cause so much collateral damage that it wiped itself out. With no way back.

It was just at this point in his musings that his bacon, sausages and two fried eggs arrived, and their delivery provided a suitable full stop to Stuart's tale of the unexpected, and a chance for Alex to assuage his hunger for calories rather than revelations. It didn't, however, stop him asking one last 'associated' question – just as he was cutting into his first sausage. This was not directly related to China's behaviour, but to the behaviour of that deadly fungus.

'Stuart,' he ventured, 'do you really think that the spores will not be waiting for our return? That they'll have disappeared by the time we get back?'

Stuart's response to this question was an enhanced focus on his own meal – of scrambled eggs – and then an extended hesitation. Only after this did he speak.

'Alex, I just can't be sure. But as I said before, we're dealing with a genetically modified organism here. And unless the Chinese had put a lot of focused effort into that modification, I reckon it will be a sterile organism. Once all those microscopic spores have drifted to the ground – which will take quite a bit of time yet – they won't be a threat. I mean, they won't be viable, and they therefore won't give rise to another generation of fungi. Which means there won't be another cloud of spores. The threat will have disappeared entirely. Or, at least, that's what I think...'

On hearing this response, Alex indulged in an internal sigh, and then nodded his thanks to Stuart before resuming his knife-work on his sausage. After the meal, he would give Stuart's words some more thought, but for now he'd just concentrate on the taste of pork and sage and maybe turn the conversation to life – as was – at Mount Pleasant. How had Stuart and Gill found it there, and how had they coped with the wind?

Fifteen minutes later, back in their cabin, Alex addressed his wife.

'They say breakfast is the most important meal of the day. But I've never heard it said that it can be the most sensational one as well. I mean, what Stuart had to say was… fantastic. But not fantastic. I mean, it was only too bloody believable. And now we're stuck in this mess. All because a bunch of resentful bastards had set themselves the goal of running the world…'

'Seems they overreached themselves a bit,' observed Debbie. 'It's just a pity they didn't just screw up their own patch.'

'Amen to that,' agreed Alex. 'If only it was still just China's problem. If only they'd kept it to themselves.'

Debbie made no response to this observation, but began to collect together small items of clothing with the obvious intention of conducting a wash. Mankind might be in meltdown, but those who remained still needed clean socks and clean underwear, and these wouldn't arrive without an active intervention. It was clearly time for Alex to find something to do and to leave Debbie to her chores. And this he did, not by attending another hastily organised bingo session, but by taking himself to the ship's library. There, he would seek out an absorbing reference book, or maybe a tale of Antarctic adventure. In the event, he did neither. Because he found that the library already contained a single occupant by the name of Derek. And Derek, Alex thought, should be apprised of the contents of Stuart's breakfast presentation.

In very little time, he had been. Derek had invited Alex to occupy the large leather wingback chair next to his own, and had then listened attentively to all that Alex had to tell him. At the end of Alex's tale, he did acknowledge the amazing revelations, but with just a smile and a 'Well, who would have thought?'

Alex felt a little disappointed. How could Derek be so underwhelmed by what he'd just heard, and so 'calm and collected'? He should have been no less than astounded. Maybe he hadn't quite understood…

'Derek, you *have* taken in what I've said?' asked Alex plaintively. 'You haven't misunderstood me, have you?'

'No,' replied a smiling Derek. 'The evil empire has been evil. Which, I think, is what evil empires do. Although not always with such catastrophic consequences.'

Alex was bemused. How could Derek be so… sanguine?

'Derek,' Alex tried again, 'aren't you just a little bit upset? Aren't you just a little bit appalled that because of what China has done you'll never see England again? That you'll never return to the country of your birth and resume your life there? A life that's been spent there for…'

'…seventy-six years,' finished Derek. 'Only, of course, my life in the England I knew came to an end many years before this little mishap.'

Alex was taken aback. What could Derek possibly mean? He'd have to try to find out.

'I don't understand. I mean…'

Derek looked his interrogator in the eyes – his own eyes weary-looking but still penetrating – and he set about providing the explanation Alex sought.

'Alex, you're not that much younger than me, are you? So, you must remember what England was like when we were growing up. And for quite a few years after that. You know, a bit scruffy, a bit naff, a bit unsophisticated and even a bit seedy. But it was our England. Even if it was a bit of a mess, at least it was our mess. And it was a *good* place; a place where fairness, shared experiences, a shared culture and a shared way of thinking made us not notice that it was a mess. Instead, we just saw it as our home, as our own special slice of the world. And a place we were proud of.

'Well, when we left it a couple of weeks ago, it wasn't the same, was it?'

Alex must have looked puzzled at this statement, because Derek then amplified what he meant.

'Alex, what if I were to say that when I walked through Shrewsbury, I sometimes felt I was in Warsaw and not in my local county town? What if I were to say that when I switched on the telly, I'd have to tell myself that I hadn't been whisked off to India or South Africa? And what if I were to say that when I visited London, I would have to try to convince myself that I was still in the capital of England and not in one of Heathrow's international terminals?'

Alex answered none of these rhetorical questions, and Derek carried on.

'Alex, my England died years ago. Long before this rotten fungus got to it. And, worse, I've not been able to voice my sorrow at its passing for as long as I can remember. If I were to point out that a visit to Stratford to watch a bit of Shakespeare had long ago become an exercise in diversity indoctrination, I would be called an unreconstructed racist bigot before you could say "Puck". And if I dared express the opinion that most other people in this world had a country they could call their own, but we no longer did, I would be damned as an ignorant and offensive peasant who deserved only contempt. And I mean that; I really do. Whenever I argued that England was no longer the property of its indigenous people, I would get shouted down. Nobody wanted to hear that, whilst we'd retained some residence rights in our own country, it had so much changed over our lifetime that we could no longer recognise it as our home.'

At this stage in his obituary for his country, Alex noted that Derek didn't sound bitter, but just resigned and somewhat tired. Nevertheless, he still had some energy to carry on.

'Of course, it wasn't just *who* was in England now; it was also the views that had taken root there. Or should I say the views that had been aggressively planted there – as a way of overwhelming our native way of thinking? I mean, why had our history as a nation – in many ways a glorious history – now become a source of shame? Why were we now so plainly guilty of so many past sins, and apparently such a bunch of odious bastards as well? And why, for that matter, did we have to "respect" alien beliefs and practices which, if not medieval in nature, were corrosive to anybody's spiritual well-being. And then why were we obliged to consider reserve and dignity as qualities to be avoided? And why did we have to worship at the altar of celebrity? And why did we have to pay homage to the half-baked ideas of youth, when we all knew that when we were youthful, our ideas were barely even browned on the surface? Wisdom hadn't suddenly broken out in the minds of the young, but we were expected to believe it had. And not just shake our heads in disbelief…'

Here, Derek stopped and his eyes fell to the floor.

'Uhm,' he continued, 'maybe I've said a little more than I should have. You must think I'm a terrible person; somebody who's long overdue for a much-needed visit from the thought police. Or even from the real police. After all, much of what I've said could land me in court…'

Here, he hesitated just a second before carrying on.

'You know, looked at another way, it's not England that had become the problem, but me. I, and many like me, had become obsolete; subversive dinosaurs who should have had the decency to fade away before this new England with its new population and its new ideas had installed itself so firmly. We had all passed our use-by dates and turned into toxic, shrivelled bigots, fit only to be ignored or despised. And certainly, without any valid claim on the country we no longer recognised as our own…'

Alex wasn't sure what to say, so he picked up on Derek's comment about landing in court.

'I don't think you'll end up before the beak,' he observed. 'And not only because there aren't any courts any more, but also because I doubt any of your fellow passengers would report you. Your views are hardly unique, Derek; just generally unspoken. And for the very reasons you've alluded to. They're not allowed any more. Or they *weren't* allowed any more. Not in what, until very recently, was a country with multiple cultures but with only one single authorised way of thinking. So, I now know exactly what you meant when you talked about *your* England disappearing some time ago, and you will not be surprised to learn that I've had some very similar thoughts myself. Although I will still miss a sunny Spring day and a misty Autumn morning...'

Derek smiled broadly. He clearly knew that he was in the company of a fellow 'nonconformist'. And whilst he must have suspected as much before, it had now been confirmed beyond doubt.

Alex finally left his friend to rejoin Debbie in their cabin, and then to accompany her to the bar. Neither of them could summon up an appetite for even a light lunch, and instead they decided to dip into their drinks ration for the day, and partake of just a few salted nuts. It was a good decision, and it enabled Alex to further debate with just his wife what they'd been told by Stuart over breakfast, and to tell her of his discussion with Derek, none of which surprised her in the least.

Neither was she surprised when, back in their cabin, Alex announced that he'd be paying a visit to the stern of the ship for a little birdwatching while she embarked on another book – and while a good number of the ship's passengers assembled in the lounge for an impromptu presentation on navigation aids. Roy wasn't among their number, because he was already at the stern of the *Sea Sprite*. He was standing on the Marco Polo's rear observation deck, binoculars in hand, and a big welcoming smile on his face when he saw Alex arrive.

'Ah, been kicked out, eh?' he asked as Alex approached him. And then he informed Alex that he'd just missed a black-browed albatross, a fly-past of some slender-billed prions, and two blonde-haired mermaids. Alex responded with the observation that the two mermaids probably wouldn't have been true blondes, and then quickly switched the conversation to China. He wanted Roy to know what Stuart had imparted over breakfast.

Roy's reaction to this denouement was not that different from that of Derek's. It was as though he'd just had a series of long-standing suspicions confirmed, and he seemed more pensive than surprised. He also expressed the view that what the Chinese had done was hardly an example of aberrant behaviour; more, it was just another manifestation of mankind's unparalleled idiocy and its immeasurable arrogance. He then went on to amplify this opinion by telling Alex that, for the last thirty years, he had been convinced that humanity was on course to destroy either every other species on the planet or itself. That he had observed the way it had bred out of control and pushed all those other species to the margins, and had wondered what would be the ultimate result of this blind and selfish behaviour: its own extermination, or that of the natural world? Increasingly, he'd thought it would be the former. With the world divided into nation states, more and more of which were run by autocrats or out-and-out monsters – and fewer and fewer of which were prepared to cooperate for the common good – he could see the undoing of humanity arriving well before it had managed to undo the well-being of all its fellow creatures. And now it had happened. Not quite in the way he had expected – a pathogenic obliteration of all humans or their frying themselves in a nuclear conflagration – but by some sort of incontinent fungus ripped straight from the pages of a trashy sci-fi novel. Oh-so-clever mankind, nil. Dumb, unthinking fungus, one. With no replay on offer. What an end! And what a fitting end to a species whose hallmark was hubris. If it weren't all so desperate, it would be a hoot.

Alex listened to Roy's views on his fellow man with the interest they deserved, but was then left with a couple of questions in his mind. And now he had to ask them.

'Roy,' he said, 'how do I reconcile what you've just told me with your expressed enthusiasm for your "new adventure"? You know, what you said last night about not being able to wait to see what the next few days have in store. Oh, and you seem to have written off mankind entirely, whereas last night you were confident that we on this ship would survive. And I think that means…'

'There's nothing to lose,' interrupted Roy. 'What I've thought for thirty years has come to pass. And those few of us still left alive might as well enjoy what we can while we can. And we may indeed survive. In fact, I think there's a fairly strong likelihood that we will survive for quite some time. And I mean for quite a few years. But that's just us, Alex. Not the other seven-point-something billion people who are no longer with us. And, in case you haven't noticed, I think the *Sea Sprite* might have a bit of a problem in becoming the cradle for a new generation; you know, one that might go on to repopulate our currently empty world. You see, by my reckoning there are only a handful of women on this ship who could produce children. Even if they could be convinced to do so. Which means that even if we survive, we will probably be the end of the line. Mankind's fucked. We're not. Yet. And for as long as we're here, let's make the most of it.'

Roy had supplied Alex with a comprehensive response to his questions, and also with a great deal of food for thought. In particular, he had brought to Alex's attention that he, Alex, had forged a close relationship with two people on this ship (and probably three if, as likely, Elaine shared Derek's views) who had not much more than an academic interest in their own survival, and who had certainly shed barely a tear for the billions of their fellow humans who had already lost their chance to survive.

In a peculiar way, he found this rather reassuring and comforting. He wasn't quite as indifferent to his own fate as they were, and he was definitely very concerned about the fate of his wife. But maybe he ought to be a little more resigned to whatever might happen. After all, he and Debbie had both had a very good three-score years and ten – and more. And life wasn't everything. It was just what one became used to…

Meanwhile, however, there was the practical and the mundane to attend to, and that included stoking up on a few more calories, this time in the form of a rather tasty Spaghetti Bolognese followed by a sticky toffee pudding. This feast was, unsurprisingly, shared with Derek, Elaine and Roy, but what was not shared was the content of Alex's earlier exchanges with Derek and Roy. Instead the conversation ranged far and wide and took in China's behaviour, the rapid evaporation of so much of human civilisation, and the challenges that might face all those aboard the *Sea Sprite* over the next few days.

Alex participated fully in this debate, albeit he found himself evaluating everything he heard within the context of the earlier revelations on the subjects of both home and humanity. None of which he would easily forget…

twenty-five

Alex was cutting into his second rasher of bacon when Jane's voice came through the tannoy. She was a little late this morning, but still in time to give her charges plenty of notice that, in about twenty minutes' time, the *Sea Sprite* would be passing just to the east of Elephant Island. Given its place in Antarctic history and its status as the marker for the imminent arrival of the Antarctic proper, she was clearly eager to ensure that none of those aboard missed it, even if there would be no opportunity to see it at close quarters. That would have been possible with the zodiacs had the *Sea Sprite* still been carrying amateur explorers, and not, as it was now, a group of amateur survivalists.

As Jane completed her announcement with the news that there would be a regular presentation at 10.30 (on *The Seals of the Antarctic*) and an irregular presentation at 3pm (on *The Deception Island raiding plan*), Alex set to work with his knife and fork with more urgency than before. Whilst his and Debbie's present breakfast companions – a smiley pair of retired lecturers from Worksop – had proved pleasingly good company, he was now keen to finish his meal so as to be back in his cabin in plenty of time for the promised Elephant Island transit. He really wanted to see what the majority of the *Endeavour's* crew had been obliged to live on for so many months.

It was grim. The *Sea Sprite* was now only a few hundred yards off Elephant Island, and it looked to Alex like the sort of place that would never be chosen as even a transient refuge, let alone somewhere one might want to spend several months of one's life. It was, after all, no more than a large snow-streaked rocky outcrop surrounded by a scum of sea ice. And worse still, it was currently half hidden behind a curtain of half-hearted sleet and snow. It couldn't have looked more uninviting.

It was the first time Alex had seen any precipitation on this voyage, and he wondered whether there was something about Elephant Island's position, or maybe its jagged profile, that induced such a dreary veiling of its form. And, if so, what that must have meant for all those left-behind members of Shackleton's crew as they huddled together in the shelter of their (second) upturned lifeboat for all those days and weeks. And then he wondered how the hell they had managed to find a spit of land that could accommodate their makeshift home. All Alex could see from his cabin-balcony vantage point were the rocky slopes that made up the island, entering the surrounding sea at an angle of more than forty-five degrees. Nowhere was there a beach or even a stretch of gently-inclined ground.

This topography hadn't, however, discouraged a multitude of chinstrap penguins from choosing this place to raise their young. There were hundreds of them, all visible through binoculars, and all clearly demonstrating their preference for elevated nesting sites and their indifference to the effort required to reach these sites. They were obviously very hardy types, just as the snowy sheathbills were very inquisitive types, and so much so that they were not averse to visiting ships as they passed their island home – and landing within just feet of their startled passengers. One had now alighted on the handrail of Alex and Debbie's balcony lookout, and was providing them with their first close-up view of this unusual bird. With its pink face, its yellow-grey bill, and the general appearance of an all-white cross between a pigeon and a chicken, it was certainly not the most handsome bird on the planet. But, in a way, it was still enchanting, simply because it was so nosy and so precocious, spending most of its life exploiting any feeding opportunities that presented themselves in a penguin colony, but also a little time exploiting any feeding opportunities that might present themselves on a passing vessel. Even if that meant indulging in a reckless proximity to that vessel's much larger creatures. Or was it really reckless? Observing this particular snowy sheathbill on the handrail, Alex began to think that these birds were not visiting ships such as the *Sea Sprite* just for food, but also for the opportunity to experience an encounter with a species of animal not found on Elephant Island since Shackleton's survivors left it. After all, this close-by bird did seem to have more interest in him and Debbie than it did in the prospect of something to eat somewhere else.

However, all too soon, he (or she) was gone, and so too was Elephant Island and its little clutch of smaller outlying islets. The *Sea Sprite* was now on its way to a whole string of equally inhospitable islands, otherwise known as the South Shetlands. The first of these was still not in view when Alex and Debbie made their way to the lounge to hear John deliver his talk on the various seals that might be encountered as the *Sea Sprite* travelled even further south. Fur seals and elephant seals, his audience would already know. Crabeater seals, Weddell seals and leopard seals, most of them would not. Nor how these three very different seals went about making a living. Soon, however, they would. And the first seal to have its habits exposed was the crabeater.

This chap, as was apparent from an image now being projected onto the lounge's two screens, is a large, rather slender-looking seal with a small head and a doglike muzzle. And rather disappointingly, it doesn't eat crabs. Instead, as John made clear, it consumes copious amounts of krill, foraging largely at night, and so successfully that it is reckoned that it is now the world's most abundant large mammal. According to John, there could be up to seventy-five million of these creatures, all of them in the Antarctic. Alex was impressed, and then further impressed when John moved on to discuss the Weddell seal.

This guy is apparently noticeably fatter than the crabeater seal, and tends to be solitary whereas its crabeater cousin is fairly gregarious. It also has a rather 'feline' face which, with upturned corners to its mouth, creates a somewhat Cheshire-cat-like smile. But what really sets the Weddell seal apart from the crabeater and all other seals is its wintertime habits. Seals need to breathe. They are, after all, mammals. To do this in the Antarctic winter, when pack ice almost doubles the size of the continent, seals have to migrate further and further away from the land mass, in order to keep ahead of the expanding cover of frozen sea. But not so the Weddell. It stays put and survives by creating breathing holes in the pack ice, which it then keeps open by constantly gnawing away at the freshly forming ice. This strategy gives it the great advantage of having exclusive access to its food source while at the same time being able to avoid its principal predators, as both killer whales and leopard seals will have disappeared to open water. Unfortunately, this advantage is eventually overtaken by an inevitable problem. The canines and incisors of these creatures do not last forever, and those of old adults ultimately wear down to the point where they become useless. No longer can the breathing holes be maintained, and the seals drown. It was undeniable, thought Alex (not for the first time), that the beauty of nature had an undesirable flip side: one of uncompromising cruelty.

This feature was also apparent in John's description of his third subject, which was the leopard seal. This guy is the scary seal; a large, fearsome-looking creature with a huge, snake-like head and a mouth which, when open, reveals a pair of jaws equipped with numerous sharp teeth. These it uses to catch and dispatch its favourite food: penguins. And, given the opportunity, to bite off the hands of careless visitors to its domain. As John explained, when travelling in a zodiac in Antarctica, one should never dangle one's hands in the water. Leopard seals not only occasionally bite the rubber of the zodiacs, but they are not unknown to try for the flesh of any nearby fingers. Needless to say, 'swimming with leopard seals' was not to be advised either. One might easily suffer a lethal attack before one froze to death…

Back in their cabin – and having taken in their first view of the distant Shetland Islands – Alex and Debbie acknowledged the quality of John's presentation, and its ability to so successfully distract them from their current precarious predicament. They were, after all, still on a not-so-magical mystery tour, and after another modest lunch and an even more modest siesta, this fact would stare them in the face. Just as soon, that is, as the raiding-plan briefing had got under way.

Everybody was again gathered in the lounge: all those signed up as volunteers, all those who had offered their services but who had been rejected (generally on the grounds of lack of fitness or lack of stature), and all those who had declined the invitation to assist in the raiding of the research stations. Proceedings then kicked off with Captain José coughing into his microphone and, when he'd secured everybody's attention, greeting them with a series of varied thanks.

'Good afternoon, everybody,' he started, 'and thank you for coming. I'm pleased to see that we have ourselves a completely full house. And I particularly want to thank those of you who have volunteered to help out in our… provisioning runs. I am more than grateful. Because I have more of you than I can possibly use, as will become apparent very soon. And, of course, I want to give a special thanks to all those members of my crew and all those members of the expedition team who have agreed to lead the errh… provisioning parties. And you won't be surprised to learn that again we had more volunteers for this than we could actually use. And that leading these guys – and organising the whole *campaign* – will be none other than our far-from-diminutive ex-Royal Marine, Mike. Which, I can tell you, is my cue to ask him to come and take this microphone and to spell out how we'll be going about relieving the first two research stations of their otherwise redundant provisions…'

Immediately, the *very* far-from-diminutive Mike rose from his seat at the front of the auditorium and took the microphone from José's hand. Then he addressed the lounge.

'Right. As my first sergeant used to say, "Keep it simple and keep it short. That way, even the bright 'uns will remember it." So, here's our plan, in three simple and very short steps.

'Step one. Captain José will park the *Sea Sprite* in the middle of Deception Island. Because, as I'm sure you'll all now know, Deception Island is what remains of a huge volcano, and its centre is now an enormous flooded caldera, quite big enough to take a whole flotilla of *Sea Sprites*. Just as the caldera rim is quite big enough to provide a home to two tasty research stations, one Spanish and one Argentinian.

'OK. Step two. When in position, all ten of our zodiacs will be lowered into the water…'

And here he stopped to check that behind him there were now two screens showing a row of three circles at their top with, below these, a further row of three circles and, below these, a row of four circles.

'Right. Zodiacs one, two and three – those three at the top of the screens – will be used to lead our first "foraging" operation, and the target of this operation will be the Argentinian research station. The Spaniards, ladies and gentlemen, will just have to wait. OK, zodiacs four, five and six – those in the middle there – they will be held back and will only join the "assault" when the landing has been secured by zodiacs one, two and three. And I mean by that, when we have made quite sure that there is no reception committee to deal with. No matter how improbable that might be. And as regards zodiacs seven, eight, nine and ten – those at the bottom of the screens – well, they will be held in reserve. They will be in the water, near our stern, each with its designated crew. But I don't anticipate that they will do any more than simply "stand by". Unless, of course, there are any unforeseen circumstances, in which case we may be very glad we have them.

'Right. Step three. When zodiacs one to six are in position at the research station, the foraging will commence. Remember, those of us in the first three zodiacs will have established that the station is clear of personnel, and the job in hand will be to "open up" the stores and transfer their contents to the waiting zodiacs. And this will be done in an orderly fashion, with zodiacs four, five and six being used as the initial transports back to the ship, and then zodiacs one, two and three being loaded for their trip back, and so on alternately until all the stores are back aboard the *Sea Sprite*. I don't know how many trips this might involve because I don't know how many goodies there might be to collect. But it doesn't matter. We will just proceed with this simple shuttle service until we've emptied the whole place. And then we'll adopt exactly the same procedure for the second research station: the Spanish one. And we'll deploy the same personnel as well; the personnel I'm now about to show you...'

This was what Alex really wanted to hear. After all, he might be one of those personnel…

'OK, let me deal with zodiacs one, two and three first…'

Behind Mike on the two screens, the circles had now been replaced with three numbered lists of three names apiece. These were clearly the nine people who would make up the three-man crews of the first three zodiacs. Alex's name was not amongst them.

'Right. As you will not be surprised to learn, I will be the leader in zodiac one, Terry the leader in zodiac two, and the very capable John will lead zodiac three…'

(And Gill will not be leading any of them, thought Alex.)

'Now, each of us will have two others with us, and I'm happy to say that Captain José's guys have been fighting for these places. And with only six places available, we had to ask some of them to lead or crew the other zodiacs. Anyway, all these guys are not just eager participants, but most of them, of course, are proper sailors. And whilst you might not recognise these six names here, or many of those that follow, I'm sure you'll recognise them when you see them tomorrow. And they'll be the backbone of our operation.

'And I think we can now look at zodiacs four, five and six…'

The screens changed and three more numbered lists appeared. Alex's name was again not there, but Roy's was. He was one of the crew on zodiac number five, one of three Dad's Army volunteers who would be joining three of the expedition team in supporting three regular crew members in their roles as leaders of the second rank of zodiacs. Alex didn't know whether to be jealous or relieved. However, when Mike had completed his brief commentary on zodiacs four, five and six, the screen changed again to show the crews of the final, reserve rank of zodiacs. And there he was: Able Seaman Alex, one-third of the company of zodiac number nine; a zodiac apparently being led by a guy with an unmistakably Filipino name, and with another crew member with an unmistakably British name – as in P. J. Smith. He recognised neither of these names, but he did recognise that he now felt just a little bit queasy and a little bit scared. Possibly, he thought, because he had much less faith in his own abilities than he did in those of two people he didn't even know. But that he would have to resolve conclusively later. Because Mike was still talking, and Alex needed to concentrate on what he was saying.

'I promised to keep this short, but before I hand back to Captain José, I need to say just two more things. The first is that if any of you volunteers who haven't been selected feel rather aggrieved – and that's probably going to be quite a few of you – do bear in mind that there are another two research stations that will need our attention in due course. So, you may have a turn even yet. And, of more immediate importance – for those of you who *have* been selected – please don't think that I've forgotten to brief you on the detail of your roles. That will be the responsibility of your zodiac leaders tomorrow, when, quite frankly, you're less likely to forget what you've been told. Just make sure you listen out for announcements tomorrow, which will tell you when and where to assemble. And make sure you report for duty on time and kitted out with all your outside gear – and, of course, your lightweight life jacket as well. And then...

well, just make bloody sure you listen to what you're being told. Which I'm sure will be delivered in commendably short and simple terms.

'So that's it. Unless, of course, anyone has any sensible questions...'

Nobody spoke, and Mike was just about to hand back the microphone to José when somebody did.

'I think I've got one.'

It was Roy. Alex thought him very brave.

Mike glared at him, but with a nod of his head he then invited him to carry on.

'Erhh... when we've completed the Argentinian "clear-out", will there be a break before we tackle the next one?'

'Good question,' responded a now smiling Mike. 'I'm glad you asked that. And the answer is "probably". But it'll depend on how the first "clear-out" goes. If it all works smoothly and we're not too knackered, we might just carry on. If not, we'll almost certainly take a break. So, I'm sorry I can't give you a firm answer, but thanks anyway for asking the question. It shows initiative. It'll go in my report.'

This conclusion to Mike's response caused a wave of laughter around the room – and a discernible wave of embarrassment across Roy's face. And Mike was still smiling broadly when he finally handed back the meeting to the captain. He, Captain José, had little to do other than to inform everybody that in a few hours' time he would be mooring the *Sea Sprite* off Half Moon Island, a tiny island towards the southern end of the South Shetlands, and here it would rest overnight. Weather permitting, he would then take the ship into the Deception Island caldera so that it was in position for the deployment of the zodiacs by midmorning. And that, to ensure that all went well with this deployment, there would be a choice of two desserts with this evening's meal, and, for those who liked it, a modest portion of Stilton and a glass of port. And the port would not be deducted from anybody's alcohol ration.

This announcement was received extremely well, and the meeting broke up with everyone seemingly in good mood. Other than Debbie. Only two women passengers had been chosen to participate in tomorrow's morning diversion (and only, like Alex, as ballast for the reserve zodiacs), and she wasn't one of them. Alex knew he would have to tread carefully for the rest of the day.

This he did, especially over dinner, during which he took every opportunity to steer the conversation away from tomorrow's 'liberation activities' and into any other area of debate he could think of. This wasn't too difficult, as his and Debbie's regular table companions seemed more than eager to enjoy their meal and avoid any discussion – or thoughts – about what might happen in a few hours' time. The newly marinised Roy was particularly helpful in this endeavour, in that on this occasion he revealed that he wasn't just a walking encyclopaedia but also an accomplished mimic. His impersonations of both Derek and Alex were remarkable, although possibly not quite so remarkable as his impersonation of Jane. He could even do her tannoy voice as well as her lounge voice. And, in a very strange way, even look like her...

So, when the port and Stilton arrived at the table, spirits were understandably high, and they were about to get higher. And this was because Derek had soon suggested that it would be a good idea to use the port to propose a toast. And the toast would be: 'To Mike and his band of brigands.

May they all have success.'

When this toast had then been conducted, the spirits of all five diners were indeed lifted even higher, not least because they now believed that Mike and his band of brigands were no doubt assured of success.

And how, thought Alex, could they possibly not be…?

twenty-six

Alex managed a black coffee and a single Ryvita smeared with Marmite. And even that was a struggle. In fact, so much so that it occurred to him that he hadn't experienced such an acute loss of appetite since his schooldays. Then, before every competitive cross-country race (he'd been one of his grammar school's 'star' runners), he'd find himself unable to eat. It seemed that the butterflies in his stomach had required some room in which to fly. And very clearly, they still did. Acute trepidation, it appeared, still had the same effect on his body. Even if, on this occasion, he wouldn't be required to drag himself over three or four miles of damp English countryside, but instead just sit in a 'reserve' zodiac and watch other people do some work. It was they, he reminded himself, who should be experiencing some acute trepidation – and maybe a huge cloud of restless butterflies.

Eventually, with Debbie's help, he was able to convince himself that there was little to concern him. And not long after breakfast he had the best distraction possible from any concerns that still remained, and this was the *Sea Sprite's* entrance into Deception Island's caldera.

Captain José had now brought his vessel south from its overnight mooring off Half Moon Island, and Deception Island had finally come into view. At a distance, it looked like an 'ordinary' island, with a curve of near-vertical cliffs rising from the sea and no indication whatsoever of its very out-of-the-ordinary interior. But as the *Sea Sprite* approached, a gap in its cliff walls became apparent. Not a big gap, but a gap just large enough to allow a sizeable vessel – such as the *Sea Sprite* – to pass through and to enter its remarkable water-filled centre.

Within a very short time, Captain José was sailing his ship through the lyrically named 'Neptune's Bellows', that one small part of the caldera walls that had collapsed, allowing a huge helping of the Southern Ocean to rush through and flood the former volcano's entire interior. And this interior was absolutely stunning. It was a gigantic walled 'lagoon' – over six miles in length and over four miles wide – and it was overwhelmingly grey and white. The water in the lagoon was a bluish grey, reflecting the blue-grey of the sky above. The ash-covered walls of the caldera were dark grey, mottled and streaked with the white and grey-white of snow. And the abandoned whaling station, near the entrance to the caldera, was just various shades of grey, with just a hint of the red of rust. There wasn't much of this place left; just a shabby-looking (grey) hangar – from a time when small planes made use of a tiny spit of land in the caldera to bring in provisions – and a jumble of collapsing (grey) buildings that once housed probably grey-looking whalers.

They had long gone, and the only people still making use of this extraordinary middle-of-the-ocean haven were the sometime occupants of the two research stations that were the object of the *Sea Sprite's* visit. Hopefully, none of these fellows would be in residence today...

Both stations were situated on the southern side of the caldera. So, it wasn't until Captain José began to turn his vessel that Alex and Debbie caught sight of these outposts from their cabin-balcony lookout. When the *Sea Sprite* was then in position – facing its exit back through Neptune's Bellows – they were finally able to examine them in detail with the use of binoculars, and discover that they were very different in appearance. And not grey. The Argentinian station was a cluster of simple red-painted sheds, each with a prominent blue-and-white Argentinian flag painted on its front or its roof – or on both. (Nobody was to be left in any doubt as to who had put a stake in the ground here.) The Spanish station was maybe half a mile away from its Argentinian neighbour and to the naked eye it had the appearance of two railway carriages coupled together, both with grey sides and yellow-and-red roofs. However, with the use of those binoculars again, it could be seen that the 'carriages' were just more conventional wooden constructions – with roofs that were giant, painted Spanish flags (of course) – surrounded by a number of smaller buildings and shipping containers, all covered in the same red paint as used next door. Perhaps, thought Alex, there had been a job lot on offer from a passing paint salesman, who was also able to supply the requisite yellow, white and blue paints for all those prominent national flags. He also thought that there was now no doubt that establishing a presence on Deception Island was much more to do with nationalism than it was with science. He just hoped that the stations being 'statements' rather than their having any real purpose didn't preclude their housing some worthwhile provisions...

He was still thinking these thoughts when a voice came through the tannoy. It wasn't Jane's, and it wasn't very cheery. Instead it was a male voice, and without any preamble it commanded the 'zodiac volunteers' to report to the Columbus Deck lounge, suitably attired, in twenty minutes' time.

Alex's trepidation reasserted itself, but only briefly. After a hug from Debbie, he was soon feeling surprisingly self-assured and more than eager to get himself to the designated assembly point as soon as possible. Minutes later he was there – with a gaggle of other Dad's Army volunteers, including Roy – and minutes after this he was being issued with an arm-band. His had a number nine marked on it – to match his zodiac number – and Roy's a number five. And when everyone had been supplied with this required sartorial adornment, a young man, whom Alex thought he recognised as the ship's purser, made a short announcement to the effect that, in reverse numerical order, all volunteers were to make their way down to the Magellan Deck landing stage at the stern of the ship. There, they would present themselves to their respective zodiac leaders, all of whom would be wearing similar numbered armbands, and who would then provide them with all the instructions they would need.

Being a number nine, Alex was soon on his way. And it wasn't long before he'd been installed on his own rubber craft – with his leader, who was one of the Filipino engineers by the name of Joshua, and with the other passenger volunteer, who was none other than the bolshie Welshman! Inexplicably, his name was Patrick, and for his time on the zodiac he had clearly decided to abandon his 'challenging' nature and instead settle for a mix of deference and bonhomie. Deference to his leader, and bonhomie in his dealings with Alex. This wasn't ideal for Alex, but it could have been a lot worse. And, in any event, there was plenty going on that required his attention. In the first place, his and the other three reserve zodiacs, all of which had now been loaded with their own crews, were being moved away from the landing stage to allow the six 'foraging' zodiacs to be loaded with their crews. It was as this was going on, and as Alex was being given his instructions (which were essentially to do nothing), that he realised that there was no sign whatsoever of Stuart and Gill's battered yacht. The captain, he thought, must have decided that it was futile to keep a wreck in tow indefinitely, and at some point must have let it go, or scuttled it, or done to it whatever one does to unwanted marine vessels in these parts. And although he had no connection with this particular vessel, Alex felt a distinct pang of regret. It was as though their mission had suffered its first casualty, and worse, the said casualty had now been abandoned and soon it would be as if it had never existed.

Fortunately, these maudlin musings were short-lived, because he had now caught sight of Captain José standing on the Columbus Deck together with a couple of his officers and a couple of Jane's people. He had a loudhailer in his hand, and he was observing the loading exercise being conducted just beneath him. So too were what looked to be most of the ship's company not involved in this process, and they were crowded together at the back of both the Marco Polo Deck and the Erikson Deck, some of them with binoculars and some of them with cameras. Indeed, why not, thought Alex. What was about to happen was not an everyday event, and it was hardly surprising that people would want to have a very good view of it or capture it on their devices for future reference. Indeed, he spotted Debbie among the throng on the Erikson Deck, leaning on the deck's handrail with her binoculars around her neck. Her focus seemed to be on the zodiacs currently being loaded, namely zodiacs one, two and three. Numbers four, five and six had already received their crews and were now 'holding station' while the front-rank trio were being furnished with their more professional crews – and a number of added extras.

Alex had now joined Debbie in watching the loading of these final zodiacs, and noticed that each was receiving not just three people, but a significant number of inanimate objects, such as crowbars, hammers, sledgehammers and wire cutters. In addition to these 'foraging aids', both Mike's zodiac and Terry's zodiac also received a large canvas bag that clanked when it was stowed. And Alex wondered whether these contained some sort of weapons, and if they did, what might trigger their use...

He might very soon find out. Because already Mike's zodiac was moving away from the *Sea Sprite,* and then, just seconds later, Terry's and John's zodiacs began to follow it as it made a beeline for the Argentinian research station. And as this was no more than five hundred yards away, it wouldn't be long before all three zodiacs were at their intended destination. Everybody on the ship – and in the other seven zodiacs – was watching them intently, and in silence. And all those with binoculars probably had them trained on Mike's lead zodiac as it slowed in its approach to the research station's small jetty in order to allow its companion craft to join it. Clearly Mike wanted to conduct a team landing, and the jetty was certainly large enough to allow this.

So, all three inflatables were now side by side, and in each vessel their crews were standing up in readiness to leap onto the jetty just as soon as this was within leaping distance. It all looked to be going very well indeed; a bunch of professional men, performing actions they'd probably performed a thousand times before, and probably in far less benign circumstances than they were dealing with today. The water in the lagoon was still pleasingly calm, and there was certainly no hostile reception committee. No one had appeared from inside any of the station's huts, and it now seemed inconceivable that they would. In fact, just about as inconceivable as Mike suddenly collapsing onto the floor of his zodiac, to be joined just seconds later by his two crewmates. Then it happened in Terry's zodiac: all three in this craft collapsed simultaneously, just before John and his own crew succumbed – with one of them falling into the water.

There was an audible gasp from all those gathered at the stern of the *Sea Sprite*. And then someone on the Erickson Deck – equipped with a pair of binoculars – let out a cry. 'They're all writhing around,' he shouted. 'They're all… they're all dying!'

He'd hardly finished this anguished announcement when Captain José's voice came through the loudhailer. He was still at the back of the Columbus Deck, and he'd clearly seen what had happened with his own eyes.

'All passengers back to your cabins and seal them, now. And I mean now! Then wait for further instructions.'

Then he leant over the handrail and addressed all those below him without the use of the hailer.

'Get those zodiacs secured ASAP. And then all of you back inside ASAP. We start engines in sixty seconds. So, move! Move now!'

Here, he turned his attention to those just beside him and began to bark some instructions. They were clearly being told to get the *Sea Sprite* away in double-quick time, and probably to make sure that it was as much sealed as it possibly could be. And just as clearly, all the guys below him were doing their very best to carry out his commands. With almost military efficiency.

Alex found himself being swept along by the desperate urgency of it all, and was even able to help with the rapid tethering of his own zodiac before disembarking even more rapidly and haring off to the possible safety of the ship's interior.

Apart from being impressed by the speed of his and everyone else's reactions, he was also impressed – and surprised – by how soon the captain was able to set in motion his formerly stationary vessel. Alex heard its engines rumbling into life as he was ascending the metal stairs to the deck above, and even before he'd stepped into the main lounge, he felt the ship's movement as it began its desperate attempt to outpace the spores. Because that's what it was doing. The fungal spores had now arrived in Deception Island, and, having bestowed a long, drawn-out, miserable death on nine of the *Sea Sprite's* company – and nine of its most able – they were no doubt now on their way to deliver a dose of purgatory to the rest before taking their lives as well. Alex, and all those aboard this vessel, might have only minutes to wait until they too were cut down. Or they might just escape.

Well, nothing else horrible had happened by the time Alex joined his wife in their cabin – and embraced her a little too tightly. But both of them were hardly at ease.

'Jesus,' he remarked as he loosened his grip, 'that was so fucking awful…'

'I know,' responded Debbie shakily. 'I had my binocs on them, and… well, it was really horrible. They all looked to be in so much pain. And so quickly. It's just… well… I mean, how can anything work that fast?'

'Search me. But I'm bloody glad old José knows all about "fast" as well. Talk about shit off a shovel…'

Alex was right. The *Sea Sprite* was accelerating in a way that he and Debbie had not experienced before. And the throbbing from its engines was intense. It was no wonder, then, that when they'd gathered themselves just enough to peer out of their cabin window, their pocket cruise ship was already on its way out of the caldera, racing at an entirely inappropriate speed through Neptune's Bellows. Alex was very relieved to see this, albeit marginally distracted by the hundreds of entirely undistracted chinstrap penguins confidently going about their business. For them, the priority was to make their way to their nesting site on the top of the caldera walls overlooking Neptune's 'doorway', and Alex doubted they would even register the flight of a passing vessel, even one travelling at such a reckless speed. It clearly meant no more to them than a passing squall.

Then it was past them. The *Sea Sprite* was now in the open ocean again, heading at speed towards the Antarctic, while all those on board were hoping that they would still be alive after the next few minutes.

They were. And they were still alive after twenty minutes, which was when Captain José chose to address them via the tannoy. It wasn't a long address, and consisted solely of a further command.

'This is your captain,' it stated. 'You are now *ordered* to stay in your cabins until further notice. Nobody must move around the ship.'

And that was it until, almost two hours later, Jane's voice came through the tannoy, not to issue another command but instead to offer some reassurance.

'Good afternoon, ladies and gentlemen,' she began. (And it was indeed after noon now.) 'Captain José has just asked me to assure you that we seem to have… well, escaped from the… erhh, situation in Deception Island, and we are now travelling at maximum speed towards the Antarctic Peninsula. And we will, of course, not be stopping until we are a long way further south. In the meantime, I would ask you to heed the instruction to stay where you are, and bear with us while we organise an afternoon snack. Which, all being well, should be delivered to your cabins within the next couple of hours. I'm sorry we can't offer you a normal lunch, but I'm sure you will understand. Instead, the intention is to organise a normal dinner for this evening, which will probably be served a little earlier than usual. Please be assured that the captain and his crew are doing everything they can to ensure your safety, but it will really help them if you conform to these arrangements, and,

I stress, stay where you are. Believe me, your cooperation will be greatly appreciated in what are these… rather testing times.'

Alex detected a slight quake in Jane's voice at the end of her message. It was hardly surprising, he thought. Just as it was hardly surprising that she had made no reference at all to the grisly deaths of nine of the ship's company, including three of her own team; nor to the possibility that a similar demise might overtake those who remained at any time. Even before that promised afternoon snack. Alex would have taken the same approach: focus on the positive and the mundane, and avoid any mention of how Hell on Earth had just gobbled up a number of one's friends, and was now, no doubt, snapping at the heels of all those still to be gobbled. No, that was something that could wait for a chat over this evening's dinner. If there were any passengers still alive to attend this evening's dinner…

There were. Everybody on board was still well, and their situation looked increasingly secure. Deception Island was now far to the north, and as every minute passed, the *Sea Sprite* was getting closer to the refuge of Antarctica. If only, thought Alex, it hadn't stopped on its way there.

That thought was debated over dinner – by the normal gang of five, none of whom, as they freely admitted, could really get to grips with the sights they had witnessed only a few hours before. None of them had even seen anybody die before, let alone embark on a near eternity of suffering before they reached a longed-for demise. It had been truly terrible, and so terrible that Roy expressed the hope that the eight who hadn't fallen into the water immediately had been able to throw themselves in very soon thereafter. That they'd retained enough sense and control of their bodies amidst all their suffering to realise that a rapid death in icy water was much to be preferred to a long, agonising crawl to death that could last for many hours.

Derek agreed with Roy's heartfelt hope, and then added that he also hoped that Captain José, and indeed all those aboard the *Sea Sprite*, would not succumb to any guilt for abandoning the brave nine. There had been nothing to do but scram, he insisted, and any rescue attempt would have been as futile as it would have been lethal to them all. And that wasn't a fanciful theory, or a sop to his table companions' possible latent guilt. It was a fact. As were the dreadful consequences of encountering those spores. It was now easier than ever to see why the world's population had been extinguished so quickly and so comprehensively. And why it was so vital that the *Sea Sprite* continued to make its way to the most inhospitable place on the planet. Even if it was now without nine of its most capable and courageous characters. And without the cargo of optimism and confidence it had carried at the start of the day…

twenty-seven

When Alex began to stir, the first thing that came to his mind was that he was still alive. It wasn't a thought he normally had as he became conscious, but there again he hadn't normally come close to death the previous day. So close that he'd witnessed nine others embarking on their own painful path to death, and then spent the next few hours in fear that the same fate would overtake him and his wife. It had all clearly left its mark, and now this recognition that he was still alive was joined by an unmistakable joy at being alive, blended with a residual fear that this joy might not last. He was now quite awake enough to realise that the threat to his life had only receded and not disappeared. That he, Debbie and all those aboard the *Sea Sprite* still faced the prospect of a sudden and awful demise.

He dwelt on this thought only until Debbie awoke beside him, when he then initiated a brief exercise in mutual reassurance, to be followed quickly by a mutual recognition that the *Sea Sprite* was not moving. The ship's stationary state caused Alex to get out of bed and look out of the cabin window, but all he could see outside was sea and sky. He therefore soon abandoned that task and began to embark on the mundane. He retired to the bathroom for a shave and a shower, and as he then got on with dressing, Debbie took over the bathroom and eventually emerged to prepare herself for the day – and to do a little pre-breakfast tidying up. There were clothes to sort out and the contents of a handbag to be audited – just as Alex needed to clean both his binoculars and his camera.

It was all very strange; this 'just carrying on', when the unimaginable had just happened and when the possibility of the unimaginable happening again was only too real. Finding oneself racked with painful convulsions leading to one's oblivion was no longer a theoretical rumination, but something that could occur at any minute and without any warning. It was no less than simply terrifying, but at the same time weirdly manageable. It must be similar to what it was like to be in a war, thought Alex. Especially something like the First World War, during which men had had to live for months on end in the knowledge that at any time a shell might land two feet away and reduce them to mincemeat and offal. And the only way to deal with that was to just get on with stuff and forget about the ever-present deadly threat. One might sort out one's rations – or one's handbag. Or one might clean one's kit – or one's binoculars. But what one would not do was become paralysed with fear and distil one's possibly final hours on this Earth into an unremitting period of mental torture. That wasn't the right thing to do, and only a fool would take that path, and not move on to his camera when he'd finally finished the cleaning of his binoculars.

Of course, there was a difference between Alex's situation and that of some cold, shivering private sitting in a trench in Flanders, and that was the fact that Alex was cocooned in luxury and had the immediate prospect of a beautiful cooked breakfast to further distract him from his perilous circumstances. And it was now time for him and Debbie to indulge themselves in that tempting first meal of the day.

It was as good as they'd anticipated, albeit the company was a bit of a surprise. It was Patrick, the remodelled Welshman, and his even more Welsh wife, Morag. This pair of short but thickset Celts had made a beeline for Alex and Debbie's table as soon as they'd entered the restaurant, and then Patrick had asked, in his new over-friendly manner, if he and his wife could join them. It had been impossible to refuse this request – from Alex's Number-nine-zodiac crewmate – and soon Patrick and Morag were sharing their breakfast and their thoughts with their slightly nonplussed companions. And most of the thoughts concerned the implications of yesterday's disastrous visit to Deception Island – and how this whole 'survival project' was likely to end.

Patrick had a lot to say. But it could be distilled into three principal points. The first was his concern that the *Sea Sprite* had not evaded what he referred to as 'the terror', but that its flight from Deception Island had merely deferred its inevitable arrival. (Which Alex thought was hardly a novel concern on this ship.) The second was that to optimise the chances of all those on board not being 'touched' by the terror, it would be sensible to focus on getting further south as quickly as possible, even if it meant no more foraging. Oh, and why was the ship not still sailing south now? Why was it inexplicably at rest? And the third point was that, even if they weren't touched by the terror for however long they stayed in the Antarctic, and even if it wasn't waiting for them when they returned to Ushuaia, what would they do then? What would a successful outcome to this project mean for their future? Would they *have* a future? Might what they were all involved in now just be completely futile?

Alex thought that this final point – what the future would look like in the post-*Sea Sprite* age – was, like the first one, hardly a novel concern. It was on everybody's mind. It had to be. However, for most if not for all on board the *Sea Sprite*, any consideration of this daunting unknown had so far been successfully sublimated into their dealing with the imperatives of the ship's flight to the south. They hadn't forgotten that they had a very uncertain future – at best – but they had allowed themselves to be consumed with the demands of their present circumstances and what needed to be done to ensure their immediate survival. Even those who weren't able to bring Derek and Roy's insouciant perspective to the matter, and who were mourning the passing of their old lives – and the lives of their children and their grandchildren – had, by and large, come to terms with the huge uncertainty of the future simply by immersing themselves in the multiple uncertainties of the present. And it really had worked. Up till now. However, given Patrick's 'third point' reservations expressed over breakfast, and particularly his reference to the possible futility of the captain's plan, would it continue to work? Would other people now be focusing on their possible return to Ushuaia, and what purpose this might or might not serve? Alex didn't know. Nor did he know whether any of Patrick's points would be addressed by Captain José in his next mandatory briefing. But he suspected they would be. Although not before he had addressed the loss of those nine good men…

It was another ten o'clock start and another full house in the lounge. However, this meeting was different. One could see it in the faces of all of those present, and one could hear it in Captain's José's voice. When he started to speak, it was with some difficulty and with a great deal of emotion. And why wouldn't it be? His first task was to acknowledge the sacrifice made by those nine men, and to call upon all those assembled to honour their memory for as long as they all lived.

There was soon a great deal of crying in the lounge, and even some loud, unconstrained sobbing. Alex had never before witnessed anything quite so painful and quite so raw. And quite so moving. Like most in the room, he had not known well any of those who had died, but he had seen them struck down. And they had been struck down in their brave attempt to help him and all the others still alive, and still with the hope of staying alive for at least a little time yet. And would any light now be shed on how realistic those hopes were? And what else, if anything, would the *Sea Sprite's* anxious passengers and crew now learn from Captain José, and would any of it be in any way encouraging?

Well, when he finally moved on from the appalling events of yesterday to his thoughts on the situation that prevailed today, he sounded pleasingly confident and like a leader who was still firmly in control. Better still, he was able to express the unequivocal view that the immediate danger had passed, and that all those aboard the *Sea Sprite* could rest assured that no calamity was about to overtake them. As he went on to explain, he, Stuart and all those aboard who had any understanding of meteorology and the behaviour of the atmosphere had together concluded that what had engulfed Mike and his colleagues in Deception Island was not a huge 'wall' of falling spores but a very small and very localised cloud of these microorganisms. And this cloud was separated by maybe tens or even hundreds of miles from the vast shroud of spores that enveloped the rest of the world. It was similar, he said, to wisps of foam ripped from the tops of waves by the wind and carried far into the air and far from the waves themselves. Only, here it was a tiny puff of deadly spores, and it was the erratic nature of the Earth's upper atmosphere that was doing the ripping, and then the casting of this unwelcome draught into Deception Island's caldera. It had to be, he emphasised. Because, if it had been the fallout from the main cloud that they had seen in action, it would no doubt have overwhelmed the *Sea Sprite* as well. Mike and his men had been incredibly unlucky. And José was now more than confident that no such terrible luck would pay them a second visit. All those in the lounge really could start to relax a little, and begin to refocus on the next chapter of their passage south, or possibly north...

This is where he switched to telling his audience where they were now and where they would soon be going. And as regards their current position... well, the *Sea Sprite* was currently some way to the west of Torgersen Island, which was, as he explained, one of the larger islands to the west of the Antarctic Peninsula and well south of Cierva Cove – which was where Captain José had planned his next foraging visit. He had wanted to get as far away from Deception Island as quickly as possible, he admitted, and he had therefore intentionally overshot his next scheduled port of call. Now, however, now that he and his 'advisers' were so sure that the spore menace was no longer a real threat, he intended to backtrack, far enough to make that foraging visit as originally planned. And that meant that the *Sea Sprite* would soon be on the move – north – until such time as it could turn east towards the peninsula proper, where it would then moor for the night in readiness for an early, next-day appointment with Cierva Cove's Argentinian research station. This establishment was, according to Stuart's information, one of the more substantial Argentinian stations and, in all probability, it would be stocked with a very attractive amount of provisions. It was not to be missed. Even if it meant taking the *Sea Sprite* and all those aboard it towards rather than away from the giant pall of peril that still shrouded the world.

It was like a rainbow of moods, thought Alex. At the beginning of the meeting, the mood in the lounge had been one of sombre reflection shot through with acute distress. Then, when Captain José had moved on to the remote likelihood of an imminent threat, the mood had changed to one of at least partial relief with maybe a soupçon of cautious elation. Following on from that, when the good captain had set out where they were and why they were there, the mood had moved on to one of enthralment. And now that he had announced that the *Sea Sprite* was to sail north, the mood had plunged into one of alarm and consternation. Could their sensible captain really be suggesting that they do the exact opposite of what everybody had signed up for: an uninterrupted voyage to the south, and as far south as the *Sea Sprite* could sensibly go?

It wasn't long before someone in the auditorium was giving voice to this new mood, and he did this by suggesting in a pretty blunt way that the prospect of getting closer to a deadly spectre of spores filled him with dread, and that he probably wasn't alone in this view. He wasn't. This was immediately apparent from the wave of concurring voices around the lounge. It looked to Alex as though Captain José might have a genuine mutiny on his hands.

However, José was clearly prepared for this reaction, just as he was clearly the ship's leader and no longer simply its captain. He very gently but very firmly made the point that he and those he relied upon for advice had weighed up all the risks, and had concluded that whatever risk was entailed in looping back to Cierva Cove was minor compared to the risk of heading further south without anything like enough provisions. And furthermore, by visiting the station at Cierva Cove, he would also be able to take the *Sea Sprite* to Paradise Bay, where there would be both shelter and the likelihood of finding even more provisions. If all those on board really wanted to sit out the dangers back in South America and the rest of the world, then, as he made very clear, they would need more provisions than were currently on this ship, and they would therefore need to accept his decision. Whether they liked it or not. He didn't remind them explicitly of his unchallengeable power as the ship's master, but this was implicit in all that he said. And ultimately, the potential mutiny fizzled out. Many were clearly still very concerned at this turn of events, but they would be able to do nothing about it, other than hope that the captain really had made the right decision. Just as they'd have to hope that this whole remarkable project was worth anything at all…

This was Patrick's third point: the possible futility of this voyage to nowhere. And now the captain, without any sort of prompting from his audience, was about to address this point. Very directly. And he started with a challenge. It was a brave move, because it could so easily have gone wrong. Especially as it needed only one voice to inflict what could possibly have been terminal damage. Nevertheless, his challenge was not only unequivocal but it was delivered in a distinctly uncompromising tone.

'Now, on a slightly different matter,' he started, 'is there anyone in this room who thinks that what we're doing at the moment – and I mean our seeking refuge in this very cold corner of the world – that this might amount to no more than just a waste of time? That it would be better and less painful for us all if we just called it a day and let events overtake us? Simply give in gracefully and then curl up and die?'

Nobody responded. Probably because nobody dared to respond. Which, no doubt, was what José had intended. So, drawing breath, he then embarked on what was almost an admonishment.

'OK. That's good. That's really good. Because I have to tell you that I did have my suspicions that there were certain people on this ship who were beginning to think that what we are doing is futile. That we're just deferring the inevitable and there is just no point in our carrying on. However, what I am hearing now – from your silence – is that, despite a number of understandable reservations, you are all firmly committed to a successful outcome to our endeavour. And that you all have confidence in its ultimate purpose. Which is for us to outlive those bloody spores!'

He now sounded quite angry, but he turned down the dial just a little before carrying on.

'You know, it doesn't matter that ultimately we may not be able to provide a future for our species. Although, of course, we may...'

Here, he paused and attempted to glare at every individual in the lounge.

'After all – and please forgive me for being so forthright – I do accept that we hardly constitute an ideal "breeding colony". And it might be quite a call to reboot the human race through just our own efforts. Or indeed even with the help of a handful of younger people who might still be alive in any of the research stations in Antarctica. Quite frankly, the likelihood of *Homo sapiens* becoming extinct within just a few years is still very high.

'But none of that really matters. We don't owe anything to our species – particularly taking account of what it has done – but we do owe a lot to ourselves. We have survived this long, and it would be criminal if we didn't try to survive for a great deal longer. And I don't mean just until we get back to Ushuaia, but I mean until we all start dropping off our perches through natural causes. We are a collection of living beings, and it is nothing less than our duty to stay that way for as long as possible. Which, my friends, should not by any means be that difficult.

'If, as promised by Stuart, these GM spores really are sterile and represent no more than a transient threat, and one that will have disappeared completely by the time we emerge from Antarctica – and if, as is likely, there will be more food and other resources in and around Ushuaia than we could possibly need for months if not years – then we can all look forward to flying the flag for humanity for a very long time yet. And may I just say that if you don't think you owe this to yourselves, then I hope you will think that you owe it to your children, to your grandchildren, to all those other relatives and friends whom you've lost – and to all those other souls who've been cut down in their billions. In fact, it's difficult to argue that, if to no one else, we owe a duty to survive and to live on to Mike and all those who met their end in Deception Island. It would be an insult to their memory to do other than come out of all this very much alive – with lots of life still to live. Even if we turn out to be the finale, the final act in the story of foolish mankind...'

Nobody said a word. Complete silence filled the room. Quite clearly everyone had been taken by surprise – and impressed by – Captain José's words. Here was a Panamanian captain who had not only taken on the mantle of leader but who had also been able to deliver a truly potent address – in his second language. Alex was certainly both surprised and impressed, and of the firm opinion that even Patrick might now be thinking that there was all the purpose in the world in seeing this bizarre excursion through to its end, and then making every effort to carry on after its conclusion. That it was nothing less than his duty – and the duty of all on this ship – not to give up. Ever. Even if it meant living in a society made up largely of ageing geriatrics – in a foreign land and with little to remind them of their former lives.

Debbie and Elaine had clearly listened to the captain's words as closely as Alex had. Because they were now discussing the possibility that José might have been a tad pessimistic in his assessment of the breeding credentials of the *Sea Sprite's* residual humans. It was now more than eight hours since he'd delivered that assessment, and Debbie and Elaine were sitting with their three usual companions at the dinner table, talking about reproduction in general and the impregnation of women by men in their eighties in particular. It was as they were deliberating this specific – as declared non-participating observers, and by reference to the success of a couple of well-known octogenarian rock stars – that Roy decided to join the debate.

He first agreed with them that there might well be a number of men on the *Sea Sprite* who were up to the job. And he then pointed out that most of the Filipino crew would certainly be able to step up to the plate even if most of the male passengers might be barely able to rise from their seats. However, the bigger problem, he suggested, was the paucity of suitable recipients for the vigour of all or any of those capable males. There might be as many as a dozen women of childbearing age on the ship, he conceded, or maybe even more. But he questioned whether any of them would submit themselves to becoming baby production units. And even if they did, and thereby produced a new (mostly Filipino) generation of children, would these children really be able to cope with the task of pairing off themselves, when they'd already be having to cope with the daunting demands of simply surviving in a devastated world?

As interesting as it was, this exchange finally began to run out of steam. So, Alex decided to bring it to a definitive conclusion by bringing up a completely new topic. He did this by asking all those around the table to name those elements of humanity that they were gratified no longer existed. In other words, whose death might legitimately be celebrated? This was a good move. Because the regeneration theme was immediately abandoned, and instead Roy leapt into the task of providing a whole battery of proposals in answer to Alex's novel question.

He started with all those monsters who used to harvest bile from caged bears, and then reeled off a whole list of other monsters who made it their job to abuse all sorts of other animals in every way imaginable. Elaine then chipped in with even more animal abusers, before Debbie reminded the company that there were many other monsters who routinely abused their fellow men – or, more often, women and girls. And so it went on, a feeding frenzy of sorts in which all those around the table made quite sure that their favourite fiends, ogres and monsters were included on the long roll of dishonour. All, that is, other than Derek. He appeared to be holding back, and it wasn't until Elaine suggested that he must have a few candidates himself that he finally spoke. When he did, he quickly introduced a rather different flavour to their hall of shame.

'Well, if you have no objection, I would very much like to include all those useless tossers who used to become political activists in a vain attempt to convince us all that they weren't just useless tossers. And all those vacuous idiots who used to populate the pages of weekend colour mags, and especially that cadre of tired and tiresome so-called feature writers whose faces would appear in every bloody issue. They were just so upsetting. Then I think there should also be room for all those insufferable practitioners of "wokeness", and all those equally insufferable "virtue signallers". And the selfie brigade. And all those billions of idiots who seemed to celebrate their ignorance. And human rights lawyers. And immigration lawyers. And all those dreadful celebs. Hell, I could go on and on. There were just so many…'

And here he smiled broadly.

'Yes,' he continued, 'I do find it really uplifting that none of those asswipes and dickheads are still with us; that they've all been done away with. Which, one cannot deny, is quite a significant silver lining to the near-total extinction of mankind.'

The other four at the table had now joined him in smiling broadly. And this was because Derek had clearly succeeded in softening what had developed into a rather callous indictment of so many of their departed brethren – by indicting no more monsters, but instead just a bunch of people who were incredibly and irritatingly tiresome.

It proved a very good way to end the day: a balanced mix of levity and catharsis. Not a bad idea when most of what one had to chew on was just concern, uncertainty, trepidation and rather too much doubt.

And in the morning, there might even be a slice of unleavened dread…

twenty-eight

As it transpired, the first thing that Alex and Debbie encountered in the morning was the sight of a new island. The *Sea Sprite* was again stationary, and from their cabin window they could see what looked like a giant castellated fortress buttressed with slopes of snow. Reaching into a leaden sky, this massive Antarctic stronghold sat in a grey-blue sea, and this sea was peppered with countless chunks of ice. Some of these chunks were little more than scraps of ice, soon to form part of the sea itself. Others were enormous, true icebergs that dwarfed the *Sea Sprite* and that would probably still be around centuries into the future. The largest of these were like huge floating slabs of fractured polystyrene, flat-topped and big enough to host a small town. Others were not quite so large, but taken together they had the appearance of a flotilla of strangely shaped spaceships; an armada of frozen spacecraft forever marooned on the surface of a watery planet, and destined never to take to the skies again. It was a breathtaking vista, and one that held Alex and Debbie's attention for quite some time.

It also made Alex wonder where they were, and before he and Debbie reported for breakfast, he insisted that they made a detour to the stern of the Eriksson Deck in order to see what was lying to the port of the *Sea Sprite*. This they did, and there they saw that their ship was sandwiched between that fortified island and the Antarctic Peninsula. It was their first view ever of the Antarctic continent proper, and it was yet another breathtaking experience. Here was a vast expanse of white; a seemingly endless vista of huge white cliffs, but cliffs that were made of just snow and ice. And it was its scale as much as its pristine beauty that robbed one of one's breath. No wonder, thought Alex, that thousands before him had been so impressed and so captivated by this place. It was somewhere very special, and not the sort of place where anything as mean and sordid as a burglary should take place. Even if the premises to be burgled were an unmanned research station and not someone's private residence. These were Alex's thoughts as he accompanied his wife to breakfast, and he still had these thoughts when he and Debbie were back in their cabin and the *Sea Sprite* had embarked on its passage south; its passage down the west coast of the peninsula towards its morning's destination and the planned scene of the crime: Cierva Cove.

They had now passed more slabs of broken polystyrene and more alien spacecraft, some of them providing a perch for groups of diminutive penguins; penguins that looked no bigger than tiny dots on the huge white slopes of these enormous icebergs. And in this giant landscape, even the whales looked small. A number of these had been encountered as well: a couple of fin whales in the distance and maybe a dozen or more humpbacks closer to the ship. They were unavoidably enchanting, even if one could see only their great black backs breaking the surface of the sea, or occasionally a wonderful arching fluke. Or even a single white flipper, looking more like a long, serrated bone than the living flesh of a living beast. Together, all these sights were almost enough to distract Alex and Debbie from what was immediately in store. But not quite. And when the tannoy system interrupted their viewing, their interest in these wonders evaporated immediately, to be replaced by a focus on what was now required. And by at least a sliver of genuine dread...

It was going to be a replay of the tactics employed in Deception Island, with a few necessary tweaks and with hopefully an entirely different outcome. The necessary tweaks took account of the availability of only seven zodiacs and, of course, the absence of the 'elite nine'. This meant that, with two zodiacs held in reserve, just five would be employed in the raid, with two of these spearheading the assault. And these two leading zodiacs would have as their captains Stuart and Gill; while in one of the following trio would be Roy and in another Alex. This he had discovered only as the zodiac-numbered armbands had been handed out in the main lounge prior to his descending to the ship's landing stage. It appeared that the captain had decided not only that Stuart's and Gill's capabilities could no longer be ignored, but also that a last-minute allocation of duties to 'those who also serve' would inject some spontaneous enthusiasm and some fresh adrenaline into the operation. However, Alex wasn't convinced. He just felt rather overwhelmed by this unexpected responsibility – and by an increased sense of dread.

Nevertheless, as soon as his zodiac had pulled away from the *Sea Sprite*, with Joshua at the helm and Patrick seated opposite, he felt surprisingly calm. His zodiac was one of only two that had the same crew as before, and he suspected that in some way this was helping his composure, possibly by giving him a sense of familiarity with his role. Even if that was not really justified at all. But never mind. He'd grab whatever he could if it meant he could keep his cool.

He also tried to concentrate on his zodiac's progress and that of those zodiacs in front. Indeed, as soon as he'd managed to wave goodbye to Debbie (stationed, as before, at the back of the Erikson Deck), he had turned his attention to the flotilla of small craft and its passage through the drifting ice. And that is what was everywhere: small and not-so-small lumps of ice that had prevented the *Sea Sprite* from entering the inner confines of Cierva Cove and instead had required the zodiacs to make what would be a fifteen-minute trip to the Argentinian research station – with their drivers exercising a great deal of care…

They had to make a judicious choice of a pathway through the floating ice. As Alex soon realised, although they float, lumps of ice have the same characteristics as lumps of rock, and even the sturdy, reinforced rubber of the zodiacs was not immune to their literal impact. Joshua, like all the other helmsmen, was having to pick a route through them that avoided all the larger lumps and respected the solidness of even the smaller ones. When having to negotiate these, he slowed his vessel down to a walking pace and edged his way through their jumble as carefully as he could. This made what Alex thought was a very unpleasant scraping sound, and not one he would ever have associated with the smoothness of ice. But there again, he had much to learn. He was but a novice in this environment. Just as he was an absolute beginner in the practice of larceny; a crime that was just about to be undertaken. Because the Argentinian research station had now come into view, and the lead zodiacs were already slowing, with their drivers preparing to take more care than ever.

It was a collection of red-painted huts, all sited on a rocky hillside well above the level of the sea, and with, of course, a prominent Argentinian flag painted on the side of one of these huts. Alex wondered whether all Argentinian research stations had this red-hut/prominent-national-flag appearance, and then he wondered whether Patrick knew the origin of this blue-and-white national symbol. He, Alex, did. Because Roy had told him what it was just a few days before. And whilst not a conclusive explanation of its genesis, it was thought that it had been conceived by Manuel Belgrano, the leader of the Argentinian Revolution against Spain, and it was supposed to represent blue sky parting to reveal a white cloud – as is said to have happened at some liberation celebration in Buenos Aires. Roy had then gone on to question how a blue sky parts to reveal a cloud (and not the other way around), and why the representation of the sun in the middle of the flag is against a white (cloud) background and not against a blue (clear sky) background. And he was right to question this, because it didn't make sense, any more than wondering about the creation process of a national flag – and how widely this was known – when one was just about to be involved in a spot of possibly dangerous thievery. Alex quickly decided that his mind had latched onto this nonsense because he was really quite scared. But now it was time to re-engage with the job in hand, especially as Stuart had given a pre-arranged hand signal to indicate that while his and Gill's zodiacs made for their objective, it was time for zodiacs three, four and five to hold back. Unlike in Deception Island, this action was to be conducted out of sight of the *Sea Sprite*, and it was essential that if anything went wrong (again) there was somebody to bear witness to this and to take the news back to the *Sea Sprite's* captain. Even if and when Stuart gave the all-clear, only zodiac three (Alex's zodiac) was to join his and Gill's. The other two would 'stand guard' and be prepared to make a fast escape.

What was also out of sight – at the moment – was the station's landing stage. This sea-level facility was hidden behind a sizeable iceberg close to the station itself; an iceberg embellished with an icy appendage that looked like a giant hand, with one finger pointing into the air. Alex was captivated by its appearance. Right up until his captivation was replaced by a sudden bolt of astonishment. After all, whatever he had prepared himself for, he had not prepared himself for the sound of gunfire...

-o-

As Stuart's zodiac rounded the iceberg, he caught sight of the yacht. It was maybe only thirty yards away. Then his attention was drawn to the three men standing on the deck of the yacht, and the fact that two of them were armed. One had a rifle and one had a pistol, and both weapons were now being trained on him and his crew. Some sort of instinct kicked in immediately, and he began to swing his craft to the left, causing one of his team to fall into the centre of the dinghy. This fall may have saved his life, because both weapons had now been discharged. And not as warning shots. One shot had whistled past Stuart's ear, and another had hit a lump of ice only feet from his craft. And then the firing continued. Even as Stuart became aware of Gill's zodiac passing his own, with Gabriel, one of her crew members, at the helm. And Gabriel was steering the zodiac – directly towards the yacht – because Gill was crouched just to his side, taking aim with her assault rifle. It flashed through Stuart's mind that Gill must have been super fast in her reactions, as well as having been super sensible in bringing her trusty SA80 A3 weapon all the way from Mount Pleasant. And would she now be super accurate?

The answer was yes. Gill fired twice, and the guy with the rifle fell to the deck of the yacht while, at the same time, the guy with the pistol stumbled backwards and fell into the water. The third guy then made a move to pick up the first guy's dropped rifle, but as a third shot rang out, he managed only to touch it before he too collapsed onto the deck. All three 'defenders' were now out of action. Two were dead or dying and one was thrashing around in ice-cold water.

-o-

As soon as those first shots had been fired, Joshua had opened the throttle on his zodiac's outboard, and in no time at all, he was racing towards the two leading zodiacs, so that he, Alex and Patrick would be able to do... whatever it was that they needed to do. However, everything had happened so quickly that when they reached the scene of the shoot-out, it was very much all over. Everybody aboard Stuart and Gill's zodiacs looked to be alive and unharmed, but on a rather handsome black yacht, tied to the research station's landing stage, were what looked to be two very still bodies, and in the water, towards the yacht's stern, was a man who was still alive but clearly in some distress. It was as Alex's attention was focused on this unfortunate chap that what would prove to be the final act of this hostile engagement took place. At first it was merely an indistinct movement in the water, just a few yards from where the reluctant bather was struggling to stay afloat. Then something broke the surface of the water. It was the head of a serpent. But then Alex realised what it really was; a leopard seal, and it was now gliding towards the subject of its interest. It disappeared again, only to reappear a fraction of a second later, its mouth wide open and ready to seize its victim by the neck. This it did with consummate ease, and then just as easily it dragged the poor guy under the water. And it never reappeared again. Nor did its unfortunate companion.

It was horrible. Alex felt sick. Patrick, he couldn't fail to notice, actually retched. And even Joshua slumped forward as though he was about to faint. A few deep breaths later, Alex was able to see that in the other two zodiacs there was a similar mix of shock and dismay, and Gill in particular looked really distraught. This was hardly a surprise. She was not a born killer. But she had just ended the lives of three people, directly or indirectly, and they were probably not even bad people. They were just protecting themselves from what they presumably saw as a threat to their own survival.

The *Sea Sprite's* little expeditionary force hadn't scored a victory. All it had done was subtract three more people from the tiny remnants of humanity, and that was very much more a loss than it was a triumph.

Nevertheless, there had been no choice. Just as there was no choice as to what to do now. The first job was to check whether there was anybody *in* the yacht, and when this had been done – and nobody found – there was then the research station to be checked to ensure that it wasn't hosting any hiding Argentinians. This finally completed, it was then a matter of organising the removal of the station's stores – of which there were plenty – whilst at the same time dealing with two dead bodies and extracting from the yacht anything that might be of use back on the *Sea Sprite.* Stuart took a lead in organising all this work, and he also ensured that Captain José knew what was going on. One of the reserve zodiacs had been dispatched from the *Sea Sprite* as soon as those on board had heard the gun fire. So it wasn't long before this had returned and the captain had been briefed on the firefight, and on who had been killed and who had survived. But he still needed to be kept informed of the more prosaic aspects of the operation; namely, the size of the cache of provisions discovered and an estimate of the time it would take to bring this cache back to his vessel. This was, after all, the primary purpose of the zodiacs' visit to the research station. And even after that painful overture, it still had to be performed. Again, there was simply no choice…

It took until mid-afternoon to finish all the work in hand, including the 'liberation' of the black yacht. Unlike the *Bluebird*, this vessel was in perfect order, and it took little time to decide that it would now be joining the *Sea Sprite* on its passage south. It would be towed behind the ship, to be used as and when the need arose. Its name was *Gũse*, which Roy decided was Moldovan for 'goose'. He wasn't certain about that, but he was quite sure that the flag flying at the back of the yacht was Moldovan, so it was odds on he was right. The only mystery was what three Moldovans were doing on a small boat so far from home, and why they had been quite so uncompromising – and so ill-judged – in their behaviour.

José decided to give the two who hadn't been carried off by the leopard seal a prompt burial at sea, and this burial was performed with due solemnity in the late afternoon. Unsurprisingly, the only Moldovan flag available was the small one on the *Gũse*, which meant that the two bodies, wrapped in white bed linen, had to make do with Union flags as a mark of respect as they were slipped into the sea. Not ideal by any means. But, as Alex thought, they were both well past taking offence…

It was one of many thoughts he had in the latter part of this day, and one of the few he could deal with. To add to the sight of nine good men cut down by those invisible spores, he had now seen – close up – two bodies with bullet holes in them, and he had witnessed one person actually becoming a body, thanks to the attentions of a large carnivorous seal. Together with his proximity to a firefight and his participation in a large-scale robbery, it was just too much to process, especially for someone who had spent a lifetime cocooned in the ordinary and the normal, and for whom death and violence were just things that happened on a screen. And then very rarely for real.

With Debbie's help, he did manage dinner – with the

usual companions – but he was more than a little detached throughout the whole of the meal, and more than a little reluctant to revisit the events of the day. Roy seemed more willing to do so, but even he was keener to look to the future and to consider how today's events would influence Captain José's plans. Would he still want to conduct a further raid on another research station? Would he risk another encounter with armed men? Or would he announce in his promised briefing the following morning that he had devised a new plan; one that sought to avoid contact of any sort with anybody else?

After the meal, Alex couldn't bring to mind much of the dinner conversation, and especially Roy's thinking aloud what tomorrow might have in store. But one aspect of his musings had stuck: the one that followed on from the possibility of José steering clear of any other encounters. And this was Roy's wondering what had happened to José's earlier declared strategy of 'no communications'. Their captain had also indicated that there would be only limited and cautious contact with other vessels, but that seemed to be an irrelevance now. The *Sea Sprite* appeared to have the Antarctic virtually to itself. However, that still left the question of communications with, say, British research stations on the continent, or maybe somewhere further afield. Was it still possible to communicate with the Falklands, or even with Ushuaia? Or were even the British outposts on the cold continent impossible to contact?

Of course, nobody at the table had been able to provide answers to any of these questions, but Alex remembered that Roy had committed himself to attempting to get some answers in the morning. That, Alex believed, might prove to be very interesting, and it might even prove to be a very effective distraction from thoughts of shooting and drowning that he feared would still be with him when he woke. They were certainly still with him now. As were thoughts of two bodies slipping underwater from beneath the cover of two Union flags. It really had been an awful day…

twenty-nine

Stuart had been dealing with his own suite of thoughts. Over the past couple of days, neither the comforts of the *Sea Sprite* nor even his evolving relationship with Gill had been able to keep at bay entirely the pain of rejection. And it was the same for Gill herself. Both of them knew that, despite their having brought potentially life-saving news to all those aboard the *Sea Sprite*, they were still regarded – by the ex-military on board, and by some of their associates – as deserters, as a couple of guys who had shamelessly abandoned their mates. That was why they had been passed over in the selection process for the raid in Deception Island. They were not wanted as comrades by those who had been largely responsible for organising and conducting that raid.

Then things had changed. Dramatically. Mike and Terry had been killed along with seven of their mates, and it was now only those undesirable deserters who could take their place for the next planned raid. Captain José had been very good about it. He'd freely admitted that he had felt uncomfortable about their earlier exclusion, but that he had been more concerned about the success of the job in hand. And that had clearly demanded the total commitment of all those involved; something that would have been put at risk if Stuart and Gill had been 'imposed' on the others. This, he'd admitted, had possibly been wrong. But of course, that was all irrelevant now. There was another raid to conduct, and it was essential that it was led by the one remaining soldier on board the *Sea Sprite,* together with a young, intelligent person who would inevitably have more confidence – and ability – than someone who had worked on a cruise ship for many years, or who had not worked at all for many years.

So, it was welcome rehabilitation time, together with the prospect of actually doing something useful and something quite demanding. Stuart and Gill hadn't hesitated for a moment, and had been only too happy to accept José's offer of a leadership role. Stuart had felt really quite elated. He was still in buoyant mood when he'd set out in that zodiac, and as far as he could remember he had then felt unalloyed ecstasy when he'd realised that all that shooting had left him and his colleagues completely unscathed. But only for a moment. The ecstasy soon dissolved into relief – that Gill was OK. And then there'd been a bizarre mix of revulsion at the needless death of three people and admiration that it was his 'girlfriend' who had been responsible for their demise. She had done exactly what needed to be done in the most polished and professional manner possible, and had even been full of remorse after the event. She had shown that she was still Gill, still a woman with the emotions of a woman, and not some crazed Rambo killer. That admiration might soon, he thought, turn into something else.

This all meant that Stuart was now experiencing a degree of mental turmoil like he'd never known before. Because he had somehow to reconcile his new leadership role with what he now knew was his serious distaste for violent confrontation. And he also had to balance his new-found respect for his partner's fighting skills with his burgeoning affection for her, both of which feelings fed into another aspect of his turmoil. Which was how best to protect Gill and himself from what might still lie ahead. Should they continue their agreeable alliance with those aboard the *Sea Sprite*? Or should he question the likelihood of this alliance proving successful and maybe consider the possibility that success – in terms of his and Gill's ultimate survival – might instead be realised by their striking out on their own? After all, there was now another yacht that could be made use of. And that opened up all sorts of possibilities.

As he lay in bed, with Gill already asleep beside him, these were the thoughts that were rolling around in his head. And keeping him awake. It wasn't until he accepted that he could resolve nothing now that he was able, finally, to get to sleep himself. Matters might become clearer in the morning, he'd decided, and particularly after the next promised briefing by Captain José. It was by no means guaranteed, but this update on the *Sea Sprite's* situation – and what was planned next – might just prove useful to somebody who was trying to decide whether to stay with the *Sea Sprite* or whether to 'jump ship'. It might leave him with only a manageable amount of turmoil to deal with…

thirty

Alex and Debbie knew very little about the Moldovan flag when they sat down for breakfast. However, thanks to Roy, with whom they shared this meal, at its conclusion they knew not only that it was a vertical tricolour of blue, yellow and red – with the coat of arms of Moldova in the centre bar – but also that this coat of arms consisted of an eagle holding a shield adorned with an aurochs' head. In fact, when they'd started their breakfast, they hadn't even known what an aurochs was. But again, thanks to Roy's encyclopaedic brain, they were soon equipped with the knowledge that an aurochs was an extinct species of large wild cattle that used to inhabit numerous parts of Asia, Europe and North Africa until it dwindled to a remnant population in Poland. This, mankind managed to eliminate back in the seventeenth century, but not before it had much earlier used these animals to create the ancestors of modern domestic cattle. Quite why the Moldovans had chosen this beast to decorate their coat of arms – and their flag – Roy wasn't entirely sure. But he did propose that it might be because there was very little chance of any other country wanting to use this poor defunct animal as part of its own national symbol. It was akin, he suggested, to choosing an image of a gerbil as your national icon. Or maybe an image of Liberace.

Alex knew what was going on here. Roy was very aware of the trauma that his friend had suffered, and his form of post-trauma counselling was a combination of esoteric instruction – if possible, about flags – and as much levity and silliness as he could get away with. And it worked. Alex felt much better in all sorts of ways when, an hour later, he turned up for Captain José's ten o'clock briefing in the main lounge. He knew he would now be able to apply himself to what was about to happen and not dwell on what had happened. Indeed, he knew he owed it to Debbie and to his friends to focus on what Captain José was about to say, and that in itself would serve as an additional useful therapy. Particularly if Roy was able to succeed in his endeavour to prise out of their leader any details of any communications he might have made. Although that would have to wait until José had dealt with his own agenda. And this started with a recognition of yesterday's events...

First there was an expression of regret. Three people had died who would not have died if the world had still been normal. However, as José was at pains to point out, it was not by any means normal, which was why, simply by approaching a moored yacht, one could quite easily get shot at. And everyone in the room, he suggested, knew what might happen then. It was a way of expressing some sincere regret, but at the same time paving the way to giving his thanks for the rapid reactions of those who'd been shot at, and particularly the outstanding performance of sharpshooting Gill. She was standing at the back of the lounge with Stuart, and José clearly wanted her to hear – before the whole ship's company – that her actions were greatly appreciated and should not be regarded as anything other than entirely proper as well as amazingly skilful. Indeed, to emphasise his point, he invited the audience to consider the possible outcome of yesterday's events had Gill not been able to defend her colleagues quite so quickly and quite so deftly. They all owed her a huge debt of gratitude. And she should feel rightly proud of her performance, free from any sort of guilt whatsoever.

Gill looked a little embarrassed at the conclusion of this eulogy, but José spared her any further blushes by moving on briskly – to discuss his immediate plans for the *Sea Sprite*.

'As I'm sure you've all noticed,' he started, 'we are still in Cierva Cove, and we will be here until about lunchtime. The chief engineer's men are currently doing some routine maintenance work, and when that's finished in about two hours' time, we will be on our way. And our way will be a south-west course to a place called Danco Island, a little further down the peninsula. There we will moor overnight, ready for a short hop to Paradise Bay in the morning, just in time to relieve another Argentinian research station of its goodies. And that reminds me. I should have told you that our zodiac heroes "liberated" more provisions yesterday than I could ever have hoped for. Although, of course, we can never have too many, which is why tomorrow we will be visiting that next Argentinian takeaway. And let me assure you now that we will take all the care we can to ensure that this visit involves no drama of any sort. And I don't think it will...'

'How can you possibly know that?' asked a brave old man from the middle of the room. 'How do you know there aren't people at this base as well?'

Captain José responded like the true leader he had become, and with an explanation that would mean that Roy would not have to quiz him on the subject of communications.

'OK. A very good question. And my answer is that I can't be sure. There might indeed be another vessel there. And there might even be some people in the base itself. But I very much doubt it. And I very much doubt it because we have picked up no transmissions of any sort that would betray the presence of either. And I know that's not conclusive. After all, we picked up nothing from the Moldovan yacht. But I still think it is highly unlikely that we will run into anybody else. I mean, it really is *very* unlikely...'

The audience reacted to this news with a ripple of murmurs and mumbles, and then José carried on.

'Anyway, talking of transmissions, I need to tell you what else our wireless officer has been up to since we adopted our policy of not communicating with the outside world. You see, even though we have been adhering to our policy of remaining silent ourselves, he has been checking on whether anybody else has been in a more talkative mode. And what he's found is very interesting and potentially very revealing. And to put it into a nutshell, he has been able to find nothing coming out of anywhere to the north. And by that I mean no transmissions whatsoever from the Falklands – and that includes Mount Pleasant – and nothing from

Argentina. Or from Chile, for that matter. It's all just total quiet. Which might mean that if there are any people up there – still alive – they, just like us, are keeping their heads down. Or it might mean… well, you know what it might mean…'

Here there was another round of murmurs and mumbles, and then José continued. And his voice had now moved from the solemn end of its spectrum to the very animated, as he abruptly announced that contact *had* been made with some other human beings…

'Well, on a potentially much brighter note, I can also tell you that we have now – very recently – broken our radio silence. And we've done this to make contact with Rothera – which, as some of you may know, is the British Antarctic Survey's largest base in the Antarctic, and a base that is still very much full of people. That's why we've been so indiscreet. We thought it important that they should know that we are around, just in case we might be of use to them. And vice versa. After all, Rothera has an airstrip, and it is one of the best established and best equipped research stations in the Antarctic. And it just seemed the obvious thing to do. There seemed to be no good reason to hide from what at some point might prove to be an essential refuge.

'Anyway, before you get too enthusiastic about this development, I should say that, whilst they have acknowledged our presence, they would not welcome our presence. They have insisted that we stay well away from Rothera, and simply keep them informed of our situation and our condition. And that's hardly surprising. After all, if any of us here were responsible for the lives of all those hunkered down in an Antarctic research station, the last thing we would want would be a ship-full of… other people turning up to overwhelm our resources.'

He had chosen 'other' here rather than 'old', but it was clear to Alex what he meant. A team of young researchers didn't want their base made into an old people's home, and one that might run out of provisions before anybody got a great deal older.

'I might also say that their understandable caution also extends to their giving us any information about their own circumstances. They have told us that they are basically in good shape, but they have refused to tell us how many of them are holed up there, what their resources are, or even whether they are in contact with any other bases, including Halley VI. That's the rather *designer* British research station on the Brunt Ice Shelf. Oh, and they haven't told us whether they have access to a plane or a ship. However, given their reluctance to have us anywhere near them, I suspect they may have both. Which can't be a bad thing. In fact, in due course, it may prove more than useful. For all of us.

'Anyway, that's what I wanted to tell you. We are not alone. There is at least one station out there with people in it. And whilst those people are currently unwilling to see us, we will keep in contact with them, and we will try to work with them. In any way that helps us all. Meanwhile, however, we will continue to look after ourselves. And that means that tomorrow there will be another exercise in international looting, and I can announce now that this plundering will be conducted by the same zodiac pirates who were so successful yesterday. I'm sure that we can all be confident that they will be equally successful tomorrow. Albeit without having to make another call on Gill's exceptional skills…'

That was the end of the captain's speech, and for many the beginning of their processing everything they had been told. And especially the knowledge that they were now in extended arm's-length communication with a British research station. It was a lot to take in, and for Alex a lot more on top of the turmoil that had still not abated entirely.

Nevertheless, there was some help on the way, and it arrived as soon as the *Sea Sprite* resumed its travels south just after lunch. It was, of course, the indescribable beauty of the Antarctic Peninsula. Here there was a channel that ran down its west coast, formed by a continuous thread of snow-covered islands parallel to the peninsula itself, and capable of immersing all those aboard the *Sea Sprite* in an almost other-worldly experience. Because it was like being on another planet; an icy, watery planet where colours other than blue, grey and white did not exist. There were no greens, reds, yellows or oranges here, but just that restricted palette of those three subdued tones. And it was all so pristine. And so serene. And so untroubled. And so 'content'. It was a place at peace with itself; the antithesis of so much of the man-made world with all its manic frenzy, its ugly squalor and its ubiquitous need for excess. Alex found it all extremely soothing, and ultimately decided that it was not a place to come to live, but a place to come to die. But by choice. Not because one had to scurry here to avoid a self-induced global disaster.

The whole afternoon passed with the soothing balm of more and more beauty, until at seven, it was time to join the meal squad for dinner. Alex, for some unknown reason, just knew it would be a good one.

It certainly started well, with Roy first of all giving his views on 'communications', then on the apparent reserve of the British Antarctic Survey, and finally on what might be assumed to be a substantial boost to the possible mankind-recreation programme.

As regards communications, he immediately questioned whether silence from the Falklands and from the whole of the south of South America really meant that there was nobody left alive there. As Captain José had rightly conceded, might the hardy Falklanders and their military companions at Mount Pleasant not be doing exactly what the *Sea Sprite* had been doing: hiding? And in the case of Argentina and even Chile, might they similarly not want to betray their continued existence? Especially if this existence was maybe hanging by a thread? Anyway, there was no way, he maintained, that a death certificate could be signed for the whole of the South American population just yet. Although, if all went to plan, in a matter of weeks this might be possible – and unavoidable – for the entire population of Ushuaia. In the meantime, the subject of the existence or not of living souls further north could be parked, and the second subject – their cold-shouldering by the British residents of the cold continent – could now be addressed.

When it was, it soon became apparent that Derek agreed with Roy's opinion, which was that he would have done exactly the same as those researcher types at Rothera. He would have told a ship-load of OAPs to keep its distance. That said, both of them then admitted that they would almost certainly be at a loss as to what to do if the *Sea Sprite* ignored this instruction and just turned up. There were probably few if any weapons at Rothera, and even if there were, there might be some resistance in the ranks to shooting people who looked and sounded like their now-departed grandparents back in Britain. And even denying their new guests a share of their rations might be a problem. As how could you seek to re-energise the human race when you've just starved to death some of its innocent remnants and actually witnessed their pathetic demise?

Inevitably, this is where Roy's thoughts arrived at the process of 're-energising', and in particular the capacity of the staff at Rothera – and maybe at Halley VI as well – to significantly bolster the pocket-sized regeneration team aboard the *Sea Sprite*. The first point he made was that it was highly unlikely that the tendrils of British gender equality legislation hadn't reached down to the Antarctic, and consequently there would be a whole nest of prospective mothers tucked away in both British bases. The debate, therefore, should focus on how the regeneration process might work in practice. How would baby-making be conducted?

It was perhaps the surfeit of new information today – on top of the chilling events of yesterday – but for whatever reason, this was the point at which considered and thoughtful debate was overtaken by unbridled irreverence. All those around the table seemed in need of a dose of no-sense-whatsoever...

Elaine was the first contributor to this session of the absurd, and her contribution was a proposal that all those with inseminating or inseminatable credentials should be paired off according to their height. This, she said, would avoid the problems associated with the inequality of stature, which could be as acute as that between Mr Bercow and his wife, and which was a source of discomfort for all those who had to observe it. And even a very tall man with a diminutive women was far from ideal.

Debbie agreed, but thought that pairing itself might warrant a review. What, she asked, would be the problem with officially sanctioned promiscuity, where everyone had a go with everyone else they fancied? Just as long as the lust was mutual. And such an approach, she suggested, would have the added advantage of stimulating shared parenting. If a man didn't know who was his child, wouldn't he want to contribute to the well-being of all the children, and therefore to the well-being of the entire new generation?

Anyway it was now time for a man at the table to put forward his views, and Alex was first to do this – by suggesting that if promiscuity wasn't a starter and a more traditional approach to child-making prevailed, pairing might be conducted on the basis of IQ. Eugenics was reprehensible, he admitted, but with such a small number of procreators to hand, shouldn't some be charged with producing the new generation of leaders and thinkers, and others, the wood-gatherers and latrine-diggers? For a few moments, three of the other diners at the table clearly thought he was being serious with these remarks. But it took only the start of a giggle from Debbie to alert her friends to her husband's buffoonery, and when their laughter died down, Roy made his own contribution to the discussion.

It was that the elders of the new order (that is to say, himself and possibly his present dinner companions) might have to institute an award system, loosely based on that Soviet ruse of making serial child-bearers heroes of the nation. After all, he said, in kick-starting humanity, there could be no room for a middle-class attitude of 'two is quite enough'. Indeed, you would have to be regarded as a slacker if you produced fewer than five little wonders. And as for those burly female geologists from Rothera and Halley VI who could manage a dozen or more… well, they'd be feted by the whole community, and statues would be raised in their honour. With maybe some smaller statues for their long-serving partners…

Then it was Derek's turn.

'We could just go the vasectomy route,' he announced. 'And then everybody could just enjoy themselves – in pairs, or in groups or in a series of huge communal orgies – and all without the prospect of unleashing another wave of humanity on the world. In my mind, this would be as liberating as it would be altruistic. And it might just get my vote…'

Derek now wore an inscrutable look on his face, and Alex, for one, thought that he wasn't joking. Even though that inscrutable expression was now being abandoned in favour of a mischievous grin.

In any event, his comments constituted a suitable full stop to the evening's proceedings and an end to a day in which Alex's turmoil had finally receded. All he felt now was the beginnings of trepidation – in preparation for the demands of tomorrow's raid – and a deep uncertainty about the wisdom of trying to reboot mankind. A world without people would, in many ways, he thought, be a much better place. It might be full of more of the sort of wonder that he'd experienced during his passage down the peninsula earlier today. However, it wouldn't have people like Debbie, Elaine, Derek and Roy. And that would be a terrible loss.

It was just as well, he decided, that he would have no part in whatever outcome was achieved or suffered. Even though he *would* have a part in tomorrow's zodiac exercise. Which he desperately hoped would not involve the discovery of a Moldovan flag, or indeed the flag of any other nation…

thirty-one

As the *Sea Sprite* had made its way down the Antarctic Peninsula, Stuart had not been oblivious of the breathtaking beauty of this wonderful part of the world. Indeed, he and Gill had spent much of the afternoon at the stern of the Erikson Deck, savouring what had been a continuous vista of unsurpassed splendour. Nevertheless, his mind had been largely elsewhere, hopping from one demanding thought to another, and all concerning his and Gill's future – from every possible perspective.

After Captain José's earlier presentation, he had more or less reconciled himself to an immediate future aboard the *Sea Sprite*. He could see no benefit in him and Gill striking out on their own. And Gill, he discovered, agreed. Whilst there was now the theoretical possibility of joining forces with a group of people of their own age (by stealing another yacht) – and this did have its attractions – there were just too many associated risks and too many reasons to stay and help

Captain José. In fact, taking the crew and the passengers together, there were about 150 reasons. Furthermore, neither stuart nor Gill had much of an appetite for making a habit of abandoning their mates. Even if they knew only a few of them by name…

So, if their foreseeable future was on this undeniably comfortable ship, sharing one of its comfortable cabins and one of its comfortable beds, what else should they now consider sharing? In particular, should they share their honest feelings for each other?

Resolving this was more difficult than resolving the issue of staying with or leaving the ship. After all, despite their now unavoidably intimate relationship, officially they were still 'just friends'. No longer the sort of friends they'd been back at Mount Pleasant, where their friendship had been that of two companions, but now the sort of friends who had a genuine affection for each other and a closeness that neither of them had experienced before. And how could it be otherwise? Sleeping under the same duvet and coming under fire during the same operation simply made that inevitable. And there was more. To start with, there was their consoling each other after their initial rejection as 'deserters'. Then the small matter of Gill saving Stuart's life. And the not-quite-so-dramatic matter of Stuart being able to reassure Gill that she was not some sort of gung-ho assassin, but instead a brave and skilful defender of lives. Captain José hadn't been the first to explain to her that what she had done was nothing to be ashamed of, but everything to be proud of.

Well, by the time the *Sea Sprite* had reached its mooring off Danco Island, Stuart had finally stopped hopping between thoughts, and had instead come to a definitive decision – concerning his relationship with Gill. And what he had decided would in no way be easy, because it would so much involve the deconstruction of a former relationship before he could properly establish its replacement. But he did manage it, helped to no small degree by Gill's reaction to his proposals. Indeed, by her eagerness to embrace and even 'enhance' his proposals. And all such relationships do, of course, involve two people...

So, when they finally retired to their bed, they were definitely no longer just friends, and within minutes they were 'officially' lovers. Not just in the physical sense, but undeniably in the emotional sense as well.

Despite a very uncertain future, and despite whatever trials they might both face in the morning, Stuart, as he was falling asleep, realised he had never felt happier. And very rarely more surprised...

thirty-two

Alex had seen Danco Island and its surroundings the previous day – as the *Sea Sprite* had arrived there in the late afternoon. But now, in the early-morning light, it was a different place. Overnight, someone had bleached all the snow and someone else had turned up the intensity of the sky. This was now bluer than ever, and a strip of it had even been taken down and laid across the surface of the mirror-smooth sea. So, the sky and the sea were now indistinguishable, and both so vividly blue that Alex doubted what he was seeing. Could anything this natural be so 'technicolour'? And so undeniably striking?

This question was debated with Patrick and Morag over breakfast. (It had now become difficult for Alex and Debbie to avoid them.) And the conclusion of the debate was that the blues and whites were vibrant bordering on the vivid because the atmosphere here was so clear. It was not adulterated with all the dust, pollen, ash and particulates found in the rest of the world. And fortunately, it was still not polluted with spores…

This aspect of the conclusion then led on to a discussion about the forthcoming zodiac venture, and the revelation by Patrick that he was confident that this one would be a little more straightforward than those already conducted. And that, as a result, he was quite looking forward to being involved once again. Alex smiled in response to this announcement, but did not admit to having similar thoughts himself. Because he didn't. He still thought that, as with Deception Island and Cierva Cove, anything might happen, and none of it might be good.

Very soon, he would discover whether his concerns were valid. Because the *Sea Sprite* was already on its way to Paradise Bay, and only an hour after breakfast there had been a call to the zodiac crews to again gather in the principal lounge to collect their numbered arm bands in readiness to board their vessels. Magical scenery had surrounded the *Sea Sprite* all morning, but when it arrived at its destination, the magic score edged up just a few more points. Paradise Bay, as its name might suggest, was something of a pinnacle in terms of Antarctic beauty; a place of azure sky and azure sea, and with such brilliant icing-sugar land separating that sky and sea that it again made Alex doubt what he was seeing. Only the incongruous Argentinian base, just five hundred metres away, managed to extinguish this doubt and replace it with another strong dose of trepidation. There was no yacht there and no ship anywhere near, but would the base itself be occupied?

Well, it didn't appear to be. It was just another collection of red huts (the largest of which had a roof rendered as a blue-and-white Argentinian flag), and it seemed to be entirely deserted. It sat at the foot of a bluff – at least, that's what Roy called it. He was standing next to Alex on the *Sea Sprite's* landing stage, and he advised his companion that, as far as he could recall, a bluff was a headland with a broad, steep face. And that was certainly the nature of the mass of rock that formed the backdrop to this Argentinian blot on the landscape; a snow-covered chunk of the Antarctic continent that rose above the base to a height of maybe two hundred metres.

The name of the base, spelled out in prominent letters on the side of that largest of the huts, was 'Brown'. This was not a description of the brownish hue of the huts' red paint, but a recognition of an Argentinian hero by the name of Almirante – or Admiral – Brown. Alex knew this because his walking-Wikipedia friend had just told him. He seemed to know everything. And he definitely knew that Almirante William Brown was an Irish-born Argentinian who was regarded as the father of the Argentinian Navy. And he had earned this title through a string of heroic actions back in the nineteenth century that had led to not only this small outpost being named after him, but also a class of destroyers in the Argentinian Navy, a few other Argentinian warships, a national college, four football teams, and even an Admiral Brown Cup, which, fittingly, was awarded to the winners of rugby matches between Argentina and Ireland. Before rugby, along with all other sports, had become extinct. Such were the rewards, Roy suggested, for heroes of a country that had few heroes from which to choose...

With that rather barbed conclusion to Roy's history lesson delivered, it was time for Alex and Patrick to join

Joshua in zodiac number three, and for Roy to settle himself with his mates into zodiac number five. And within no time at all, these and three other zodiacs were on their way to the Almirante Brown base, with, as before, the other two held in reserve at the *Sea Sprite's* stern.

Alex realised that he was beginning to feel somewhat excited rather than embarrassingly nervous. This was in part due to what would be the reassuring proximity of the *Sea Sprite* to any 'action' that might arise, and in part to the likelihood that there would be no 'action' whatsoever. The research station still looked completely unoccupied. No window coverings were open, no doors were ajar, and there was not the slightest hint of the slightest movement within. In fact, he now thought that he could already make out that the landing stage just below the base was covered in pristine un-trodden snow. Although, of course, that wasn't conclusive evidence of there being no residents, he told himself. If there were no vessels in sight, other than the *Sea Sprite* team's own, it would not be surprising that there were no footprints on the landing stage. And it was still possible that the station's complement of fit and aggressive Argentinians had been deposited here some time ago, and were now hunkered down in their sealed redoubts, waiting to spring out and deal mercilessly with any intruders…

His nervousness was returning. He needed to tell himself that he was being stupid. And that was what he did. And so convincingly that, by the time Stuart and Gill and their respective crews had secured their zodiacs to the landing stage, he felt nervous no more. And when they approached the first of the red huts and Stuart banged on its door to announce their arrival, Alex would have been flabbergasted.

if anyone had opened it and greeted the newcomers with a cheery '*Buen día*'.

It was indeed as deserted as the station in Cierva Cove, but, because the *Sea Sprite* was so close to hand, a lot easier to relieve of its provisions. It did take some time and some effort (the access to the station from its landing stage involved a lot of steps), but by mid-afternoon, Almirante Brown had lost all his valuable stores and, with that earlier theft from Cierva Cove, the *Sea Sprite* was now packed with more food than it had been when it left Stanley. Not the same sort of food granted, but food that would still allow all those aboard to be fed for the duration of the planned stay in the Antarctic.

Captain José was very happy. He said so in a brief tannoy address in the late afternoon. And he also made a point of thanking all those who had once again been brave enough to make an unannounced visit to an Argentinian 'warehouse', and who, on this occasion, had fortunately not had to resort to violence. Although, as he stressed, he was entirely confident that they would have done whatever was required of them in this respect, had the need arisen.

When the good captain signed off, Alex felt that the rescheduled voyage of the *Sea Sprite* had come to some sort of full stop. The ship was now where it would probably stay for the next four or five weeks, and it was stocked with all that was needed to do this. It was also full of people who had reconciled themselves to this immediate future, and who were probably thinking – as Alex was – that they could now relax. At least to a degree. Fate might still present them with all sorts of unpleasant surprises, but for now the chores had been completed – without further incident – and they could all figuratively put their feet up. Even if some of them might need the company of their friends over dinner to remove any last vestiges of concern.

The company on hand this evening was ideal. On a table for seven were the usual gang of five – and Stuart and Gill. And it was Gill who opened the conversation by asking her older table companions for their views on violence. Maybe, thought Alex, she still had a few demons to chase away; demons who had appeared when she'd made use of her gun. And demons who were still loitering in the middle distance despite all the assurances she'd received that what she had done had been both necessary and proper.

Roy was the first to respond to this question by suggesting that all normal people had an aversion to violence, but at the same time very few would rule out its use when it was unavoidable; when violence had to be met with violence. And rather than using Gill's own actions at Cierva Cove to illustrate his point, he told her of his earlier concerns about violence breaking out on the *Sea Sprite*, and how he and the other four oldies at the table had made a pact to watch each other's backs. Implicit in this, he maintained, was a willingness on the part of each of them to perpetrate violence on others if this was the only way to 'watch a back'. And that could even have meant killing someone, some formerly polite old cove who was now wielding a fire axe in an attempt to do some killing himself.

The other oldies nodded their agreement, and, like Alex, they displayed no anger or alarm at Roy's revelation of their 'secret' pact. And why would they? After all, the likelihood of insurrection breaking out on the *Sea Sprite* was now so low as to be essentially non-existent. What all those aboard had witnessed over the past few days had in some way bound them all together, and everybody knew this, passengers and crew alike. So, any move to form a clique or to challenge the status quo would have been regarded not just as an affront, but also as a breach of trust. That wasn't to say that mayhem might not still break out if the ship's company ended up starving, but that would not be the sort of internecine situation that had led Roy to make his original mutual protection proposal. It would be... well, just a messy end, in which survival would probably not be an attractive proposition. And, in any event, starvation now seemed a very remote possibility indeed. Thanks to Captain José's actions and those of some unknown Argentinian quartermasters, there was on board, in Roy's own words, enough food to sink a ship.

Gill seemed to welcome Roy's analysis of people's attitude to violence, and she must have been further gratified to hear Elaine stating that her own views on violence were exactly in accord with those of Roy, and that she had not been in the slightest bit appalled by what had happened at Cierva Cove. As with most people on this ship, she explained, her experience of violence had previously been restricted to what she had seen on a screen. But these were different times now, where the extraordinary had become the ordinary. And if someone shot at you or your friends, it was the most normal – and justified – thing to fire back at them. With the intention of delivering what she referred to as 'a Clint Eastwood conclusion' to the exchange. No winging them with a view to bringing them to a 'justice system', but a bullet planted wherever was best to bring them to an immediate full stop instead.

Alex was fascinated to learn how his closest shipmates were applying their views on the use of violence to the situation in which they now found themselves, and it made him wonder how they now viewed their predicament in more general terms. Were Derek and Roy still as indifferent to the outcome of their venture as before? And what of Stuart and Gill? Surely they had a rather different outlook to those of the more-than-middle-aged at the table. And this latter question he would now try to resolve. And he would do this by asking Stuart and Gill how they currently viewed their long-term future.

It was Stuart who responded to Alex, and his response was a revelation.

'Well, I suspect that – ultimately – Gill and I will end up leading a somewhat solitary life,' he announced. 'I mean, forgive me for saying this, but we do plan to get to your age. Which means…'

'…you won't be sharing a table with us in twenty years' time,' finished Debbie.

'Errh… precisely.'

'Aren't you forgetting the crew,' interjected Roy, 'and maybe even some of the guys from Rothera? They'll still be around…'

'You're right,' agreed Stuart. 'But by then I doubt Gill and I will…'

'Why not?' asked Roy.

'Well, we'd be only too happy to help out in setting up a new community – you know, some sort of base where you and all the other guys on this ship could live out your lives. But… well, frankly, I'm not so sure we'd be too keen to take part in any sort of new world order…'

'You mean you wouldn't want kids?' suggested Elaine.

'Spot on,' confirmed Stuart. 'We think that bringing kids into what might remain of the world might not be too good an idea. And well… we're not exactly huge fans of our own species either. I mean, look what it's done…'

Here he hesitated before going on.

'So, I don't know how welcome we might be in any sort of community that thought otherwise. We might soon be regarded as outsiders. And even if we weren't, we might still feel just a little uncomfortable…'

'So?' encouraged Alex.

'Well, I can't say for sure…'

And here Stuart looked at Gill before he continued.

'…but I suspect we might want to make off on our own. You know, maybe take a yacht and maybe even make a life on that. Roaming around the world until we couldn't roam any more…'

Here, he hesitated again, and then rushed out an embarrassed apology.

'Hey, don't get me wrong. We both consider ourselves really lucky to be where we are. With you and all the other guys on this ship. And we'll do anything that's needed to… you know…'

'I think you've already proved that,' remarked Alex.

'Yeah, well, you asked about the future. And I was just being honest. And it doesn't mean that we won't still be eating together in…'

'Leave it at "ten years' time",' interjected Roy. 'Some of us might just make it that far.'

This is when the other four oldies at the table started to laugh, and when Stuart was relieved of any remaining embarrassment. Indeed, it wasn't long before he – and Gill – were relieved of any guilt for holding such an unenthusiastic view of the future. First it was Derek, assisted by Elaine, confirming that both of them were very much fatalistic about the future, and that neither of them would get too concerned about any eventual outcome. Their investment in this future was very limited, they said, and whether humanity survived or not was a matter of near-total indifference.

Roy wasn't that indifferent. He said so. However, he also said, to nobody's great surprise, that his interest in the future was very much that of an impartial observer. His major concern, he admitted, was that he might not be around to witness the final outcome: the successful rebirth of humanity or its total demise. And what a book it would make! With him as its author…

Eventually, it was time for Alex to reveal his attitude to the future, and he did this by asking Debbie to act as their joint spokesperson, having first made it clear that, as with Stuart and Gill and Derek and Elaine, he and his wife shared exactly the same views. It took her only a little time to do this, because it merely entailed telling the others at the table that their outlook involved combining fatalism with a little dash of hope and more than a little dash of regret. Their fatalism, she explained, bordered on the indifference to the future of humanity as already expressed by the others. The dash of hope was for a good, peaceful outcome for them all, and particularly for the younger people on the *Sea Sprite* and for all the 'youngsters' in those Antarctic research stations. And the regret was that, without a future generation of humans, there would be no more individuals of the sort they had known as friends, a handful of whom were sitting at this table right now.

Alex was concerned that Roy might accuse Debbie of giving a politician's explanation of their joint perspective on the future; one that was designed to offend nobody. But he didn't. Probably, thought Alex, because he would know it was true. He would know that these two friends of his had no great affection for humanity as a whole, but a deep affection for a small number of its members, all those people with whom they had chosen to share some of their lives.

It had been a good dinner. By sharing their thoughts, the bonds between the 'senior five' had been strengthened some more, and new bonds had been formed with the youthful pair of Stuart and Gill. All that remained to be seen was whether these bonds would be further strengthened by all seven of them sharing even more time together in their forthcoming Antarctic isolation. And there would potentially be plenty of time to share...

thity-three

As it transpired, they shared some time together the very next morning. Roy had suggested the previous evening that they all gather on the stern of the ship – on its Marco Polo Deck – for a concerted exercise in joint wildlife observation. This they did. And although the wildlife was a little sparse – just a few humpback whales in the distance, a passing unidentified seal, and the odd swimming and diving chinstrap penguin – it was a time 'enjoyed by all'.

While they were here, they were also able to debate what Captain José might include in his afternoon presentation. (This had been announced over the tannoy system just after they had started their wildlife observation, and it was due to commence at 2.30 sharp.) Derek thought it would be a series of warnings and unchallengeable diktats to underpin the forthcoming period of martial law. Roy, however, thought it would be just a barely disguised pep talk. And as it turned out, he was nearer the mark. Albeit the pep talk did have a significant sting in its tail...

When the presentation started, the captain sounded just as happy and upbeat as he had in his broadcast address of the previous day, and at least to start with he had only good news. The *Sea Sprite* was now well stocked with all sorts of provisions, and not just extra food but also extra fuel for the zodiacs, and even extra toiletries and medicines. Albeit some of the labels on these extra supplies were in Spanish. He was also able to report that he was still in contact with the base at Rothera, and whilst they were still reluctant to give away any information on their own circumstances, those in charge there had agreed to maintain contact and to provide aid and assistance if this was ever needed, and if they could do so without endangering their own situation. It was, Captain José explained, an arm's-length, fairly cordial relationship that he'd been able to forge, but one in which the overriding feature was caution. His contacts at Rothera did not want to be drawn into the role of nursemaids for all those aboard the *Sea Sprite*.

This revelation seemed to surprise or upset no one in the crowded lounge, and nor did what Captain José had to say next. This was that the *Sea Sprite* would be staying in Paradise Bay for an indefinite period. And whilst this decision would be kept under constant review, there was certainly nothing at the moment to suggest that there was anywhere better to sit out the scourge of the spores. He then went on to say that everything would be done to make this period of enforced waiting as bearable as possible. And whilst being confined on a ship might prove to be something of a trial, he was very confident that Jane and her team would soon come up with all sorts of irresistible diversions. There was even, he advised, a large supply of jigsaws on board – although not, unfortunately, a set of deck quoits. Probably, he mused, because the *Sea Sprite* lacked the requisite decks...

This admission set off a round of laughter in the lounge, which was probably what the captain had intended. Because he was now about to invite the ship's doctor to speak, and little of what he was about to say would raise even a smile.

This was the Ukrainian doctor, Dr Kovalenko, and although he had not before addressed the assembled ship's company, and although he was hampered by a rather thick Ukrainian accent, he immediately came over as a confident public speaker – and one with a decidedly brisk delivery. He kicked off by reminding everyone of his comprehensive services and by encouraging all those in the room to avail themselves of these services sooner rather than later if they felt at all unwell. But at the same time, could they please avoid the need for other of his services by being ultra-careful? Broken bones and deep cuts were always bad news, and, accordingly, rushing around the ship and racing down stairwells were not to be advised.

He proffered these warnings not as a joke, but with all the seriousness he could muster. So that there wasn't quite the jolt there might otherwise have been when he moved on to the principal subject of his address...

Alex noticed that Captain José, who was standing to the side of Dr Kovalenko, looked decidedly uncomfortable at this stage of the proceedings. And that was because he no doubt knew what was coming. And then it came.

'I know this is a subject we don't want to think about,' the doctor began, 'but as your physician, I believe it is my duty to remind all of you that, however remote, there is still the possibility that we will be visited by the spores. And I doubt I need remind you that, once exposed to these spores, there is the prospect of only a drawn-out and painful death.'

The temperature in the lounge seemed to have dropped by ten degrees. Dr Kovalenko had just broached the taboo topic of the spores; something that most people had probably been able to push to the back of their minds in readiness for a well-provisioned period of indolence in fantastic surroundings. But there was something even more unmentionable to come; something connected with that likely drawn-out and painful death.

'Well,' Dr Kovalenko continued, more briskly than ever, 'Captain José has authorised me to tell you that, following our visits to Cierva Cove and...'

Here he pointed to the lounge windows on the port side.

'...that place over there, I have been able to assemble a whole range of medicines and... precursors, that I wouldn't normally be carrying on this vessel. And, well... with these additional resources – and with my own supplies – I will very soon be able to provide every individual on this ship with the means to avoid a protracted and agonising death...'

Alex became aware that his mouth had dropped open. He also became aware that elsewhere in the lounge there was a large helping of stunned silence. But the good doctor just carried on.

'What I am talking about is a drinkable liquid that is very similar to that which you might have seen injected into one of your pets, when that pet had reached the end of its life. It kills... almost instantaneously. Which, I think you'll agree, is very much more preferable than twenty or more hours of excruciating pain.'

At this point, nobody expressed agreement or otherwise, and the doctor ploughed on with his engrossing revelation.

'Of course, nobody will come under any pressure to make use of this... errh... remedy. But what I would ask is that all of you give it your serious consideration, and if and when you decide that you *do* want this... remedy, please visit me in my surgery. I will then provide you with one vial per person, to be stored somewhere in your cabin. It doesn't need to be refrigerated, but it does, of course, need somewhere where it won't be trodden on or sat on. Clearly, given the nature of the spores and the possible suddenness of their arrival, it would make no sense for me to attempt to distribute the vials when... well, when they might be urgently required. So, just to sum up, I will soon be able to provide, to anybody who wants it, an alternative to a horrible death, should the unlikely happen and we are overtaken by a cloud of spores. In fact, from around tomorrow lunchtime. But you must let me know whether you want this alternative. It should be your decision. I am, remember, a doctor, not a vet. And you're not a roomful of sick and ageing pets...'

Alex thought that this ending was a somewhat miserable attempt by the doctor to finish his announcement with just a soupçon of levity. But if it was, it didn't work. As he looked out at his audience, all the doctor would have seen was a sea of almost expressionless faces, the sort of faces one observes on people who are just emerging from shock. However, Alex was already pretty sure that, when the shock wore off completely, many if not most of the *Sea Sprite's* passengers and crew would be knocking on the door of the doctor's surgery in order to take out their very own (very sensible) 'death-insurance' policy. He knew he would, and he knew Debbie would as well. They would both be fools, he thought, if they didn't.

Inevitably, the wisdom or otherwise of taking up Dr Death's deadly potion was the first subject discussed over dinner just three hours later. Stuart and Gill had apparently been asked by the captain to discuss the communication arrangements with Rothera, so it was just the gang of five at the table this evening, and all five were keen to express their relief that there was now a painless route out of their existence should the need for one arise. In fact, Derek expressed more annoyance than relief, and questioned why it had taken a global cloud of spores to furnish him with something he had wanted for at least twenty years: a clean, swift way to end his own life at a time of his own choosing.

Nobody questioned his irritation. Nor the wisdom of having a lethal insurance arrangement. They all knew that they were still not safe from the threat of spores, and their continuing vulnerability was underlined by Roy. And in particular by some of Roy's 'interesting facts'. In this instance it was his listing of some latitude figures and what they might mean for their chances of not encountering the spores...

To start with he informed his friends that they were currently moored in a position that was approximately sixty-five degrees south of the Equator. Rothera, the BAS's main base, was, he then went on to inform them, about sixty-seven degrees south, and Halley VI, the BAS base on the Brunt Ice Shelf, was at seventy-five degrees. These positions compared to that of the supposedly super-safe refuge of Franz Josef Land of *eighty-one* degrees north of the Equator. In other words, they were nowhere near as far south as

Franz Josef Land was north. And how could they be? There was that huge Antarctic continent that constituted a bit of a barrier to navigation. But the fact remained that their current presumed safety was very much predicated on the assumption that a polar location was more important than an actual proximity to a pole. If in fact the latter was more important, then they might still be very exposed.

This latest chapter of Roy's collected compendium of facts caused a slight hiatus in the conversation. Maybe emphasising the vulnerability of all those aboard the *Sea Sprite* – in such a clinical manner – hadn't necessarily been the best move on Roy's part. And it certainly hadn't been conducive to stimulating a feel-good mood. Roy must have realised this, and quickly attempted to repair the damage by informing the company that his major concern with the deadly cocktail on offer was that he might not be able to manage it. Not because it was deadly, but because he found vials almost impossible to deal with. They were in the same category as beer bottles, he explained, and he could never drink beer from a bottle. He always had to ask for a glass.

Derek assured him that, if and when the time arrived, he would in no way associate a small vial of poison with a beer bottle. And even if he did, and he couldn't manage to swallow the vial's contents, then he would almost certainly be more than happy to just chew on the damn thing, glass, contents an' all. In fact, he assured him, he would find it a 'piece of cake'. Even if not quite as tasty as regular cake.

On hearing this, Roy looked very relieved, and then positively happy when Derek moved the conversation even further away from latitude statistics by asking all those around the table whether they had any projects in store to while away the next four or five weeks. After all, he said, there were only so many presentations one could attend.

His wife was the first to respond. Elaine's plan, it appeared, was to document life on board the *Sea Sprite* with her camera. She had two 4-gigabyte memory cards, and she wanted to fill them completely. It would be important, she maintained, that some record was kept of this unique period in their lives, and she would appoint herself as the record keeper.

Derek's reaction to this idea was not particularly helpful or well-judged. It was to point out that in a Stone Age world – which in all probability was imminent – a digital record of events might not be terribly useful. Elaine, however, took this caustic observation in her stride, and suggested that if she couldn't slot her memory cards into a working device, then she had somewhere else in mind where she would slot them instead.

Derek looked pretty unperturbed by this suggestion, but then sought to remove any mental image it might have created by asking Roy what, if anything, he planned to do.

That was easy, responded Roy. He would offer his services as a quizmaster. Jane was bound to want help in keeping everybody occupied, and what better way to do this than by putting on a series of quizzes? He could even do one on flags!

Debbie said that she thought this was a great idea, but that her own occupational therapy would involve her finding a bridge partner and some suitable opposition. She would initiate a bridge school. She hadn't played in years, she said, but here was a golden opportunity to brush the rust off her game and enjoy herself as well. And if that worked out, and there was still some time, she would probably see whether there were any other souls on the *Sea Sprite* who might be interested in forming a strip-poker school…

Alex raised his eyebrows at this point, but then compounded the risqué element of his wife's proposal by revealing his own solution to a month of potential boredom. This was to compile as many bawdy limericks as he could manage, and maybe even to invite everyone else to do the same, with a view to making it into a competition. At the end of their internment, he explained, all the limerick writers could present their efforts to the whole ship's company, who would then be invited to select a winner.

This idea won the approval of all those at the table. And then, with a bit of prompting from his wife, Derek revealed how he planned to fill the next four or five weeks of his life.

'I will read books – from the library,' he announced. 'And these will be bad books; books that are so bad that it will be a struggle to finish them.'

'Why?' challenged Debbie.

'For the sweet taste of victory,' he responded. 'As you are all no doubt aware, I have become a serial loser of late. I had already lost my country and any respect for its modern values before I came on this trip. And I've now lost my liberty and I might still be on track to lose my life. So, I just need to be a winner – in some small way. And if I can defeat a bad book – by actually finishing it, against all the odds – then that makes me a winner. I will have clocked up a victory. And if it's ten books, then that's ten victories. And that will make me the happiest person on this ship. I shall be simply radiating happiness and joy.'

This prediction brought the house down, and the laughter only stopped when Roy asked him how he would identify all these bad books. Derek's answer was that as about 99.9 per cent of all books published were bad, it was highly unlikely that he would end up with a good one.

This triggered another round of laughter, and the mood at the table was now far removed from the earlier chill caused by Roy's discourse on comparative latitudes. It then only got better as the conversation lurched from one non-death/non-spore-menace topic to another. It even managed to lurch in the directions of the sticking power of religions in the face of enlightenment, the rapid demise in the initial popularity of hula hoops, the (disputed) inferiority of spatial awareness in women, and whether, in counting the steps up to a platform, it was legitimate to include the platform itself as one of the steps (ie the final step). It also managed to convince Alex that he and Debbie would be able to manage the forthcoming confinement with ease. Not only would they find plenty to keep themselves occupied, but they had already found a group of people who would no doubt help to sustain them to the end of this confinement and beyond.

Alex also knew that those people had the very same thoughts themselves.

thirty-four

It was just 8.30 in the morning, and Jane's voice leapt out of the tannoy. It sounded breezier than ever.

'Good morning,' she sang. 'And what a morning. If you've peered out of your window, you'll already have seen that not only are we in "paradise", but we have the weather to match. Blue skies, no wind, and even a balmy minus two degrees already. In fact, perfect weather for a bit of sightseeing…'

Here she stopped. She was clearly waiting for that start of her message to sink in.

'You see, Captain José has told me that, given what we've all been through and what we've all achieved, he thinks it's only right and proper that you're provided with a bit of a treat this morning. And this treat will be in the form of a zodiac ride around Paradise Bay. Starting with a visit to a formerly well-stocked Argentinian research station…'

The message then went on to deal with the zodiac loading arrangements and their timing, but Alex was already busy working out how he might make his own arrangements to ensure that his and Debbie's zodiac was shared not only with their three long-standing friends but also with their new younger companions. After all, this might be the last time that Captain José allowed this welcome reversion to an 'expedition cruise activity', and he was keen that it should be enjoyed with all of his closest friends.

It wasn't straightforward, but with a bit of pleading and a bit of forbearance on the part of other passengers, Alex succeeded in his endeavour. And shortly after ten, he was in a zodiac with his five chosen companions – and his wife – and with Nick at the business end of the craft with his hand on the tiller. Three minutes later, all aboard were stepping onto the Almirante Brown landing stage and preparing to have a nose around the empty research station – before contemplating a climb up that substantial bluff that overshadowed it.

The 'research station' was not very interesting. Principally because it was little more than five mostly empty sheds, in which any evidence of any former research was as difficult to find as any evidence of comfort. Whichever poor sods had been deployed to this place, thought Alex, they must have craved a comfortable settee and a comfortable bed even before they craved the company of a woman. And they would all have been men. This place had the distinct feel of a military outpost, and Alex doubted that the Argentinian military had been at the forefront of gender equality. Especially when they were posting their 'forces' to somewhere with very limited facilities. And very limited opportunities for segregation.

The bluff was better. It was quite a climb through the deep snow, and only Stuart and Gill made it to the very top.

But even from a viewpoint halfway up this huge mound of rock, the view was not so much breathtaking as heart-stopping. How snow-covered peaks and a flat sea under a plain blue sky could create such wonder was, to start with, something of a mystery to Alex. But when he stopped to think, he realised that those peaks in the distance, lying under the strong Antarctic sun, were literally radiating whiteness, and that this whiteness was being reflected in a pool of magic blue below, with more of this magic blue above. And this was when he began to solve the mystery. Quite simply, this was the inanimate at its best, and it was almost too beautiful to absorb.

Easier was the beauty of the imperial shags. The eight sightseers had now reboarded their zodiac, and Nick had taken it around the other side of the bluff, where high up on its other sea-facing side was a shag colony. There were maybe a score of nests here, all apparently built on turrets of guano, and all occupied by one of these magnificent birds. How long each bird sat before he or she was relieved by his or her partner was something that even Nick didn't know. But what all of them did know was how privileged they were to be witnessing this sight. More so because they were amongst just a handful of people on the planet who could still witness anything.

This thought was in Alex's mind as Nick then made for the other side of the bay, which appeared to consist of the long, low front of one enormous glacier. And it was. And it was truly enormous. As the zodiac approached it, this became more and more apparent. Specific parts of it that Alex had taken to be the size of a small parish church, say, were in fact the size of a gigantic cathedral. It was as though his brain, when it had initially been charged with processing the information being fed to it by his eyes, had simply not been able to handle the scale of this vast block of frozen water. Only when the zodiac was a mere two hundred metres from its enormous ramparts could Alex's brain finally cope with the truly gargantuan size of this fabulous glacier.

Not for the first time, Alex felt humbled by the grandeur of this Antarctic realm, and by the almost incredible scale of its features. And, as if to emphasise his humble status, some alarmingly loud rumbling suddenly punctured the quiet of Paradise Bay. All aboard the zodiac then looked in the direction of this outsized sound, and saw what had caused it. Because there, above and beyond the glacier's face, were the powdery remains of a giant avalanche, already being consumed by the giant snowscape around it. To have been in that collapse of snow would no doubt have proved lethal. To witness its immediate aftermath from a distance was to witness no more than an inconsequential puff of white dust, a mere nothing in this vast polar setting. It really was indisputable, thought Alex; the hallmarks of the Antarctic had to include grandeur and scale; enormous, difficult-to-comprehend scale.

The seals might not have agreed. To them this place was just home. And a good place to find a small iceberg on which to take a nap. And it didn't matter what sort of seal you were. A small, flat-topped iceberg made an ideal bed whether you were a Weddell seal, a crabeater seal or even a leopard seal.

Nick found a Weddell seal on one iceberg, two crabeaters on another, and a leopard on a third. All were 'half asleep', their eyes closed but not always, and each of them not entirely unaware of the nearby zodiac. Alex was delighted that he was able to get such a good view of them all, and also very pleased that he could distinguish one smooth-bodied grey seal from its similarly smooth-bodied grey cousin. He'd remembered what he'd been told in the late John's lecture, and here were those three featured seals in person, all displaying the physical characteristics that enabled even a novice to tell them apart. The school lesson had been followed by a visit to the zoo. And this visit had proved to be a fitting end to this unexpected circumnavigation of Paradise Bay. Alex suspected he was not alone in thinking that Captain José, in allowing this round of excursions for all his passengers, couldn't have made a better decision.

He was right. All the others with whom he had shared the trip agreed that their captain had made what amounted to an ideal decision. They had now swapped their seats on an inflated roll of rubber for seats around a restaurant table. Here they would share their lunch and their impressions of their ride around the bay. All of them, including Nick, who had been to Paradise Bay before, expressed their delight in the magic of this place, and their hope that Captain José might punctuate the forthcoming lockdown with more such expeditions. If, that is, there was time between all that reading, all that limerick composition, all that photography, and all that card playing and quizzing.

Yes, with lunch over, it was time to embark on some of those self-help diversions, and when Alex and Debbie were back in their cabin, they made an immediate start. Debbie wrote a note to go on the ship's noticeboard in reception, requesting that anybody interested in bridge make contact; and Alex actually composed his first two limericks. Then they both embarked on another activity planned for the duration. Which was an extended siesta. Absorbing the marvels of Paradise Bay had obviously proved exhausting for them both.

Dinner was a dinner for seven: the five oldies and the two youngsters. And although the main course was clearly based on something that had lived in an Argentinian tin for some time, it was again a really enjoyable meal. By now, Stuart and Gill knew their fellow diners well enough to know when they were being serious and when they were being flippant (something that was no less than essential when listening to Derek or Roy). And this shared familiarity, as well as leading to a fair amount of jocularity, made for a truly amiable exchange of views; views that concerned just about anything other than their present situation or the regrettable loss of most of mankind. Nor was there any discussion of the future after Antarctica.

They were all in a bubble. After that full stop to their 'adventure' two days before, a feeling of well-being had grown on the *Sea Sprite*, and if one were fortunate enough to be one of the diners around their table of seven, this feeling of well-being was probably acute. It certainly was for Alex. In fact, he felt so very well and so very content that he was on the edge of feeling guilty. Given everything that had happened to so many people around the planet – and to Mike, Terry, John and their mates, and to those three Moldovans – he wondered whether he and his friends should be so happy. Because they undoubtedly were. Whatever the future had in store, they were together, they were relaxed in each other's company, and they were reassured by each other's company. And they all knew that they had this almost blissful state of affairs to look forward to for at least the immediate foreseeable future.

What's more, Alex had already dreamt up some rhymes for limericks number three and number four, and Debbie had no less than seven bridge players lined up for tomorrow morning. And Derek had even found in the ship's library a copy of Martin Amis's *Yellow Dog*...

four weeks later

thirty-five

It had become a routine for Alex and Debbie: quite early out of bed, but then, wrapped around with enough quilted outerwear to keep themselves warm, anything up to an hour sitting out on the cabin balcony, taking in the ever-present beauty and tranquillity of Paradise Bay. After that it was ablutions and breakfast, a walk around the outside of the Marco Polo Deck, and then their attendance at their respective 'group planning meetings'. There were quite a number of these, all instigated by Captain José, and all involving the participation of selected members of the *Sea Sprite's* passengers and crew, and all intended to achieve two ends. One was to prepare the ship's company for whatever they might face back in Ushuaia, and the other was to give the ship's passengers something to occupy them that might actually be of real use.

Debbie was in the group charged with establishing how the new colonists of South America might put together a mini health service. Not surprisingly, it was chaired by Dr Kovalenko, and it had been devoting much of its time to exploring how any medicines and medical supplies in Ushuaia could be gathered and stored and, given the age profile of those on board, which medicines and medical supplies might be those most in demand. There was then the issue of what to do when these supplies eventually ran out, and how feasible it would be to replace at least some of them with home-made alternatives, using any natural or synthetic materials that could be foraged in and around Ushuaia. There was also the small matter of how to support the skills of three of the handful of doctors who might still be alive on the planet. (There were possibly a number tucked away on various Antarctic research stations, but here on the *Sea Sprite* there were definitely just three: Dr Kovalenko, and two others who had been travelling as passengers and who had only recently retired.) All in all, as Debbie had reported to Alex, it had been quite an interesting and quite a challenging use of her time, and she had even decided that what her group had been doing might prove really useful, if not critical, to the survival of all the *Sea Sprite's* unlikely pioneers.

Alex – and Roy – were in the group that had been asked to deal with something entirely different, and this was the development of a constitution that might serve the purposes of… well, the residue of mankind. Alex had initially thought that this was a joke, just something to occupy a bunch of men and women who had none of the skills necessary to do anything else. After all, stuff like food procurement, fuel procurement, and even entertainment had already been handed out to others (as had 'security', despite Alex and

Roy's roles in the raiding operations), and clearly Captain José had been obliged to dream up something else to mop up the dregs.

However, it had soon become apparent that, far from being at the worthless end of occupational therapy, working out how a group of people would live together – and avoid their regressing into some sort of feudal and possibly brutal society – was no less than a critical task. Especially when one took into account that this group would comprise a bunch of old folk, quite a few younger folk (with a predominantly Filipino culture), and a miscellany of various 'other types'. There were just so many questions, principal amongst which was who would rule this rump of humanity, and who would choose this ruler? Would the new society be a democracy or an autocracy? And how about the laws? Who would establish them, and who would enforce them? And would there be a separate judiciary, and how would that work? All these questions could, of course, have been made redundant if Captain José had announced that he intended to remain in his present role and make every decision that needed to be made in respect of every aspect of everybody's life, in much the same way as he was doing now. However, he was the first to insist that this would not be an acceptable way to proceed, and that, as soon as his captaincy duties came to an end, his leadership needed in some way to be shared with or passed on to others. There were, he maintained, wiser heads on this ship than his own. And if that was debatable, then there were indisputably many on board with more experience, and this, he suggested, should be seen as a reservoir of resource and a reservoir that needed to be tapped.

Alex had, very early on, begun to enjoy this 'constitutional construction' work. As had Roy. It was a genuine mental challenge, and an opportunity to contribute something of real worth to everybody's future. It was also like nothing he'd done before. That alone made it constantly absorbing, and maybe even more absorbing than compiling all those limericks…

It was now four weeks since that first ride around Paradise Bay, and Alex had written forty-four limericks, all of which he intended to enter into a limerick competition that he himself had launched the day after the ride. This writing was something he did in the afternoons, when he wasn't attending a presentation on *Pelagic Birds, The Secrets of Ancient Greece, The Flora of the Falklands,* or *The Recollections of a Customs Officer* (which was Patrick's very own 'uniquely bemusing' contribution). Or, indeed, when he wasn't struggling with one of Roy's quizzes or struggling even more through a rubber of bridge with a partner whom he had decided was card-suit dyslexic. The two of them together soon established themselves as serial losers.

Combined with the continued provision of imaginative food, the continued remarkable forbearance of the entire crew – and another six zodiac rides around the bay – all these intellectual and not-so-intellectual demands made for a very manageable time aboard the *Sea Sprite.* And if one added in the frequent sightings of humpback whales, assorted seals, a good number of penguins and quite a few other birds, it was more than just manageable; it was almost idyllic. And, whilst not something that Alex could have imagined doing indefinitely, it was certainly far more than just bearable. Every day, at some point during the day, he would stop to ask himself why he – and his wife – had been spared the carnage that had been visited on the rest of the world and had instead been delivered into such a sybaritic haven – on a well-appointed, well-provisioned ship, well out of harm's way. Or, at least, it seemed to be out of harm's way. Despite those terminal preparations recommended by Dr Kovalenko (of which Alex and Debbie had availed themselves), the spores had not returned, and in most people's minds they were very clearly no more than a distasteful fragment of history; a passing blight that had overtaken the old world but that was not about to overtake the new world down here on the *Sea Sprite*. Or even when the new world docked back in Ushuaia. The spores were definitely has-been spores. Everybody on this ship knew this for sure.

Alex, however, wasn't quite so absolutely sure. So, every day he checked that his and Debbie's vials were still intact and still ready for use. Nevertheless, he had to admit to himself that he was finding it increasingly difficult to keep alive any sort of raw fear. Now it was more like an intermittent dull toothache, the occasional unwanted realisation that a dreadful death might still descend from the skies and put an end to the lives of all those aboard the *Sea Sprite*. But only in much the same way as a boiler explosion might, or a fire in the galley that got out of control. Terrible prospects, all of them, but all of them not a great deal more than a theoretical possibility. And especially in the case of the spores. After all, one only had to consider how they were spread: through the upper atmosphere and then by descending to ground level – everywhere other than at the two poles. How, then, could what was now a five-week hiatus fit into that model of distribution? It couldn't. It simply wasn't possible. And hence that intermittent, ever-duller toothache that Alex was experiencing – rather than acute fear. Indeed, so much had the fear diminished that yesterday he had even forgotten to check on the vials. Although that may in part have been because he had heard a rumour – that today, Captain José would be making a significant announcement...

All the planning groups had been given a deadline to complete their deliberations and produce a report. And that was two days ago. This was to give the captain a little time to study the reports before their contents were presented to the whole ship's company, probably in a series of lounge gatherings, and probably when the *Sea Sprite* was on its way back to Ushuaia. He was apparently keen to energise his charges in preparation for their having to confront the reality of their new lives, and he believed that engaging them in all the practicalities of these new lives – as examined by the planning groups – would be an ideal way to do this. It would also mean that the findings and recommendations of each of the groups would be fresh in everybody's mind.

So, if that was his thinking, and he now had all the reports – and it was now just over four weeks since the beginning of the *Sea Sprite's* 'rest' in Paradise Bay – it was odds on that an announcement was imminent. The odds then shortened considerably when Jane informed her listeners over the tannoy that at the conclusion of today's afternoon presentation on *The Night Skies of the Southern Hemisphere*, Captain José would make a short address, for which he would welcome everybody's attendance. And that, thought Alex, would not be to tell his assembled audience that he was a keen stargazer himself.

It wasn't. It was, as all aboard the *Sea Sprite* suspected, to announce the end to their sojourn in Antarctica. Captain José started by telling them that the guys at Rothera were being as inscrutable as ever, and he had now formed the view that they regarded the *Sea Sprite* as no more than a potential threat to their own chances of survival. They wanted to avoid any contact with his vessel if at all possible, because they wanted to avoid any responsibility for all those aboard it. This was unfortunate, he said, but almost inevitable. And, in any event, it wouldn't have any bearing on his own plans. Which involved setting off for Ushuaia the very next morning! Tomorrow, immediately after breakfast, the *Sea Sprite's* engines would be started, and it would embark on its journey north, with Ushuaia as its intended destination.

His tone, throughout the whole of his address, had been very upbeat, even when he'd reported on Rothera's indisputably selfish attitude. ('It's very much their loss, not ours,' he proposed, 'and they'll probably come to regret it.') And to top off this upbeat theme, he concluded the address by informing everybody that tomorrow evening, the first evening of their journey 'home', there would be a grand Captain's Dinner. With all the trimmings. The kitchen staff were already beavering away to prepare what would be a very special meal, and there would even be a suspension of the alcohol rationing system. Wine would flow. And all the ladies would be expected to attend in their poshest frocks and all the men in their smartest gear. There would even be cocktails before the meal, at which there would be the opportunity to choose the winner of the limerick competition. It would, Captain José emphasised, be a night to remember. Albeit not, of course, in the *Titanic* sense.

This, his last remark, earned him a long-lasting round of laughter, and that it lasted so long was probably a function of the general mood in the crowded lounge. This was one of enthusiasm and anticipation, and a sense of almost childlike excitement at what the immediate future might hold. And if there were any concerns, or any doubts, or indeed any fears still lurking in people's minds, for the moment at least they were forgotten. Although that didn't mean that they wouldn't be remembered when the band of five plus two gathered again for this evening's more modest dinner.

In fact, the subject of fear in the singular was the first topic of discussion. Stuart was interested to know whether his companions at the table felt more or less fearful now than they had when he'd addressed them in the main lounge well over a month ago – to reveal his knowledge of the spores.

The consensus around the table was a definite 'less'. That initial shock – of learning that the world of humans was being rapidly devoured – had certainly instilled a huge amount of fear in everybody's minds. But now, as all agreed, it was very different. Alex, it appeared, wasn't the only one at the table who hadn't been able to sustain that early level of raw fear indefinitely. Indeed, it also became clear that, for all seven of the diners, the mood of cautious anticipation that now suffused the ship had largely overtaken even the residue of that initial fear.

Nevertheless, not everybody's emotions were entirely positive. And certainly not Elaine's. This became clear when she admitted to feeling a little embarrassed and almost ashamed to be on the threshold of a brave new world, but a new world that would be in the hands of a bunch of people who had done little more than hide themselves away. Pioneers, she maintained – and settlers and trailblazers – were almost exclusively courageous and resourceful types; stalwarts who were prepared to undergo hardships and all sorts of dangers to realise their dreams. They crossed seas in tiny vessels, they endured near starvation and all sorts of diseases in their attempt to build for themselves new lives. And they very often had to fight for their lives. Well, she conceded, this remnant of humanity on board the *Sea Sprite* had lost nine of its number at Deception Island, and there had been that singular display of outstanding courage at Cierva Cove – by just a handful of other brave souls. But, by and large, the ancient mariners aboard this vessel had adopted a very passive approach on their road to a new Jerusalem. And it couldn't be denied that they had run away. (And here, Elaine made clear that she was referring to the *Sea Sprite's* dash south, and not Stuart and Gill's 'escape' from the Falklands.) What's more, she said, they had been obliged to endure no privations of any sort, and essentially had been able to continue a pampered cruise while the rest of humanity had been writhing in its death throes. And all that, she concluded, could hardly be characterised as heroic. It had all been far too easy, far too straightforward, and just not the stuff of building a cautious new world, let alone a brave one.

Alex could see her point. The passengers and crew of the *Sea Sprite,* he thought, had simply been lucky. (Or at least, those of them who hadn't been taken at Deception Island, and who hadn't had to earn their luck through some sharpshooting at Cierva Cove.) But he also thought that in a way they were all as much the victims of the super-spores as were all those who had perished. Their old lives had been ripped away, and they'd reacted in the only way they could. And they now had before them the considerable task of creating new lives; something that would be a real challenge no matter how much enthusiasm they could sustain. And it might yet require some heroic efforts.

Similar thoughts to these were already being expressed by Debbie, but before Alex could add his own voice to the discussion, Roy decided to take the discussion in a different direction. And he did this by pointing out – politely – that it was always fruitful to look at any situation from other than a human perspective. Especially when that situation involved humans.

Elaine was right, he said. There was very little that was heroic about the *Sea Sprite's* odyssey so far, and whatever those aboard it could establish as a new beginning would be built on foundations composed mostly of passivity cemented together with bucketfuls of 'self'. But that hardly mattered. Because what *did* matter was the world, the whole world, and not just the speck of brave new world that might be fashioned by either the *Sea Sprite's* scraps of humanity or by those still tucked away on Antarctic bases.

Here, he began to elaborate on his theme. And he did this by suggesting to his table companions that, if one regarded the world not as a large rock circling the sun, but as a complex web of life that had taken billions of years to evolve and now represented something of untold beauty and wonder, then perversely the world's future had just become infinitely brighter. For years it had been under attack from one small element of all that complexity, otherwise known as man. Indeed, this 'man' had already inflicted so much damage that an extinction event had been triggered that was destined to shred more of the Earth's beauty and wonder than had been managed by a giant asteroid in the dim and distant past. But now, through chance, 'good' fortune or maybe Gaia's design, that toxic element had been almost entirely removed, and even if a tiny residue of toxicity remained and was able to increase in size, it was indisputable that 'the world' could look forward to a healthy future for thousands of years to come, if not for a lot longer than that. It was a simple question, he proposed, of deciding what was the real toxin: the spores, or those affected by the spores? And in coming to that decision, maybe the nature of the foundations of the new humanity was not that important.

To her enormous credit, Elaine did not appear to be in the least offended, and her only response to Roy's gentle broadside was a smiley 'Touché'. She clearly knew him too well to think that there was an iota of malice in his remarks, and just as clearly she didn't resent being reminded of that other-than-human perspective. After all, one could not dismiss the fact that humanity, whatever it managed now – and if it survived at all – would be a bit player for thousands if not tens of thousands of years to come. And it was only right and proper that it relinquished its roles as the centre of attention and the only thing on the planet that mattered.

After Roy's heartfelt contribution to the discussion, there was still much of the evening to come, and initially Derek assumed the mantle of the group's self-critical conscience by suggesting that whatever the *Sea Sprite's* cargo of humans did when they got back to Ushuaia, it should not countenance the revival of any of those dreadful religions that for so long had put humans on a pedestal and relegated every other life form to the status of useful, edible, sport-worthy or just plain worthless. In fact, he promised, if a born-again Christian or a Hindu or a Muslim crawled out of his shell, he might just have to knock his head off. And if any cult appeared, he would insist it was strangled at birth…

Following on from this laying down of the rules concerning the lack of religious freedom in Derek's new world, the conversation moved on to some less 'strident' topics. Debbie brought up the subject of music, and whether there would be any way to listen to all that wonderful music from the '60s and '70s ever again. Gill wondered aloud how she would get through life without the services of a professional dentist. And Alex finally rounded off the evening by asking Debbie whether her group's consideration of the medical needs of the *Sea Sprite's* senior citizens had extended to their need for Viagra or one of its generic equivalents. And, if so, had they possibly formulated how this 'assistance' might be located and, if it was, how it might be distributed to those in need? He didn't get an answer, but he did get one final round of laughter on this last evening in Paradise Bay. And he did ensure that all those at the table left it with smiles on their faces, even if, as they dropped off to sleep in their respective cabins, they brought back to mind Roy's salutary comments on their rather overdue insignificant status…

thirty-six

As Stuart lay in bed, still very much awake, he was not thinking about Roy's salutary comments. Instead, he was thinking about whether he and Gill should participate in Captain José's return to Ushuaia. Every day he tested his earlier decision to throw in his lot with the passengers and crew of the *Sea Sprite,* and so confirm in his mind that he was doing the best for Gill and for himself. Up to now this test had always come up with the same result: stay and assist Captain José in any way that he and Gill could, and reject any other course of action. Especially a yacht trip to Rothera.

However, tonight, it wasn't so clear-cut. He realised something had changed. And what it was, of course, was the fact that the voyage back to Ushuaia would mean the closing down of any real opportunity to abandon the *Sea Sprite* in favour of the currently reachable Rothera base. He and Gill might not be welcome there, and they might even be turned away if they did arrive there. Stuart knew this only too well.

Just as he knew that he had always come down in favour of sticking with the *Sea Sprite* not because of this probability of rejection by Rothera but instead because of the attachment he and Gill had formed with so many of those on board this vessel. Nevertheless, there was still that niggling attraction that could not be ignored; the attraction of the company of people of a similar age. Even if he and Gill might ultimately decide to go their own way.

He could not help admitting to himself that whilst he and Gill had made some real friends on the *Sea Sprite*, and not least the famous five, these friends were predominantly old friends – as in years, not duration. And bluntly, how long would they live? And even more bluntly, did he want to become one of their carers? How easy would it be for him and Gill to sail off into the sunset if it meant deserting real friends when their needs had become acute?

He stayed awake until the early hours trying to come to a decision, and finally he realised that the ties he and Gill had already formed on this ship with so many people meant that abandoning these people would be far, far worse than their abandoning all those poor sods back at Mount Pleasant. And for what? Merely to be with a bunch of people of their own age whom they didn't even know. And it would also be to ignore the fact that this ship had saved their lives, and that so many of the people aboard it had welcomed them with open arms, to say nothing of then providing them with weeks of comfort and sustenance – and genuine friendship.

Yes, friendship above all else still bound Stuart – and Gill – to this vessel. Gill, maybe even more. Indeed, hadn't she told him all too often how she had been overwhelmed by the warmth of this big bunch of grandpas and grandmas, and he could simply not conceive that she would willingly break so many newly formed bonds. That would take something quite extraordinary to happen.

He wasn't in the situation he wanted to be in. But when had he been? Certainly not back at Mount Pleasant. So, he had just better accept that for better or for worse he was one of the *Sea Sprite's* company, and his fate lay with theirs. And even if that meant he was making the wrong decision, then at least he was making the wrong decision for the right reasons.

He and Gill would be going back to Ushuaia aboard the *Sea Sprite*, and that was final.

thirty-seven

On their last morning in Paradise Bay, Alex and Debbie once again followed their normal routine, albeit they were more reluctant than ever to quit their established cabin-balcony survey of the bay's superlative charms. The weather was perfect, and the bay looked no less than stunning. And, of course, tomorrow morning they wouldn't be here to judge whether it still looked stunning or not. Because they would be gone. This was their final chance to drink in the early-morning splendour of one of the most beautiful places on the planet, and they wanted to gulp down as much of it as they could. Even if it meant turning up rather late for breakfast.

They did just make it in time, and they were still able to share their meal with Elaine and Derek, who, it appeared, had also lingered over their last morning view of Paradise Bay. And it must have been the finality of this act – for all four of them – that was responsible for the distinct air of melancholy at their shared table. It was so distinct that Alex thought he would try to smother it with a cloak of futile questioning. He would ask Derek whether he was now prepared to reveal the conclusions of his 'top-secret' planning group; the one he'd asked to be allowed to join and the one that had been given the innocuous-sounding title of 'clearance'. Because it had been charged with examining what might need to be done to clear the multiple dead bodies they might find on the streets of Ushuaia...

Derek maintained the reluctance he'd shown for the past four weeks to discuss any aspect of this group's work, and informed Alex that he would simply have to wait. The group's findings would, he assured him, be made public in one of the forthcoming plenary sessions. Or, at least, those of its findings that wouldn't cause too much distress. However, this answer merely spurred Alex on, and he therefore asked Derek to give him just a hint of the nature of the more distressing findings. He would be so grateful, he said, and he and Debbie would promise not to tell another soul.

It was no good. In the first place, Elaine told Alex that Derek had disclosed barely anything to her, despite four weeks of her asking. And in the second place, Derek's expression was beginning to betray the fact that he was really relishing being the custodian of some 'secret' information, and that he intended to keep it secret. Even from Alex and Debbie – and Roy. He was sure, he said – with a very wide grin – that in his situation, all three of them would do exactly the same.

He was right. And Alex had known from the outset that his questioning would be futile. It had, however, dispelled that air of melancholy at the table, and he now sought to ensure that it didn't return by supplying his table companions with his own speculations regarding what might be extremely distressing about the clearance of corpses from Ushuaia's thoroughfares. This wasn't too difficult. There was little about what this might involve that *wasn't* extremely distressing. So, he started off with the state of the corpses, which he imagined would be terrible, before moving on to their number, which he suggested might be enormous, and then to the actual clearance techniques, which he proposed could be the most distressing aspect of all. Fortunately, his table companions had finished eating by the time he'd adopted this further avoidance-of-melancholia tactic, but that didn't stop him being reprimanded by his wife. She conceded that the reality of Ushuaia might be something they all needed to come to terms with very soon, but she questioned why it had to be made a topic of conversation at the breakfast table. And while they were still in the magical surroundings of Paradise Bay.

No sooner had Debbie delivered this reprimand, than she and her three table companions became aware that the *Sea Sprite's* engines had sprung into life. It seemed that they would very soon be leaving those magical surroundings...

Within minutes, Alex and Debbie were back in their cabin, observing their exit from the bay as their vessel embarked on its long trip north, and what very quickly became apparent was that they had by no means left the magic kingdom. The scenery – everywhere – was, just as they'd observed on their journey south, superb. And so simply enthralling that they'd soon taken themselves to the stern of the Erikson Deck to provide themselves with a more panoramic view of what they were passing. They spent much of the morning here – before then spending quite a bit of time in the bar. Debbie, in particular, wanted to save her appetite for the evening's gala Captain's Dinner, and was happy to let a large bowl of peanuts serve as her and her husband's lunch. This also meant that they could spend a little more time at the stern of the ship before turning up for this afternoon's lecture on *Giant Icebergs and South Georgia*. It sounded just interesting enough to persuade them to forsake even more scenery viewing. At least for three-quarters of an hour.

Most of the other passengers appeared to have come to the same conclusion, so that when Tony began to tell his audience that in recent decades several icebergs had been observed passing close to South Georgia that were nearly the size of the island itself, he was addressing a virtually full house. It soon became an attentive full house as well. Tony's presentation was really very interesting indeed, and it held everybody in its thrall, right up until about ten minutes from its scheduled end, when they all began to realise that the *Sea Sprite* was slowing…

Tony carried on, now deep into a discussion about the Ross Ice Shelf. But he was beginning to lose his audience. And it was lost forever when Captain José entered the lounge with Jane and strode quickly towards where Tony was standing, while, at the same time, a voice on the tannoy was demanding the immediate attendance in the lounge of all those who had not been tempted by a top-up of their knowledge of giant icebergs. Captain José then relieved Tony of his microphone, and used it to tell the assembled company that he would wait just a couple of minutes to allow others to join them, after which he would make an important announcement. He looked grey, and his voice had lost something of its usual confidence. He occupied himself for the pregnant two minutes by whispering to Jane and Tony, but his appearance, and the manner of his appearance, had already reduced the atmosphere in the lounge to one of acute alarm. Everybody could clearly sense that something was very wrong. Then finally he spoke. His voice sounded almost strained.

'Ladies and gentlemen,' he started. 'I am going to make this announcement as short as I can. For reasons that will soon become apparent. And the first thing to say is that I have recently been in radio contact with Rothera. They called to tell us that last night they had been unable to raise Halley VI. That, you'll remember, is the British base on the Brunt Ice Shelf, well to the south and east of Rothera. Initially, they weren't too concerned. They've had communication problems in the past. But then they couldn't raise another base; a Chilean one to the south-east. And then another one, and then yet another. And this was against a background of an unusual air mass moving in a north-western swirl towards them...'

'Jesus!'

It was an involuntary shout from the middle of the room, and it formed a prelude to a far more chilling revelation from the captain.

'I am very sorry to tell you this...'

And here it sounded as though he was about to dry up. But then he gathered himself and continued.

'...but while I was speaking to the base commander, I began to hear... well, quite a lot of noise in the background. And then he... well, he just said something like "They're here", and "God help you" or "God help us". I can't quite remember. And then there was nothing. Other than some more noises in the background. And then… screams and howls…'

Here he did dry up. Not that anybody likely noticed. Too many of them were clearly processing what this news would mean for their chances of seeing out this day. Alex was no different. His stomach felt completely empty and his mouth as dry as old parchment. He then realised that he had his arm around Debbie's shoulders, and then that Captain José was speaking again.

'There can be no doubt,' he announced, 'that the spores are in the Antarctic, and that they are heading north-west…'

'So why are we slowing?' shouted a woman from the back of the room. 'Why aren't we making… you know, full steam ahead?'

Captain José responded to this question without hesitation. Because he knew the answer only too well.

'Our reading of the swirling movement of that air mass tells us that it might miss us entirely. And I emphasise "might". Frankly, it's just about impossible to tell where it will go. However, we certainly can't outrun it. No matter how much we "steam ahead". And there's as much chance of our running into it if we continue as there is if we drop anchor here and… well, just hope that it passes. But as your captain, I can tell you that I would much rather we were stationary if and when we encounter these spores than our being on the move, when we might quickly find ourselves without anyone on the bridge who can steer this ship or even bring it to a safe stop. Given the nature of the spores, you would be quite justified to argue that whether we are stationary or moving, it would make little difference. But that's more than *no* difference. And if we cannot judge whether we will be safe here – or further north – or indeed somewhere further back south, I think it makes no sense to do other than find a good place to moor where we are now, and… await our fate.

'So, ladies and gentlemen, I am now going to ask you all to return to your cabins, close your doors, close your windows – and just wait. And, of course, listen for any tannoy announcements. I know that doesn't sound like much of a plan. But it's all we can do. Other than hope and maybe pray that since we've got this far, then we'll be able to get a little further yet. Like to Ushuaia. And sorry, but no questions. There just isn't time. I want you to move now!'

His shocked audience had become children again, and without any rebellion, they now began to follow their teacher's instructions by filing out of the lounge. Not by any means in a panic, but rather slowly, and with faces that betrayed that they were possibly already reconciled to whatever might await them. Alex and Debbie joined the moving throng, and soon found themselves with Elaine and Derek – and Roy. No words were exchanged, and there was no need for words. Instead, transient hugs and a few tears did the job. And it was similar for Stuart and Gill. They had been swept out of reach, but not before their five 'grandparents' had made clear their feelings for them with a combination of hopeful smiles and a few more tears. Alex immediately wished they'd all been given just a little more time.

The ship was now stationary. The crew had performed a slow 180-degree turn to bring it to the edge of the peninsula. And back in their cabin, Alex and Debbie were setting about the task of giving each other some much-needed reassurance. But it was difficult. Especially when they admitted to each other that their immediate priority should be to look out their two doses of death. Dr Kovalenko's wonder potion had to be put on standby without any delay whatsoever. This they dealt with, and then they embarked, as instructed, on the task of waiting. This was even more difficult than those mutual reassurances, and it required the employment of one Kindle, one book, and the pretence that they could both take in anything of what they were supposedly reading. Alex was doing no more than seeing consecutive lines of words on a page, and then Debbie told him that this was her experience as well, which was when they both turned their attention to the view outside their cabin. From Alex's not-entirely-reliable observations and calculations, the captain had moored the *Sea Sprite* somewhere to the north of Danco Island, and this meant it was parked in another 'area of outstanding natural beauty'. And, unlike a book or a Kindle, the view through the cabin window promised to hold Alex and Debbie's attention for quite some time. There were numerous icebergs out there. And whilst none of them was the size of South Georgia, they were all more than fascinating and all far more than handsome.

Nevertheless, time passed rather slowly, and the only 'thrills' all afternoon were two tannoy announcements and a delivery. The first announcement was merely to emphasise to the ship's company the importance of remaining in their cabins, and the second was to advise all passengers of the forthcoming delivery. A knock on their cabin door would herald the arrival of some bottled water and a couple of sandwiches, which, the announcement said, should be gathered up quickly and then the cabin door re-closed as soon as possible. For Alex and Debbie, this happened within only minutes of this second announcement. And only minutes after the admission into their cabin of the sandwiches, they were gone. After that bowl-of-peanuts lunch, they had both become extremely hungry.

The sandwiches kept the hunger at bay for some time, but by early evening it was forcing its way back in again – for both of them – and that's why Debbie wondered aloud whether, if the Captain's Dinner was now highly unlikely to take place, there would be another delivery to their door – of something more substantial than prawn mayonnaise sandwiches. Even though those earlier ones had been delicious. She had done this aloud-wondering from her position on the bed, while at the same time Alex had been looking out of the cabin window. It was then that he put his own wondering into words, and he did this by saying, in a bemused tone of voice, 'I wonder whether that's Stuart and Gill.'

He had caught sight out of the window of the *Gūse,* the yacht that had been towed at the stern of the *Sea Sprite* ever since it was first commandeered. Only now it was moving away from the *Sea Sprite* in a southerly direction, and on its deck were two people, a man and a woman.

Debbie had now joined Alex at the window, and they both stared intently at the diminutive craft. Against the grandeur all around, and compared to the huge icebergs all around, it looked smaller than ever.

'It is them,' she announced. 'I recognise Gill's jacket. And Stuart's, for that matter...'

'You're right,' confirmed Alex. 'But where are they going? They can't be going to Rothera. That'd be suicide...'

Debbie looked into her husband's eyes.

'They always wanted to be together. And they've had so little time...'

'Yeah, but they didn't have to do that. It's just crazy. Anything could happen.'

'I think they know that, Alex. But they'll be together when it does. And I think that's what they'd want...'

Alex felt helpless and angry. No matter what his wife might be suggesting, what Stuart and Gill were doing was not right. And they were putting themselves in so much peril. If only they would come to their senses. Before it was too late.

Captain José must have had similar thoughts, because his voice was now coming through a loudhailer. And whilst Alex and Debbie found it difficult to hear his every word, he was clearly pleading with Stuart and Gill to come back to his vessel. As soon as they possibly could.

However, that wasn't going to happen. As the captain was still projecting his voice towards the yacht, Gill fell over and started to writhe around on the deck of the *Gūse,* whereupon Stuart, without any hesitation whatsoever, scooped her up in his arms and jumped with her into the sea. He then seemed to pull her towards the hull of the yacht, and then beneath it. He could only be trying to make their end as quick as possible, and while he still had Gill in his arms. And soon it looked as though he'd succeeded. As much as Alex and Debbie studied the surface of the sea all around the yacht, they could see no signs of their friends and no signs of life. The spores had done their work. Which meant that the spores had arrived to do their work on the *Sea Sprite* as well...

Alex felt his heart pumping, and then he noticed that Debbie was crying. She started to wipe the tears away with her hand, and then, with a big Debbie smile on her face, she addressed her husband.

'Well, we gave them a bloody good run for their money,' she said. 'And, you know, I'm not so sure I ever wanted to live in Argentina…'

Alex smiled at her, and then told her that he pretty much agreed with her on both counts, after which he asked her a question.

'How do you want to play this?' he asked. 'I mean, shall we wait a bit, or shall we do it now?'

'Not yet, Alex. This was going to be a special night, remember. And it still should be. Which means, I think, we should get appropriately dressed. I certainly don't want to step into eternity wearing just an ordinary sweater and an old pair of slacks. And it won't take us long. I'm sure we've got time.'

'Too true,' confirmed Alex. 'I mean, we can hardly let humanity down by going out looking like we didn't care. And we're certainly not going to get another opportunity to dress up. So, let's get going…'

And they did. They got going by sorting out the clothes they wanted to wear, and by Alex commandeering the bathroom for a while before Debbie then took it for her own use. While she was sorting herself out in there, Alex went to the cabin window and looked out to see whether the *Gūse* was still visible. And whether there was any trace of Stuart and Gill.

There was nothing. The yacht must have drifted out of sight, and his friends' bodies must have sunk out of sight.

The scene outside the window had reverted to its normal undisturbed, pristine beauty. And this had its inevitable effect; it captivated his attention to the exclusion of everything else. The whites out there seemed whiter than ever; the blues bluer than ever. And the icebergs; they were simply stunning. Indeed, one huge iceberg just two hundred metres from the *Sea Sprite* was no less than painfully beautiful, and completely mesmerising.

He could no doubt have stared at the vista without indefinitely, but he knew he had other things to do, and finally he began to turn his attention away from the view through the cabin window. However, just as he did so he observed a little movement in that outside scene, and his attention was captured again. How could it not be? That movement heralded the arrival of whales...

There were four of them, four humpback whales in a tight group, spoiling the glassy-smooth surface of the channel with their rising, blowing, diving and splashing. Although whether they were feeding, bonding, playing or just relishing their existence, Alex couldn't tell. But it didn't matter. They were a joy to behold. And Debbie would no doubt want to behold them as well. He should get her to the window...

'Debbie, there's some whales out here. Four humpbacks. You should come and see them. They're really close.'

Debbie was soon walking towards him from the bathroom – still fiddling with a reluctant earring in her left ear.

'Four of them?' she inquired.

'Yeah. Just to the left. Over there.'

She had now joined her husband, and, having secured the reluctant earing into its designated earlobe, she was soon peering through the window to locate the promised four cetaceans.

'Ah yes,' she exclaimed. 'Fantastic. And look, did you see that fluke? It was pale underneath…'

'Well, if it wasn't, you'd be a bit concerned. They are humpbacks, and their flukes are supposed to be pale underneath. Just like we're supposed to have a crease in our bum.'

'Don't be vulgar,' she responded. But her words were delivered with a smile, and she then spoke again.

'Just look at them,' she said. 'Aren't they sublime?'

'Sublime and… happy. At least, they look pretty happy. And I must say, it's difficult to imagine that they're not. After all, they've got this wonderful place to live in and they've got each other as well.'

Debbie turned from the view of the whales to face her husband.

'Just as *we've* got each other,' she said. 'As I'm sure you've not forgotten…'

'Sorry,' responded Alex, 'it's just…'

'…time we got ourselves ready,' interrupted Debbie. 'And I'm nearly there.'

'So am I,' declared Alex. 'I just want to put my boots in the wardrobe and sort out the safe…'

He knew very well that it was quite bizarre to be concerned about the tidiness of either the cabin or the safe in their present circumstances, but it was just the way he was. And Debbie would understand. She was very much the same, and had already put away all her unwanted clothes. Nevertheless, on this occasion, Alex's emotions were about to override his natural inclinations, and he decided that his boots and the safe could wait just a while. And this was because he had now registered the wonderful appearance of his wife.

'Debbie,' he pronounced slowly, 'you look beautiful.'

And she did. No longer young, she still retained her essential good looks, and in her brand-new wine-coloured dress and her favourite wine-coloured shoes, she looked absolutely splendid. And so too did her eyes. Their sparkle matched that of the icebergs outside. Although, unlike the icebergs, they radiated warmth.

She acknowledged Alex's compliment with a small nod of her head, and then she spoke.

'Thank you. I thought I should make an effort.'

Alex hesitated, and then he went into the walk-in wardrobe, and was soon back out again, holding in his right hand his bright-blue linen jacket.

'Might not be up to your dress, but I've brought it this far, and it hasn't got that many creases in it. As long as you don't look at the sleeves...'

Debbie grinned.

'It'll do just fine. I mean, just absolutely fine. In fact, I think that together we will be the best-dressed couple aboard. No matter how many creases...'

'Bloody right,' confirmed her husband. 'Absolutely bloody right.' And then he approached her, threw his jacket on the bed and embraced her tightly – and held her in this embrace for quite some time. When he finally released her, he then spoke.

'I love you,' he said slowly. 'I always have and I always will. In fact, I may love you more now than I've ever loved you before. And if that sounds stupid...'

'It doesn't,' interrupted Debbie. 'Because I feel just the same. I mean, I really do. So… it can't be stupid, can it?'

Here she gave her husband a generous smile, and then she closed down this ultimate emotional exchange by reminding Alex of the need to attend to the practical. She had a face to check and he had his boots and the safe to attend to. So, after another not-quite-so-long embrace, they both got on with their respective duties, until finally they were standing together in the cabin, Debbie in her wine-coloured dress and her wine-coloured shoes, Alex in his bright-blue jacket and a pair of dark-blue trousers. They were now ready to embark on their plans for the evening. And this was just as well. They had already heard some unusual noises that sounded as though they were coming from the bridge, and there now came the distinct sound of screaming from somewhere below.

Debbie lay on the bed first – on its left-hand side. As she was doing this, Alex collected the two vials, opened them, and then carefully sat on the right-hand side of the bed. He handed one vial to his wife, kissed her, and then lay back himself. Debbie was left-handed and Alex was right-handed. This meant that they could still hold each other's hands while they used their favoured hands to deal with the poison. It was then only a case of saying, in unison, 'I love you', before bringing the vials to their lips and drinking their contents in one quick gulp.

They were both dead before the vials dropped to the floor, and well before the screams arrived just outside their cabin.

thirty-eight

It was the start of a new era, but for all those creatures that now had the planet to themselves, just the start of a new day.

The four humpback whales were still around. They were just yards from the *Sea Sprite*, and they were still rising, blowing, diving and splashing. Still doing what whales have done for aeons, but now without the threat of being harpooned, and without the threat of their food source being stolen by a fleet of oversized krill trawlers. They had a golden future to look forward to, as did all their cetacean cousins, and none more so than the champion giant of the seas, the majestic blue whale.

There were two of these magnificent creatures swimming together to the east of South Georgia; two of the tiny number that remained after a century of hunting that had seen nearly four hundred thousand of their number massacred and then butchered for their flesh. They too now had nothing to fear from their upright mammal cousins, and in all likelihood they would be able to play their own part in restoring their global population to its rightful pre-carnage levels. And in time, even their race memory of grotesque murderous chases, explosive harpoons, cries of pain through the water – and places like Grytviken in South Georgia – would all be expunged. Not for them the grisly prospect of being 'processed' to near extinction; but instead just a near-infinite future of feeding, migrating, breeding and, despite being the largest animal in the world, gliding effortlessly through all the world's oceans and seas.

Of course, they shared this water-aided agility with many other creatures, including the fur seals and elephant seals that long ago had recolonised Grytviken after its whaling days were done, and that had been around when the *Sea Sprite* had stopped there just a few weeks before. Then, these new colonists had still been sharing this abandoned facility with a small but steady stream of two-footed visitors and the more permanent two-footed residents of the nearby King Edward Point. And, although certainly plentiful and all too evident, they had not overwhelmed the place. Their caution had clearly kept their numbers in check. But not any more. In some way they had already sensed that the rusty remnants of the whaling station and all the land surrounding this stain on South Georgia's coast had been bequeathed to them by those now-disappeared intruders. So now there were hundreds if not thousands more of these creatures occupying every nook and cranny of the station itself and indeed the whole of the cove in which it sat. One huge bull elephant seal had even used his prodigious weight to flatten part of the white-painted fence around the tiny whalers' cemetery, and was now sprawled across Ernest Shackleton's grave. In making himself comfortable, he had knocked over Shackleton's headstone, the tall granite column carrying a quote from Robert Browning that would never again be read. It was as though he was reclaiming every last aspect of this former unwanted outpost of humanity, even if it meant desecrating the last resting place not of a whaler, but of one of humanity's recognised heroes. Maybe for too many seals – as for too many whales – humanity wasn't something they associated with any sort of heroics…

Back in Ushuaia, it wasn't just desecration going on. It was more an outbreak of mayhem. And gorging. The rats were the first on the scene, but as the red foxes in the surrounding countryside noticed that Ushuaia had lost its noise, its smells – and its hostile, potentially dangerous air – they too arrived. And then there were the hawks and the caracaras. In their hundreds. And what all of them were doing, with some urgency, was what Derek's planning team had anguished about for four weeks: clearing away the former apex species of the planet that had now been reduced to no more than an all-you-can-eat buffet, and that would soon be just a scattering of bones. It was gruesome. But not in the eyes of the feeders. And theirs were the only eyes to bear witness.

It was a similar story around the globe. Every village, every town and every city had become an omnivore's and carnivore's paradise, and the omnivores and carnivores hadn't waited for an invitation. There were cougars and bears – and rats and crows – in Seattle. There were tigers, vultures and rats in Delhi. And there were hyenas, leopards, rats – and honey badgers – in Johannesburg. It wouldn't last for long, of course. Even eight billion people can't feed a world of opportunistic feeders indefinitely, and the mayhem would eventually recede. Albeit the pressure on humanity's past realms from the wildlife they had formerly excluded would not. Crops were already being consumed by every grazer and every browser that could reach them. Monkeys, baboons, opossums, raccoons and a whole host of other animals were already busy in people's homes. And the first sprouts of Himalayan balsam and giant hogweed were pushing up through the pavements of countless cities and countless towns; the spearhead of a huge army of trees and bushes that would one day bury them under thick vegetation. Eventually, they'd even manage to engulf all those new radiation hot spots that had once been mankind's nuclear answer to its energy needs; needs that very definitely no longer existed…

But, back to that new era. Because the beginnings of a permanent change in the world's appearance – and all that grisly chaos – did presage a new chapter in its history; one in which a certain balance had been fortuitously restored by the actions of the one species that had been well on its way to upsetting that balance – irreversibly. No longer would a majority of the Earth's residents be under the threat of extinction. The Holocene extinction, the extermination of tens of thousands of species and tens of millions of individual creatures that had been triggered by man's selfishness, blindness, greed and sheer weight of numbers, had been brought to a shuddering stop. From now on, all the world's fauna – and all the world's flora – could recover and then thrive, and not have to face a future of culling, starvation, hunting, dispossession, clearance, trashing, felling or man-made fire. The world was going to be mended. And all those animals, and all those birds, fish, insects, trees, shrubs and bushes that hadn't already been wiped from the face of this planet could look forward not just to a temporary (albeit extended) respite from man – as postulated by Roy – but to a permanent respite from his relentless and malignant activities.

They were the fortunate ones. They had been facing unparalleled perils, but now the principal architect of those perils had been removed. And whether they were, in some way, aware of it or not, they would soon be savouring the sweet, long-lasting taste of… survival.

Afterword

I conceived this story in 2019. I began writing it on 18th January 2020. I first heard of COVID-19 at the beginning of February 2020.

David Fletcher

Matador